# LAST MAN TO SURVIVE

CHEVALIER PROTECTION SPECIALISTS - BOOK 4

LISA PHILLIPS

Cover Designed by: Ryan Schwarz

Edited by: Christy Callahan, Professional Publishing Services

❋ Created with Vellum

## 1

The sun had begun to set in Last Chance County. Dusk brought with it a chill Badger enjoyed—just so long as it didn't start to rain or snow. Given it was November, either was possible. At least the face of the mountain wasn't icy. That would make things difficult.

Badger wasn't about to look down, but for a second he took his gaze off the rock face in front of him and looked up.

Halfway.

Sweat dripped down to the small of his back. He lifted one foot and ensured it was secure in a notch above a protrusion in the rock. Once he had steady footing, he lifted one hand and then the other, raising himself another two feet up the face of the mountain.

The whole face was maybe forty five feet to the summit. Not exactly one of the tallest spots to climb in Last Chance County. But considering what he'd been through in the last few months, Badger was arguably taking it easy even doing this. He intended on reaching the top without much difficulty. Even if he had to pretend.

He could take a photo from the top, then send it to his teammates. The ones who thought he wasn't ready to return to active duty as part of Chevalier Protection Specialists, despite the fact their doctor declared him healed-ish.

If Zander, the team leader, knew Badger could do this, he had to rethink keeping Badger benched any more than necessary.

Badger zeroed his focus. This section of the rock face was the trickiest part of the whole climb, except for that last foot where he had to haul his body up and over the edge onto flat ground. He didn't need to be distracted when he had no tether or anything else to secure him. One slip of a foot or hand could send him tumbling to the ground.

After having inhaled a single drop of a deadly chemical a couple of months ago, and then more recently being forced to defend himself against an attacker, he didn't exactly want to wind up back in the hospital. Or dead. All because he made a misstep.

Six or seven feet above that spot, he heard people approach below. Badger didn't turn to look. He needed all his strength for the last part of the climb.

"What are you doing?" one of them called up.

He figured out who it was—Andre, Zander's number two guy and one of Badger's best friends, for years now. But the answer to Andre's question? As if it wasn't obvious given he was most of the way up the rock wall at this point.

Someone else spoke, but the words were a murmur from this distance.

Every second of being hurt had sucked. More than just the fact Badger had been unable to blow off steam in any of his usual ways—most of which involved exertion. He needed this. He needed the win of making it to the top to prove he was back up at full strength, capable of being put back on active duty.

His breath hitched on an inhale. Badger stilled, hugging the wall. After a few long breaths he would be fine, back to scaling the mountain.

"Don't worry," Andre called out. "We'll get set up just in case you don't make it. Judah can sprint to the top and lower a rope. Haul you up."

That was enough to get Badger moving again. He gritted his teeth and sucked in a breath, hauling himself up another couple of feet. The whole team was probably down there watching him. Assuming he was going to fail, although they probably wished he wouldn't. He knew they cared about him. That was why they refused to let him self-sabotage instead of recovering.

But he was good now.

Badger looked at the summit again, just to see how far it was.

Zander peered over the edge. His head and those broad shoulders carried the weight of their team.

Badger couldn't read the expression on Zander's face from this distance, so he ducked his chin and concentrated on moving. The longer he stayed stagnant, the more his momentum drained away. But if he kept going, then sooner or later he would make it to the top.

As his head neared the top of the wall, Zander crouched.

"I want to be back on full duty." Badger's voice was breathier than he would have liked. But it couldn't be helped.

Instead of responding, Zander got up and stepped back out of sight.

Badger set his footing and curled his upper body over the edge. He found a dip in the dirt, tested it would hold, and pulled himself over. He rolled over to his back, breathing harder than he wanted to in front of his team leader.

The satisfaction he felt at the fact Judah, their British team member, hadn't even made it to the top yet, let alone had time to lower a rope and try to "rescue" him, caused Badger to grin.

"Yeah, yeah. You made it." An answering smile tugged at Zander's lips. "How are you going to get back down?"

Badger narrowed his eyes.

Zander wandered over to the edge and looked down. Badger didn't see what he did with his fingers. What had been communicated between him and the men on the ground?

Badger's arms burned enough that pushing off the ground wasn't going to be a good idea. He clenched his abs and used his core to lift his shoulders and get into a sitting position, his arms limp on his thighs. Chest heaving. No matter how many times he held his breath at the top and then blew out slowly, it took longer than he wanted to steady his breathing.

"How are the lungs?" Zander said.

"The doc said my lung capacity is back to normal."

"Yeah, but there's normal, and then there's us. So how are they?"

Badger wanted to make a face, but the respect he had for Zander overruled almost anything.

The guy had been his sergeant in the US Army. His team leader before and after they left the service. He would have told anyone that being part of Delta Force was a more demanding job than his life now as a member of Chevalier Protection Specialists. But given some of the missions the team had been on lately, it might be considered untrue.

"A little tight," Badger said.

"Probably the exertion."

"That wouldn't rule me out of some missions, though. Right?"

"You've made your point. But you know my process for reinstatement. Especially after six weeks where you were almost entirely on bed rest." Zander held out his hand.

Badger clasped his wrist, and his team leader assisted him in standing. Not because he needed it, but because Zander needed to know Badger would rely on him if necessary. That he would accept assistance instead of going off alone…and climbing a mountainside.

"There are things you can do," Zander pointed out.

Badger started to object.

Zander cut him off. "They're not all at the house. Some of them are in the field, like visiting Isaac."

"You think he'll talk to me?"

"The rest of us have tried. And failed," Zander said. "It's worth a shot."

Badger nodded. *Finally* something to do.

Getting through to Isaac was going to be difficult. Their former teammate was a trained CIA operative. The member of an elite covert organization none of them had been able to pin down despite knowing they operated in the US. A few weeks ago Isaac had turned himself in to the military, along with a suitcase nuke stolen from the government.

Now Isaac was in federal prison.

Why he'd done it, none of them could decipher. And anytime they tried to visit him, no one could get an answer.

But Zander was right. It was worth a shot.

Thoughts of Isaac made Badger think of Hannah as well, though that was the last thing he wanted. She'd occupied his thoughts entirely too much the past few weeks while he'd been laid up in bed. At first he'd tried calling. Then texting. She hadn't replied to either, not talking to him at all since he'd driven her home after Gladstone's arrest and made sure it was safe for her to stay there.

As if all that time they'd spent together transporting evidence and handing it over to the feds, getting to know each other, meant absolutely nothing to her.

He figured now he knew where he stood. It was time to move on.

"Okay," Badger said. "I'll pack a bag and go pay a visit to Isaac. See if he'll talk to me."

Zander nodded. "Still trust me?"

Badger frowned.

"Because I know how you're going to get down." His team leader took a step toward him, one that caused Badger to back up in response.

Toward the edge.

"You want to risk your life?" Zander said. "Do it on someone else's payroll."

Zander kept coming. Badger had already accepted what was going to happen when Zander pushed out with two hands and shoved him over the edge.

---

AFTER THREE WEEKS of undercover work, it was finally happening.

Rochester PD Detective Hannah Yassick watched the window on the computer monitor tick past as the files copied. Even though she was the only one there that night, she still wished it would go faster.

She'd made a copy of the clinic director's office key a week ago. The flash drive would copy all the files on the computer without leaving a record of her activity. All she had to do was wait for it to finish and get out of here. Difficult, but not impossible with all the tricks she had learned.

The clinic was closed now. At just after eight in the evening, she was the only one who remained in the office after letting the head nurse know she'd be staying late to finish the paperwork. Just not this late.

A flicker of nervousness walked up her spine as the ticker approached complete. Instinct, or fear. She didn't know where the sensation came from.

Hannah had learned to ignore both her gut and the way her mind seemed determined to paralyze her. As if she wanted to sabotage her own actions by relying on her *instincts*. What a terrible idea.

It was better to just get on with the job. After all, her entire profession dealt in evidence. It was all about obtaining physical proof of someone's guilt or innocence. Without that, they had nothing. She certainly wasn't going to rely on a fallible gut instinct. She didn't even want to think about the way her intuition had led her astray over the years.

As much as she wanted to listen to her instincts, what was the point?

Hannah fiddled with the door key. They needed the contents of this computer, or the task force investigating this clinic for both insurance fraud and suspicion of money laundering had nothing.

The sound of a car door slam echoed from outside.

Hannah waited two seconds. The documents finished copying. She clicked to complete the file transfer and ejected the flash drive. She locked the director's office and went to the rear door. The clinic had a low budget, and that included their security system. Even if she wanted to look at the footage to see who was out there, Hannah would have to boot up the computer at the front desk—something that would take several minutes.

She headed toward the door just as it swung open and the director, Dr. Barbara Mathers, breezed in, followed by the head nurse, Pam Weston. Both spotted her immediately.

"Sarah, you're still here?" Nurse Weston was older but kept fit, even outside of a demanding job. Her silver cropped hair and customary bright eye shadow topped a trim figure.

Hannah, working under the alias Sarah, nodded. "I'm about done with the filing and cleaning up a bit for tomorrow. I was just about to head out."

Dr. Mathers, a physician with a bustling practice she charged practically nothing for, sized her up and down. "Dedication. I like it." Then she flashed a smile as though meeting in a dark hallway was an everyday occurrence with the new receptionist. Mathers was a former Iron Woman competitor who had won trophies several years running about a decade ago and seemed to have worked hard to maintain her athletic ability since.

Both of them were back at the clinic after hours, but neither appeared nervous at being discovered. Hannah/Sarah followed them to the break room where they removed winter jackets and hung them in their lockers.

"Is there an emergency with a patient?" Hannah headed for the counter beside the refrigerator. "I can put on a pot of coffee if you'd like."

"That would be great." Dr. Mathers tugged on a white lab coat before heading out of the room.

Hannah turned to Nurse Weston. "Is it something serious?"

"Just a patient who prefers to come in after hours." Weston never gave much away in her facial expressions. She may as well have been a brick wall, but Hannah was determined to find a crack. "You aren't going to want to see this guy, and we'll be busy taking care of him. So once you're done with the coffee, you should head out." She nodded as though satisfied with her statement.

"Of course." Hannah smiled in reply. "If you think of anything else I could do to be useful before I leave, just let me know. I'm happy to help out."

Undercover work walked a fine line between ingratiating herself with the person she was trying to get close to and doing her best to not appear sad and desperate. Hannah liked the challenge. People made things interesting when they didn't often react in ways that made sense. And it was a whole lot better than her regular life right now. Undercover work was simpler and yet more complex in many ways, all at the same time.

When the chance to join a federal task force and go on this assignment in Maryland had come up nine weeks ago, she'd jumped on the opportunity for new scenery. After three weeks of surveillance, they'd finally decided to send her in as the new receptionist. Without information from the inside, they couldn't figure out what was going on in this clinic.

A mystery to solve. One where Hannah got to catch criminals and serve justice. It was what she had dedicated her life to ever since she'd decided to become a police officer.

Being here definitely beat drowning in open cases. Or listening to her partner complain about his mother-in-law. Dodging her adoptive parents' phone calls. Trying to figure out what she would say to her half sister the next time they spoke. Purposely not thinking about a particular guy who had made her sit up and take notice of him—the first time that had happened in a long time.

Or all the ways any of that could go completely wrong.

The way it always did.

After all, nothing ever worked out like she thought it should, and in the end she would only realize she'd been hoodwinked again. Someone innocent would suffer, and she'd have to live with the fact life had proven to her again that she couldn't trust her instincts.

What she needed was evidence.

Nurse Weston glanced over, eyeing her. "I might take you up on that. Not tonight, but soon."

"Great." Hannah breezed to the locker she'd been given, the one with painter's tape on it and S-A-R-A-H written in permanent marker. She pulled out her purse and jacket. "I'll see you in the morning."

As she walked to the hallway the flash drive burned a hole in her pocket. There was little point sticking around, even if she did want to know which patient warranted a late night return to work. The clinic served primarily low-income families from the neighborhood, referrals from other clinics where the patients had no insurance, and patrons of the homeless shelter close by.

Everyone who came in was seen, something that would usually warrant pride. Hannah would believe they were doing good work if it weren't for the fact the director had several offshore bank accounts under family members' names totaling nearly twenty million. Nurse Weston had her own net worth, though only a measly fifteen million. She also had a boat that made up the difference, currently anchored in

Miami. Which explained the number of long weekend trips she took.

The director's son, Craig Mathers, also worked here as a physician's assistant. His net worth was hidden in a series of mansions in major cities and regular trips to Aspen with his girlfriend—the one he'd met at a strip club down the street.

Meanwhile, the clinic regularly begged local residents and authorities for funds. All the equipment was secondhand. The furniture was threadbare. And supplies, not to mention pharmaceuticals, came in spurts when someone with plenty remembered the clinic existed.

Hannah used the back door they had entered and headed for her car in the rear parking lot.

As she climbed behind the wheel, a Mercedes SUV sped up to the back door. Several men climbed out, hauling a limp man between them. The doctor opened the back door and allowed them entry.

Hannah drove away with a wave the doctor wasn't going to return, as though nothing was amiss. She parked a block away in an alley behind a Chinese restaurant, gathered her surveillance equipment, and hiked back to the corner where the clinic was. It didn't look like anyone was inside, but a yellow light glowed behind the frosted glass window around the back.

Hannah climbed a fire escape to the top floor of the building across the street, where she had a full view of the back door. The Mercedes SUV hadn't moved. Sooner or later, whoever had been brought in would be transferred back to his car. Dead. Or alive, if the doctor had managed to save him.

She took several pictures of the license plate.

Now all Hannah had to do was wait for them to exit. Her

camera ready to snap a picture of the doctor's after hours patient. As she waited, Hannah pulled out the burner phone her handler had given her and sent a text requesting a meeting before the morning.

Her phone pinged with a reply.

AGREED. THERE'S INFO YOU NEED. NOT CASE RELATED.

Hannah frowned. Not case related?

What could it be about?

She'd left her life—her confusing, topsy-turvy life—behind when she took this job. Except for the occasional call with Nora Gladstone...now Nora O'Connell. She was getting to know her sister.

Anything else? Not interested. Hannah already had more than she could handle, which should be clear to Badger from the last few weeks of radio silence.

She just wanted to do her job. Take some time to figure everything else out.

Several hours later the man was walked out of the rear door of the clinic. Hannah's shutter worked overtime for a few seconds.

Long enough to capture an image of José Suarez.

She sent a follow-up text to her handler.

SCRATCH TOMORROW. WE NEED TO MEET ASAP.

## 2

---

The wind whipped at Badger's back as he fell through the air. His thoughts vacillated between straight fear and the knowledge that Zander would never have shoved him over the edge had there not been a way for him to survive the fall. It was tempting to twist and look. Probably in time to smash his face into the ground. Considering Zander was at the top staring at him, he didn't give in to that flash of concern.

Badger hit the net at the bottom.

Andre, Judah, and Eas surrounded him, holding onto the springy fabric as he bounced to a stop. Then they lowered the net to the ground.

Badger stared up at the sky, unable to see Zander anymore. The guy was probably making his way down.

"I think he might need a minute." Judah chuckled. "Or a cup of tea."

Badger immediately rolled, pushing himself to stand. "Not your kind of tea."

He didn't even drink a different kind, but it was the principle of the thing when it came to their British teammate. The guy had some freaky ideas about what foods went together. Badger could say that because he'd grown up in Hawaii eating all kinds of things that had seemed normal at the time.

Zander jogged toward them from around the corner and the path that led to the top of the hill. He didn't even seem winded, which wasn't surprising. The boss held them all to a high standard, and as their team leader, the standard for himself was greater.

Andre stared down at him. "Are you done trying to kill yourself now?"

Eas gave him a similar expression—one that told Badger he agreed with Andre's sentiment, but he also understood.

"That's not what this was about," Badger said. "I made it to the top, and Zander gave me an assignment."

Even though it wasn't full active duty, visiting the teammate who had betrayed them was still considered a mission.

Andre nodded. "Good."

Judah slung an arm around Badger's neck and tugged him over. "I'll go with you. Is it going to be exciting?"

Badger punched Judah's kidney until the guy yielded and quit yanking on Badger's neck. "Maybe I'll ask your sister to go with me. I heard she's a better shot than you."

Judah was just about to retaliate when Zander clapped. "Let's get to the car, children. Or no one gets treats after they eat all their dinner."

Badger angled for shotgun on the ride home, even though Judah called it. He elbowed the British guy out of the way. Successful, until Andre hip checked him and nearly sent him sprawling on the ground.

"I get the front seat," Andre said.

That left Badger, Eas, and Judah crammed in the back row. But thankfully they never bought or rented team vehicles they couldn't fit into. What was the point? They were all grown men, and they needed grown-men-sized seats.

Still, Judah sat with his elbow permanently in Badger's side, acting clueless. "So what's for dinner?"

"Depends what you're making," Andre said from the front seat.

"We should order in from the diner," Eas said. "Stuart told Aria he was making brisket sandwiches this week."

Zander nodded. "Sounds good. Order enough for everyone."

Eas and his former flame, Karina, an operative herself, had settled in Last Chance County years ago. The place the team called home. Together they had a high school age daughter and a dog the entire group had claimed. Aria now worked at the diner a few days a week after school and on Saturdays.

The team had expanded in the last few weeks. Zander was married to Nora. Andre had reconnected with his estranged wife, Lucia, who Zander had recently cleared as a full team member. Ted, the team's technical expert, was planning a Christmas wedding to his police detective fiancée.

Judah and Badger were the only single ones left in the group. Things had been changing a lot, but would feel normal again if Badger could get back to active duty. Better than him being laid up at home while the rest of the team hopped on the plane and went on missions. Even if it was different now, he would still be himself back on the team. If he could bring to the group what he always had in the role he occupied.

Zander pulled up in front of the massive house where

they lived. Even given there were ten people and a dog living there, it still didn't seem cramped.

As they all climbed out of the vehicle, a silver Nissan made its way slowly down the long drive toward them.

"Looks like a rental." Badger glanced at Zander.

His team leader was already pulling out his phone. Zander pressed buttons on either side and held them down, using it as a walkie. "Ted, get Aria and Nora to the panic room."

Karina was in town, teaching a couple of back-to-back workout classes, so they didn't need to worry about her.

Ted's reply came quick. "Copy that."

They faced the approaching vehicle as a group. The driver was a female with blonde hair, someone they knew well.

"Lana." Badger put everything he felt about the woman into his tone, almost able to taste his dislike.

As she parked and climbed out, the front door of the house opened. Lucia shut the door behind her and stood on the front step holding a shotgun across her body.

Badger had only ever seen Lana in surveillance video and photos, but he knew she was the leader of an organization that skirted the law and seemed willing to do anything it took to achieve their goals. He just had no idea what the ultimate goal was. Every image he'd seen of her, Lana wore tactical gear. Tonight she had on a dress that hugged her strong figure and heels. The kind of outfit a business manager might wear —or a fiftysomething government director.

He wondered which of those she was pretending to be.

Lana glanced over at Lucia by the door. "Planning to order me off your property?"

Lucia lifted her chin. "Depends on why you're here."

Lana rounded the front of the car and opened the passenger door. Each of them reached for a concealed weapon, except Badger, who only had a knife on him. Lana lifted a file from the front seat and straightened. She waved it. "Just paper. Hardly lethal."

She strode toward Zander but stopped far enough away they could each stretch out a hand and transfer the file between them.

All of them were on edge. This woman was unlikely bearing gifts, and she always had an agenda.

Lana glanced at the house, then the warehouse beside it —with its basement bunker. "Where is she?"

The skin around Zander's eyes flexed. "You really think I'll tell you?"

Given how they felt about Lana being Nora's mother, it shouldn't be a surprise that Zander's feelings were twice as strong. Nora wanted nothing to do with the woman who had birthed her, a woman who'd put their friends—their family— in danger too many times. She'd done unconscionable things for her own reasons.

Badger was pretty sure Nora had no idea what to think, but he also figured she would come to terms with it in time. Figure out a plan.

She held out the file. "I'm here to hire your company for a protection detail."

Zander didn't take it. "You have people. Put one of them on whoever this is."

"Who this is," Lana said, "is none of their business."

Did she want to keep a secret from her people? Badger reached over and grabbed the file while Lana and Zander faced off with each other.

He flipped the file open.

"Z." It came out of his mouth before he even realized it.

Inside the file was a Rochester Police Department personnel record, and the photo at the top corner of a woman in uniform. Detective Hannah Yassick.

Nora's sister.

"She's also your daughter, right?" Badger didn't need to betray the attraction he'd felt for her from the moment he met her, months ago now. Still, he figured a woman like Lana didn't miss the inflection in his question. No one around him was unaware of the fact he'd been ghosted over and over. Or that he'd since given up waiting for her to respond.

Why bother?

But if her life was at risk, he wanted to know about it.

"She's gone dark. Undercover with a federal task force." There was zero emotion in Lana's expression. She could have been talking about the weather.

Andre hissed. His wife had been with a federal task force that turned out to be entirely dirty. The odds of that being the case again were extremely low.

Badger figured they didn't need to worry about that. But still.

"The mission went wrong?" he asked.

Lana shook her head. She held herself back from them, not looking fully at anyone except Zander. Because she was genuinely worried about Hannah? She needed help her people couldn't give her. "There's a price on her head. She might think she's laying low, but they'll find her."

Badger turned to Zander. He had nothing to say.

Zander nodded. "Go."

Badger turned to Lana. "Because of you? Because who you are puts her in danger?

The woman didn't betray an ounce of emotion. But then again, she never did. "Are you going to do this or not?"

Badger went inside to pack a bag.

---

THE FOLLOWING day Hannah stowed the cell phone in a hidden compartment at the bottom of her purse before climbing out of her car. Her handler's reply text meant she was back at work waiting out the chance to talk face-to-face, which he'd requested at ten tonight. Nearly twenty-four hours later.

After he'd dropped a bomb about info she needed?

But there was nothing she could do about it.

She'd still sent the photo of last night's patient to the secure email address the task force kept on hand for anything she might gather. They would run the image, and they'd realize what she knew. Tonight she could give her handler the flash drive.

And find out what he had to tell her.

The idea that José Suarez was linked to Director Mathers —for whatever reason brought them together—put an entirely different spin on this operation. She'd been sent undercover to gather information about the medical center and find out what was happening here. They'd suspected a connection to illegal operations, which meant the clinic laundered money for certain criminal elements.

The idea they did it for one of the most notorious cartels made Hannah want to shiver even though she had her thick winter coat on.

She'd lived in Upstate New York most of her life. Winters weren't something she was unaccustomed to. In fact, she wasn't sure she would know what to do anywhere it was warm this time of year. Or still light, late in the evening.

She kept those thoughts uppermost in her mind as she used her key to enter the back door of the free clinic.

Nurse Weston poked her head out of the break room. "Good, you're here."

"I am." Hannah peeled off her coat even though she wasn't warm yet. They kept it far too hot inside the building, but that was for patient comfort and not her preference. Though, it gave her a reason why she might come across as uncomfortable. "It's chilly outside this morning."

Nurse Weston lifted a coffee cup to her lips. "Supposed to reach a high of forty-seven." She took a sip.

"How did things go last night?" Hannah kept the question light as she stowed the coat in her locker and poured her own cup of coffee. At least the stuff here was better than the thick brew that passed for java in a police station.

Nurse Weston leaned back against the counter. "Oh, fine. Nothing to worry about." She took another sip. "We had a big donation come in this morning, so buy the portable X-ray machine that's in your email. I sent you a link."

Hannah nodded. "Sounds good. I'll get on it before any patients come in." Then she breezed out with a smile, playing the role she had been sent here to play. Biding her time until she'd gathered what it would take to prove what the feds suspected about the free clinic.

Maybe it was already on the flash drive, physical evidence of money laundering. Or, given the sudden donation and the identity of the man who'd been here the night before receiving emergency treatment, it could be more than that.

In the end, it didn't matter which.

Hannah would find the truth.

She opened her email and looked at the price tag for the portable X-ray machine. She felt her eyebrows rise. Fifteen thousand dollars? No doubt José Suarez had paid handsomely for the treatment he'd received after hours and under the table.

As she made the purchase and then admitted patients throughout the day, Hannah thought about her research the night before. Nothing official, as she didn't have the federal computer she'd been loaned when she came on board with the task force. No, her research had been done entirely using the internet. Newspaper articles. Sites that gave a biography she'd found scarily detailed until she had to shut down her search, or she wouldn't sleep a wink thinking about things the Suarez cartel had likely done.

The guy lived in Miami, Florida, and in Mexico City. How he wound up in Baltimore was curious, unless he also had holdings here. Something she wasn't sure the feds knew about.

But they would soon.

Hannah turned down an invitation to lunch from two medical assistants who helped Nurse Weston with patients. Dr. Mathers had a salad delivered, which she ate at her desk. By the time Hannah closed the front door of the free clinic, the tension in her neck and shoulders had brought on a headache.

Just a few hours, and then she'd be able to check in with her handler.

She headed to retrieve her things and heard the murmur of voices before she stepped into the break room.

"...soon enough. Or he'll be gone by the time we get to it." That was Dr. Mathers.

Nurse Weston responded in a low voice. "How do we

know last time wasn't a fluke? We could be in for a world of hurt if things go wrong."

"So we outsource help." The doctor's tone indicated she didn't seem too concerned.

"From unknowns?" Nurse Weston hissed. "That's too risky. I don't like it."

"We need the money, or the clinic won't last much longer."

Hannah didn't make a sound. Out in the hall, she hugged the wall and listened. Both women had considerable stashes they could dip into if the clinic needed money. Or were they only in this for themselves first, and the clinic continued to be an afterthought? Maybe they were in over their heads, and the deals they made with cartel leaders who paid for concierge care didn't cover the bills.

Criminals weren't always good with money. And these two being stressed out when there wasn't enough would make anybody react on emotion instead of sense.

Hannah breezed in since their conversation had died down. "I'm headed out now." She grabbed her coat and purse and waved to both women. "See you tomorrow."

One day she wouldn't. The task force would move in and make arrests. These two women and Dr. Mathers's son would be detained, their assets frozen.

Justice would be done.

Five hours later, Hannah pulled her car into the parking lot of a flooring store that had gone out of business several months ago. She drove around to the rear of the building, where employees parked. The place was empty, but it was normal for her handler to wait for her to show up and then reveal himself.

A few minutes later, he walked around the far corner of the building.

She watched him approach, confirming his identity as he strode from under a streetlight that should've worked into the light from its neighbor that did. Then under the next light, also dark. Back into a beam. It was him.

Hannah turned off the interior light and cracked her door, then left it open a fraction. She waited for him to reach her, fiddling with the flashlight in her pocket.

Special Agent Brad Pearson of the FBI lifted his chin as he approached. He wore a wedding band on his left hand and recently had his silver hair trimmed. Instead of a suit, he wore jeans, boots and a wool overcoat. "We've done a full workup on Suarez."

Hannah said, "Good." That meant they knew even more than she did. Plus they had the personnel to devote to it while she worked on the clinic.

She handed him the flash drive. "This is everything from the director's computer."

He accepted it. "Great. Hopefully we can get what we need from this, and it won't be long before you can be done."

She told him about the conversation she'd overheard. "It's not much, but it could lead to something in the next day or two." Time enough to go over the flash drive and add to their picture of what was going on.

Pearson nodded. "Okay, sounds good. Are you doing okay?"

She knew he was only asking because her psychological state played into the success or failure of the investigation. Having an unstable undercover cop in a volatile situation wasn't good for anyone.

But she still wasn't going to open up to him as a confidante. Hannah kept her own counsel, the way she always had.

So she told him, "I'll sleep better tonight than I did last night."

"Good deal."

"If you tell me what else you came here to say."

He stilled for a second, then nodded. "Got an envelope for you to take with you." He patted the breast pocket of his jacket.

"Not gonna tell me what it is?"

"It won't change what's doing here," he said. "But it's personal and up to you to decide what you want to do with it."

She nodded.

Hannah had worked with other officers who insisted on prying into her personal life until she had to clearly explain that she would never open up. It was pretty much how it happened with every romantic relationship she had, but that was another issue she didn't need to get into right now, even in her head.

"I'll contact you if Alanson wants a meet," Pearson said. "Assuming you want in when we take these guys down."

She was about to reply when the pop of a gunshot cut through the night air. But the bullet didn't hit her.

Pearson fell to the ground.

A bullet hole through his neck.

**3**

———

B adger spotted the muzzle flash from the shot. A rifle. The shooter had taken up position on the building's roof. He'd aimed down at a steep angle but managed to hit his target.

Hannah immediately crouched. Even with police training, anyone in her position might need a second to orient themselves over what had just happened. She rallied before he expected her to, shuffling along the ground to her handler.

Badger heard the echo of the roof door in the quiet night.

The shooter was on the move, headed away in retreat most likely. Now the job was complete, there was no reason to stick around. Except the job wasn't complete, because it was Hannah's handler who lay dead on the ground. Not her.

He could be coming up close to finish things.

Badger raced toward her.

Hannah spun and raised a weapon. She spotted him on approach with his own gun drawn.

He ignored hers. She wasn't going to shoot him. "You good?"

She gasped and lowered her gun a fraction.

Badger squeezed her shoulder and moved past her to the man on the ground. "Keep your eyes open. I think he's headed down from the roof."

Blood had pooled under the body. Now it moved in a slow trickle toward a flash drive that had fallen from the man's hand. He swept the device up and pocketed it before turning back to her. "Get out of here, fast. Take the car and go to a motel. Pay cash, no ID."

"But you'll—"

"I've got this. Just go." He needed her to be safe. "Text me your location when you're settled."

She didn't move.

"Go, Hannah."

She headed for her car and then backed the vehicle up before circling to exit the parking lot.

Badger found the handler's cell phone and dialed 911, then wiped his prints from the phone and headed back toward his own car.

He peered around at the corner of the building in time to see the shooter exit the side door and look both ways.

Badger ducked back behind the corner and waited a second before he looked out again. The shooter crossed the street, carrying a rifle case in one hand. He was leaving.

Badger's brain spun. All the guy had done was warn Hannah that her life was in danger by taking out her handler. For him to be leaving now, the shooter had to know how to find her.

Or, at least he was confident he could.

Or he knew Badger would fight him if he tried again. Or...

There were so many other possibilities. Variables. Whatever his reasoning, this guy was determined to fight another day.

As if Badger would let him get away.

His free hand curled into a fist as he crossed the street and followed the shooter, staying twenty feet or so behind him.

If this guy thought he'd find her later, he was in for a surprise. Instead of Hannah, all he would come up with was a former Delta Force soldier. Because no matter why Lana wanted them to protect her, Badger would do his job. He didn't like it when innocent people were targets. Especially when they had no idea why.

Probably she was caught in the middle of some rivalry. How she connected the two sides was a mystery, but it didn't matter.

She wasn't going to get hurt.

Badger reached his car, climbed in the driver's seat, and watched as the shooter got into a pickup truck and pulled out.

Badger followed, grabbing his phone to call Judah. As soon as it connected, he hit Speaker and set the phone in the cupholder.

"Hey. Nothing here." Judah had been at the clinic, searching for anything that might indicate a connection to someone trying to kill Hannah.

Badger explained about her handler.

Judah reacted immediately. "I'm on my way."

"Actually, finish up if you need to. Cops can take care of the dead guy. I'm in pursuit of the shooter."

"Two of us can box him in easier than one."

"When Hannah hits a safe place, I want you to sit on her."

"You don't want that detail for yourself?"

Badger gripped the wheel. "Soon as she gets it to me, I'll send you the address."

He hung up on Judah and tailed the guy through the streets of Baltimore. All the while wondering if he considered tonight a success or a failure. Anyone who was a professional wasn't going to allow personal feelings to cloud their judgment. He'd done what he could, and despite Badger's assumption that the guy would keep coming until he finished the job, evidently he intended to wait until Hannah was caught unaware again.

But now she knew someone was coming.

It would be a game of cat and mouse until they faced each other again. Not that Badger intended to allow it to happen.

The guy circled a couple of blocks and took several random turns. Making sure no one was following him.

Badger doubted the guy was aware he had a tail but wouldn't rule it out.

The shooter pulled into the parking lot of a bar. Lights blazed from every window, and people spilled onto the street in front of the building. Thumping music could be heard even above the mess of people and the insulation provided by Badger's car windows.

This could just be another wrong turn. Or it could be his destination.

Badger parked as though he intended on being a patron, then jogged around the building.

The shooter climbed a wooden staircase to the floor

above. He used the key on the door at the top and went inside.

Badger used his cell phone to alert Ted of the location. He asked for the name of the person who owned or leased the place, along with a full rundown.

The rear of the bar backed up to an all-night burger place. He bought a double cheeseburger and a milkshake and sat where he could watch the door.

Thirty minutes later, Hannah sent him a text with the address of a motel and the room number. He'd half expected her to tell him she no longer had his number. After all, she'd seriously ghosted him after the last time they parted ways. He'd assumed she deleted him entirely from her life.

But apparently not.

He texted back,

SIT TIGHT. YOU OKAY?

The reply consisted of three blinking dots. They disappeared. A second later, the dots blinked again. Then disappeared.

Badger set his phone facedown on the table, needing to focus on the door and not her response. It didn't really matter what she had to say. The fact was that Chevalier Protection Specialists had been hired to safeguard her, and that was what was happening here. Not anything personal, which would not only be unprofessional but would also muddy everything.

His phone buzzed. He flipped it over and looked at the screen.

I CALLED MY BOSS AND LET HIM KNOW WHAT HAPPENED. HE SAID POLICE ARE ALREADY AT THE SCENE.

Did she want to keep this strictly business as well? Fine by him. In fact, that was preferable.

Badger replied,

Stay where you are until I get there.

He figured there was at least a chance she would do as he said. At least up until she realized she didn't need to take orders from him, and she headed either to the free clinic where she was working undercover or back to the office where the task force was located.

Didn't matter. He would be there to make sure she was safe. There was no other option.

He finished the burger. Lights in the upstairs apartment above the bar glowed yellow behind the shades. In one spot the blinds were broken, but Badger couldn't see inside without binoculars or a high-powered camera.

He sipped the milkshake slowly. If it took more than thirty minutes to finish the thing, he'd start to stand out. Someone would remember him as an oddity, which he didn't need. His whole life Badger had perfected the art of laying low. Blending in, because sticking out and getting noticed drew attention he didn't want or need.

Until it counted.

Ted sent an email with detailed information about the tenant living upstairs, along with a photo. Of *her*. The resident was a woman.

The shooter had used a key.

Boyfriend, or relative. A friend she'd let sleep on her couch.

Or something more sinister.

Badger wandered over to the bar and headed inside. The heavy beat of music hung in the air as thick as smoke. He wove through the crowd to the bar, ordered a drink he didn't plan to consume, and tipped well enough that the bartender noticed. "Hey, question."

The bartender waited.

"Lady that lives upstairs. You know her?"

"Sure." The bartender shrugged. "She owns the whole building. But she's been gone for a few days, so if she owes you, it ain't time to collect. And if cops come here about a break in, I'll show them your photo on my security tapes. Feel me?"

And yet he'd just told Badger there was no one upstairs. "Roommate?"

He shrugged again. "How should I know?"

"Thanks." Badger tapped the bar with two fingers and left, circling back around the building. He sent a text to Ted and Judah letting them know what he was about to do. Then he silenced his phone, so he wasn't distracted by their replies.

Within two minutes, he had the lock on the door picked.

He pulled his pistol and twisted the handle. The door eased open, and the first thing that hit him was the smell.

The second thing weighed less than he did but packed a punch.

---

HANNAH'S JAW ached from clenching it so hard to not say what she wanted to say. *Stay where you are until I get there.* As if.

The second she'd read that text, Hannah had grabbed her purse and walked outside the motel room. Like she was going to be managed? Nah. No way.

Badger actually, seriously wanted her to sit around while he took care of things? Not just that, but his buddy and teammate sat outside in his car watching. She'd known because Judah got out of his car about three seconds after she left the room.

Hannah blew out a breath. In the shock of what had happened, she'd forgotten the envelope Pearson said he had on him. It couldn't be about her mother. She already knew that.

So what was it?

"Don't worry." Judah glanced over from the front seat. "Soon as we get there, you can tell him exactly how you feel."

"Unless it's all burned out by then." She huffed. Being mad at Badger was better than being mad at herself.

"Shame. I'd like to see it."

He really wanted to watch her yell at Badger? Maybe he thought his friend deserved it. But then, what kind of friend was that?

Hannah stared at Judah. "That's not what I'd have thought you'd say. I figure you'd want me to be all grateful that he saved my life or something." Even though Badger hadn't shown up until after the shot was fired. She'd actually thought for a second that he was the shooter. Then he'd ordered her around and disappeared after the guy.

Hannah's phone buzzed. She flipped it over on her leg and saw it was an email from her supervising agent.

"Anything I should know about?" Judah asked.

She wasn't going to tell a civilian proprietary federal information, but she figured Judah and his team weren't ordinary civilians. Still, she tried to follow procedure as much as possible. Chevalier Protection Specialists might be here on the job, but they weren't involved with the investigation, even if they seemed to have taken over.

Hannah said, "I need to get my boss the flash drive I had. The one Badger took from the scene."

She'd seen it happen but hadn't been able to do anything about it, considering she'd been in shock for a few seconds after the shooter took out her handler. She still couldn't believe he was dead. Every time she closed her eyes, she saw him jerk and fall all over again.

She glanced out the side window and squeezed her eyes shut. She hadn't even known the guy all that well, and now this?

Hannah blew out a breath.

She figured Judah would offer her some meaningless statement meant to comfort her. The same way her parents had whenever she was hurt or failed at anything. Curiously she was interested to hear what it was.

Before he could, though, his phone rang. Judah had already connected it to the car's Bluetooth, so the music quit, and the ringing sound filled the car.

Judah swiped the screen. "Go ahead."

"It's me."

Judah glanced at her. "Hannah is in the car with me."

"Copy that. Hi, Hannah. It's Ted."

"Um, hi, Ted."

"He's our tech guy," Judah said.

Hannah nodded, not really feeling like she needed to say anything. He and Ted started talking anyway, and it didn't require her input.

She already knew plenty of the people with Chevalier Protection Specialists, even if she'd only met some. She hardly needed to know more, let alone all of them. How would that help her with this clean break she had going on?

The whole point of being undercover with the task force was to lay low, under the radar for a while. It served more than one purpose—like being away from anything to do with Badger and his "boys" and whoever else was with them now.

Ted said, "…hired from the dark web."

Hannah blinked and glanced at Judah. "What was that?"

"The guy who shot your handler. He's a pro. Contracted to kill you through a dark web server that handles that kind of thing."

Hannah swallowed. "He can't be that much of a pro. He missed."

"That might not be the pertinent point here, Han." Judah turned a corner. Headed toward wherever Badger currently was.

"Not just that. But now I *know* someone is gunning for me." She folded her arms. "It's not like I'll give him a chance to strike again."

"You always do that?"

She glanced at Judah. "Do what?"

"Brush off the threat? In my experience, it pays to be cautious. You don't know what could happen."

"What are you, some kind of sage?"

Ted's exhale crackled across the speakers. "Maybe I should leave you two to figure this out. I'll update Zander."

Before she could object to that, Ted hung up.

"Why would he need to update Zander?" Hannah asked.

Judah said nothing, punched the indicator lever, and pulled into a parking lot.

"Jude."

"Han." He used nearly the exact tone she had.

She rolled her eyes. "Tell me why you guys showed up here."

Even though she figured she already knew. A dark web contracted hitman? Didn't take a genius to tie up the threads of that investigation. Case closed.

"So y'all flew across the country just to protect me out of

the kindness of your hearts?" Of course, Badger wasn't here for any other reason. This was a job for him.

"What would you do if we did?" Judah backed into a space and put the car in park, so they faced the busy bar. "Nothing owed, no expectations. Just doing the right thing. Would that be so bad?"

Before she could answer, a shatter of glass caught her attention. There was no time to figure out the source before a man came sailing down from the floor above the bar and landed on the pavement.

Hannah winced. *Ouch.* She climbed out of the car, her badge on her belt even though this wasn't her jurisdiction. Things had been too crazy tonight, and she needed the normality of being Detective Hannah Yassick right now. Not Sarah, the free clinic receptionist. Or the cop assigned to a federal task force. Just her.

"Back up." She held out her palm as people started over. "Police. Everyone give him some room."

Hannah half expected it to be Badger, but it wasn't. The shooter? She crouched beside the guy's hip while someone in the crowd said, "I called 911."

"Good." She rolled the man to his back and winced. "Sir, can you hear me?"

His glazed eyes didn't focus. He'd been injured, beaten badly. Though from the abrasions on his knuckles, he'd put up a good defense, so maybe it had been a fair fight.

Until he sailed through the window.

"Sir?"

When he still didn't respond, she glanced around. Judah had climbed out of the car with her. Now he was nowhere to be seen.

She looked up at the window he'd fallen from. The white

curtain billowed out the shattered glass. Badger could still be up there, maybe hurt. She had to stay with the injured man—likely the person who'd killed her handler. At least Judah would figure that out.

It almost made her miss having a partner. Almost. And not *her* partner. More like just having a partner in general.

"You okay, cop?"

She blinked and looked up at the guy in front of her. White towel over his shoulder. The bartender? Hannah swallowed. "Yeah, long night, you know?"

"I do know." His eyes smiled. Given half an inch of room he'd have made a solid attempt at flirting.

Some guys liked the strong, independent woman thing. She could kick doors in and take care of herself, and they liked that. Then there was the kind of guy who only wanted to protect the woman he cared about, usually by taking over, giving orders, and expecting everyone to jump when he said so just because he used to be Delta Force. Now he was on some protection squad that faced down national threats or whatever.

Hannah had no interest in either.

The guy on the ground moaned. Thankfully in the distance, she could already hear police sirens. As soon as she got her supervising agent to confirm who she was, she'd be able to get this done and get some sleep. Hannah intended on being at the clinic first thing in the morning.

If she was in danger, it had to be about the investigation.

After all, this guy had hit her handler. It could be he'd planned to kill both of them, but she'd ducked out of sight too fast.

And then Badger had been there, messing everything up. Interfering the way he had since Chevalier Protection

Specialists walked into her life and every corner of it flipped upside down.

Now she had no idea who she was.

Who she was supposed to *be*.

Hannah blew out a breath. She didn't want to see Badger right now. Those few seconds after Pearson died had been enough. She didn't care about him or his "do what I say, and we'll get along fine" attitude. Ordering her around. As if.

She heard the injured man exhale.

Hannah looked down as the guy's eyes fluttered open. His gaze zeroed on her and widened.

"Yeah." She straightened to stand over him. "Better luck next time."

She turned and waved over the uniformed officers and the ambulance that pulled in behind their purposeful stride.

Hannah was a cop.

She didn't need to be anything else.

---

## 4

Badger shifted on the bench seat of the diner booth. He lifted his tiny mug, but only the drip at the end of his coffee remained. He glanced over at the waitress and waved the mug.

She headed for the insulated carafe.

Judah sat beside him so Hannah could take a seat opposite. He halfway wanted to ask Judah to get lost, but it was for the best that his teammate was here. The guy would run interference while Badger fought off his attraction to her.

At least now he knew why she'd been ghosting him the past few weeks. At least to an extent. She was busy with this undercover assignment and hadn't had the time to start a relationship. Not that he assumed that's what they'd have. Maybe she only wanted to be friends. Or nothing.

Maybe he was just kidding himself that she'd only not called or texted back because she was busy undercover. The truth was, she'd obviously found him lacking. Meanwhile, he'd been captivated by her. Those few days spent watching out for her, helping her gather the evidence against Stephen

Gladstone, escorting her as she moved in to make the arrest? They'd been unlike any other time in his life.

And the fact it happened without his teammates…

Badger wasn't sure how he felt about that. He didn't need their interference. They'd done enough of that since the airplane explosion, where former president Raleigh's wife had been killed.

She breezed in the door then, not quite able to hide that determined police detective stride. Then again, if she figured no one in her undercover life would see her here, maybe she didn't feel the need to disguise it.

But she caught his eye, along with several other guys in the room. Judah let out a breath. Yeah, a woman like her just hit a guy a certain way. Whether he wanted to acknowledge it or not. The strength and confidence she exuded blended with her classic features and that long dark hair into a package that turned heads. Enough Badger had to remind himself this was just business.

"Hey." She slid in across from them, tugged off her coat, and bundled it beside her.

The waitress refilled Judah's coffee. He grumbled something about awful tea and had her pour him another cup of coffee.

Hannah inverted her mug and said, "Thanks."

"Sleep okay?" Badger didn't care what Judah thought about him asking that. Neither was he interested in the guy's reaction.

Hannah's eyes narrowed. "Why, do I look tired?"

Judah snorted, dumping those tiny containers of half-and-half into his coffee and stacking the empties in a tower.

"You were up half the night," Badger said. "Just like the rest of us."

And they didn't have the benefit of being able to lighten things with makeup. Which she seemed to have done expertly, considering it was hard to tell if she had on more than a basic amount. And thinking on it further would only mean he sat there staring at her.

Badger pulled out his phone and unlocked the screen. He found the image they had of Lana and showed her. "Do you know this woman?"

Hannah lifted her mug. "It's usually me asking those questions."

"Any idea why she would ask us to protect you?" He had no idea if she knew any of this.

Hannah glanced down at the phone, her mouth tight. "I've never met her."

"We're still putting together exactly who she is."

Zander had given him permission to share anything he needed to with her. However, she might not require all the information when she was in the middle of an undercover operation. She probably needed—and wanted—to stay focused.

Badger had no problem looking out for her while she completed her investigation. "Did your boss assign you a new handler?"

"I talked to my supervising agent this morning. Alanson is going to be my handler himself until they can assign a replacement, which will be done after they figure out why that guy killed Pearson."

"Do they know if he was aiming for you?" Judah asked.

"We can't be certain he was." She shrugged one shoulder. "Not until the investigation is complete."

"But we know he was hired to kill you," Badger said.

"Why would he have killed your handler instead of you? He had to have been aiming for you and missed."

"I guess I'll find out." She sat back against the seat. "I've got an appointment to speak to my supervising agent later. He can tell me what the shooter said."

Badger bit back his initial reaction and swallowed. "That's good."

He figured he could convince Alanson that Hannah should be taken off the undercover assignment and stashed away somewhere. Protected.

He didn't know why he was surprised she'd made contact and set up a meeting. He shouldn't be. But then again, he'd assumed she would be fully focused on the undercover operation. Instead, she apparently planned to pull double duty working the clinic and helping her colleagues investigate Pearson's death. They wanted to speak to Badger as well, considering he'd been there. Zander had been fielding calls from her supervising agent all morning asking for his time.

Badger had to concentrate on protecting Hannah. Not just because Lana had hired the team to protect her daughter. In fact, it wasn't really because of her at all. It was because Hannah's life was in danger.

"You really don't know that woman?" He tapped the screen of his phone but didn't unlock it again.

He needed her to open up a little, let him into what went on below the surface. Something he didn't figure she had much practice at. For the last few weeks he'd been the same way, while his friends and teammates had tried to dig for the reason why he'd been out of sorts.

Okay, so he'd been downright moody.

But falling for a woman the second he saw her and then

having her brush him off didn't exactly fill him with confidence.

"What do you know about her?" Hannah took a big bite of her omelet. Probably so he couldn't ask her a question in response.

"Her name is Lana, former Soviet operative. Double agent. These days she runs an organization of mostly ex-military, some former spies. That kind of thing. Picks people off the streets and trains them to go on missions."

"What kind of missions?"

Badger said, "They don't contract with the government, as far as we know. Unless it's some kind of off book CIA thing. But we know she has an agenda, and she's not afraid to order an assassination to get it done."

Hannah's expression gave nothing away. "And for some reason, she wants me protected?"

Judah said, "I'm guessing the reason is that someone hired a guy on the dark web to end your life."

"It's probably about the undercover job. Someone doesn't want me digging into the clinic and what they've been up to." Hannah shrugged, taking another bite. "What else would it be?"

Badger focused on his pancakes for a while, getting most of the way through them while he thought over it all. "We can go back and ask her," he finally said. "But if you don't know your connection to this, I'm not sure we'll get it out of her."

"And I'm not sure I care who she is." Something flickered in Hannah's expression. He couldn't quite grasp what it was. "Or whether she thinks I'm in danger." She shrugged. "I can take care of myself."

Badger wasn't convinced she was straight up lying to him

—but she also wasn't being completely truthful. At the least, she didn't trust him.

He had to admit that stung. They'd spent time together. He'd watched her back and helped gather evidence Zander thought Lana had sent them. Maybe she hadn't.

Hannah had to know he was good at his job by now. But if she wasn't going to open up, then maybe she didn't think he'd be able to help her out.

Which also stung.

She was going to go back to being undercover in that clinic. Maybe her life wouldn't be in the line of fire while she was behind the reception desk, but given the fact her handler had been killed by a sniper, she couldn't assume she was safe. Why would she dismiss him watching out for her?

He, of all people, knew there was strength in numbers. That was why he worked with a team and not solo.

"I have to get to the clinic." She gathered her things, left some cash on the table, and headed out.

Judah nudged his elbow. "We aren't just going to let her go, are we?"

"Of course not." An idea came to him. "Now that I think about it, my shoulder doesn't feel too good. Maybe I hurt myself last night, and I should get seen by a doctor."

Judah grinned. "Maybe there's a free clinic around here somewhere."

"You read my mind."

HANNAH HESITATED a second before she stowed her phone in the locker. Sarah. She should think of herself as Sarah, or she might end up slipping out of this undercover role at the wrong moment.

*Lana.* Her mother's name was Lana.

She squeezed her eyes shut for a second so the information could sink in.

All Hannah had up until now were a couple of old photographs and a fake name. She knew the person her mother had been during the marriage to Stephen Gladstone had been fabricated. That had been easy enough to spot.

But the rest of it? Former Soviet double agent. CIA stuff. Even with all the things she'd been part of, that was way above her pay grade.

Badger had handed over the information. Which only made her wonder what else their team knew and hadn't told her.

She made her way to the front reception desk in time to watch Nurse Weston unlock the front door.

"Mindy is late again." Weston rolled her eyes. "At least you get here on time."

"But I'm not qualified to even take a temperature." Mindy was a certified nurse's assistant, along with Bethany. The only male who worked in the office was Craig Mathers, Dr. Mathers's son, a physician's assistant.

"At least you get the patients situated until they can be seen." Nurse Weston waved at the coffee pot in the corner. "It was a good idea having one of those."

Given that the people who occupied the waiting area tend to be sick, Hannah had to disinfect the carafe's handle every time someone poured themselves a cup. But it didn't take that much, and the tradeoff was fresh hot java she didn't have to walk far to obtain.

She'd only finished two mugs worth of coffee at the diner,

and those were tiny anyway. Given how much sleep she'd gotten, Hannah figured she was about four cups behind at this point.

"Rough night?"

She was surprised Nurse Weston even asked but had prepped her answer just in case.

Hannah/Sarah nodded. "It was a long one, that's for sure." She'd always thought that sticking as close to the truth as possible was the best way to play any role as an undercover. "I ended up talking to the police."

Nurse Weston's eyes widened.

Hannah said, "It started with phone calls. That's nothing new—the harassment. My ex called me, and then when I stopped picking up, he called from a different number. So I shut my phone off. But he came over and was banging on the door. I called the police, and they told me I should file a restraining order." She shook her head as though frustrated with the whole situation.

Hannah had met plenty of women who had every right to file a restraining order. Just as she had met plenty of men entitled to do the same. Abuse didn't originate from one gender but crossed all lines and happened in every social circle. She'd seen it in every form. She had helped the victims and done what she could to bring justice.

She knew the system wasn't perfect.

"He didn't hurt you, did he?" Nurse Weston looked her over as though surveying her for injuries.

Hannah shook her head, calling on recent frustrations to harden her expression. "Even if he got in, which he didn't, I've taken so many self-defense classes, and weapons training classes things would certainly be different than the last time."

"Good for you." Nurse Weston looked her up and down as though not entirely convinced.

Hannah leaned against the front desk, lifted one foot, and showed the knife in a sheath at her ankle. She didn't show her the gun holstered on her other leg. That was her backup revolver. Purely for emergencies.

Weston stared at the knife. "Well, then."

Hannah went around the desk and settled in her seat. "I've had some ideas about fundraising that I've come up with."

Nurse Weston nodded. "You sure you know how to take care of yourself?"

"I do what I can to be safe. No one else is going to do it for me." That was also something that had proved true in her life. "I'll send you an email about my ideas."

Nurse Weston stayed where she was. "We already have an idea. Doctor Mathers and I came up with something, and we might need some help if you're interested."

Given the nurse's body language and her expression, Hannah decided to forgo excitement. Though she did perk up a little in her seat. "What is it?"

Before Weston could tell her, the clinic's front door opened, and Badger strode in with a slight limp but also holding his shoulder. Hannah kept her expression blank, even though Weston wasn't looking at her, and said, "Good morning."

What was he even doing here? It took effort to maintain her composure.

Waltzing in here, like he had every right to invade her work. The guy didn't have any sense of boundaries. Or her capability as a cop. Otherwise, he would've trusted her and kept his distance. It was doubtful he was here to pass on some kind of message, considering he could've just sent her a text. She hadn't blocked him. She just hadn't replied or returned any of his calls after Judah drove her back to that motel.

And she wouldn't, when it was clear he still wanted to take over her life. If she gave that proverbial inch, one day she would wake up and realize he'd taken the whole mile. Maybe it wouldn't be bad. She might even enjoy that kind of life. But there was no way she could still be who she was if she was absorbed into a world that he took charge of.

Hannah would rather call the shots in her own life.

Badger hissed out a breath and put a hand to his ribs. "Any chance I can get seen before I've gotta be at work? Boss doesn't like it when I'm late."

"Of course." Hannah handed him a clipboard with the intake form already on it. And a pen. "Just fill these out, and we'll get you back there."

Nurse Weston studied him with the eye of someone accustomed to reading people. Hannah could have told her that Badger was her dangerous ex-boyfriend. She didn't have to pretend he was just some anonymous patient who came in the door just now. He had to know she could've reacted to him, milked the situation. Had him forcibly removed.

She could have destroyed his ability to watch over her from the same room. Though, what he planned to do when he was inside the exam room was another story. Unless he'd brought surveillance cameras with him and planned to plant them as soon as Weston left the waiting area.

She could have easily ruined whatever plan he had going on here. Instead, she kept up with the pretense that he was nobody to her. It really was the best way to deal with this attraction that seemed to zing back and forth between them. Badger thought he had to be in control all the time, and she was going to have to let him—at least in this situation—if she was going to be Hannah and not Sarah, desperate to have her ex out of her life.

The person she was under the police shield she wore, even when it wasn't clipped to her belt, wasn't a liar. She knew a lot of cops were prepared to skirt the lines if it was necessary to get a dangerous criminal off the streets, but she wasn't one of them. She'd never compromised. And even if it might be momentarily satisfying to see Badger kicked out of the clinic, she wasn't willing to be that person.

Nurse Weston glanced at her. "Are you good?"

Hannah nodded. "We'll talk more later?"

"Tell me first," Weston said. "How do you feel about Robin Hood?"

"Robbing from the rich to give to the poor? People should put in the work if they want something. No one ever gave me a handout." She wanted to wince, but the words were already out. Hannah had been born with nothing and raised in a family who had little to their name despite working long hours. Some things were simply ingrained, and her work ethic was one of them. But she still needed to convince the woman in front of her. "When it comes to getting what I need? I'm willing to do whatever it takes."

Nurse Weston's eyebrows rose. "I'm happy to pay more than well for this. I'll text you later. Don't be late."

She strode from the waiting area to the back hall. As soon as she was out of earshot, Badger wandered back over with the clipboard. Hannah lifted her chin. "All finished?"

"Can anyone see us?" He nodded as he spoke, as though in answer to her question.

"No one checks the camera feeds."

He pulled out his cell phone. "Good. If your computer flickers, it's just Ted getting into the system."

"And my flash drive that you stole?" She would have nothing on the clinic's financials if he didn't turn it over to her to pass to the task force supervising agent. Or anything else that had been on the director's computer. As it was, the drive was no longer admissible. But they still needed the information.

"It's safe."

She glared at him. Of course, he would hold onto it until he felt as though it needed to be handed over. She wanted to give him what for, but another patient entered. Badger wandered back to his chair with that self-assured stride of a highly trained operative who knew what he was capable of. And the situation he was putting her in.

Whatever Nurse Weston had going on, Hannah was willing to go so far as praying it brought this operation to a close.

Then she could walk away from Badger and the whole mess that was her life.

Again.

## 5

"You think she was telling the truth—that she doesn't know Lana?" Zander's voice was low through the phone line. "Nora wanted to tell her, but Hannah just changes the subject. When she replies at all."

Badger held the phone to his ear as he crossed the street, headed to where Hannah was meeting with her supervising agent. That was news to him. But then, he'd been concentrating on his recovery. "She's good as an undercover. She may be lying, and she knows all about Lana."

All day while he watched the feeds of the lobby and listened to every conversation she had, he wondered about it. Only the fact Ted had managed to hack her phone told him she likely didn't work for Lana already. Unless she was deep, deep undercover, weeks into a ruse where Chevalier Protection Specialists might have been the target.

But he didn't want to think about that. It was all too reminiscent of Isaac being assigned to their team...and then betraying them.

He wanted to believe Hannah was just a police officer—if

she could be "just" anything. Given what'd happened the past few months, the reality was none of them really knew her. Even if she was Zander's sister-in-law. Lana's daughter.

So far Lana had proven to be a mystery, aside from her relationship with Isaac. Their former teammate had been ordered by her to get close to them.

Now they knew his true colors. Just not why he'd done it —or why he turned himself in to the authorities. Something Badger was supposed to be trying to figure out.

"As soon as Hannah is safe, I'll go talk to Isaac."

The guy had turned himself in at the same time he'd returned a stolen suitcase nuke to the military authorities. Now Isaac was in federal custody, and they had permission for one of them to go see him. It was the investigating agent's last-ditch effort to get Isaac to talk. The guy hadn't said one word to anyone, even after he'd been threatened with life in prison.

Badger figured they probably threatened him with more than that. The guy was a former CIA agent, so he'd know all about black sites where due process meant little in the face of national security. No one wanted to believe that places like that actually existed, but the world was a dangerous place.

Zander said, "Copy that."

Badger spotted Hannah in her car, waiting for her supervising agent to show up. He didn't want to think about the night before, and how she'd seen a man shot in front of her. As far as he knew she didn't break down or anything, but considering the time she'd spent alone last night after she dealt with the police, he realized she might have cried herself to sleep for all he knew.

It wasn't as though she would openly admit anything of the sort.

At least not to him.

She spotted Badger before he was close enough he'd worry about her spatial awareness. The woman looked worn out, something he was hoping her supervisory agent would notice. Not that anyone would be given a day off in the middle of an undercover investigation—especially one that involved the death of another agent.

She climbed out of her car. "Seriously?"

"I was hired to protect you."

"From my boss?"

Badger shrugged. "Federal agent or not doesn't matter. What matters is your safety."

She came close enough he could touch her, but neither of them did that. "You don't think I'm protected? There's risk inherent in undercover work, sure. But that's why I meet daily with my handler."

"He's dead."

"You're impossible."

"Maybe. But you'll be alive when this is done."

"And if I hate you by then?"

"I get paid whether you like me or not. That's not the job." He managed to get all the words out. Telling himself her feelings on the subject didn't affect him failed to account for *his* feelings happening to suck right now. The closer she got, the more he felt the attraction between them.

Hannah either refused to acknowledge it, or she felt nothing for him—except maybe disdain.

He wished he knew whether she felt *something* for him. But what would that help? It wasn't why he was here.

"That your guy?" He motioned with his chin to the man approaching them. Suit and tie, silver hair. Middle-management type. He could've worked in a bank or some office just like any other. Pushing paper instead of affecting real people's lives.

Ted said the guy had commendations and whatnot, but that didn't mean Badger was about to trust him. Honor wasn't something that could be faked in person. He'd be able to tell if it was a pretense.

But then, why hadn't he known something was off with Isaac?

Hannah blew out a tight breath and turned to watch Supervisory Special Agent Ken Alanson approach. "You're seriously going to stay for this?"

He smiled to himself. "Zander already cleared it with his boss." Badger leaned close and whispered in her ear. "I'll be your shadow for the remainder of this investigation."

He spotted a muscle in her jaw flex and had to smother the amusement. It was probably unsportsmanlike to be so pleased she was out of sorts. As long as she didn't get in his way or hinder his ability to cover her six, they weren't going to have a problem here.

Special Agent Alanson sized him up. "Chevalier?"

He stuck his hand out. "Ryder Samuel Huaka'i. But everyone just calls me Badger." His mother had called him Sam, and everyone at school used a name he wasn't supposed to say out loud.

Hannah twisted around to stare at him.

"Okay, then. Badger." Alanson turned to Hannah. "How are you?"

She brushed off whatever that was about his name. "Do I really need a babysitter?"

"Considering Pearson is dead?" Alanson shook his head. "Yes. And being as it's additional resources I don't have to account for in the funding, why would we say no?"

Hannah pressed her lips together.

"You won't even know I'm there," Badger said.

She didn't seem convinced.

Until he produced the flash drive. "This is the evidence from the clinic, a copy of everything on the computer, right?"

Hannah glared at him. "Did your people make their own copy?"

He'd figured it wouldn't be admissible in the investigation given he was an outsider, and he could've tampered with it before he turned it over. Erased anything that could incriminate him—or made alterations. The feds had no idea, and he was an unknown as far as they were concerned.

Badger shrugged one shoulder. "We don't have a great track record with federal task forces or higher ups in agencies. But we have a good friend in the bureau."

Hannah said, "So you'll freely interfere in the chain of evidence in a federal investigation like it's no big deal?"

Alanson pocketed the flash drive. "Let's hope there's something good on it anyway." His expression darkened. "Because we've got nothing else that connects the guy in custody to the death of Special Agent Pearson."

"Except eyewitness testimony?" Hannah asked.

He figured she was talking about him or herself. Maybe both of them, which would mean more time spent together.

Alanson nodded. "You're headed out tonight to meet the crew from the clinic?"

Ah, yes. Badger brushed off thoughts of spending more time with Hannah in favor of this Robin Hood thing.

He didn't have a good feeling about whatever Nurse Weston had invited Hannah to participate in tonight. She needed to complete the investigation. He knew that because he would if he were in her situation. But he also had zero problem scooping her out of any trouble that got too hot and protecting her on the run—whether she liked it or not.

Badger figured she knew it. Nor did she like it. But her handler was dead. She wasn't going to walk away from this.

Hannah said, "They've definitely got a plan."

"I think I might have an idea what it is." Alanson shifted his weight to take the pressure off an injury Ted mentioned was on the agent's medical record. "We found an open case. Local. Someone ripped off the Chinese after hours. A laundry. We think they were running games out the back. All their cash was gone, and the guys working that night were tranqued with pharmaceuticals." Alanson sighed. "We only know it happened because Baltimore PD has a guy in vice undercover. The Chinese thought it was a rival gang and went after them, but he wasn't convinced. Managed to get the bloodshed to a minimum because they couldn't be sure. No one wanted to start a war over it, even if their money was gone."

Hannah blew out a breath.

"Yeah," Alanson said. "Their guy took a serious risk, but it paid off."

Badger frowned. "You think it was Nurse Weston and her boss?"

Hannah said, "I think we're gonna find out."

Badger nodded. "Very good."

"There's something else." Hannah glanced at Badger, as if she didn't want to say this in front of him. But she did. "Pearson had an envelope on him when he was shot."

Alanson nodded. He pulled one from the inside of his suit jacket.

Hannah pocketed it without even looking.

"He informed me…" Alanson pushed out a breath. "Just be careful."

HANNAH WAS across the street a little ahead of schedule. Sitting in the driver seat of her undercover persona's car.

"Do you get nervous before this kind of thing?" Badger's voice was almost warm in her ear. Comforting, at least.

She didn't shake her head. If anyone was watching, they didn't need to see her communicating with someone—or looking like she was.

Or losing the battle to look in that envelope and allow herself to be distracted. Which was why she'd left it with her things.

Hannah lifted the paper cup of coffee she'd bought at a drive-thru to her mouth and spoke behind the rim. "What's to get nervous about? I'm just doing my job. And whatever happens, it's a part of my job to deal with it."

She figured Judah was also listening, considering he was on her protection detail as well, though she hadn't seen him since he drove her to the bar last night—in time to see that guy fly out the window.

Badger still hadn't told her what the shooter had said to him during their altercation. Before he supposedly jumped out of the window. That could mean he'd said nothing. But she didn't take anyone's word for anything.

The latest email update from her boss was that police had identified a deceased woman in the apartment above the bar as the resident. She'd been dead nearly a week. Shot, presumably in a home invasion. Why the shooter had returned to that place, no one knew.

He might have known he was being followed and chose somewhere that would offer a defensive position and give away nothing about who he was. Or he'd killed the woman, and it'd also been a job. He needed the police to process the body so there was confirmation of a kill.

She figured when the investigating detectives worked the case they would find nothing to connect the shooter to the dead woman.

Unless he confessed, which she figured was unlikely given he was a professional hitman.

The guy had been transferred into federal custody and was now awaiting whatever charges would be filed.

She didn't figure he would come after her again if he was released on bail. But then again, anything was possible. People's actions didn't always make sense to her.

If someone had hired him, then maybe they'd hired someone else as well, as a backup plan. It could only be a matter of time before the next attempt on her life.

As if that was going to stop her from doing her job.

Badger spoke up. "The address Nurse Weston gave you is the residence of a local lawyer. You think that's the target?"

"We'll find out in a minute." She glanced both ways on the street, looking for someone she knew.

"You think the clinic staff are the ones who knocked over that Chinese gambling den?"

Hannah blew out a breath. "I thought you were being paid to protect me. Not get involved in a federal investigation."

In her experience, the more people were interested in something, the muddier it got. Until no one knew who was responsible for what. It was hardly an effective way to get anything done.

She lowered the paper cup and swallowed. "I don't need to toss ideas around. Feelings don't get convictions. Evidence does."

"You never acted on a hunch?"

"Why?" Hannah frowned. She had, once—though it had been more like doing nothing because the hunch had been that the kid involved was innocent. The resulting devastation wasn't something she ever wanted to go back and revisit. "The truth is the truth. Instincts can be biased all too easily."

"So tell me what the deal is with that envelope?"

Hannah didn't respond. He was pushing, trying to get her to open up to him, and she had no intention of allowing that to happen.

The envelope was a window into her past and who she was. She didn't even know what was in it, hadn't opened it, and she still knew that. It was a test—another way to ensure her feelings had no control over her.

She was going to open it later. And not tell Badger what was in it.

Ever.

Thankfully, Hannah spotted Nurse Weston on approach, coming up behind the car. "Gotta go. Bye."

"Have a good day at the office, dear."

His use of that expression caused a hitch in her throat so that when Nurse Weston rapped on the window, Hannah was partially choking. She hit the button, and the window rolled down.

"Are you sure you can handle this?"

Hannah cleared her throat. "Maybe if I knew what this was?" She motioned to the house where the lawyer lived.

"That isn't where we're going. Two houses down, the gray one."

Hannah frowned at the gray house. A high wall and a big gate. "Who lives there?"

"Your job isn't to ask questions." Weston looked at her

watch. "I'll see you there in two minutes." She pulled a gun from under her coat. "Carry this and do what you're told. You'll get paid well."

Weston turned and strode toward the house. Hannah spotted the doctor and her son—the PA who worked at the clinic, Craig Mathers. She hadn't spoken to him much, as he tended to keep to himself.

The three of them were definitely up to something, like knocking over a Chinese gambling den and taking off with all the money.

Hannah climbed out and pocketed her car keys. She didn't bother locking the car, just in case she needed to make a quick getaway.

"We're moving in." Badger's tone in her earpiece was clear and professional, as though he knew she was focused now.

Enough of that intuition business she wasn't interested in listening to. He was a soldier, which meant he had plenty of skill. The company he worked in now would've given him plenty of knowledge to go along with that. Experience layered on top.

But in the end, he wasn't a cop, and this wasn't his case. There was no time to respond to his comment. If his intention was to interfere, that was one thing. But she hoped he was only purposely trying to keep her safe, as was his job.

Hannah tried to look like a clinic receptionist and not a cop as she held the gun and walked through the gate, following Nurse Weston to the front door.

The entryway was lit up. From down the hall, she could hear shouting. Nurse Weston disappeared into a room at the end of the hall, to the right.

Hannah made her way after her and stopped at the

entrance to a vast study. She still wasn't sure whose house it was.

She turned and looked in the room. Her mind blanked, only coming up with one thing.

*Blood.*

Judah got on comms, his British accent thick with irritation. "Ted has intel."

Hannah just stared at the scene in the room while her mind struggled to process. The Chinese had been subdued with tranqs.

And yet, here was the doctor—doing damage to some guy tied to a chair.

Judah said, "The house is listed under a holding company with known ties to José Suarez and his entire cartel. Looks like after he came to the clinic and the doc realized how much money he had, she decided to do a little fundraising of her own."

"She's not even listening." Craig stepped in front of her, waving his hand in front of Hannah's face.

She blinked and looked up at him. Anyone would be shocked at what she had just seen. Even a cop with a long career investigating homicides. Including ones where every square inch of the room was covered in castoff.

The doctor had made a serious mess.

"Why is she here?" Craig glanced over his shoulder at his mom, who was clearly the one in charge.

The clinic director held both a gun and a knife. She had the foot soldier tied to a chair at the desk. "You really want to talk about this now? We need the code to the safe, or we're all sunk, and we get nothing."

Craig grabbed a handful of Hannah's hair and tugged her in front of him.

Hannah hissed out a breath.

Craig said, "I just don't see why we need four of us here."

There was no time for Hannah to respond, even if her brain was coming up with ideas now. Which it wasn't.

Nurse Weston glanced over at him. "You know why." But she didn't explain.

The director turned back to the man strapped to the chair. Her back blocked Hannah's view of him while Craig held her close to his front and breathed on the side of her face. She tried to wiggle out of his hold, but he didn't let her go.

The man in the chair twitched and thrashed. Whatever the doc was doing, it caused a moan behind whatever had been tied across his mouth.

"You're going to tell me?"

Another moan, this one in agreement.

The doctor shifted. "Go ahead."

The man spewed obscenities at her. Dr. Mathers jerked her hand toward him, and the man screamed. Seconds later, his body went limp.

*React like a receptionist.*

"You just killed that man." Hannah inhaled a gasping breath as though she had never seen anything like this before.

The doctor glanced at her son. "Let her go, get over here and blow the safe. We need to get the money out before anyone comes back."

Nurse Weston shoved past Hannah and headed for the hall. Craig let her go. The two of them bumped against her as if she were in a pinball machine. Hannah just stood there in shock—which wasn't too far from the truth. If she were honest with herself, it was at least *partially* shock. All she could think of was Pearson. His body jerked. He fell to the ground.

No one could be entirely numb to something like this. Not when this much blood had been shed.

She tried to shake it off and focus. What was her role here? They had to have asked her to come with them for a reason.

The doctor came over and shoved her back against the wall, pressing her forearm against Hannah's collarbones. "Don't look at the safe."

Over by the wall behind the desk, Craig stuck plastic explosives to the face of the safe.

"As soon as it blows, grab one of those duffels and start filling it. It'll take all of us to carry the money out of here."

Hannah swallowed.

"And if you double-cross me," the doctor said, "you end up like that guy. Got me?"

## 6

B adger crouch-walked between the stone wall and the bushes, then ducked down so he remained out of sight. Nurse Weston watched from the window. On lookout, probably for any of the cartel guys in case they came home before the group was done ripping them off.

"You see anything?" That was Judah, still in the car. Waiting to be the getaway driver if they needed to make a quick exit.

Badger said, "Did you mute us on Hannah's end?"

"Before she went in."

That meant Judah had gone into the app on his phone earlier—the one that controlled their earpieces. He'd toggled Hannah's settings to exclude their audio. It was a complicated setup, but sometimes one of them needed not to be distracted by everyone else's conversation.

Badger made his way along the row of bushes to the hedge that separated the garden from the entertaining area. Over there he would be as close as possible to the nearest entry in case he had to use it. Which he would, even if it meant running for the door exposed him to Weston's watchful gaze.

If he had to get inside, it wouldn't matter because if Hannah needed him in there, he was going to race straight across the grass and run inside.

"Andre would have it blown open already."

Badger smiled to himself. "Andre wouldn't be blowing the door and burning up any of the money at all."

Judah chuckled over their comms.

He could still hear them in the room. Waiting for Craig to set explosive charges on the safe, as though blowing it wouldn't damage the contents. Maybe they thought the salvageable bills would be worth it. Assuming the entire thing was stuffed with money. They had to have done some kind of recon, or the doctor had shown up here to collect the fee for treating Suarez, and she'd seen it with her own eyes.

"Did you tell Alanson we're in position?"

Judah scoffed. "Uh, duh. But the feds are holding off. They're going to sit tight and wait for Hannah to say the word that means they need to move in."

"Why don't they just bust in and catch them in the act?"

"Apparently they'd rather sit in their vehicles. Because if they wait for the crew to leave the house with the money, they can grab them on the street. Alanson wants to flip the doctor, her son, *and* the nurse. Get them to give the feds intel on Suarez and anything they know about his operation. Or any other operation."

Badger blew out a breath. "Of course. How silly of me to not realize they didn't want to stop a crime in progress."

Instead of one burglary crew, they were going to go after a cartel.

"I'm moving closer."

Judah said, "Copy that."

Badger got far enough he could see the study window, though the curtains were closed. He set one hand in the dirt to steady himself and caught an inhale that felt raw deep in his chest.

"That sounded painful."

"I'm okay," Badger said. "Sometimes it feels like breathing in sandpaper."

Windermere, the team doctor for Chevalier Protection Specialists, had given him a clean bill of health several weeks ago. But it didn't mean that after inhaling a single drop of a deadly chemical, Badger still didn't feel the aftereffects.

The whole thing happened nearly two months ago now. He'd been laid up in bed for the first month, letting his lungs heal. Taking all kinds of meds and vitamins until he could inhale a full breath. Now doing it didn't hurt for the most part.

"Cover your ears." That was the doctor, her voice distant over the comms, even though he figured she stood right in front of Hannah.

The police detective didn't give anything away. Hannah acted like the part of a scared clinic receptionist in over her head. He'd wondered why they'd brought her here—until they said she was to help them load the duffels. Just another pair of hands to carry the load. Badger couldn't help thinking she might be set up as a scapegoat if the worst happened.

Only because they didn't know she was an undercover cop.

If they did, they would probably shoot her and leave her here for the cartel to think the feds were the ones who ripped them off.

He pondered that while the pop of the explosion echoed

through the earpiece. It crackled and shut off for a second, going quiet so that he had no idea if Hannah was okay. Or if she was dead.

Crouched in a bush wasn't the place he wanted to be. Not a guy like him used to being in the thick of it. Even protecting her, he'd been relegated to outside.

If they'd had more time to set this up, he'd have played the part of her boyfriend and forced the doctor to include him as the skilled third party he'd be introduced to them as. In a longer operation, it might've worked. But with no time to plan something like that, they'd had to just roll with the night's operation.

Which meant sending Hannah in there alone and unprotected. Even with her team down the street and him outside because they didn't know him well enough to clear him to be part of it, even if there was time.

Nurse Weston turned back from the window. Badger burst out from behind the bush and raced across the lawn. He slammed into the wall beside the window just as she turned back. He saw her mouth move as she said something but didn't catch what it was.

Over comms, he heard the guy ordering Hannah to fill duffel bags with cash while she whimpered as a terrified captive.

Badger heard the noise he made, low in his throat.

"You're going inside, aren't you?"

It figured Judah remembered the compound a couple of months ago when Andre had gone inside to rescue his wife. Lucia had been a DEA agent, captured while on an operation much like Hannah was on now. Except that there was no romantic relationship between him and the police detective.

"I guess I shouldn't really be surprised." Judah sighed

across the comms line. "Everyone knows how you feel about her."

"That isn't what this is." Badger slid his back along the wall and headed for the side door he figured led into the kitchen. He twisted the handle and crept inside. It was dark, the air warm and musty. He'd have argued more with Judah, but what would it serve?

They weren't trying to get Isaac to open up to them because Hannah was in danger. There wasn't any other reason why they'd sought her out. And with Lana being involved somehow, no way could they have ignored it.

Nurse Weston called out, "A car just pulled into the driveway."

"Let's go."

Badger heard the hurried word with one ear and through the comms earbud in the other. He figured it was the doctor. The pattering of feet headed his direction down the hall. Badger ran his hand along the counter and ducked down behind the breakfast bar.

The group hurried through the kitchen. Flashlights bobbed in the dark, illuminating the valance over a window. Breathing came heavy as they raced for the door. There was a thud, and Hannah whimpered. She'd bumped something.

His next inhale burned.

"Let's go." That was the guy with them, the doctor's son Hannah had mentioned.

As soon as they cleared out, he would follow. Sticking to the bushes again as he made his way after them. Judah could pick him up, and they'd be able to pursue Hannah to her destination. Watch the feds do the takedown.

As long as he could get out before the cartel showed up.

Quiet echoed in the kitchen. Badger eased around the breakfast bar and heard a faint whimper. He paused.

Heard a shuffle.

They were gone. He should go.

"What is it?" Judah asked.

"I think there's someone else here." Badger pulled his phone and flipped on the flashlight. "How long do I have?"

"Maybe a minute. More, if I can give you a distraction."

"Do it." Badger approached the pantry in the corner, twisted the handle, and eased it open.

Inside, a dark-haired girl, probably high school age, crouched in the corner. Tears ran down her face, her eyes wide with fear.

"I can take you to the police." It was a risk. Maybe that wasn't somewhere she would be safe. "There's a woman outside, a detective, and she can help you." That might not be any better. What was he supposed to say? "Do you want to escape this house?"

The front door crashed open, and the sound echoed down the hall.

Badger whispered, "Come on. We have to run before they see us."

---

"WELL?"

Hannah glanced over at Dr. Mathers as they ran. Craig was right behind her. All of them carried duffel bags, except Craig, who had two. Nurse Weston slung one over her head to lay across her body.

They rushed as a unit to the sidewalk, headed toward Hannah's car.

Dr. Mathers laughed as they crossed the street. "She's speechless."

"Probably never had that much excitement in her life." Craig's breathy chuckle was far too close behind her.

Even Weston seemed amused. As though each of them got a rise out of ripping off dangerous criminals, ones who would probably come after them if they ever found out who was behind the theft. They hadn't left any witnesses, and if they got out of there quickly enough…

It was still far too risky as far as Hannah was concerned.

Maybe the plan was to give up Hannah as the one behind the break-in and the theft of all the cartel's money. And wasn't that a terrifying thought?

She would wind up carved up and left in the desert. After the Suarez cartel tortured her—probably for days—all to find the location of the money. She would have no clue, and they wouldn't believe any of her pleas for mercy.

Cartels were ruthless. But a cartel that had been robbed would be twice as deadly.

This was how the doctor funded her clinic?

Hannah could hardly believe they had that much bravado. But the whole Robin Hood thing was likely intoxicating. Considering they'd gotten away with it before, and now they might have done so again.

They piled into Hannah's car with Craig in the driver's seat, whether Hannah agreed with it or not. Nurse Weston slid across the back seat while the doctor got in the front passenger side. She was supposed to get in. Instead, Hannah glanced over her shoulder and spotted Badger running down the driveway along with a young woman wearing no shoes.

The cartel would see them.

Hannah needed out, so she could go help them. "I don't want to be part of this."

Craig hadn't shut his door yet. He glared at her. "You stay here, and they'll kill you."

She took a step back. "I'm not getting in the car."

"Your funeral." He hit the gas, and they took off. The open rear door swung shut on its own.

Thankfully she hadn't left anything incriminating in her car that would lead them to her real identity. The vehicle was completely clean in terms of her undercover persona, and the envelope was in her jacket, but that wasn't what she needed to worry about right now.

Hannah turned and raced toward the stone wall.

Badger and the girl were halfway down the driveway. "Come on." He beckoned to the girl. Beckoning her to angle right with him, leaving no room for error.

Hannah could see the pain on his face from every inhale. His lungs must be hurting.

Hannah had the gun Weston had given her. She spied around the wall where two men raced out of the house. She saw the second they spotted both the girl and Badger.

She steadied her stance, aimed the gun, and squeezed off a shot. It clicked. Empty. Had Nurse Weston given her an unloaded gun?

One of the cartel guys lifted his gun and pointed it toward her.

Hannah had nowhere else to go, so she raced across the driveway in front of them toward Badger. A shot kicked off the asphalt behind her. She caught up to the girl just as Badger twisted around, planted one knee on the grass, and fired twice.

The girl screamed.

Hannah collided with her but caught herself before they both went down. "I'm a police detective."

That might not make the girl feel any better, but if it was possible to reassure her, then Hannah would do that.

"Keep going," Hannah said. "We need to get to their vehicle."

She had no idea where Judah was right now. Hopefully hurtling in their direction in the car, coming to pick them up. Meanwhile, the feds would be closing in on her car and taking down the crew who had just robbed the cartel.

Adrenaline flooded her, making her hands shake as they raced along the sidewalk in front of the neighbor's house.

A bullet slammed into the tree as they passed it. The girl screamed again. Hannah wanted to tug her close, but it would hinder their running and provide the gunmen with a bigger target. "Keep going. Come on."

Badger fired another shot behind them.

She heard the scream on impact and a body fall. How many more were there?

He said, "Copy that."

Hannah glanced over her shoulder as they ran. "Judah?" She couldn't hear anything through the earpiece they'd given her.

Badger said, "Thirty seconds. He'll pull a U-turn on the street."

Before that could happen, car tires screeched from behind them. She assumed it was a group of cartel guys for a split second, enough to completely overwhelm them. But then she heard doors open and the thud of boots. One of the SUVs belonging to the task force.

Hannah heard the call of, "Federal agents! Put the guns down!"

She grabbed the girl and tugged her behind the nearest tree, slowing them both to a stop. They both swung around and took cover, just in case the cartel guys decided to fight back.

Badger moved close to them. "Are you both okay?"

Hannah brushed off whatever feeling wanted to take root. She didn't much care to entertain it. Not when it came to Badger and his insisting on calling all the shots. Despite knowing exactly how to work on a team, he seemed to forget everything when she became part of the group.

The cartel guys were thrown to the ground and cuffed. Supervising Special Agent Alanson strode over to her. "You okay, Detective Yassick?"

"Yes, sir."

"Good. Let's go talk about the colossal mess tonight has become."

Badger glanced at her, but Hannah didn't look at him. She just followed her boss as he strode toward the SUV he'd pulled up in.

Hannah said, "Did the other agents pull over my car and get the crew and the money?"

"When a gunfight kicked off here?" Alanson's eyebrows rose. "We split into two groups. The group on the car is in pursuit."

"They're going to do the takedown on the road?"

"That's not something you need to worry about right now. Not when you were supposed to be in the vehicle with them, playing along so you can maintain your cover in case we need to utilize it at a later date by putting you in holding with one of them."

Alanson paused a split second, not long enough for her to respond. "And yes, I understand that in the heat of things we sometimes have to switch up our direction. But to save your boyfriend, who only came here to protect you? Not good enough. You're putting your life in the line of fire to save him." He shrugged as though he had no clue why she would do that.

"I had a gun. I saw he had an innocent with him and that the cartel was in pursuit, so I broke off and went to provide him with backup." Hannah hoped he understood without her having to explain in greater detail. After all, it was only going to sound like she thought Badger couldn't handle it. Or she let her emotions cloud her judgment.

But Badger did have a girl with him now.

She continued, "I'm sure there was a reason why he pulled her out of the house. Maybe she can provide us with intel on the cartel, given she was in there?" That sounded a lot better than her getting dragged down by her emotions. Thinking for a split second that Badger could lose his life here trying to protect her. Turning around to go help him.

Not just because she would much rather be where he was than in a car full of suspects who would be at the top of the cartel's hit list soon enough.

Alanson folded his arms. "I'm not sure I require your presence on this task force. Clearly, your judgment is questionable."

She started to argue.

He cut her off. "Given what was in that envelope, maybe it's not so much of a surprise."

Hannah gaped. "You…"

Alanson turned away.

Rage blinded her. A message for her, and he *read* it?

"What is it?" Alanson barked.

Not only did he read it, now he was kicking her off the

task force because of what was in there. Hannah couldn't believe this.

She whipped the envelope out of her jacket and tore the top open.

The agent who jogged up to them shook his head as he approached. "Suarez wasn't among them. All we've got is four soldiers."

"And a witness." That was Badger.

They might want her out, but she'd still be part of this one way or another. They couldn't avoid that. She didn't look up from the paper, just slid it from the envelope and opened it.

She could feel their gaze on her. Did everyone know what was in this?

Hannah walked several feet away, but it did nothing to distance herself. She parted the folds and looked at…a report.

A DNA match, but she already knew Nora was…

It wasn't Nora's name on the paper. The DNA had been run from an inmate in federal prison trying to ascertain his identity.

Hers had popped up in the system because, as a cop, she was on file. She'd come up as a familial match.

With *Isaac Amrakov.*

Hannah whirled around.

Badger walked over with the girl, who hugged herself, looking scared and freezing. Then he pulled off his coat and wrapped it around the girl's shoulders. "If you go with these agents, they can make sure you get a hot drink and somewhere safe to stay."

Hannah glanced at Alanson, trying to figure out what to say.

All he did was glare at her. "Collins, take the girl to a car and have her sit tight."

"Yes, sir." The agent led the girl away.

Badger and Hannah both waited for him to continue.

Instead, he pulled out his phone and looked at the screen. "You'd both better pray we get something out of all these people we just scooped up. Because of the doctor and her crew in your car? Our people lost them."

Hannah's gut tightened. Her DNA matched a criminal, so now she was a suspect too.

"Since you're not in the car with them, guess who's responsible?"

## 7

B adger paced up and down the driveway of the cartel house. Hannah had been dragged back inside by agents and local cops so she could walk them through the scene and tell them what happened.

He was interviewed as well, but it didn't take nearly as long as hers. Mostly only so he could explain how he'd found the girl and knew nothing about her. Also why he was here when he lived nowhere near Baltimore. What Chevalier Protection Specialists was, and yes, how they were the same crew who were on the ground when former president Raleigh's wife was killed. The ones responsible for Stephen Gladstone's arrest. For taking down Franklin Burgess. And more recently, for the arrest of Rei Wen Chang and all that business with the guy who had turned out to be Eas's twin.

It turned out to be a longer explanation than he'd thought. But once the agent he spoke to confirmed with Supervising Agent Alanson, and both of them called Zander, they considered him free to go. Assuming he would stick around town if they had any further questions.

The cops mostly ignored his pacing after that.

Special Agent Alanson strode out the front door a while later, tugging off gloves that kept his prints or DNA from contaminating the scene. He strode over to Badger. "When she comes out, the two of you are free to go."

Badger nodded. *Free to go.* As if they'd been detained? "Care to tell me what's going on?"

He didn't especially like having to protect her from a spot where he couldn't even see her. However, given she was surrounded by cops, he figured there wasn't much room to argue. Alanson was acting weird, though.

All the agent said was, "I want a meeting first thing."

Badger wasn't assuming Hannah would want to go off the radar, even if it was for the best. "Just tell us when or where, and we'll be there."

He and Judah had a rental house they were using, with a full security system. Judah had gone to the motel to check Hannah out just so she wasn't charged more than she needed to be. He was also going to fetch whatever personal belongings she'd left there.

He figured Sarah, her undercover persona, had a place she was staying. The fact Ted hadn't been able to find it only said good things about the task force and their security.

Badger said, "Your people are continuing the search for the doctor and her cohorts?"

"When we find them, I'll let Hannah know." Alanson's expression shifted, a flash of irritation there. Probably at the failure to catch the car full of medical staff and money.

Whether Alanson managed to flip them for intel or not, bringing them into custody would likely be a big win for the task force. But when things started to go wrong, he put the blame on Hannah. As if it was her fault she'd turned around and headed over to provide him backup.

Alanson didn't get to be mad at her for doing something good. But Badger wasn't going to tell him that because the guy probably wouldn't take it well.

Even if Badger agreed with him. At least in part.

Alanson strode away, headed for a group of his people.

As far as Badger was concerned, they'd let Hannah swing in the breeze without much protection. Sure, it'd maintained her undercover identity to keep from swooping in and taking over. Hannah hadn't used the code phrase that would indicate she was in distress. But still, she could have been seriously hurt—or killed. Especially when she'd broken off to help him.

Badger needed to ask her about that envelope but wasn't sure it was his place. Did the contents play into him protecting her?

"What's going on?"

He spun to find her on approach. Badger pressed his lips together and shook his head to keep from spilling out everything. He would only wind up sounding like a nutcase, and she didn't need that right now when she looked absolutely exhausted.

He turned to the side and motioned down the driveway. "Let's head out. We can talk on the way."

Hannah blew out a breath as they walked. "I've seen the aftermath of a murder. But I've never seen both sides. Before the person died, as well as the emptiness when they're gone."

"That guy in there, the cartel guy, you saw him die?"

She nodded. He still couldn't decipher the look on her face.

Badger had the curious urge to take her hand in his and

hold it as they walked to the car he'd brought. Judah had his own ride, so they could separate if needed. Take each other's backs if needed. And still, Hannah had tried to do Judah's job.

Not exactly disobeying orders, even if she'd known what Alanson expected her to do. But at the moment, it wasn't to double back like one of the Chevalier team.

"I didn't need help, by the way." The last thing he wanted was for her to think he wasn't capable of doing his job.

"With the girl?" He saw her glance at him from the corner of his eye.

Badger scanned the street in front of them, just in case another assassin was out there, even if a rifle shot would come out of nowhere. They'd have no way to take cover in time if a sniper already had them in his sights. He knew because it was part of his training.

"What if she was killed, or you were?" Hannah shook her head. "You think I was going to let that happen?"

"Judah was on his way."

"Oh, so I should've just left you to die and gotten on with my job?"

"I'm not saying I'm unhappy that your instinct is to save lives." So often his had been to take a life rather than safeguarding one. But he'd always known she was a better person than him.

"It wasn't instinct." She stopped at the passenger door of the car and turned to him. "I'm not going to let an innocent bystander get caught in the crossfire."

Badger said, "Get in." He held the door for her while she settled, then shut it and jogged around the front end of the car.

He was neither innocent nor was he a bystander. But

maybe she just didn't know how it worked being part of a team. She didn't need to. Hannah had a partner she worked with as a detective. Being on the task force, she was alone, working undercover. But she had support. Operating as a small squad? Not something she did every day.

Badger lived and breathed Chevalier Protection Specialists. The way he had lived and breathed Delta Force before that. Following Zander and Andre out of the army into civilian work had seemed simple at the time.

And it definitely hadn't turned out to be boring.

"I guess it's mostly over now." She let out a long breath. "Case closed." She made a face, which he took to mean that it would be when the doctor and her cohorts were found, and the paperwork was done.

"You'd rather do this stuff than return my calls?" Or Nora's.

The question was out before he realized he'd even spoken aloud. He should be telling her how Alanson wanted to meet tomorrow. Instead, he was dredging up things they didn't need to discuss.

She sighed again. "I want to say it's simpler. But only because relationships aren't my… I don't connect. I never have."

"You are with Nora, aren't you?"

"I think Nora wants something I can't give her." She blew out a breath. "And now…"

Badger hadn't heard anything like that from Nora. Then again, did the woman ever get frustrated about anything? In comparison, Hannah was like fire. "I don't think your sister is after anything. Except just to get to know you."

"I don't know how to do that. Why do you think I took

this job?" She sounded lost and completely alone, even if he was in the car with her.

He should be keeping this professional. Instead, they were treading into dangerous territory where his emotions came into play.

Taking this job had been about proving to Zander that he was capable. That his friend and team leader's confidence in him was justified, even if Zander was reserving judgment.

If things with Hannah got messy, and she was put in even more danger, it wouldn't look good for his future with Chevalier Protection Specialists. The team might not be able to afford to lose anyone else. Badger was going to get sidelined anyway. They'd all believe his injuries had sent him down a path that made him more of a liability than a help.

A guy who made poor choices.

The past hurtled toward him like the headlights of an oncoming car, ready to smash into his present with relentless force. He shoved the memories back. Sealing them in the box where he kept them, deep in his mind.

No one needed to know about any of it.

Which was why he couldn't allow himself to get even more hooked on Hannah. Maybe it was inevitable, but he at least had to try and fight it. It wasn't like she felt the same.

She was asleep by the time he reached the driveway of the rental house, and she didn't wake up. Badger lifted her into his arms and headed for the front door.

No, he didn't need to fall any harder for her than he already had.

This had to be about work and nothing else.

HANNAH STIRRED her coffee even though it didn't really need it. They were back at the same diner where she'd met Badger and Judah the previous morning. Only this time, she was side by side with Badger in a booth waiting for supervisory Special Agent Alanson. Judah sat across the room, facing them at a table where he could provide backup if necessary.

Sitting here, knowing Isaac was her brother. *Isaac Amrakov.*

The teammate who had betrayed the Chevalier guys was her flesh and blood, and she didn't want any part of it.

Hannah wanted to get up, walk out of the diner, and just…go.

"Sleep okay?" Badger said.

She glanced over. Instead of warmth and interest, he had an almost blank look on his face. Asking her the exact same question as though the question was perfunctory and not one of concern for her. She wasn't going to take the bait. "Thanks for letting me stay at your place."

He'd slept on the couch while she took one of the rooms, and Judah had the other. She'd heard them moving around through the night. They probably switched spots and made sure one was constantly on watch while the other slept and she rested.

It probably should have bothered her being woken up. But the sound of them was oddly comforting, considering she lived alone and had always slept alone.

He took a sip of his coffee as though he hadn't said anything.

She stared at Badger. "Are you just not a morning person?"

Across the diner, Judah grinned behind his mug at her question. He'd heard her through the open phone line tucked in Badger's pocket. The Brit gave her far more engagement than the man sat beside her—the one who had been nice to her last night. Which meant that she'd said too much. Exhaustion, or the lingering adrenaline. She didn't know which it had been. Just that she wouldn't normally have opened up to him and admitted she didn't really know what she was doing in relationships.

She must've drifted off in the car because she'd woken up in a bed later with no shoes on. After that she'd heard them taking care of her. This morning, Badger was back to being the guy she'd ghosted—the one who'd shown up to do his job even though he was mad at her.

It was probably because of what she'd said last night. Maybe everything he was learning about her put him off. He'd changed his mind, he didn't want anything to do with the disaster that was her personal life, and he didn't even know about her criminal connection.

The whole situation was unreal.

Not that she wanted him to fall harder for her than he already had when it would only complicate things when she was trying to keep it all simple. Feelings didn't need to get involved. Enough was going on with the investigation and her work here in Maryland. Things of the personal variety didn't need to get all messy. She had enough to deal with.

Her boss came in.

"Let's just keep things professional," Badger said. "No one needs to know we have history."

She glanced at him. He thought they had a history?

Alanson made his way over, shook both their hands, and settled in the seat facing them. As though he were a stranger, not her supervisor. One DNA test and every ounce of rapport they'd built was gone.

As if she could change her blood.

Across the room, Judah seemed to have taken an intense interest in the artwork on the walls. Whatever that was about.

Alanson said, "How are you both doing this morning?"

Badger just shrugged.

Hannah said, "Good." It wasn't like she wanted to get into small talk. "Have there been any developments overnight?"

She wanted him to tell her the crew had been apprehended, along with money stolen from the cartel. And that the girl Badger rescued didn't know anything, so she couldn't be used as a material witness and was being placed with kind people. The way Hannah had been adopted as a baby.

The waitress wandered over before he could answer, and they all ordered breakfast.

When she'd wandered off, Alanson said, "We're still looking for them. Your car was found abandoned at a state park, so we know now that they're on the run."

"They know the task force is chasing them?"

He shrugged. "We have to assume so. Or they know the cartel at least is on their tail. If they believe they're in serious danger—which they have to if they're smart—then they should just turn themselves in. After all, we're going to treat them a whole lot more fairly than the Suarez cartel is going to."

Hannah nodded because she agreed with him even if most criminals proved a whole lot more pigheaded than seeing reason and turning themselves in.

Badger said, "Is that even likely?"

"We can hope."

Hannah said, "It would be better than cleaning up the mess the cartel is going to make if they find them instead."

Talking about police work was a whole lot better than

thinking about Badger and the attraction that ricocheted between them. Sitting beside him meant she didn't need to worry about trying to avoid his gaze. Or the fact he avoided hers all too often.

She had no problem being professional. It was what she did every day.

But if her life really was in danger, and she needed protection because she was a target, then maybe she could talk to Zander and get one of the others—like Judah, since he was already here—to stay with her. Or use that underground bunker Nora had told her about the last time they'd talked when she'd updated Hannah on everything that had happened with their teammate who always wore a mask.

The one who had been on the FBI's Most Wanted list.

Nora hadn't wanted to share with Hannah before the situation had been resolved. Likely because she knew Hannah the cop would have had to turn him in. There would be nothing else she could do in a situation where her back was up against the wall and her professionalism was on the line.

It was how she knew things weren't going to work. As much as she wanted a relationship with Nora, things were far too complicated.

Although, given what she had just discovered? She should have at least one conversation with her half sister. Otherwise, they would never know if Isaac was Nora's brother as well as Hannah's.

It was all so confusing and complicated. Being adopted with no clue who she was or where she came from had been better than this. Why had she ever wanted to know?

Badger's presence here made her feel hemmed in by her own feelings, trapped in a way that wasn't entirely uncomfortable. It was nice to be swept up a little in an attraction. To know it was reciprocated. But acting on it brought way too much pressure.

"As far as the assassin who took out Special Agent Pearson," Alanson said. "That's a whole other story."

"He talked?"

Alanson shook his head. "Not in the way you think. Greg Benton is claiming his brother's the assassin while living here with a woman above the bar. He said the brother killed his girlfriend, and he only went to your meeting to try and stop him from killing Pearson as well. He didn't even mention you, so we don't know if you were the original target or not."

"Did he say where his brother is?" Hannah had heard some wild tales told by people trying to get out from under police suspicion before. This was an interesting one, to say the least.

"He doesn't know. But he wanted the girlfriend's body to be found, so that's why he led our friend here to the apartment." Alanson motioned at Badger. "He claims this guy broke in and attacked him, then threw him out the window."

"Benton threw himself out the window." Badger sat there with zero expression on his face. "Are you here to arrest me?"

She couldn't tell if he cared or not. Or if he would be concerned if someone slapped cuffs on him and took him away.

"You at least need to give me a statement about what happened. But the fact of the matter is, I believe this man is lying about being the one who shot Pearson." Alanson paused. "Did you see a second person at the meeting?" He glanced between them. "Either of you?"

They both shook their heads.

Hannah had been in a daze, in shock after she watched Pearson die in front of her. But she'd rallied fast enough—

forgetting entirely about the envelope—when Badger told her to head to her car and find a safe place to lay low. She'd managed to hold it together until she got to the motel and checked in.

"He had the gun, didn't he?" she asked Badger.

"He took it with him to the car," Badger said.

Alanson nodded. "We searched everywhere in the apartment and his truck. No guns."

Hannah blew out a breath as she tried to figure it out. She glanced out the window to stare at the bustle of the street while she thought through everything. "So maybe his brother was there, and that guy is the one who took the shot."

"We're looking into Peter Benton."

Hannah blinked. Across on the other side, standing on the sidewalk, was a man she knew. At least, the boy she had arrested six years ago was still there in his features. He was older now, a young man and no longer a child.

Those dark eyes stared at the diner as though he could see her.

Hannah scrambled from the seat and strode to the door, unable to comprehend what she was seeing.

Joseph Ricker was here.

"Hannah!" Badger called out, and she heard him rush after her. Alanson said something, but she didn't understand what it was. She just needed to go see. She had to see.

Was it him?

She pushed outside and was buffeted by the November wind.

A bus barreled past and headed up the street.

When it moved away, she looked at the spot where he had been standing. There was no one there.

Ricker was gone.

## 8

"What you mean he was released?" Hannah gripped the phone, sat beside Badger in the front seat of the car.

After she thought she saw someone on the street, it had taken him and Judah all the convincing they had in them to get her from the diner and in the car, where he could take her back to the rental apartment.

It had been all they could do to keep Alanson from believing she may have lost it. That relationship was already on shaky ground—why, he didn't know. Neither of them opened up about it. But he'd tried anyway to convince Alanson she hadn't had some kind of episode where she saw someone who wasn't there. As it was, the whole situation was up in the air until Alanson saw her next, and the entire thing had blown over.

There was nothing normal about her state right now.

"You're seriously telling me that Joseph Ricker was released from juvenile detention, and no one thought to give me a heads-up?" Her breath came in short waves. "This is unbelievable. There were specific instructions in the file that I was to be notified no matter where I am and what I'm doing."

Joseph Ricker.

Badger had no idea who that was. He needed to find out one way or the other. The guy was obviously some kind of trigger for her. Someone she had arrested, maybe? She'd said juvenile detention, so the guy couldn't be too old. That at least narrowed it down.

"Yes, Captain." She sucked in a breath and blew it out slowly. "I understand that."

Hannah squeezed her eyes shut. It made Badger want to reach over and lay his hand on her knee. Offer her reassurance of some kind. If he thought she would accept it, which he highly doubted.

But since he'd determined to be professional and not let his feelings for her get involved in this job in any way, he needed to stay hands off. Even when she was so clearly battling something.

Badger knew all about demons from the past. Those memories haunted him every time he closed his eyes, determined to tear apart his resolution. Not to mention the belief in him that everyone he knew had. The one that drove him every day.

"Yeah, because of *me*."

He pulled up at a stoplight and glanced over. The pain in her eyes was raw, but he saw no tears gather. Just the anger and frustration of someone powerless to stop the inevitable from happening.

Badger wasn't going to let it get to that place. He knew what it was like to live those feelings and their aftermath. To have to walk that road while everyone around him grieved and pointed their fingers.

He sent a quick text to Ted, just the guy's name and a question mark. All he had time for before the light went green.

"I understand." Hannah hung up the phone. She stabbed the screen with her index finger, and for a second he thought she might be contemplating rolling the window down and throwing her phone out.

He tapped the gas. "I could just keep driving. We could disappear and go somewhere no one will find us."

Why did it sound tempting to do that when it would be with her? He'd never considered it on his own. His team was his family. But getting lost with Hannah seemed like a dream —or an enticement.

"Exactly what will that achieve?" she asked.

He heard the brokenness in her voice. The way she had been shattered, and now tried to live her life, never allowing it to happen again.

His foot slipped off the gas pedal. She might have some clue of the things he had gone through. But it was too much to hope that she might understand. It'd never happened in his life up until now. People said they got it, but they didn't know how it felt to fail the way he had.

"Who is Joseph Ricker?" Badger figured he could protect her from assassins, but he likely couldn't protect her from herself. Especially if she didn't open up to him.

"Where are we going?"

As if he was still considering making a run for it. And he wasn't about to let it slide that she hadn't answered his question. But did he need her to? Badger wanted her to trust him. It would mean they had grown closer as friends and associates. But the truth was he didn't need her to give him all the information. Ted could find it out quickly enough.

The kid could find out anything. Which was why Badger had never assumed Ted didn't know everything about him.

Badger said, "We're going to the rental house."

"Good." She shifted in the seat. "I didn't take a shower this morning, so I should do that."

It was on the tip of his tongue to tell her that what she needed to do was trust him. But if she wasn't willing to do that, then maybe it told him everything he needed to know.

If she found out exactly how hugely he had failed, she would probably never accept him as capable of protecting her. She would force Zander's hand and arrange for Judah to be the one with her instead.

The selfish part of him wanted to keep all his secrets, so that never happened.

Maybe after she took a shower, then she would open up. But hopefully, by then, Ted would have already found out everything Badger needed to know.

"I'll make us something to eat," he said. "Since we didn't get to finish our breakfast."

"I don't want anything. Except maybe more coffee."

"Whatever's happening, you don't think you'll need fuel to deal with it?" It was something Zander drummed into them. The life they lived, and the physical exertion it included, meant they had to eat. Otherwise, they wouldn't have the strength to face their enemies.

They walked from the drive through the front door in silence.

Until she said, "You carried me all this way last night?"

He nodded. She didn't say thank you, so he didn't offer her a "you're welcome" either.

She looked away.

Badger didn't move from the entryway. "Is there something I need to know to keep you safe?" She couldn't think lying or withholding information was going to make this easier. "Maybe about what was in that envelope?"

She blanched.

A second later, it was as though the expression never was.

"I probably didn't see Joseph Ricker." She shook her head. "It's just a crazy coincidence there was some guy who looks like him on the street this morning." She headed down the hallway, leaving him standing there. "I'll be back out in a bit."

The bedroom door closed.

He pushed out a long, slow breath. The unspoken hung in the air like a cloud.

It was for the best, though. If she opened up for real, that would only lead to her expecting him to do the same. He'd never told anyone he knew now about what'd happened when he was a kid. What he'd done. Not even Zander or Andre.

His phone buzzed with the text. Ted wanted him to get on video chat.

Badger set up the laptop on the coffee table and waited for it to load. As soon as it did, and he saw Ted's face, Badger asked, "Did you really get an answer that fast?" He half expected this to be about something else.

Ted shrugged. "I didn't need to look far. And I didn't have to hack anything because all of it was in the file Lana handed over about Hannah. She gave us Hannah's whole file."

Badger felt his eyebrows rise. "Every arrest, every case she's ever worked?"

Ted shook his head. "Not that file. The one with notes from her conversations with the department shrink. Something mandatory for a while after she arrested Joseph Ricker. Seven plus years ago now."

Badger sat back on the couch and ran his hands down his face. "Did he just get released? Because she thought she saw him on the street." She hadn't told it to him straight out. But from the conversation he'd heard, it was pretty clear that'd happened.

"That part I had to look up." Ted nodded. "He's eighteen and a half now. The judge let him go provided he checks in with a doctor at a psychiatric facility regularly, as well as his parole officer."

"What did he do?"

"From what I read"—Ted winced—"it started out as a welfare check, then the cops got involved because it was clear the kid was being abused."

"And he ended up in juvenile detention?" That didn't seem right if he had been the victim.

"Because he burned down his home. Dad, stepmom, and baby sister were inside. He killed them all."

Badger stared at the laptop screen until his eyes burned. "All of them?" And a little girl?

"Tried and sentenced. Three counts of murder, and now he's back out on the streets."

Badger closed his eyes, but all he saw was a little girl in a short skirt over a sparkly mermaid bathing suit. Her long blonde hair was in pigtails, wet from the ocean spray.

And then lying in a casket.

Cold.

HANNAH BRACED her hands against the wall of the shower, pressed her head between them, and let the water pound down on her back.

She could still smell the smoke from seven years ago. Taste ash in her mouth, and the way her breath hitched because the smoke had gotten in her lungs. She'd thrown those clothes away, unable to contend with the smell that lingered in the aftermath of what the Ricker kid had done.

And just how thoroughly she had gotten everything wrong.

It didn't matter how much therapy she'd gone to or who had tried to tell her she wasn't alone in her mistake. It didn't change a thing.

In the end, she'd told the doctor what he wanted to hear, that Hannah didn't blame herself. Even if the dad wasn't exactly an innocent victim, the stepmom—his young girlfriend—and her baby hadn't deserved to have their lives ripped from them in flames.

She could still remember the look on Joseph Ricker his face as he stood across the street, watching the house burn down.

While the firefighters had piled out of their rig to battle the blaze, she'd known it was too late. She'd confronted Ricker, realizing exactly how wrong she had gotten everything, and put cuffs on him while he struggled to watch the fire turn the house to nothing but ash.

No matter how many times she asked him why he'd done it, all he did was smile.

The sob worked its way up her throat. Hannah didn't bother to fight it. What was the point? She'd always known that she felt things deeply. Bottling it up only made the situation worse when everything finally exploded out of her because it couldn't be contained any longer.

In her first case as a detective with her first partner, he'd seen her fight the urge to empathize. After that, he'd made a big deal whenever she showed emotion. Until she'd learned it was better to wait and do it in private.

That way, she didn't have to deal with anyone else's expectations or judgment about what she felt. Why. How she processed it.

Even her adoptive parents hadn't understood why she felt so deeply.

They'd been almost benign in comparison. Meanwhile, Hannah shed a tear over every fish they had lost. Or every friend who had slighted her, leaving her out of their plans the way kids did without considering others' feelings. It was just the way things were, and no tears were going to change that.

But the fact of the matter was that she could've seen it.

Hannah had taken Ricker at face value and trusted her gut reaction—that he was a victim. She'd jumped on the chance to rescue him, the way she'd wanted to be saved so many times in her life.

She had seen herself in his eyes.

And then her ability to trust her gut had gone up in flames, along with that house.

Hannah shut off the water, dried herself off, and got dressed in clean clothes from the bag Judah had retrieved for her. Trying not to think about any of it.

Maybe she hadn't seen him at all.

But considering Ricker had been released two weeks ago, she couldn't believe it was a coincidence. There was no way he'd have shown up here in Baltimore precisely where she was for any other reason than to continue tormenting her.

At the same time frame, her birth mother had gone to Chevalier Protection Specialists and hired a bodyguard.

A woman she had never met but who evidently kept close tabs on her.

Hannah pulled a hairbrush through her tangles, hacking at them to get them to unknot. As if it was that simple to make things straight. Like she could use brute force on her life and wind up with no damage, determined to sort out everything.

It didn't work like that.

She emerged from the bathroom just as Badger opened the door to the bedroom and peered around it.

"I brought you coffee." He stepped in, holding the steaming cup.

She took it with two hands, embracing the warmth. "Thanks." Not just because he'd made her a drink, but also because he hadn't pushed her until she snapped and told him everything. She could see he wanted to ask, but thankfully he respected her enough to allow her to tell him in her own time. If he hadn't already had Ted give him the whole rundown.

"Do you need anything else?"

"What is Nora like?" She sat on the edge of the bed, holding the mug.

He frowned, then shoved back hair that had fallen to his eyebrow. "You mean like her personality?"

Hannah nodded. "I just want to know if she shows emotion easily."

While Hannah had been taught that was a bad thing, maybe Nora was allowed to keep her emotions on her sleeve for all the world to see.

"She's more reserved than that." Badger set an elbow on

the top of the dresser that came up to his ribs. "But she's one of the most caring people I know. Why do you ask?"

"To see if we're alike at all." Hannah shrugged one shoulder. "I know Gladstone wasn't my father, but maybe she and I share things we got from our mother."

But if their mother had felt deeply, fought hard, and loved fiercely, then why had she walked away from both of them?

"You are alike in some ways." He stared at her with a gentle expression on his face. "You're both caring and incredibly strong."

Hannah blinked away tears. "How can I know what's just me and what was given to me?" Before he could ask what she meant, she continued, "I looked into my mom. When I found out Nora and I are related, and it wasn't through Gladstone because I had them test his DNA after he was killed." She took a shallow breath. "I looked into her mom. I found photos, but it was clear pretty fast that the whole identity was fake."

"You knew who Lana was?"

She bit her lip. "I'd seen her picture. Before you showed it to me."

He looked mad. "Has she ever approached you?"

Why she was telling him now, she wasn't sure. Hannah shook her head. "I've never met her or seen her in real life. If I did, what would I say? She hired someone to protect me, but she doesn't warn me herself that I'm in danger. Who does that? She left Nora. She had me adopted out. Obviously she doesn't want to be part of my life."

And now Isaac was in the mix.

Hannah had no idea what to make of it.

"Maybe that's how things had to be." Badger spoke softly. "You know the circles I operate in. You're not too far removed from all of that, especially with Lana involved in your life. Maybe your mom did what she had to do to keep you safe."

"Like now that I know about Nora, it put me in danger somehow?"

He shrugged gently.

"I'm on an undercover assignment. A kid I arrested six years ago is out. I can't even begin to deal with all the family stuff on top of that."

"You think the first thing Joseph Ricker did was come and find you?"

It wasn't an accusation. But part of her still stung. "He made it clear that there was no way I would be forgetting about him. Ever." Not when he'd sent her all those letters.

"Do you think he hired an assassin to kill you?"

Hannah shook her head. "Not his style."

Although given he'd been locked up for six years, maybe she didn't know his style anymore. That made him completely unpredictable. This could go wrong really fast if she wasn't prepared.

At least she had the guys from Chevalier Protection Specialists watching her back. Otherwise, she might be nervous.

"Ricker is going to do whatever he'll do," she said. "But right now, we have the find the doctor, her son, and Nurse Weston. Otherwise, the money is still out there, and we can't take down the cartel." She winced. "The task force can't."

She doubted she was even part of it anymore. All because Isaac was her brother, and so she was being let go.

Hannah would head back to Rochester with her tail between her legs, as it were. Only, was she going to be bringing an assassin with her?

He stared at her for a second. She wondered what he would say about her fallback of diving into work instead of dealing with what was inside her. It was much better to focus on the external.

Badger said, "Surely Doctor Mathers and her crew will show up somewhere."

"If they do, the task force is going to know. Every account they had was frozen. One move, and it will pop on radar. No one showed up at the clinic today. Alanson's morning email said they would spend the day looking at the residences and other assets, trying to find a lead on where they might have gone."

Because yes, she still got task force emails. But knowing she couldn't participate in what was going on stung.

"You think they're hiding?"

"I know why Doctor Mathers killed that guy. It's the signature of Suarez's enemies, and it was supposed to look like their rivals ripped them off. But by now, José has to know it was the doctor. He'll be gunning for her, whether she thinks she got away with it or not."

Before he could say anything, her phone rang.

Hannah swiped her thumb across the screen and put the phone to her ear. "Detective Yassick."

"Yeah, this is Detective Olden, Baltimore homicide. Your boss, who is apparently FBI Special Agent Alanson? He said you'd be interested in what I'm looking at."

"And what's that?"

"The body of Pam Weston."

"Text me the address." Hannah hung up the phone and headed to find her shoes. She hesitated before picking them up. Her hand stretched out.

"What is it?" Badger said.

Alanson had told the cop to call her. Because she was a homicide detective, or because no one on the task force could be spared, and she got to do the leg work while they all worked the important stuff?

Did it matter? Going to work beat sitting around here, thinking about her messed-up life.

This was something she could do. This was normal.

She swiped her shoes from the floor. "The cops found Weston, which means you get to see how we investigate a murder."

## 9

B adger followed Hannah as she strode to the house. Ted had confirmed the residence had a mortgage that listed Pam Weston as the homeowner, with a considerable outstanding balance that she hadn't used her hoarded millions to pay off.

The entire yard had been cordoned off with police caution tape. Plenty of officers hung around, along with a couple of detectives by the look of it.

As Hannah and Badger approached the uniformed officer at the tape, a suited man broke off the conversation with his associate and approached them. "Detective Yassick?"

She held out her badge. "Rochester PD. Nice to meet you."

"Hmm." He didn't return the sentiment. Just handed her badge to the uniformed officer, who wrote down Hannah's information on his clipboard. "I'm Detective Olden."

"You said Special Agent Alanson wanted me here?"

"Apparently, on the task force you're on, you're the resident murder expert."

Badger wasn't sure if Hannah blushed at hearing that, but it was likely close even if her cheeks didn't turn red. Then he turned to her and realized she didn't look happy.

Maybe this wasn't a positive sign, but more of a sideline assignment. Busywork. The cops here probably didn't think so, even if it was true for the task force.

Olden glanced at him. "And you are…?"

Badger was about to answer when Hannah said, "He's with me."

"You've got your own entourage?"

Hannah said, "More like a bodyguard."

It was clear Olden wanted to make a joke but waved at the house instead. "Given the mess in there, if you're involved at all, that's probably a good call. But he doesn't go in the living room."

Badger folded his arms across his chest. "She'll be within my eyesight at all times."

Olden studied him. "Fine." He'd taken Badger's measure and likely had determined that arguing with him wasn't worth it.

"Good call," Badger said.

Hannah glanced between them. "If you guys are done posturing, maybe we could go see about this dead body."

Olden's lips twitched, but he turned to lead the way. The guy looked to have Hispanic heritage, with threads of silver at his temples. A ring on his left hand. He probably had a wallet full of pictures of kids and grandkids, the kind that reminded him why he put the police shield on his belt every day.

Hannah followed him inside, and Badger hung in the entryway. As much as he intended to protect her no matter what, he also didn't figure he needed to interfere in police business. The two of them were professionals at assessing a murder scene. He was only a professional at creating messes like this.

The last thing he wanted to do was get in the way and potentially compromise anything. He didn't need Zander getting a phone call to say that Badger hadn't worn gloves and had left a fingerprint where he wasn't supposed to. He wasn't supposed to touch anything anyway. Especially if it pointed to him as the suspect in a murder.

He could smell the odor of death from where he stood, feet planted hip width apart. Same smell as that apartment where the bar owner had been murdered—by the assassin or the brother.

He crossed his arms. None of them needed to know there was a gun under his jacket, though he figured they weren't dumb. They probably already knew he was armed, and yet they let him walk in here with a cop they didn't know. Evidently, federal weight meant something, which could play in his favor.

Two police officers stopped in front of him. Blocking his view of the living room. But he could hear Hannah talking to the detective and knew she had crouched beside where the body was sprawled on the couch.

"Got some ID?" an officer asked.

"Sure, I gave it to the guy at the tape. The one with the clipboard." Badger had handed it off before they came up the front walk. Something the two of them would know, considering it was procedure, and he hadn't drawn any attention the way he would've if he came in here without anyone realizing.

"I've seen you on TV." The officer glanced at his buddy. "Haven't we seen him on TV?"

"Yeah, harboring that guy who was FBI Most Wanted."

Ah, so they knew about his association with Eas.

Not that Eas had been a criminal. However, his twin brother had been sure to implicate him in plenty of crimes. As though any of that affected these cops and their ability to do their job. Which was precisely what they were aiming at now. Ruffling his feathers so they could prove they were real men.

One glanced at the other. "Aren't they the guys who had that suitcase nuke everyone was looking for?"

Badger sighed. He was all for banter, but these guys just wanted to get a rise out of him. Probably because they were bored. "So my security clearance is higher than yours." He shrugged. "Is that a surprise to any of us?"

One of them opened his mouth, but before he could speak, someone called out, "I need two volunteers for cone duty, and you two look happy to step up."

Both officers glared at him. "Sure, Lieutenant," one said. "No problem at all."

As they cleared out, Badger spotted Hannah over by the body in a chair with the back to him.

She turned her head so she could look over her shoulder. At him. Her expression asked a question.

Badger shook his head. She didn't need to worry about him, not considering she had plenty to do here. "How's it look?"

Detective Olden glanced at him, then continued his assessment of the victim's wounds. "How do you think it looks?"

Hannah winced. "He was right about it being nasty. Both her hands were cut off, and it looks like her tongue was removed."

"The Suarez cartel?" Badger felt his eyes widen and

hoped he didn't look like an excited kid given a chance to watch a horror movie. He should be freaked out, but any time the team went up against someone big, it all worked out in the end. Why would this be any different?

He figured if he got in over his head, he could just call Zander. Having the boys here would make protecting Hannah easier. She was family, even without Lana being her mother. Hearing her talk about that stuff only made him all the more determined to protect her.

The look on her face made him wonder otherwise. Maybe it wasn't a good thing that a cartel was involved. Did she know something he didn't about killing like this?

Olden straightened, his face paled. "This is their MO. But a nurse?"

Hannah said, "Let's just say she had a run-in with them recently."

"This is how they usually retaliate?" Badger knew she felt more secure talking about work than anything personal.

She nodded. "Nurse Weston took something of theirs, so they took her hands. Only the ME can tell which was cut off first, the hands or the tongue, but it's not an exact science. Though, I'd guess the hands came first. If she wasn't mute from the shock, they'd have continued with the torture trying to get her to spill what she knew."

*If* she knew anything. Badger tried to guess what the nurse might have told them about the doctor and her son. How did cops figure this stuff out?

Olden glanced at what remained of Pam Weston. "What did she have that they wanted?"

"Money she stole from them," Hannah said. "Did any of your people find a black duffel?"

One of the forensic technicians turned. "There was one

in the bedroom with the open suitcases, but there wasn't any money."

"She was packing?" Hannah asked.

Olden nodded. "It appears she was making a run for it when they showed up here and did this." He motioned at the body. "She robbed the cartel?"

The movement displaced air in the room. Badger took a breath through his open mouth to try and relieve his nose of the smell. "So they got what they came for?"

Weston hadn't had the chance to disappear and start a new life with the cartel's money. Instead, all her assets had been frozen, the duffel was empty, and she was dead. They had at least part of their money back, right?

Not the end Weston had likely anticipated when she'd been rushing out of that house to the car. Or packing for her trip.

*Now look at her.*

Badger winced.

Olden shook his head. "If they did this to her, they want their money. Someone got here before them and took it from her, or she hid it and didn't tell them." He waved a technician over. "Recheck everything. If the money is here, we need to find it."

"Yes, Detective." The technician offered a bow he seemed to think was amusing and wandered off.

Badger turned to Hannah. "You think she held out against torture like this?"

"Not if the others have her share. I'll bet she was double crossed before the cartel got to her, and when they try to find out where it was, she had no idea."

Badger glanced at the chair again and winced. Not a situation he'd ever want to find himself in. Which made him all the more desperate to get Hannah away from it.

So far, they'd faced down an assassin. Dr. Mathers and her crew seemed content to leave Hannah behind, thinking she was only their receptionist. Now this Joseph Ricker guy was potentially out there with his attention on Hannah. He didn't need a cartel in the running as well.

Who knew where the next threat would come from?

If the task force didn't cut her loose for real, Badger might have to talk to Alanson and get her relieved. After all, the feds wouldn't want her personal situation putting any of the rest of them in danger. Or hindering their hunt for the stolen money.

He watched Hannah continue studying every aspect of the scene and realized then that she could be it for him—the person he wanted to spend the rest of his life with. The way Zander had married Nora and Andre had reconnected with Lucia. Now Eas and Karina were talking about the future. Only he and Judah remained single. Given the fact he never intended to tell anyone what he'd done, that was the way it would stay.

Even if Hannah *could* change his mind.

She'd known before he did that it wouldn't work. Now he knew that when this was over, he was going to walk away from her—this amazing woman who didn't need his mess in her life.

"You okay?" she asked. She wore a frown on her face.

Badger didn't answer her question.

He took her in. The complete package. Strength, competence, and deep concern. Because she cared about him.

He never needed her to learn that he didn't deserve it.

HANNAH GLANCED at the back of Weston's head, still able to picture the body in its gruesome state, then back at him. She half expected him to have a look of disgust on his face, but he didn't. He was looking at her with…she didn't know what.

Over the past couple of days it had become clear to her that he had secrets of his own. Plenty. The way she did. Though she'd started to come clean, spurred by whatever after seeing Ricker on the street. And while he hadn't decided to trust her with his, she wondered if maybe it was enough that he looked at her like that. With the kind of look she had seen Zander give Nora.

Still, even if he didn't seem bothered by the dead body in the room, she probably shouldn't drag this out.

Hannah turned to the detective. "I appreciate you letting me take a look."

"Which means you're planning on leaving me with all the paperwork."

She grinned. "If I get involved, there will only be more."

The detective made a *hmm* sound behind his closed lips, but she caught the slight twitch. "I suppose that's true enough."

"I'll let the rest of the task force know to tell you if they find anything that could prove helpful." If Detective Olden pushed too hard, he could wind up a target of the cartel. Not just him, but people he cared about. "I'd be remiss if I didn't advise caution in pursuing this."

"I've got eight other open cases on my desk, so any help I can get from the federal task force on this one means more time I can spend working those." Olden shrugged. "If they want the case, it's theirs."

She nodded, glad he got the gist of what she said. "Sounds good."

Hannah stripped off the gloves as Badger moved aside, and he followed her down the hallway to the front door. Halfway down the driveway, he said, "Was that some kind of police detective shorthand?"

She hadn't thought so. "The task force thing?"

"What's going on here that I don't know?"

She glanced at him. "I'm not keeping you in the dark. You were in there. I didn't have any conversations you weren't privy to."

"So why does it seem like the detective isn't all fired up to find the person who did this to Weston."

"Maybe because the task force is already working to take them down. Just because they have federal funding doesn't mean they're completely protected when the cartel inevitably targets them. But it'll go better for the whole team and all the support staff than it would for one detective."

"So basically you're protecting him."

Hannah shrugged. "I guess, but he doesn't need this on top of everything else. And he knows that."

Badger was quiet as he scanned the street. They climbed in his car, and he pulled out. Finally, he said, "Is there a way you can warn Doctor Mathers and her son? Have some kind of press conference, and tell them they're being hunted, so they should just turn themselves in. That kind of thing?"

"Sure we could, but the Suarez cartel will go to ground if they know we're on their tail," she said. "Even if we have physical evidence and witnesses, who's to say we'll ever find one of them to arrest? They could cut and run as soon as they get their money."

"Leaving you with at least a short timeframe where you could grab them before they flee the country."

Hannah tapped the seat beside her knee, trying to figure out where the doctor and her son would go. If they knew of any hideouts, the task force could raid those places. The more buried they were, the better. Whether the doctor and her son were hiding together or apart, they would go somewhere familiar. Somewhere that wasn't easily traceable.

She glanced at Badger. "Do you think Ted could find any residences the task force doesn't know about? Or transportation. Something they might use to disappear."

Weston had a boat, but the task force knew about that. Which meant they would have someone sitting on it, watching in case any of them showed up.

"Sure, we could ask." Badger handed her his phone, sliding his thumb across the home button to unlock it. "He's in my favorites."

Instead of having an awkward conversation, Hannah sent Ted a text asking for what she needed. She even laid out what she knew about the three of them and things she remembered from the research she'd done.

All of it was technically confidential federal information. Something she wasn't supposed to share with anyone. But considering the reach Ted's skills had, she figured either no one would find out, or he could somehow get retroactive clearance for the job. Like as a consultant.

When she was done, she replaced the phone in the cupholder.

He glanced over at the next light. "You do stuff like that a lot?"

"Text Ted?"

"You know what I mean. Bodies like that."

"It's never pleasant," she said. "But that was particularly gruesome. I don't care what they've done. Nobody deserves to be carved up."

"I wonder if she saw it coming. Or did they just rob a cartel without even considering how bad it could get?"

Hannah blew out a breath. "Hubris can be blinding. If they really thought they'd prepared enough, they were going to get away with it, then no. Probably they didn't even consider the fact they might wind up on the run with the money."

"Being hunted down and carved up by a cartel."

"You've seen stuff like that before?" He hadn't gagged or seemed disgusted by the sight of it. She didn't know where he'd been with the army. But the chance he'd been in Delta Force and never seen anything like that was pretty slim.

"You're right." He nodded. "No one deserves to get carved up like that. Especially not innocents."

Hannah knew then that he had seen many terrible things.

She reached over and squeezed just above his knee so he would know she understood because they shared some of those experiences. "I first met Joseph Ricker as the victim of a possible abuse case. It was my early days as a patrol officer." She exhaled a breath. "He worked it. I'll give him that. He had me all the way fooled when he described, in detail, the things his dad had done to him."

Badger sat quietly while she spoke.

"We removed him from the house and put him in foster care. The dad still had his girlfriend and their baby living there. Though, she was in and out, sometimes staying with her mom. I spoke to her at length, warning her of what might already be happening." Cases with children were the ones that ate at her soul.

"We thought it was over. Dad was arrested and then bailed out by the girlfriend. The case was going to trial, and Joseph was in a safe place." She blew out a breath. "A week or so later, the house is on fire. Dad, the girlfriend, and the baby were inside at the time. I got a call from the lead detective on the case because I was the one who spent the most time with him. And when I roll up to the house, Joseph is in the middle of the crowd. Smiling."

"He killed them? Like, in retaliation for what his dad had done?"

"I have no doubt his dad did what Joseph told us he did." Bile rose in her throat. "But that's not what created the sociopath he turned out to be. At least not on its own. Fourteen years old, and he had no conscience. No emotions. He fooled everyone, including me." And that was the worst of it. "That kid is pure evil. I nearly lost my job over him, and now he's back on the streets."

Hannah closed her eyes. Badger slid his hand across hers. She flipped it over and entwined her fingers with his, squeezing for dear life because she needed something to hold onto. She didn't always want to be alone.

"Is it possible he might have hired the assassin?"

Hannah shook her head. "Not his style. He's way more up close and personal."

"Why is he not in some kind of facility?"

"A kid like that? He probably fooled every psychiatrist he spoke to the last six years. All that time spent in juvenile detention, who knows what he's become." She couldn't even fathom what went on in that boy's mind. He'd sent her letters for years, but she stopped reading them a long time ago. "He's supposed to check in with a facility as well as his parole officer."

"But he's basically a ticking time bomb."

She couldn't even speak the word to agree. But he was exactly right, and Hannah had both a task force appointment that had turned into a fully out-of-control investigation, plus a potential hitman situation. How on earth was she going to deal with Joseph on top of all of that?

"Huh."

Hannah glanced over. Badger's attention was on the rearview mirror. "What is it?"

He frowned. "Grab my phone again. Call Judah." He unlocked it for her.

Hannah didn't waste time dialing.

Judah picked up. "Yes, Jeeves? Is my Lobster Thermidor ready?"

"Bro, there's someone behind me."

"Uh, duh." Judah dropped the thick Queen's English and settled back into his usual London inflections. "He's been following you for four blocks. You only just noticed? That girl is distracting you."

Hannah's cheeks flamed. But there was no time to worry about it.

They had a tail.

## 10

H annah turned around in her seat to look out the back window. Badger glanced at her for a second and saw the pink tinge high on her cheeks.

Pity there was no time to talk about what that was. Probably a reaction to Judah's comment about Badger being distracted. He also figured she was only embarrassed because they both knew he had a crush on her, and she didn't feel the same way.

Why else would she be embarrassed?

Maybe it was better they didn't talk about it. Otherwise, he would be the embarrassed one. And right now, they had other things to deal with than the attraction he was purposely trying to avoid thinking about.

Judah was still on the phone.

Badger said, "Confirm for me which car it is that's in pursuit."

Hannah pulled out her phone as well.

Badger's mind went through a series of scenarios, possible

ways they could get rid of the tail. Or turn the tables on whoever was back there.

Judah said, "Silver, four-door compact. You want me to call Ted with the license plate?"

"Memorize it. We'll tell him later if we need to." There was a slim chance the guy would get away, and they'd need that information to find him.

Success was never guaranteed. Mostly they tried to cover as many variables as possible to get the outcome they needed. Most situations wound up somewhere in the gray area of acceptable, along with manageable fallout.

The minute he, or any of the team, or anyone else in their line of work started to assume they would be victorious? That was when failure became predictable.

After all, look at Nurse Weston. It could be argued she'd brought the consequences down on herself by ripping off vicious bad guys. Because she had returned to her own home to pack before she left town. Instead of simply disappearing, going somewhere that cartel would never find her.

"Yes, this is Detective Hannah Yassick. Rochester Police Department. Badge number..." She rattled off a series of digits.

"Is she calling this in?" Judah's voice came through the car speakers.

Hannah glanced at him. The phone against her cheek. "We are currently being pursued by a silver four-door." She shifted the phone away. "Judah, what's the license plate number?"

There was a beat of silence. Then he said, "Can't read it from this distance."

Hannah frowned.

Badger just shrugged off her unspoken question.

"Yes, if you could. That would be great." She refocused on her call. "I would appreciate it." She gave a few more details and then hung up.

Judah was silent the entire time. Badger kept one eye on the car behind them, driving aggressively to keep up with them through downtown Baltimore. Eventually, he would need to turn, or they would wind up in the harbor. But that wouldn't happen for a few minutes yet.

Hannah said, "What was that about?"

Badger glanced at the rearview. "What was what?"

"I needed that license plate. Judah?"

"Yes, Detective?" There was a coldness to his tone Badger had rarely heard. It made him want to wince.

Hannah sat back in her chair. "Is that how it is?"

She folded her arms. And considering the fact they were both keeping secrets from each other, he didn't press the matter.

"He's on approach." Energy had returned to Judah's tone. "You might want to brace."

Badger spotted a turn coming up. He flicked his gaze to the rearview and saw the silver car barreling toward them. At the last second, Badger used a two-handed grip to rotate the wheel all the way to the right in a sharp move.

Hannah flung toward him in her seat. Her shoulder slammed into his. "Sorry."

Badger straightened the wheel. He hit the gas. "No worries."

Seconds later, the silver car flung around the corner, the back wheels nearly spinning out as it struggled to make the turn in pursuit.

"Not a professional," Badger muttered.

She held the phone in a white-knuckle grip. "What was that?"

"The way he took that turn. He's not trained in defensive driving."

"I wouldn't worry about that guy. Cops will be here soon." She waved her phone at him. "I'm guessing it'll take them minutes to dispatch the closest patrol car."

Badger didn't have time to get into all the issues of this. In many ways, they were similar, but sometimes it felt as though they were on opposite sides of a divide that couldn't be breached.

"What are you thinking?" Judah asked. "The Topeka Special?"

"No." Badger had already dismissed that idea. "The Topeka Special takes three vehicles and a rocket launcher."

"Oh yeah, I always get that one confused with Buffalo Salad."

"What are you guys talking about?" Hannah asked.

Badger took another turn. The silver car followed. Behind it, he spotted Judah in the truck. "Buffalo might be a good idea."

Before he could get into that, a black-and-white police car with the lights and sirens going approached them in the oncoming lanes. As soon Badger passed them, the vehicle swerved in a U-turn in the middle of the street, bumped over the central reservation, and headed up behind them in pursuit.

Hannah shifted in her seat. "We should all pull over. Just to be on the safe side."

Badger wasn't going to slow, but he did change lanes. Cars pulled to the side in both directions as people got out of the way. He watched through the rearview, keeping one eye on the road in front of him.

The cop car pulled up tight behind Judah's car.

"I'm pulling over." Judah slowed down, and Badger saw the police black-and-white slow with him. "Actually, I think I'm *being* pulled over."

The silver car never slowed. It accelerated toward Badger as they put more and more distance between them and Judah, who was now fully stopped.

"I'll call them again. Tell them they got the wrong car." Hannah fumbled for her phone.

The silver car slammed into the back of them.

They both jolted forward in their seats. Hannah's head slammed the dash, and she dropped her phone. She hissed and touched her forehead.

Badger hit the gas and took another corner. If he could make three more right turns, he would wind up back behind the police car. That would show them that the pursuit was still happening. The cops would get the right idea instead of pulling over his friend.

He wasn't worried about Judah. He was more concerned about the car coming up behind them again.

Badger surveyed the area. They were surrounded by warehouses, close to the river.

A good place to park and turn the tables on the silver car.

Hannah twisted again. "It's only one guy. Just the driver, no one else."

"So the cartel didn't send a whole hit team. Just one assassin? That's comforting to know." Two of them and one bad guy behind them, and she thought he couldn't handle it? Enough she had called in reinforcements.

Now Judah would get a speeding ticket or whatever, just because she didn't think he could handle this.

"What are you going to do?"

He figured she asked because she was fully aware he would have a plan. Badger took a right turn. He just needed to find a good spot to get out of sight. Then when the silver car came around the corner, they would both be waiting. Doors open. Guns pointed at the driver.

It wasn't as though this situation needed to last much longer.

"Just hang on." He didn't need her doing anything else.

"I can't believe you're mad I called the police. You remember how I'm a cop, right? We call for backup. That's what we do."

Badger hissed out of breath. "Some of us don't have the luxury of backup. Especially when it just got pulled over."

Judah was probably steaming. But playing nice and using the classiest British accent he could muster to try and talk his way out of the situation. Especially if the cop was a female. Judah fell in love at least once a week.

"He's still right behind us," she said.

Badger turned the next corner. Just about to tell her that he knew exactly where the other car was.

The pedestrian came out of nowhere. One second it was clear, and the next second he saw blonde hair and a stroller— a runner pushing her child.

He swerved to avoid the woman.

The car hit a curb and flipped upside down in the air.

Hannah screamed.

Any second now, the car would hit the concrete.

As soon as that thought dropped in his mind, they splashed into the water.

HANNAH SWALLOWED THE SCREAM. She gasped in a breath and scrambled for purchase as the car descended to the bottom of the river.

Ice cold water rushed in on all sides.

She tried to turn her head but could only gasp. Fumbling around, she found the belt buckle, hit the release, and tumbled down onto the roof, splayed out awkwardly. The car descended, and she scrambled to her knees.

"Badger."

His eyes were closed, his body still. Unconscious.

She didn't want to snap him free of the seatbelt. He would fall and be injured more than he already was. She would only do that at the last second before she got them out of this.

*Think.*

Seatbelt. Window.

Water poured in. Soon enough, the vehicle would be completely filled. They would be able to push the door open when the pressure equalized.

The whole breaking the window and swimming out thing wouldn't work. It would only let more water in. That was for when a car hadn't gone below the surface yet.

*Think.*

It was almost completely pitch-black and seriously freezing. They had to get out of here. But she had to balance between acting too quickly and putting them both in danger, waiting for the right moment to get free of the car.

The difference would be a matter of seconds. She just needed to hold out for the exact time.

She felt under the water pooled at her legs. The car groaned.

Hannah managed to remove her shoes because those would weigh her down. She removed Badger's, and her fingers found his phone.

Hannah brought it to her face so she could see the screen. *Please work.* Her cold fingers fumbled the buttons. She didn't know what she was pressing. A sob worked its way up her throat and puffed out her lips.

The phone speaker crackled. "Go ahead."

What just happened? Hannah pressed a couple of buttons.

"Go ahead." Pause. "Badger?"

Hannah couldn't get her finger to swipe the phone symbol on the lock screen. If she could do that, she could make an emergency call.

"If this is Hannah, press the power button and the volume down button simultaneously. Use it like a walkie-talkie."

She did as instructed, trying not to think about how crazy the situation was. "Hello?" She let go of the buttons.

"It's Ted, and I can hear you. What's going on?"

"We were run off the road. Into the river. The car is submerged, and the water is coming in fast." She could barely get the words out. Her chin shook as shivers wracked her whole body.

"Where's Badger?"

She held down the buttons. "I think the impact knocked him unconscious. The car is—" The whole thing started to turn sideways. She squealed, then knocked heads with Badger as the car flipped from the force of the water. Another scream emerged.

"Hannah. Can you hear me?"

The car settled right side up but still descending. How deep was the bottom? It was pitch-black except for the glow of the phone screen. She squeezed the buttons. "We flipped over. We're right side up now."

But there was no time for chitchat. She jabbed at the seatbelt holding Badger down.

The car slammed into the bottom of the river.

They were going to have to swim out, and he was still unconscious.

She patted his face. "I really need you to wake up right now." Otherwise, she would have to pull a serious lifeguard move and drag him to the surface. She pushed out a breath, preparing herself to do exactly that. The water crested her elbows. She patted Badger's cheek again. "Of *course* you're unconscious for the good part."

"Judah is on his way."

Hannah pressed the buttons. "Tell him to bring a dive team."

She didn't want to think about their earlier reaction to her call for backup during a high-speed pursuit—where she was the one being pursued. Situations like that could get out of hand fast. Something that should be pretty clear on account of the fact the car was completely submerged.

Rapidly filling.

Almost to her shoulders now. It was hard to keep the phone out of the freezing water.

Hannah shifted, so her knees were on the seat. She wouldn't be able to open the door until the pressure equalized and she could force it outward so they could swim free of the vehicle. She would have to get Badger from his chair and drag him across the car. Or open the door on his side and push him out first.

"Hannah."

She responded, "There's maybe a minute, then we'll be swimming to the surface." She tried to sound confident. Badger seemed to think he was the only one who could take charge of a situation. Which just proved how little he knew her.

The frustration burned hot in her abdomen.

She was going to use that. Energize herself with irritation and prove she was capable by dragging him from a car.

She didn't hear what whoever was on the other end of the phone said. She stowed the cell under the water in her back pocket, realizing she should probably remove her jeans otherwise they would weigh her down. Like the shoes would.

However, the idea of pulling off her pants in freezing water didn't seem fun. And there was no time anyway.

She started to drag Badger as soon as the water reached her chin. She pushed up on his shoulder blades from the back, trying to keep his head out of the water. Only a few seconds later, the water reached the roof of the car.

She threaded an arm under him, across his chest from the back. His head knocked into hers, but she ignored it and shifted to the door.

Hannah pulled the handle and used her foot to shove the door open.

Emerging from the car was like swimming into a void of nothing. She couldn't even see the surface above them, just the pitch-black freezing-cold water. But she knew the surface was there. She had to trust that, even though she couldn't see it. Both she and Badger were counting on her, and if she didn't make it they would die down here.

Hannah kicked with her legs. Badger's deadweight made it slow going, but no way was she going to give up. She could imagine the guys on the other end of the phone. Freaking out, knowing she was in danger and they were far away. Frantically calling Judah.

She didn't need anyone else. Not a sister she barely knew or a mother she'd never met. A father who was nothing but an idea. A team who wasn't here. A task force that didn't want her. Colleagues she barely knew. The man she couldn't face her feelings for.

She'd always dealt with everything alone. Why would this be any different?

On that thought, her head breached the surface.

Judah yelled, "Hannah!" A second later, she heard a splash.

She concentrated on treading water, kicking her legs constantly. Holding up Badger while his teammate swam to them.

"I got him." Judah's arm came between her and Badger. "Come on."

Her energy drained, and her body wanted to sink below the surface. But with both arms free, Hannah kicked her legs and made strides through the water. Trying to remember the few swimming lessons she had taken as a kid—enough that she wouldn't drown. But she was hardly proficient.

Judah swam to a dock with stairs leading up to the street level. He shoved Badger onto the pier. Badger rolled over onto his back. Judah pulled himself from the water and knelt beside his teammate. He leaned down and listened to Badger's face.

Was he not breathing?

The thought was enough to put a hitch in her stride.

Hannah's face sank beneath the water for a second before she kicked back up and made it all the way to the dock.

But she had no strength to pull herself up.

She grasped the edge and held on.

Judah linked his fingers and started pumping Badger's chest. Two seconds later, his teammate rolled over and coughed out water. Judah scrambled over to her and held out a hand. "Come on."

He dragged her over the edge. Hannah hunched over in a seated position, lacking the strength to sit upright. All she could do was stare at Badger. The rise and fall of his chest. The water now on the dock that had been in his lungs.

Badger groaned. "Why does it feel like an elephant sat on me?"

He glanced at her. Hannah quickly swiped at the tears on her face, not wanting him to see them. She looked up at the overcast afternoon sky. Wished she could see the sun. Anything but that heavy gray and the chill.

Police sirens rang out.

It should have been a comforting sound, as it always had been. But it wasn't now.

"Hannah?"

Both of them were watching her. She could tell. But she didn't look at Badger, even though he'd called her name. She shook her head and looked up at the dock. Waiting to see the first sign that rescue was here.

Joseph Ricker stared down at her.

## 11

---

"Hey." Badger shuffled around and inched closer to Hannah. "What?"

She'd made a noise, low in her throat. A sound of distress. Her face was pale, but given what they'd been through, he wasn't surprised.

Badger was cold to his bones. And his chest really did feel like an elephant had sat on him. He touched her elbow and followed the line of her gaze.

Up at street level, the young man stared down at them.

Badger said, "Jude."

Judah jumped up. "On it." His feet pounded across the dock to the stairs, and he raced up. The kid had already disappeared out of sight.

"Judah will get him," Badger said.

Her wide eyes met his. The blue there was dim now so that it almost looked gray. Her blonde hair was darker. Wet and plastered against her cheeks.

He touched her cheeks. His fingers were probably as cold

as the skin on her face. "Judah will get him." He tugged her closer.

She started to lean against him, then shot back to sitting straight up. "You're hurt."

He didn't care about that. "You saved my life, didn't you?" He touched his chest. It hurt in a deep way that had nothing to do with his lungs, more like a giant torso-sized bruise. "I think Judah might have tried to kill me. Probably so he can steal you away."

Her gaze lifted to his. Badger realized he'd said too much. More than he should have, when he was so determined to walk away from her after this was over. But that was before she'd hauled him by herself to the surface.

Tears filled her eyes. More ran down her cheeks.

He swiped them away with his thumbs. "You saved my life."

If he let her, she would do it again and again every day. Saving him in all the best ways that a woman could make a man's life worth living. That was the power she had over him. And maybe it freaked him out more than he wanted to admit when his life was about controlling the variables and doing what he could to ensure a win.

Relationships were a risk he had never before wanted to take. Keeping things casual with anyone he met, never committing to more than he was prepared to offer. But she'd been different from the start.

Hannah represented everything he wanted.

Her fingers curled around his elbows, hanging onto him as though she needed his strength. That was fine with him because right now he felt the same way.

"Thank you," he said.

"You're welcome." Her voice was little more than a whisper. The remnant of fear and the shudder of adrenaline leaving her system. Soon enough they would both be too shaky to do anything, but the cops would show up before then.

As much as he might want it, Badger and Hannah didn't have all the time in the world.

Badger leaned in, even though they were both freezing. He decided to push away all logical thought and just seize the moment to have a quiet second here with her where there weren't any doubts.

Her nose touched the side of his. He wasn't sure who moved those last few inches. He heard a soft exhale and turned his head slightly to the side so he could touch his lips to—

The dock rocked back and forth underneath them.

Badger glanced over and saw an officer and two EMTs, his eyes able to catch the uniforms but not the details. He closed them for a second and sucked in a breath between gritted teeth.

His head was pounding harder than he wanted to admit to himself. The amount of time he'd spent ill or injured the past few weeks? No. The last thing he wanted, or needed, was to be down again. Recovering. He hated just the idea of it.

The EMTs had them separate, shifting apart to sit beside each other instead of with Hannah practically on his lap. Badger wanted to complain but figured they'd think it was amusing more than anything.

Both of them were wrapped in emergency thermal blankets, and the EMTs shone a light that was far too bright in his eyes. "We need to get you guys out of those wet clothes. But they can do that at the hospital if we head out ASAP." The guy glanced between them. "Any injuries I can't see?"

"He lost consciousness for a while."

Badger shot Hannah a look for ratting him out. *Is she serious?*

"Well, you did." She didn't look apologetic at all. Just glanced away and spoke to the cop then, "His associate chased after the man I think ran us over."

The cop nodded. "My partner went with him."

Badger decided he'd been sitting long enough, and considering he was soaked, he was ready to get himself and this situation moving. He shifted his legs and stood. The EMTs grabbed his elbows and helped him. Which turned out to be a good thing since he was more unsteady on his feet than he'd thought.

When he was stable, he shifted out of their grasp. "Ready?" He held his hand out to Hannah, wanting to be the one who helped her up.

She grinned. "Seriously?"

The EMTs helped her up also. The two of them were walked by first responders up the stairs toward the ambulance. One bus for both of them. A good thing, considering he wasn't about to let her out of his sight. Sure, she was the one who had saved his life. But protecting her was the job, and he intended to do it.

"Let's get you in there, and you can lay down." The EMT guided him onto the ambulance, whether Badger wanted to do that or not. Soon as he could, Badger was going to call Dr. Windermere.

Hannah got in and sat opposite him on the bench seat, where he could see her. Both of them were wrung out. There was plenty to say and even more than that to do. But he was too exhausted to start with any of it.

He decided not to argue for now. Until he spotted Judah

jogging over.

Badger didn't lie down.

He waited while Judah drew near enough to say, "That little squirrel ran off. Got into the car I was following."

The cop was right beside him.

Judah glanced at the guy. "It was definitely the one who ran them off the road."

Badger's head swam just remembering the sensation of sailing over the edge. Upside down. The moment they hit the water, he'd blacked out. Become deadweight. The victim.

The EMT grabbed his elbow. "Easy. I'm gonna help you lie down now."

Badger called out, "Give the cops your statement, Jude." He then turned his head, which stabbed like an ice pick behind his eyes. But he saw Hannah's expression. That same look he'd seen earlier, now there on her face again.

She said, "You want to involve them now?"

"Seems like they already are."

Her expression shifted to something he couldn't read. But it didn't matter because it was done already, and the cops weren't likely to let them walk away without a lengthy explanation. After all, it was their job to know what was going on.

The more help they could get with this, the better. Not only would the cops want to clear everything up and be given answers to all their questions, but they would also be on the lookout for Joseph Ricker. With more personnel at their disposal than Chevalier Protection Specialists had—even if the rest of the team was in town.

The team.

Badger shifted to find his phone in one of the pockets on him. Last he'd seen it, the thing had been in the cupholder.

"Are you looking for this?" Hannah held out the phone.

"No calls until you get to the hospital." The EMT looked adamant. "I need to check your vitals."

Badger took the cell, thanking God that it was water-proof, and squeezed the power button and volume up. He pressed both simultaneously twice. The screen flashed and showed the "all clear" symbol. Badger dragged it to the top of the screen, where it would send a notification.

He got a text in reply seconds later.

Copy that. Team en route anyway.

The boys were coming. Probably Lucia, too. Badger figured that was good. If he and Judah could protect Hannah, then the entire team could do it even more effectively.

"What is it?" she asked.

He tried to respond, but the words got stuck in his throat. His thoughts weren't tracking all the way. He felt kind of sluggish, even when he attempted to lift his hand. Let alone keep the grasp he had on his phone.

It slid from his fingers.

And everything went black.

---

"Badger! Badger!" She shook his shoulder.

The ambulance's rear doors slammed shut, a sound so foreboding her entire body shuddered. Though, maybe that was down to the cold.

The phone Badger had been holding slipped off his shirt. Hannah caught it before it hit the floor, grasping the phone with numb fingers.

It beeped. A raspy voice said, "Go for Zander."

The EMT glanced at her, a frown on his face. She didn't

much care what the guy thought. They didn't know each other.

"Just take care of him." She fell back on that police bravado only she knew was a total fake. Every part of her body felt frozen. Stiff. Her fingers were turning purple. She tugged the insulated blanket around her, but with the soaked and ice-cold clothes against her skin, all she could do was shiver.

"Badger?"

She nearly dropped the phone. Hannah tried to remember the buttons, pressed what she thought was right, and lifted the phone close to her mouth. "He passed out."

A second later, the phone started to ring. On the screen, caller ID said *Nicholas Fury*. Which made no sense.

"Hello?" She couldn't keep the shiver from her voice.

Zander spoke. "You said he passed out?"

Exhaustion seemed to hit her like a wave. Her vision blurred, and she lost focus on Badger's fingers that she realized she'd been staring at.

"Hannah."

"Mmm?" She let her eyes close.

The phone was lifted from her fingers. "This one isn't exactly up to conversation, whoever you are." The EMT paused. "My ambulance, my rules." Another pause. "Copy that…*Nicholas Fury.*"

The phone landed beside her.

And then the EMT was in her face, swaying with the movement of the vehicle. "You with me?"

Hannah managed to say, "Cold."

"I'll bet." His fingers grasped her wrist. "We'll get you warm, though."

"I know." She wanted to fall asleep. Maybe if she did

that, she would be free of the nightmare where Joseph Ricker stood over her when she woke up. Those eyes bore into her as though he knew everything.

Smarter than her, or at the least far more cunning. Full of evil.

She shivered again. Running them off the road wasn't exactly his style. He wanted to make a statement, and they'd wound up in the water. He couldn't have known that would be the end of it. More likely he anticipated they'd have had a confrontation on the street. He might've even claimed she was harassing him, as though she were the aggressor.

The ambulance stopped. The EMT caught her before she toppled over. "Let me get him out, and then I'll help you."

Hannah didn't know if she managed to nod or not.

The doors opened. When the EMTs tugged out Badger on the stretcher, it was Judah who climbed in. "Come on, hun. Let's get you moving." His British accent was enough to wake her out of the semi stupor.

"Zander called."

"I know." Judah lifted her into his arms.

"You're warm."

"Not really. You're just freezing." He dipped his head so the skin of his cheek pressed against her forehead.

The heat was almost overwhelming.

She didn't want to ask but had to. "Did you find Ricker?"

"Don't worry about that right now, Hannah."

"Where's Badger?" She tried to grasp his sweater, but it was damp. Her head clouded like a storm moving in, and there was nothing she could do to stop it. "Don't let me alone."

Hannah had no idea if she even made sense...

And then her world was swallowed up in darkness.

Things drifted for a while. When she woke up, Hannah was wrapped in a cocoon of warmth. Even though she was still chilled, the heat felt good.

Before she even opened her eyes, Hannah knew something was wrong. All she could think about was seeing Joseph Ricker up at street level. Where he stared down at them.

She sucked in a breath, and her eyes flashed open. It took a minute for her to realize she was in a hospital room, with a handsome black man in the chair beside her. His head back and eyes closed. Fast asleep, if the steady rise and fall of his chest was anything to go by.

Hannah turned her head enough to spot her cell phone on the table beside her. Assuming it wasn't waterlogged or trashed in some other way.

No, that wasn't her phone. She had a different case, and that was an entirely different brand.

"Hi." Judah blew out a long breath and stretched.

"Where's Badger?"

"Story of my life." He rolled his eyes. "The ladies always want to know where Badger is."

Hannah frowned. Even if her brain managed to operate, she wasn't exactly sure how to respond to that. So many questions flitted through her mind she didn't know where to start. Or if she should say anything at all.

"Okay, update." Judah sat forward in the chair. "If you're ready for this."

"Tell me."

"Badger is okay. His body just shut down faster than yours because of all the damage it sustained recently. They also think he has a concussion, but it might only be mild. We're waiting to see on that." He checked his watch. "Zander and the rest of the team are due to land in about thirty minutes. They should be here soon."

"What about Nora?"

"She wanted to see you."

Hannah bit her lip. *Isaac.*

Judah said, "She might be with them, but if you'd rather wait to see her until you feel up to it then I can tell Zander and we'll accommodate that."

"I want to see her." Hannah hesitated. They did need to have a conversation. "But if Joseph Ricker is out there, and someone is targeting me, how can I be around even more people? It was bad enough with just you and Badger in the line of fire. Now I'm supposed to put my sister in danger, along with everyone else on your team?"

"More people means better security."

"It also means there's a higher chance someone could get hurt because of me."

"True." Judah nodded slowly. "And you're used to going it alone, aren't you? It's hard enough to let people in when you wouldn't be putting them in danger."

His comment brought a question to her lips. But this wasn't an interview, and his life wasn't an incident for her to delve into, so she stayed quiet.

"Zander had me call Special Agent Alanson. To see if he wanted to head over and see you, or if he had any information for us on the cartel investigation."

"What did he say?"

She would rather talk about Dr. Mathers and her son or even investigate Weston's death. Falling back on the professional was her default for a reason, much like checking her email instead of calling her parents. They enjoyed their retired life in Texas and contacted her for a video chat once a month. Beyond that she just never thought to share more with them.

Especially not the fact that she had discovered a half sister.

Now a brother, too.

"They have the investigation covered," Judah said. "He suggested you take a week and use some vacation days. Lay low for a while so they can figure it all out, and you can take care of your stuff."

Hannah winced.

"He just gave you a vacation. Isn't that a good thing?"

"He told me to go on vacation. That's basically benching me because I am a liability and not an asset right now."

"Ah." Judah shrugged. "But it gives you more time to focus on staying safe and maybe finding Joseph Ricker. Right?"

As if she wanted to take on board all of that. After her colossal failure the last time, how could she even know she'd be able to best him? She couldn't just arrest him—not if he hadn't done anything. Harassment was one thing, but she needed to do this right and not in a way that made her look petty.

Judah stood up. "I'm going to get an update on Badger. See if he's awake."

A flash of fear rolled through her that he was going to leave her by herself. Hannah shook it off. She lived alone and worked alone. Why would this be any different? Just because she'd had a hair-raising day.

Judah leaned down and pressed a kiss to her forehead. "I won't be long at all."

She nodded and watched him close the door behind her.

It was fine. She was fine. Just because she was alone didn't mean anything would happen to her. Judah wouldn't have left her if there was a chance of that.

The clock ticked on the wall. She watched the hand jerk around the face of the clock until her eyes burned. No way was she going to close her eyes and fall asleep. If she did that, she would only wind up back in her nightmare. Cold, submerged in the dark.

Alone.

She needed coffee.

The phone beside the bed rang, far too loud in the silent room.

Hannah's whole body clenched. She extracted one arm from the warm blankets and reached for the handset. "Hello?"

"Did you get my letters?"

## 12

B adger sat on the edge of the bed to pull up the sweats Judah had brought him over his hips. His British teammate emerged from the bathroom. The doctor had insisted on admitting him, and that had been fine while his body wanted to sleep. But now he was awake.

It was time to get going.

Judah shot him a look. "You know she's fine, right? I left her resting, and the doctor was going in to look at her anyway."

"Don't you dare say—"

"We're in a hospital. What could happen?"

"Maybe you haven't been paying attention." Or it was that most of Badger's material came from stories at the hospital in Last Chance County. Even with increased security measures, it always seemed the worst things happened when people let their guards down.

"The last hospital we were in, everything kicked off in the garage. Not up in one of the rooms."

"Yeah?" Badger said. "And when Lucia shot one of her colleagues from a hospital bed?"

"Oh yeah." Judah nodded. "That was crazy."

Badger stared at him. "And you can't understand why I might be a little apprehensive about leaving Hannah alone?"

"There's a security guard on the door," Judah said. "It's not like she's completely unprotected. You just care about her more than you want to admit, so you're going to wade in there and micromanage every moment of her protection."

That wasn't what he was doing. Badger was pretty sure, at least. But he wasn't going to argue, or this would turn out to be an even longer conversation than he wanted. "Why don't you go tell the doctor I'm ready to leave."

"Yeah, because you just check outta hospital like it's a hotel." Judah folded his arms across his chest. "Why don't we wait till Windermere gets here, and you can have him do the paperwork?"

"I can read, you know."

Judah frowned. "Where did that come from?"

Right. He didn't know. Badger winced. "The 'too long, didn't read'—pun completely intended—is that I slipped through the cracks of my local education system. When I joined the army I didn't know how to read. Had to have them get classes for me so I could learn."

"You didn't graduate high school?" It wasn't an accusation. That was the only reason Badger let the question slide.

"They gave me a diploma just so I would leave." Badger tugged a hooded sweater over his head, so he didn't have to see the expression on Judah's face.

"Doesn't seem to have slowed you down. Or hindered what you're capable of."

Badger glanced over. "Thanks."

He'd worked hard for months learning to read. After that, he'd absorbed every book he could get his hands on. Mostly adventure stories, science fiction, and fantasy. Worlds he'd been denied because he hadn't been able to decipher the words on the page.

He'd also learned that there was a percentage of adults who grew up without learning to read. Whether because of disability, or a failure of the people who should've taught them, they still had to navigate the world as adults.

It was probably what drove Badger's need to be viewed as skilled and a valuable team member. Because he had been forced to earn for himself every single inch of respect.

And yet, Judah gave it without reservation.

Instead of picking apart Badger's story and asking a hundred questions about how it had come to be or why it was even possible. Turning his personal experience into a discussion. Judah simply accepted Badger exactly how he was—and even went so far as to applaud his achievements.

Instead of feeling inadequate, Badger got the chance to feel like an equal.

"Thanks," he said.

"Maybe you do have a concussion. Because you already said that." Judah grinned, back to his normal self. The guy could be serious for about five whole minutes before he brushed off whatever it was and got back to being the jokester.

"Let's go. We need to make sure Hannah is okay."

Badger headed out the door first. She wasn't far down the hallway, but before he got there the entire team stepped off the elevator at the end and headed their way.

Greetings were called up and down the hallway between Judah and the guys. Nora, Lucia, Andre, and Zander. Dr.

Windermere was with them. Eas had evidently stayed home —with his family.

Badger ignored everything and headed for her room.

He needed to see Hannah more than anything else. He was here to protect her, which meant he wasn't in a different room while she was alone.

The security guard stepped aside, and Badger strode in.

She looked up, her eyes wide. Face pale. She had the handset of the phone against her ear.

What was—

Hannah slammed the phone down hard enough he heard the plastic crack. Then she grasped the whole unit and threw it on the floor. It hit the ground. The plastic splintered this time, and he heard the discordant busy tone through the tiny speaker.

"Hannah, what—"

She looked at him and screamed, "GET OUT!"

A feminine hand tugged at his sleeve. "Let's give her a minute."

He didn't want to, but he allowed Nora to tug him back. A nurse squeezed between them, slipped into the room, and shut the door.

Then Zander was in front of him as well.

The two of them ushered Badger back.

"Sit," Zander ordered.

Badger's legs buckled. They caught his elbows before he landed in the chair. He let out a long breath, elbows to his knees. He hung his head and covered his face.

"She didn't look good." That was Nora.

"Did you see her throw the phone?" Lucia asked.

"Something must've happened." Andre so often seemed to be the levelheaded one, even though he was also plenty crazy on his own. The group just balanced each other out. Which was good, because right now Badger felt like he was caught in a tornado. Spinning out.

He lifted his face. "One of you needs to find out who was on the phone."

He wanted it to be him, but the look on her face…

He wasn't sure she would ever speak to him again at this point. Or she just needed some time to process.

Either way it might be clear to her that he'd failed her. She was the one who rescued them from the car. The assassin he took down might not have been the shooter. In saving someone's life, she had turned back to help him instead of doing her job.

Exactly what had he done that made her life better in all of this?

"Take a deep breath." Dr. Windermere stuck the end of his stethoscope down the back of Badger's hoodie. He listened to Badger's breathing through the thin material of his T-shirt. Low in his lungs, where the raw scrape began every time he breathed.

After a few seconds, Windermere crouched in front of him. "Headache?"

"Maybe you could just go ask the doctor who treated me."

"Because you told him the truth?"

Beyond the doctor, Nora glanced at the closed door to Hannah's room. Probably wanting to go in and see if she was all right. The two of them might not know each other very well, but they were half sisters. Now that he knew it he could see the resemblance, though it was slight beyond the similarity in their hair color.

And both of them bore a resemblance to Lana.

"If I go talk to the doctor," Windermere said, "Then you're going to be lying down in the bed they gave you. If you want to be done here, then you answer my questions yourself."

Badger let out a breath. He wasn't going to do that when the rest of them were standing around listening, entirely too interested in his physical state. "Someone go and see if Hannah is okay. It doesn't matter who it is."

Maybe all of them could go in there and find out what was going on.

Zander glanced at Andre and motioned toward the door with a tip of his head. Andre said nothing. He headed for the door, waving Lucia and Nora inside. That left Judah watching their backs—yes, even in a hospital hallway—while he spoke with the doctor and Zander.

"They said *mild* concussion." Badger said, "and you know for us, that basically means we're fine."

"Fine is not a medical diagnosis." Windermere shone a tiny flashlight in Badger's eyes until he winced. Probably trying to get him to wince on purpose. The moment he yielded, the doctor saw the truth. "What about your ribs? Judah said he had to expel water."

"Doesn't feel like he was trying to save my life." Badger rubbed his chest with a hand and grinned.

Zander was still frowning. "I think you need a couple of days' downtime, either way."

Badger started to argue.

"Don't bother. We're all taking tomorrow off. You know Hannah needs it, and we're going to lay out everything. Figure out the next step."

"Okay." If it made Hannah safe, who cared what he had to do?

THE NURSE HEADED for the door. Hannah had managed to convince her that everything was fine. She glanced at Nora, Lucia, and Andre. "You guys should just leave. I really don't want you in here."

She could have had the nurse throw them out, but it wasn't like that. They meant well. Nora wanted to get to know her, and while Hannah felt the same, the fact was that life always got in the way—until she could say she rarely got what she wanted. Except maybe making detective, but that was something she'd earned.

Hannah had nothing she didn't possess simply because of hard work.

She didn't look at them. It wasn't worth seeing the looks of pity on their faces. What would be the point, except to focus on what was in front of her so she didn't have to think about that phone call?

Tears gathered. One slipped down her cheek.

There was a slight dip in the mattress as Nora settled on the edge of the bed. Older than Hannah by several years, she was refined where Hannah had hard edges. Like two different types of glass. "Who was on the phone, Hannah?"

The soft tone of her voice sent another tear falling. Hannah swiped away the betraying moisture. "His name is Joseph Ricker. I arrested him years ago, and he was recently released."

She could still hear the echo of his voice in her ear. Enough it made her want to scrub her ear canal just to get rid of it.

Hannah shook her head to displace the thought. She caught Andre tugging out his phone. To check his email or send a text. He could be ignoring her and working, but he could also be communicating everything she said to the rest of his team—or Ted. Either way, she figured she was about to have their entire team standing with her.

They were going to stand with her, even if she'd just yelled at Badger.

She knew they would.

Since Nora was waiting for her to say more, Hannah figured she may as well explain it once and get it over with.

"I need to talk to you about something else." Not all of them, just her sister. "But Joseph is the one who ran us off the road."

"And he just called you?" Lucia frowned. "How would he have gotten the number?"

Nora glanced at her, then back again. "What did he say, Hannah?"

"He asked me if I got his letters. He was locked up for six years, and he sent me one every week." Hannah shook her head. "At first I read them. After that, I let my sergeant know, and they sent someone to tell him to quit writing, but he didn't. I moved to a new house, and he sends letters there now. Whatever threat they attempted, Joseph didn't care. He just kept writing to me."

Lucia shifted. "Did he ever call you or send someone over to harass you?"

She sounded like the federal agent she had been up until a few weeks ago. Any other time, Lucia would likely have been someone Hannah got along well with. That meant she had two women in this room she could easily come to count on. Women who could share her life and whom she would consider friends.

But right now, she would only put them in danger.

146 | LISA PHILLIPS

"There wasn't much he could do except posture. He was locked up in juvenile detention." Hannah pushed aside the fear and thought about the phone call. "When I told him I threw all the letters away, he wasn't exactly happy. But it wasn't the reason why he called."

She was still trying to process all of it.

"There was a girl, or a woman, on the line. I don't know how old she was. I just heard her whimper." And if they'd left her alone, she would've called 911 to report it.

"He has someone with him?" Nora seemed to be reserving judgment before she jumped in with a reaction. Gathering all the facts first.

Hannah said, "I think he kidnapped her. That before or after he ran us off the road, he took a girl. He's going to hurt her."

"Because he wants your attention?" Lucia said with that "cop" stare Hannah saw on colleagues all the time in cases like this. Trying to distance herself from the empathy and work the case. "He starts by revealing himself and the fact he's out. Then he escalates and kidnaps a girl. He runs you off the road."

"He wasn't trying to kill us. That was an accident." She didn't want them to think she was defending him, so Hannah added, "I think he was trying to confront us. If we turned the tables and forced a confrontation with him on the street, he'd have told me that he had a girl. And if I did anything to him, we would never find her."

The pieces she hadn't managed to put together yet clicked against each other in her mind.

Hannah continued, "I'd have wanted to arrest him, but I wouldn't have been able to do it if there was someone out there. If he had intel on a victim."

Nora said, "You think he's playing a game with you?"

Her half sister wasn't a cop. Hannah needed to remember this wasn't anything Nora had dealt with. Even if Nora had endured plenty as Stephen Gladstone's daughter, both over the years of her life and in the last few months. She knew what it was like to be manipulated and how to survive it.

But there was still a difference between Gladstone and Ricker.

Gladstone had used people to make money and get what he wanted. Joseph was simply evil. If he was determined to destroy Hannah, using innocent people was the best way to do it. He knew exactly how to get into her head and create fissures in her resolve.

"I think whoever he abducted doesn't have much time left." Hannah winced. "I told him I never read his letters, that I just threw them away because they were trash. He escalated it and told me he had a girl. Dangling that piece of information so I couldn't just brush him off and walk away."

"Now he knows he has you hooked." Lucia shifted, a determined expression on her face. "And this girl might not mean anything to you, but she will be used."

Nora winced.

Hannah said, "You didn't need to come, but thank you anyway."

Nora's expression softened. "When we heard the two of you had taken that dive into the river, we all headed here." She paused. "What else did you need to tell me?"

Hannah shook her head. "Later."

For now, she wondered if "all" included the guy she had only ever seen wearing a mask. The one who'd been revealed as one of the FBI's Ten Most Wanted in the past month or so.

The last news article she'd read about him sat at the front desk of the free clinic working undercover. He had a twin. His whole birth family had been destroying his life for their own ends.

It was just another reason why she hadn't been all in to connect with hers. Even if she only knew Nora was part of it, there couldn't be anything good about opening that door. She wanted to know the woman who sat close to her. But only because Nora seemed like a good woman. Someone who garnered the respect of the good people around her.

Could Hannah even say that about herself?

Let alone the others connected to them. Lana. *Isaac.*

"I'm glad you're okay." Nora squeezed her hand.

Behind her, Lucia made a face. Hannah almost laughed. "Lucia doesn't agree with you."

Before Hannah could explain, Lucia said, "She might be out of the woods in terms of hypothermia. But my guess? Hannah is far from okay."

Nora began to bluster.

Hannah just laughed. "To be fair, she's not exactly wrong."

But maybe she had been when she'd shut out the whole team. So far she'd only had to deal with Badger and Judah, and that was enough. But having all of them here? Surely they could find Ricker. The feds would work through the cartel investigation. She'd go back to Rochester and her position in homicide.

"Okay," Andre said. "Ted did some digging. Social media, local law enforcement channels, and those neighborhood sites where you report a missing dog. There's a girl who lives in a West Baltimore neighborhood. It's all over those sites. She was abducted this morning."

Nora gasped.

"Teachers called her mom because she never showed up for school. There are people out looking, and they found her phone on the side of the road where she walks to school."

Hannah opened her mouth to ask how on earth he knew this was the girl Joseph Ricker had been with when they were on the phone.

Before she could, Andre said, "Her name is Hannah."

Then he walked out of the room.

## 13

B adger stared at Andre as he explained. Of course, given the explanation that happened in the first two minutes after he exited the hospital room, it told him nothing about Hannah's state of mind.

And after she'd screamed at him to get out.

"He's taunting her." Badger was the one who wanted to scream now.

Zander said, "I'll have Ted send me everything he can get on this guy."

Badger spun to his team leader. "Get a hold of Special Agent Alanson at the FBI."

Zander stared for a second. Then he gave a brief nod and pulled out his phone. As he did that, he reached up and squeezed the back of Badger's neck. Whatever his intention, it worked. As far as Badger was concerned, that was all he needed to get his head together and be in a position to help Hannah.

Badger realized how much he drew from their strength by

standing there with his teammates around him—excluding Eas, but it would be the same if he was here. Pushing them away for weeks hadn't helped him at all. In fact, he would wager it made things harder. But then again, he hadn't wanted their help dealing with Hannah ghosting him.

Badger turned to Andre while Zander made the call. "How was she?"

"There's a lot going on there."

"You think I don't know that?"

Andre held up both hands. "Easy. You know what I'm saying. And with this guy purposely taunting her, on top of everything else?" He blew out a breath. "I thought dealing with Burgess was bad. Now we've got multiple things kicking off at once and no idea where an attack will come from next."

"She won't care about that. She's just going to want to try and rescue this girl." Badger knew that the same way he knew that if the team told her it wasn't possible to find Joseph and his victim, Hannah would walk away and work the issue independently. Completely unprotected.

Andre scrubbed his hand down his face.

"What about with Nora?" Badger asked. "How was that whole thing?" He wanted Hannah to tell her himself. But Andre's read on the situation would give him a baseline at least.

His friend shrugged. "Hannah said there was something she wanted to tell Nora. But there was no time when it's clear this Joseph guy has a victim he abducted."

Badger nodded. He wanted to know what Hannah had to say to Nora. He wasn't about to interfere in the relationship of two sisters getting to know each other, but if he could do anything to ease things for Hannah, then Badger wanted to. And he knew exactly how that made him sound. Even just to himself, Badger knew that he was all in with Hannah despite his determination.

Except that it seemed she wasn't as all in with him.

"Here." Zander held up the phone. "Alanson."

Badger put it to his ear. "You have people looking for Joseph Ricker and this girl, right?"

He didn't want Hannah to be a part of the chase, and hopefully a rescue.

He wanted to do whatever it took to keep her separate from it. Even knowing how cut up she would be that there was a victim out there, in part because this guy was obsessed with Hannah. He still wanted to keep her from seeing the worst. Feeling the guilt.

"Not my jurisdiction," Alanson said. "And given that debacle with the car in the river? You can tell her for me that she's off the task force. Not just on vacation, but done. If you or her, or anyone, sees Doctor Mathers or her son, or you hear one whisper of the Suarez cartel, then I'm the first to know about it."

Badger couldn't believe this. "You're just going to let her swing?"

"Some guy she arrested years ago isn't my problem. I've got enough already." Alanson wasn't backing down. "But you tell her that if she ever wants another appointment in this town, my advice? She gets that brother of hers to talk first."

*Brother?*

The realization dawned on Badger. "Isaac."

There was no time to ask any questions because Alanson had already hung up.

"Isaac...what?" Andre asked. "They're looking for this girl, right?"

"I imagine someone is." He shut his eyes and tried to comprehend it all. "But it's not her task force supervisor. And she just got fired." Before either of them could ask, he said, "Unless she can get Isaac to talk."

Of course it was Isaac. What else would any of this be about? A brother, who needed to talk? *Of course* Isaac would know about it. *The envelope.* That was the thing she'd needed to tell Nora.

Zander frowned. "What would Isaac—"

Badger moved between them before Zander could finish his question. He twisted the handle and let himself into the room where Lucia stood with her back to the wall, and Nora sat on the edge of the bed talking low with Hannah.

Both of them turned to him.

Nora said, "What is it?"

"I need a minute." He looked at Hannah. "And no more hiding."

She stared right back at him, not backing down a single inch. Which was something he seriously admired about her. "Because you don't have any secrets?"

Minutes ago she had been all but shattered over what was happening. Now she seemed to have wrapped that resolve back around her. He was piecing together precisely who she was, not just the kind of cop she made but also the type of woman that resided underneath.

She didn't trust her feelings or instincts. The cop preferred physical evidence to anything else, and he figured the woman wouldn't mind proof either.

The fact she knew someone was being hurt, and there

was no way to stop it immediately meant she would be struggling.

"I know what it's like to feel guilty. Not just because everyone around you blames you for something that happened, so you should feel bad about it because they think you should. But because you had a lapse in judgment as a kid and in a moment of selfishness, the worst thing possible happened." He shook his head. "But that's not what happened to you. You didn't know Joseph was like this or that he would do any of it."

He knew what it was like to take the blame for something. Deep down, he knew it was fitting that he had the responsibility laid on his shoulders.

Tears filled her eyes. "So it's not my fault that girl was taken?"

"You didn't even know he'd been released." He knew when blame should be assigned. She'd taken responsibility for another person's actions when there was no way she could have stopped it. "Him kidnapping that girl has nothing to do with you."

"Then you're really not going to like my idea."

No, he figured she was probably right about that.

"Get me a phone," Hannah said. "Find out the number he used to call me here. I'll call him back and tell him that I'll trade myself for the girl."

He started to object when Zander strode in. "Did you all cover the Isaac thing? Is everyone up to speed?"

Badger blew out a breath.

"Because the next thing already hit." Zander had his phone up. "Hannah is getting a call on her FBI phone. Ted is going to put it through to me."

"I'm not even going to ask how you guys can do that."

She motioned for his phone. "Just give it to me. It could be Joseph."

The phone buzzed.

Zander said, "Here it comes. And we'll all be listening on speaker."

He didn't hand over the phone, just tapped the screen. Badger watched Hannah's face intently. She looked like she was about to be sick, and she definitely didn't want to do this. There was nothing in her which embraced the situation. She was scared, and he wanted to take all the bad from her life.

But given what he'd just told her and the differences between the guilt they both carried, he doubted she would even let him.

Hannah said, "Hello?"

"Sarah? Is that you?" The voice through the phone was female and crackly. Not Joseph.

She frowned. "Doctor Mathers? Where are you? How are you? What's going on?"

"Pam is *dead*. You need to get out of town before they kill you, too."

Hannah gasped. Probably more to buy herself time to figure out what to say than for any other reason.

Doctor Mathers said, "I'll help you get away. We need to meet."

---

HANNAH GRIPPED THE PHONE. "Yes. We should meet. I think someone has been following me, and I don't know where to go."

Dr. Mathers was the boss. She'd also killed that man at

the Suarez house. She would want to be the one in control, and Hannah could use that in her favor.

Even if she was in a hospital bed, they could make this work.

"Good." Mathers rattled off a location, the corner of two streets. "Can you be there in an hour? I'll pick you up."

"I'll be there."

The phone call ended. Zander said, "She hung up."

"Seemed pretty hot to help you." Lucia frowned, approaching the end of the bed. "A little strange, considering when you left the house it was everyone for themselves, right?"

Hannah barely had time to nod. Someone had filled the former DEA agent in on the whole situation. Probably Judah.

Lucia continued, "But now Pam is dead."

Nora said, "She sounded worried about what would happen to you, in the light of what happened to her friend."

"I would believe it if she was nowhere near here. But if she's been kicking around town for hours?" Lucia shook her head.

"I would be halfway to Miami by now," Hannah said. She actually wouldn't, considering she preferred cold climates to perpetually warm ones. Plus, south was where the cartel operated. It made far more sense to go north. Probably into Canada, hiding somewhere they would never think to look for her.

Badger said, "I'll call Alanson back and give him the update."

Hannah locked gazes with him. She could tell he didn't want her anywhere near this. That was why he had to understand. "We need to be finding the girl Joseph has. Maybe I'm the one who needs an update on that, and Doctor Mathers can go fend for herself if she thinks she can rip off a cartel. But an innocent young girl? That's who I want to help." She didn't exactly care about the doctor and her problems—or a task force she was no longer part of. Not when there was someone far more vulnerable at risk here.

"Maybe Alanson has a blonde agent who can take your place."

Hannah winced and shook her head. "Not in time to do this. And the minute Mathers sees her, she'll know it's over." The doctor would put a bullet in the head of whoever was sent to play Sarah. Not much of a ruse unless they were only there to arrest the doctor. "Alanson is going to want the doctor to lead them back to her son. Then they'll sweep in and take both into custody so the feds can flip them for info on the cartel."

She pushed back the blankets covering her legs. Nora assisted, saying, "We need to get you some clothes."

The rest of them filed out. Lucia grabbed a bag from Andre, handed it to Nora, then disappeared as well.

Hannah glanced over and saw the honest look on her face. How Nora simply accepted that she would do this. The faith her sister had in her, or maybe it was just understanding, made a difference in Hannah's life. No one had ever understood her in a way where they just let her be who she was. Not even Badger, although she was pretty sure he was getting the gist of it.

Given what he'd told her, she knew now there was something in his past. He could understand how she felt about missing what was right in front of her face with Joseph Ricker. She also knew he understood the guilt of being responsible when someone else was hurt.

She wanted him to open up. Just because he hadn't yet

didn't mean he wouldn't. With so much going on, there had hardly been time so far to dive deep. She hadn't wanted to trust him. But it was becoming clearer to her that putting her faith in him and the men and women of Chevalier Protection Specialists would be far better than colleagues she hadn't worked with long.

Alanson had already made up his mind that her shared DNA with Isaac meant she would be painted with the same brush as him.

Never mind that Nora was all class and kindness. Her father had been a manipulator and criminal who dragged her through the mud. And yet she had survived it. People now knew she was good.

Would the same thing happen with Isaac?

"Do you know…" Hannah didn't even know how to begin.

"The thing you were going to tell me?"

"I got some news yesterday." Hannah took the clothes, turned her back, and kept talking so she didn't have to see the look on Nora's face. "When Isaac turned himself in to the military, and they handed him over to the feds, his DNA was run so they could see if it matched any open cases. Or if they got hits in any database."

"And they had one?"

Hannah glanced over her shoulder. "Yeah, but the match they got wasn't to a case. It was to me."

Nora's brows raised.

"Isaac is my brother. The match was a half sibling, like you and I." Hannah lowered the shirt over her head. The clothes didn't fit precisely, but it was near enough she could deal with it for the time being. There wasn't long before she was supposed to meet with Dr. Mathers, pretending to be

Sarah. She had no idea what the doctor intended, but it couldn't be anything good. That was why she had to get all this said between her and Nora.

Nora said, "Do you think he's my half brother?"

Hannah shrugged. "It's possible, since Lana is both of our mothers, that she's also his mother."

Nora nodded. "That would make a lot of sense about the relationship they have. He's tied to her, and it's far deeper than simply respect for a person in authority over you. I bet she is his mother." Her face blanched. "That means Isaac is my brother."

Hannah gave her a second simply to absorb that.

"I always wanted a brother." A second later, she winced. "My dad can't have known. He tried for a short time to set us up. But it always seemed like we could be friends, and anything more would be strange."

"I always wanted a brother as well. And a sister." Now Hannah had both, there was no time to even enjoy it.

She also had a birth mother she'd never met, but one who evidently kept tabs on her because she'd known that Hannah was in danger. Instead of coming to protect Hannah herself, she'd hired the best people Hannah knew for the job.

Having the Chevalier Protection Specialists team here, along with her sister, was the best Hannah could have asked for. And yet, the chance to know her mother was like an ache deep inside her. Even with her and her parents' relationship, there would still always be that missing from her life.

Nora held out her hand. Hannah slipped hers into it, and they exited the hospital room together.

"Let's go." Zander led the way.

Andre and Lucia walked ahead of him. She glanced over her shoulder and saw Badger close behind her. Judah at the back. The whole team, surrounding her. The wealth of skill and knowledge with her was humbling. Hannah had years of experience as a police detective, and yet with them she almost felt like a vulnerable client their company was being paid to protect.

Mostly because she kind of was.

Hannah glanced at her sister. "Have you ever spoken to Lana?"

As they stepped into the elevator, Nora shook her head. "Not for years, and I don't know what I would say. She left when I was twelve. You were born after that. Isaac is older than both of us, so he was born first. Three kids, and Isaac is the only one she sees. Their relationship isn't exactly healthy. But maybe what we have is better, because we don't know her. Things can't go bad because they just…aren't."

Lana stayed away because it was better not to have a relationship than to see one go bad. It was a theory. But then again, Hannah considered her own situation. How she shied away from connection because it was easier to be safe and alone than it was to put herself out there and get hurt.

Again.

Was she pushing Badger away because all of this family stuff came unavoidably with him? It was easier to bury her head in the sand than risk Nora not wanting to be a family to her.

"I might talk to her one day," Nora said. "But until then, I have everything I need right here. In this family, who will risk everything to keep each other safe, I don't need anything else."

Zander wound his arms around her in a hug and pulled her close to his front. Nora settled in his arms with a smile.

Hannah didn't look at Badger until the elevator doors opened.

The longing on his face, observing Nora and Zander, made her want to try. To see what was between them.

But first, there was work to do.

---

## 14

The task force command center was a fifteen-passenger van with blacked-out windows. The seats inside had been removed and replaced with a bank of computers and enough swivel chairs for Alanson and the guys he had ordered into it with him.

Badger hadn't been invited. Not that he'd expected to be.

Being even out of arms reach of Hannah didn't sit well with him. Not when he was supposed to protect her, and how he was feeling now that she'd saved his life. Both of them had gone through an ordeal in the last day. But she wanted to do her job, and he could understand needing to see it through to the end if it was possible. She could avoid bloodshed by putting herself in danger—and he knew exactly why she volunteered for that.

Chevalier Protection Specialists had been divided into two groups. Zander, Nora, and Judah were in one SUV. Andre, Lucia, and Badger were in the second.

As usual, Andre had confiscated the keys and was driving.

Badger sat in the front seat, which put Lucia in the back row. But it didn't sound like she was idle. It sounded like she was assembling an arsenal. Checking and rechecking every weapon they had. Ensuring it was all squared away just in case.

No one wanted to get into a gunfight on a city street. It would be avoided if at all possible. But there was a dangerous cartel involved, and frequently, in their work, people's lives were at stake.

Up ahead Hannah, back in her undercover role as Sarah, the clinic's receptionist, drove a borrowed car to the spot where Dr. Mathers had arranged for them to meet. Weaving in and out of traffic.

"Anyone else getting a vibe she drives like Judah?" Zander's voice came through the car speakers. They could've got on comms, but it was best not to run into interference with the federal personnel in the area and their own setup. They didn't need anyone listening to their conversations so they had called each other and connected the two cars by phone line.

Through the speakers, Nora began to chuckle. Judah said something, but it cut off.

Andre said, "Yeah, I'm getting serious Judah vibes."

Badger frowned. "She's late for the meeting. People's lives are at stake."

"Next time we're hanging out," Zander said. "You and she can go and pick up the pizzas. Then we'll have more data."

Badger lifted his chin, even though his boss wouldn't see it. "Deal."

Right then, there was nothing he wanted more than for

Hannah to be part of their team. The one that was more like a family to him than the family he'd been born into.

Andre pointed ahead. "She's pulling over."

Zander said, "Copy that."

On the corner of the streets Masters had told Hannah to meet her at there was a chain pharmacy next to a local donut shop. Badger's stomach rumbled.

Andre slowed in the line of traffic and glanced over. "When we're done here, we eat. Badger needs to fuel up."

"Understood."

Zander would probably have Nora get on her phone, searching up local restaurants where they could all get a big breakfast. Or someplace they could load up on foot-long sandwiches. It didn't matter if Badger told them he didn't need to eat yet. Zander was fastidious about being at full strength.

The amount of exertion they put into their jobs meant they needed enough fuel to be strong and have energy left at the end of the day. No matter what they were doing.

Andre reached over and squeezed the back of Badger's neck.

Badger only allowed it because he knew that he would be doing exactly the same if the situation were reversed. Taking care of his teammate as well as getting the job done.

The federal van pulled into the parking lot on the opposite side from where Hannah had parked, outside the pharmacy. No one knew what car the doctor would be driving or if she would approach on foot. Although, she had said that she would pick up Hannah.

Zander took the opposite corner, across the street to the west of the pharmacy. Without Badger having to ask him,

Andre pulled into the gas station just down from the pharmacy. It wasn't a great angle, but they would be close if everyone needed to move in and intervene to save Hannah's life.

In that situation, the last place Badger wanted to be was across any street. Dodging traffic. Watching the worst happen to her.

It brought back too many memories of another time in his life, where he'd watched with foreboding and been too far away to do anything.

That time he'd been surfing with his best friend, Timo. Just a couple of twelve-year-old boys who wanted to goof off all day. Only they were saddled with his friend's eight-year-old sister. They'd left her on the beach and paddled out, waiting to catch waves.

Badger had been riding a wave back into the shore when he saw the man grab Alexis and run back to his pickup with her. Too far away to stop it from happening. He'd watched the entire thing.

Her body had been found two days later.

"You okay?"

Badger didn't look at Andre. Lucia was quiet in the back, finished with her task. She didn't like inactivity any more than he did.

Nor did he like the idea of having to explain it all. How he'd been selfish and done what he wanted. How he'd watched her get taken. Unable to get there fast enough, although he'd almost drowned trying. Then he'd rushed across the sand. Falling. Crying.

But she'd been long gone.

"Bro. We've been through this before." Andre glanced over. "Maybe you should just tell me."

"It doesn't matter." Badger shook his head. "It won't change anything."

Badger was the only one who could change things. By not being selfish. By being where he could make sure the same thing didn't happen to Hannah. If she became a permanent part of his life, he was going to tell her everything.

The aftermath, all of it.

How his family and Alexis's family had blamed him and Timo as though they were the ones who'd killed her. And in a way, they'd been right. Two years later, Timo had killed himself.

As soon as he could, Badger had left Hawaii. He'd left Ryder behind and become a different person. The man he wanted to be. A guy who would never let something like that happen again.

Because he *couldn't* let it happen.

But the truth was, his friends didn't know the real him. They only knew what they saw. What he chose to show them. Badger didn't ever want them to know that he was someone entirely different. He only wanted them the way they were.

He never wanted the guys of Chevalier to look at him the way his family, or Alexis, had.

He didn't want the boy Ryder had been to be a part of Chevalier. Otherwise, Badger would only end up causing pain all over again. He would fail. It was inevitable.

No, it was better they didn't know. That they thought he was good.

The alternative didn't even bear thinking about. The guys would consider it a good thing if he opened up. They wanted him to tell them everything because they would try and prove to him that it didn't matter to them. But that wouldn't work either. Never mind that their intentions were good. Eventually he would mess up, and they would know precisely why. They would see the truth that lived inside of him.

"There's a car approaching." Andre handed him a pair of binoculars.

Badger watched as someone pulled in beside Hannah. He trained the view on the driver and focus. "It's Mathers, but she's the only one in the vehicle."

Judas said, "Confirmed," through the car speakers.

"Are we tapped into the FBI comms?" Badger figured it was possible whether the feds knew about it or not.

"Ted has it." Andre showed him the screen of his phone. Ted was transcribing the federal channel so that it appeared as a long message thread. Or maybe he had a program that did it for him. "He'll alert us if something is pertinent."

Badger nodded. He wasn't going to relax until this was done and they could get to the rental house. But with a missing girl out there, he doubted Hannah would stop moving until all her cases were closed. She would push through anything and everything until the job was done.

It was enough to make him want to fall in love with her.

But given the way he'd already tumbled hard, and everyone knew it, Badger figured she had to make the first move if anything was going to happen between them. Otherwise, he would make a fool of himself all over again when they all found out she didn't feel the same about him at all.

As Badger watched through the binoculars, their windows came down so they could converse side by side. Still in their cars.

DR. MATHERS HAD ALMOST white lips. Dark circles ringed her eyes, which carried in them a kind of frenzied look. "Sarah, you're here," she said, almost as if she didn't believe it.

"I saw Pam's death on the news." Hannah sniffed, recalling the moment she saw Joseph last to sell the fear. Thinking about that missing girl—and what might happen to her. The fate of the clinic crew mattered little in light of that. For all she'd given to the task force their aim seemed so meaningless now.

A girl had been kidnapped.

It suddenly seemed so wrong to be here. But with nothing else to do except wait for Ted to get them a lead on where Joseph or the girl might be, Hannah had jumped on the chance to get a win *somewhere.*

"I've been hiding." Hannah leaned over and whispered, "I didn't know what to do."

The doctor's eyes flared. "We'll figure it out. Together."

Hannah nodded. "I'm so glad you called." She shook her head. "But where is Craig?" She let all her fears about the worst that could happen to that abducted girl, Hannah, simmer to the surface.

Meanwhile Dr. Mathers looked as if she wanted to be sick. "Get in my car. We shouldn't be here this long." She rolled her window up.

Hannah grabbed her coat from the passenger seat. The gun Alanson had given her sat in the folds of the jacket, which she slipped into the back of her waistband as she emerged from the car and pulled the coat over her shoulders.

She glanced around nervously as she rounded the car. No one on comms said anything. Then again, they didn't need to give a pep talk or remind her of everything they'd drilled into her in the minutes while she'd been waiting, and before that as she drove to the pharmacy to wait.

Still, she knew they were happy to put her in danger if she got them a win on this. Task force or not, Hannah had signed up for a life where she risked herself to bring justice. It was what she did every day as a cop.

This was no different.

They weren't being reckless with her safety. She knew the drill.

Hannah climbed in the front beside the doctor and took a look at the back seat. It was clear. Was all the money in the trunk?

She needed to focus on what was happening here, right now, where she could affect the course of things. Not with some girl she didn't know, who they couldn't find. Yet. But they would. The entire Chevalier team had promised her that, while Alanson hadn't even mentioned the abducted Hannah.

Mathers pulled out of the space and turned onto the street.

"Thanks for coming to get me. I've been terrified, and I didn't know what to do." Hannah blew out a long breath, pushing away the dichotomy of feelings inside her. "Where are we going?"

"It doesn't matter. As long as we keep moving."

"Okay." In the tone of her agreement was the unspoken fact that Hannah would defer to the doctor. In doing that, Mathers would believe she was in control. She would play the role of savior in this scenario, and Hannah only needed to ride that out long enough to find out what happened to Craig, where the money was, and what Mathers wanted with Hannah.

For as long as this lasted, Mathers needed to think she was the one calling the shots here.

Hannah watched as she drove, assessing the other woman's movements. Trying to act nervous herself. Meanwhile, the doctor kept her foot heavy on the accelerator, taking erratic turns that made no sense. Hannah wasn't overly familiar with this area of Baltimore. And given the amount of cover she currently had behind them but out of sight, she wasn't scared no one would ever find her again. But still, the doctor probably shouldn't be the one driving.

Hannah waited for a quiet stretch of road and assessed the vehicles behind them in the side mirror. Just because she couldn't see the rest of them behind the car didn't mean they weren't there.

"Are you going to tell me where Craig is?" Hannah asked.

The entire task force could hear their conversation. Everything Mathers said would end up on the official record and probably be brought back up in court if the case went to trial.

The doctor hissed out a breath, grasping the wheel with a white-knuckle grip. "He's dead. Just like Pam."

Hannah gasped. "Oh no. Those people whose house it was…did they find him? That's who killed Pam, right?"

For all she knew, the doctor could've been the one who killed Pam. Or Craig. Even with the method of murder, it could have been Barbara Mathers that took the nurse's hands and her tongue. The doctor had known what she was doing in the house.

Mathers glanced at her. "You have no clue what's happening here."

That might be true, but it didn't mean Hannah was without options. "What are we going to do? They want their money back, right?" She didn't mention how it might not have been a great idea to rip off dangerous people. But the sentiment was there in the air, nonetheless.

"Of course they want their money."

"What are we going to do?" Hannah figured it was possible Sarah wasn't anticipating a life on the run with a doctor she barely knew. Especially not one she had seen kill a man in cold blood.

"You're going to shut up and let me think."

Didn't she have a plan?

Hannah had nothing that the doctor wanted. They'd taken the duffel bags of money she'd carried and loaded them into the car—her car.

As Sarah, she hadn't been given anything by the group. No one confided in her or let her keep any of the money. Pam was supposed to have paid her later. So why swoop in now as the savior instead of just leaving town?

Unless the doctor didn't think she could get clear of this. Not without doing something. And it involved Sarah.

Mathers might have called her so that Sarah could take the hit instead of the doctor.

Hannah wondered about the man who had shot Pearson. If there really was a hit out on her, then Joseph Ricker showing up was far more effective than one sniper had been. She felt like her entire being was coming apart knowing he'd abducted a girl. Whether the girl shared her name or not, Hannah wanted to find her.

On the heels of a professional hit—if that's what the shooter had been—Joseph showing up was a little too coincidental. Was he the second wave? Someone trying to take her out.

Like Sarah was to Mathers, she could be a means to an end. Someone to use.

But if there was a person out there who wanted her dead or incapacitated, that meant a subtle attempt to keep her from doing her job. Or maybe it wasn't so low key given she and Badger had ended up in the river.

The FBI wanted the crew and the cartel. They could solve the problem without her, but she'd made an obligation to them and was determined to see it through.

If she got in trouble with Mathers, they would move in. But the fact of the matter was that she was the one at risk here. Alanson wasn't going to swoop in until Mathers gave up more than she already had.

At the next traffic light, Mathers shifted in her seat and pulled out a cell phone. The old flip kind. Probably prepaid from a grocery store, and she hadn't registered it yet. Nor did she have any plans to.

Mathers typed in a phone number and listened.

Hannah could hear nothing of the other end of the conversation, just the doctor's side. Hopefully even that would give the task force enough to go on.

Mathers said, "It's the doctor." She paused, and Hannah imagined the reaction from whoever was on the other end. "If you want your money, then shut up and listen to me."

Hannah gasped and twisted around in the chair, as though *so* surprised Mathers making a deal with the cartel. In reality while she was *kind of* surprised, she wasn't all *that* surprised. Mathers had dug herself too deep, and now she had to get out of it before she wound up carved up like Pam and Craig.

The doctor didn't even look at her. "A trade. The money, and I'll throw in something extra. In return, I walk away the same as I came in, and you never see me again." Then she glanced over.

Hannah sat there with as stoic a look on her face as she could muster up.

Mathers said, "This one will be a real money maker."

## 15

Badger stared at the string of messages that formed the transcription of the conversation happening in the doctor's car.

Andre said, "What is it?"

"The doctor is going to hand over Hannah and the money." Badger's stomach churned. "She wants to make a trade with the cartel for her own freedom."

Lucia spoke from the back seat. "I'm assuming the intention is for Hannah to be a source of income for the cartel. Am I right?"

Badger could only nod, his focus on the words. Until his eyes burned, and he had to blink before hot tears gathered.

"We're not going to let that happen." Andre sounded so sure.

Badger drew strength from it. And the fact the entire Chevalier team were here, backing him up. They hadn't let Hannah out of their sight. Nor would they.

Whatever the doctor had planned would fail.

"Right, Badge?" Andre glanced over as he drove. "We're not going to let that happen."

He nodded again. He managed to choke out a yes. Only because Andre wouldn't let up until he did. That was the way it worked. Confirmation had to be given verbally because it couldn't be assumed that agreement was given until that happened, especially in high-stress situations where assumptions could too easily be made. People got hurt when erroneous conclusions were drawn.

Like the assumption he and Timo had made that Alexis would be fine on the beach, playing by herself while they were distracted and surfing. Too far away to help when a sick monster had spotted her. Taken her for himself.

Badger swiped at his face.

Lucia leaned forward and squeezed his shoulder. "We aren't going to let her get taken. But if she does? Do you think we're going to waste even one second not pulling out all the stops to get her back? And we would do that even if no one knew how you felt about her. Because it's the right thing to do."

Zander's voice came to the car speakers. "She's right, Badger. You know this."

"I do." But the last thing he wanted was a long, drawn-out conversation that delved into his feelings for Hannah. Or any of their fear over what might happen next. "Distract me. Talk about something else while we wait."

The car was moving fast.

The feds were also in pursuit. But even with all that forward motion, it felt as though they were standing still. Waiting for an inevitable crash, like crash test dummies careening toward a wall at eighty miles an hour. Just hanging there to see what the final destruction would look like.

"Hannah found out that Isaac is her brother."

The comment came through the car speakers. *Nora.*

It took him a second to remember she was on the operation with them. It didn't happen often, but they didn't leave anyone unprotected while the rest of them went out in some situations. Even if going put them in danger. They banded together and watched each other's backs.

Through everything.

Badger glanced around. Andre and Lucia didn't even react. Neither did anyone else in the other car. "You guys all know?"

There were murmurs of assent.

"Why did nobody tell me?"

Nora said, "Hannah only mentioned it to me in the hospital. But there was no time to talk about it. We had to shelve the conversation until later when everything kicked off with Joseph and then Dr. Mathers."

Two situations, one of which they were dealing with now. The other they were trusting Ted to get them a lead on. And praying for the girl who had been abducted.

Not that he put much stock in prayer since it had never done anything for him.

His mind reeled. Isaac really was Hannah's brother. That had to have been what was in the envelope, the thing she hadn't shared with him. Maybe she would have, but now they would never know.

Badger said, "Nora, do you know if he's your brother as well?"

"Ted is getting what we need to run the test." Nora paused. "Right now I have no idea, but since Hannah is my half sister, and Lana is both of our mothers, then I guess we all may have the same mother."

Zander took over where she left off. "If Isaac is the son of Lana's Soviet handler, then Isaac really did claim his birth name when he turned himself over to the military with the suitcase nuke. And Yuri Amrakov was killed before Hannah was born. So he's not her father. My guess is different dads, but the same mom."

Lana had given birth to all three of them. And yet, only Isaac had known her for any length of time recently. Nora had grown up with her mother in her life until she was twelve. After that, she had believed Lana was dead. Until a few weeks ago, when she'd seen Lana's picture and realized the leader of that clandestine line private organization was her mother.

A woman who would stop at nothing to get what she wanted.

Nora's father had been killed in prison a few weeks ago. No one seemed all that upset, but considering she'd been close to him for years, there was no way she wasn't grieving over it. Even if it felt wrong to cry for the loss of someone who turned out to be evil. They'd been each other's entire family for most of Nora's life so far—until she met Zander.

"Hannah was given up for adoption, wasn't she?" Lucia asked.

Badger said, "Yes, but I don't think her parents have any idea who her birth mom and dad are. She told me everything about the adoption was sealed, and there was no way to find out who they were."

She'd wanted to know. He had seen the yearning in her voice when she spoke about the people she had come from, the ones who gave her up for adoption.

Now that he knew her mother was Lana, it was easy to brush it off as the best thing for her to have no contact. Being given up for adoption might have saved her life. It had been a way to keep her safe, as Karina had done by raising Aria in secret. Despite the fact Eas hadn't even known he had a daughter, she had been safeguarded so that now they could build a relationship. In peace.

Eas was still part of the team, but he would be going on limited missions for a while. He needed to spend time with his family and not get caught up in everything going on out here.

The heartbreak on his face when he realized he had a daughter wasn't something Badger had seen. But given the lost look in Hannah's eyes, he could imagine it well enough.

She had to be reeling. To go from not knowing anything and dealing with the fact she never would to being told through official channels that she had a brother she never even knew about. One who was currently on the opposite side of the law from her.

He continued, mostly just to distract himself by talking aloud, "That's what Alanson meant when he said that if she wanted another appointment in this town, she needed to get her brother to talk."

Lucia huffed. "Typical fed speak. Tit for tat, if she wants another position on the task force, she has to give them something in return. It's just how they operate. No one likes it, but it's how the job is done. Trading favors and making sure you get what you want."

Andre glanced back at his wife. "None of us have ever worked like that."

"I know, babe." Lucia sighed. "Why do you think I'm here and not still working with them?"

Judah's voice came through the speakers. "I thought it was for Zander's pancakes. I don't know about the rest of you, but it's why *I'm* here."

Badger realized what Judah had done and picked up on it immediately. "Oh, really. You're saying to us that there's something American that's better than something British?" He wanted to smile but couldn't quite make his mouth do that.

He needed to talk to Hannah. Make sure she was okay because he wanted to be there for her as her friend.

"I didn't…" Judah sputtered. "That's not…"

A commotion of laughter rippled in their car and through the speakers.

Badger said, "Don't worry. You know what you really meant. We all heard you."

Judah argued. Zander got into the banter with him, and Andre backed up their team leader. A release of pressure so that the fear they all had for Hannah didn't build too high. When this kicked off, they all needed to be levelheaded.

The phone buzzed in his hand. Badger looked down and skimmed the conversation. "The feds think they've figured out where Dr. Mathers is taking Hannah. The last turn she took will eventually take her down to the Mexican Embassy."

Andre hissed out a breath. "We can't get to her inside there."

Lucia said, "The second she steps inside, Hannah will be on foreign soil. Going in there would be an invasion."

"We have to cut them off." There was no choice as far as Badger could see.

Zander came back quickly. "Badger—"

"No." He wasn't asking for permission. "We can't let the doctor hand her over."

A message came through on the phone from Ted.

Badger said, "This isn't good."

HANNAH FORCED her mind away from the full implication of what Mathers had insinuated on the phone. *Chevalier will never let that happen.*

No matter that meant she had almost zero faith in the task force, even if they were supposed to be the ones protecting her. She could too easily get lost in all of this.

Hannah might disappear without a trace, the way so many people did when they were caught up in trafficking. One day living their life, the next missing. Usually, the kind of people with no one to care or raise a fuss about the fact they were suddenly gone.

It was a heartbreaking reality of law enforcement work that there were so many they could never save.

But Hannah knew the kind of men and women who made up Chevalier Protection Specialists. There was no way they would rest until she was found.

It was the only thing that kept her from losing her cool.

Mathers took a turn onto a downtown street lined with high-rise office buildings, some modern and some much older established businesses that had been here for years. This was where they were meeting the cartel? She'd expected some kind of seedy, out-of-the-way place. The back of a bar. Or an abandoned home in the middle of nowhere.

Along the street were law offices and banks. Tech businesses.

Farther up, there were a couple of embassies.

Hannah didn't know which they were headed to, but much like with abductions the second a door closed behind the victim, the harder it was for anyone to find them. Only the fact there were three cars in pursuit, and all of them were determined to not lose anyone in this operation, allowed her to continue. But her composure was wearing thin.

If it did, she would snap.

Hannah knew herself well enough to be aware nothing could stop her after she'd had enough. It was the way she was. And now that she knew Lana was her mother, maybe there was an explanation for that. Some latent genetic tendency to reach that place where nothing else mattered but what she wanted to do. Not exactly selfishness, just the strength of will to ignore everything and get what she wanted or do what she had to.

Strength or weakness, it was what had been given to her.

And while her parents had raised her with their Christian values and tried to instill in her pacifism she didn't understand, biology was hard to overcome. Sometimes she felt like two people. Who she was inside, and the person they thought they'd raised.

"We'll have to go in the back entrance," Mathers muttered to herself. "If they can't circumvent security, that's their business."

"Strange they want to do this in daylight and in a public place." Hannah realized it wasn't exactly what Sarah would be concerned about. But at this point, it hardly mattered that a bit of her police persona shone through. She figured she didn't need to be happy with Mathers anymore. Not now it was clear the doctor had no intention of helping her. She was only going to trade Sarah for her own freedom.

"You don't need to worry about that, do you?"

"Thanks to you," Hannah said. "I'm not sure I need to worry about anything anymore. Is that right?"

Mathers winced. "It's nothing personal. I'm sure you understand."

"Oh, I understand plenty." It was the doctor who was confused about Hannah. Not the other way around. And she would find out soon enough that she'd been entirely wrong about a woman she thought would allow Mathers to trade her to people who would use her as a commodity instead of a person.

Mathers eased off the gas as they passed a stone building. Iron gates. Flags flew above the front doors, where armed men guarded the entrance.

The Mexican Embassy.

Given the cartel's influence and how much money they funneled in and out of the country, Hannah was hardly surprised at the connection. Whether this was happening under the nose of the officials who worked out of this building, or if they were entirely complicit in the cartel's activities, it would happen regardless.

And once Hannah was through those gates, there was nothing the task force could do to get her back. They would have to contact the State Department. Go through official channels. Then the officials who worked for the Mexican Embassy would have to admit to her presence there. All that would take days, if not weeks. If it ever happened at all.

By which time she would be long gone from here. Thrown into whatever life they had planned for her. Because this doctor wanted a life free of the threat of them coming after her.

Hannah's stomach muscles clenched so tight it was as though they turned to cement.

Mathers had one hand on the wheel, the other holding the gun loosely on her lap.

Whatever Lana had given her flared to life. Hannah

didn't even know the woman, but she knew this was the legacy she'd been born with.

Hannah made a fist with her right hand. Angled it at the side of Mathers's head in one move and slammed it into the doctor's temple. Smashed the bone.

The doctor jerked the wheel and lifted the hand with the gun in it.

Hannah grabbed her wrist. "Uh, uh, uh." She took possession of the gun. "I don't think so."

Conversation erupted in her ear. It was tempting to pull out the earbud so the task force couldn't yell at her, asking what she was doing, but she just ignored it instead.

Hannah pointed the gun at Mathers's head. "You don't know this, but I've had a horrible week. So listen up because I'm going to tell you how this is going to go."

Mathers glanced at her. "You're ruining this. You're ruining everything."

"Only for you."

"They'll come for you," the doctor wailed. "If they don't get their money, they'll kill all of us."

"Surprise. You'll be going to jail." There was no amusement in Hannah's expression. She knew that much. "But I'm sure they can make it, so you will be protected."

"You're a cop?"

"You say that like it's a bad thing."

Mathers started to tap the brake.

"No, keep driving until I tell you where to stop."

"I can't go to *jail*."

"It's the only way you'll stay alive," Hannah said. "By testifying and being given protection in exchange for your testimony. The cartel won't get to you."

Mathers barked a laugh. "Of course they will."

184 | LISA PHILLIPS

"No one who followed the rules of witness security has ever been lost. At least, that's what they tell everyone," Hannah said. "You have critical information about the cartel. The feds want to know all of it, and in exchange you get to live. Do you think the cartel is going to give you a better deal than that? It's a shot at a life, Barbara." There were some fine details to work out, of course. But it was all up to Mathers and what she was willing to turn over. "Unless you want to end up like Pam and Craig."

Mathers's hands shook on the steering wheel. "I can't believe this. I'm going to kill you."

"No, you're not." And not simply because Hannah had both of the guns. "Pull over into this parking lot."

The windows of the business were boarded up, and a sign hung over the front door. No one would be here to get caught in any crossfire.

"Put it in park."

Mathers did as she asked.

"Hand back on the wheel."

Once she did that, Hannah used her free hand to turn the car off and remove the keys. "You can stay right there until you're told to exit the vehicle."

Hannah slid the keys into her pocket, grasped the door handle behind her, and retreated out of the open door.

She stood there, between the door and the frame. Gun pointed in the door.

Mathers started to cry.

They were surrounded by federal agents in less than a minute, and the doctor was ordered out of the vehicle. There was nothing she could do to fight what was happening.

Hannah turned over the doctor's weapon and the one she'd been given to an agent who bagged both. Sure, Hannah could have retained hold of her own. But she had a feeling she wouldn't need a gun registered to the federal government for much longer.

Not given the look on Alanson's face.

He strode over to her, his expression as though he were about to spit fire. Or roar at her. Several other agents turned away, not wanting to witness the coming inferno.

Hannah gathered all her thoughts, the arguments she would use to justify the direction she had gone. None of it would mean anything. Alanson probably wouldn't let her say a word while he railed at her that she'd done other than he'd instructed.

As if she would have allowed herself to be taken into the Mexican consulate.

But before he could get to her, Badger called out, "Hannah!"

She turned to them and caught a glimpse of the look on his face.

She frowned. "What is it?"

## 16

"Joseph sent a video." Badger heard the words come out of his own mouth, but they were the last thing he wanted to say just then. Coming off of that mission, the one where they'd all contemplated losing her for good.

But Hannah was here. She had extricated herself from the situation and skillfully taken down Mathers such that the doctor was no longer a threat.

He was so proud of her.

Before Hannah could say anything, Special Agent Alanson strode over. The expression on his face registered. Badger tugged Hannah behind him and met the man's approach. She squeezed his arm as Alanson walked all the way into Badger's personal space and said, "One of you is going to tell me what that was."

Badger wanted to tell the guy it was nothing to do with Chevalier but that would mean throwing Hannah under the bus, and he wasn't about to do that.

Behind Alanson, the crowd of agents got Dr. Mathers cuffed and patted down. Ensuring she carried no weapons into custody. She would be processed today and put through the wringer about everything she knew. He didn't envy the woman having to go through that.

It almost made a person want to make sure they never ended up in the same situation.

That alone was enough to keep Badger on the straight and narrow on any given day. Not because of anything he'd been brought up to learn, or even the respect his teammates showed him by entrusting him with his part of the mission. Any mission.

"I can't talk about this right now," Hannah said. "Something has come up with another case." She tugged on Badger's arm, and he shifted slightly but didn't move.

"Something's *come up?*" Alanson yelled the words. "This is unbelievable. You just royally screwed this mission, and you have the gall to tell me we're going to talk about it later?" He shook his head, a vein in his neck popping. "I don't think so. In fact, as far as I'm concerned, you're a material witness. And that means you'll be spending the rest of the day in interrogation just like Doctor Mathers."

Badger swung around and started walking, tugging Hannah with him. "We're out of here." There was far too much to tell her about Joseph and the girl he had kidnapped. Hannah needed to know that she was alive as of just a few minutes ago.

"This better be good," she muttered, keeping pace with him. But not because she wanted to—or agreed.

After thinking all morning that she could be dead, Hannah needed to know the teen was still alive. There was still a chance for the feds running the case to get her back to her parents.

188 | LISA PHILLIPS

"You think I'm just going to let you walk away?" Alanson followed them to the car.

Hannah yanked her arm out of his grasp. She shot Badger an angry look and spun to her task force supervisor. "I'm happy to provide a statement. You have Doctor Mathers, so you don't need me right now. There's a girl out there who didn't ask to be abducted, and I might be the only one who can find her."

Badger wasn't sure that was true when there were qualified feds already working the case. Hannah didn't have any leads, but she might have a clue into Joseph Ricker. Just not enough to know where the girl was. Otherwise, she would have told him. Which meant while she could provide information that might be helpful, Hannah didn't need to get dragged into whatever game Ricker was playing. As far as he was concerned, she could be nowhere near this case, and it would still get solved.

But he was still going to tell her about the video. And he knew her well enough to know she'd *want* to be in it.

"An abduction? I suppose I'm meant to believe that." Alanson folded his arms. "For all I know, you and this entire team are on some kind of crazy mission. And I'm not getting swept up in their antics."

Judah muttered, "Seems like our reputation has preceded us."

Badger winced.

Andre said, "Not in a good way."

"This isn't a mission," Hannah said. "They're only here to protect me."

"Funny, I thought you were part of a federal task force," Alanson said. "Not some kind of freelance mercenary running around blowing stuff up."

"You're the one who told me to take a vacation. A young girl was abducted and needs my help." Hannah's expression blanched, and tears filled her eyes. "You dragged me back here to meet with Mathers. I didn't have to come, but I did. Now I'm doing what you asked me to do and taking a break."

"Don't worry." Alanson shook his head. "I won't ask for your help again."

Badger had no idea what the guy's intention was, but he was done with the runaround. Whatever beef Special Agent Alanson had with Hannah or any of them, Badger didn't really care. The fact of the matter was the guy wouldn't be part of Hannah's life for much longer.

Alanson turned and strode away.

Hannah walked a few steps to the car, ran her hands through her hair, and bent forward. She took a few big breaths, both palms on her knees.

Badger went to her and ran his hand between her shoulder blades.

She stood up, waving him off. "Not right now."

He figured she might not be blowing him off entirely but it still stung. "We need to get out of here."

"Just show me the video. I want to see it." Her gaze didn't meet his eyes, darting around at anything else rather than him.

"She's alive. The girl he took, she's still alive." Badger took a breath. "And Joseph might be trying to drag you into this, but it's not your problem to solve."

She didn't need to be anywhere near it. Not just because Lana had hired them to make sure she was safe, but because of a whole lot of reasons Badger didn't want to get into right now. There were entirely too many emotions close to the surface right now.

He could have lost her if Mathers had shot Hannah. Or if she'd made it inside the consulate.

He didn't want to face the idea of losing her, and he was prepared to do whatever it took to stop that from happening again. He wasn't going to watch while someone else was hurt because of him. While he did nothing to stop it.

"Just show me the video." She stared at him. "Why are you stalling? I'm a homicide detective, so it's not like I've never seen anything like this before. Just give me the phone."

She didn't get it.

Badger needed to figure out how to explain that it wasn't about her job. "I know you're a cop. You deal with lots of stuff like this. But you've also had a crazy couple of days. It's okay to let someone else take care of this."

She didn't respond to him. Just played the video he had already watched.

On the phone screen, a young girl of high school age sat in a wooden chair, her hands bound to the arms. Tears rolled down her face. Across her eyes was a blindfold.

"Say it," Ricker commanded.

The girl whimpered. "My name is Hannah. I was adopted." She dissolved a little, as if fighting against the tide of fear.

In his mind he imagined Alexis in the same situation. Her parents had never received a video as far as he knew, but she became that little girl he hadn't helped. The one he couldn't save.

"And the rest," Ricker said.

"I don't deserve to live."

Badger glanced away. He heard Hannah sniff and caught her wiping away a tear out of the corner of his eye. "He could have killed her already, but he didn't. She's still alive." He took the phone back, unable to even look at the screen again. "We sent the video to the feds working the case. If there's anything to get from it, they'll do it. They'll find her."

He had to believe that.

If he didn't, the flimsy construct of his psyche would come crashing down. Badger would have nothing to stand on because his faith in what he believed would've failed so spectacularly that he was left with nothing to trust in.

One girl might have died because of him. But there was no way it would happen again. God wouldn't be that cruel, not when he couldn't save this girl any more than he could have saved Alexis. Or any more than he could've helped Timo when his friend had descended into the darkness and taken his own life.

"If the feds have the video, then I'll go talk to them." Hannah lifted her chin. "I'm going to help them find her."

Badger shook his head. "You're not going anywhere other than with us to a safe house, and that's final."

---

HANNAH BLINKED. Had he actually just said what she thought he had? "That's final? Are you serious?"

Her brain blanked. Entirely out of thoughts or ideas after that. Badger was doing it again. He was taking control of the situation. Telling her what to do and where to go. As though she wasn't a competent law enforcement officer.

More like he considered her the person he was supposed to babysit because the woman who birthed her and then abandoned her thought she was in danger.

Most of Chevalier stood watching. The feds were clearing

out, having taken Mathers. They would go and interrogate her.

No doubt, in the same building, federal agents would be working the missing girl case. And with the video, they might be able to get the lead that meant they would find her.

And instead of jumping in to give what could be invaluable assistance, Badger wanted her to walk away. To let him take the reins and whisk her off to somewhere she would be secure—and completely unable to do her job.

"Hannah, just get in the car."

She took a step back.

Badger frowned. He moved toward her.

"What are you going to do, shove me into the car like I'm some unruly client?"

But he didn't put his hands on her. If he had, he would learn pretty quickly how she felt about that.

Hannah continued, "I'm not going to walk away and let that girl suffer when I could do something about it." She couldn't even believe he would think she might do otherwise.

"There's someone out there who wants to take you out."

"And I wouldn't be safe in a federal office?" She was in more danger, standing on a city street arguing with him. Even having the team around them in formation. All of Chevalier was on duty right now. Protecting not just her, but Badger as well. As if Joseph Ricker was out there watching her and not somewhere terrorizing a girl.

"Like it or not, you're in danger. It's the whole reason why we're all here."

"Seems to me like you've been there every time so far. When Pearson was shot, and when we found the assassin. Then you were there in the diner." She folded her arms.

"Maybe I'm not the only target, and your being with me actually makes it worse, not better."

She spotted that as it hit him.

Badger frowned. "Doesn't matter. Once we get to the safe house, you won't have to worry."

"What about that girl in the video? Does she need to worry?"

He couldn't possibly feel anything when there was a girl out there being tortured. She absolutely couldn't believe that a guy like him would walk away from a situation like this. What was in him that made him want to pack her up and take her elsewhere? There had to be a reason why. Most capable people would want to help. Even if law enforcement didn't need assistance from those they didn't know, muddying up the case.

She could still prove useful, even on the periphery of what was happening.

Hannah just couldn't let it go. This girl had her name, and Ricker was going to kill her. She couldn't walk away from it.

Hannah grabbed the phone from him and showed him the video. Paused on the girl's face. "You think she deserved this?"

He said nothing.

"You think she deserves to die while we do nothing about it?" She even gave him a little shove in his shoulder. "And then her parents have to bury her. Is that what you want?"

She knew she was pushing. But if she didn't get to the bottom of this, he wouldn't let her get involved. Hannah would have to leave all of them and walk away. She just didn't believe this was only about his job.

After she'd just reached a place where the entire Chevalier team was here helping her, on her side. That kind of support wasn't something she took for granted. It felt like her heart had been expanding. Encompassing all of them, so that now she wanted to spend even more time with him. With all of them, including her sister.

As much as she'd tried to push them away, the truth was that she wanted them in her life. She wanted to go with Nora and see Isaac and listen to what he had to say.

Badger wanted to take that away from her. Because he would force her to walk away again when she couldn't handle the constraints of following his dictates. And it was the last thing she wanted to do.

Hannah wanted Chevalier Protection Specialists to be part of her life. Badger had given her that gift, and she didn't want him taking it away.

"We have to help her," Badger said. "Or we as good as killed her."

Something snapped in Badger's expression. "It's not my fault! Just because I couldn't stop it doesn't mean I killed her." His face reddened. His body tight.

Hannah took a half step back. Not exactly afraid, but something was going on here.

Andre and Zander got between her and Badger. Nora tugged on Hannah's arm, and Judah showed up by her other elbow. They walked Hannah to the SUV, leaving her with no choice but to go with them. But she wasn't going to let them shut her in.

Hannah turned around to see what was going on.

Andre and Zander both dipped their heads to speak low in Badger's space, alternating talking. But she couldn't make out the words they were saying. Badger stared off into nothing with that lost expression on his face. As though something inside him had broken. Because she pushed him too hard? She'd had no idea he was going to react like that.

Hannah turned to Judah. "What's going on?"

"They'll take care of it." Judah squeezed her elbow. "We just have to trust they know him."

She'd caused this, whether she liked it or not. Badger had suffered some kind of damage, and it was Hannah who dealt the blow. She sucked in a breath that broke.

Nora said, "They know what they're doing."

"I didn't know he would react like that. What was he talking about?"

Nora glanced at Judah and simply shrugged. "He doesn't tell us what's going on with him. We barely knew what was going on with you, let alone something he's buried so deep even he doesn't want to believe it still exists."

And she had dug it out.

"Something happened to him."

Nora nodded, concern on her face.

"I didn't mean to hurt him."

But she had, in the same way that her actions had messed things up for the federal task force. She probably wasn't going to get that job back. It was the last thing she cared about right now. Still, her mind insisted on reminding her of her failure. As if she needed to be dragged even further under the surface.

Then there was the guilt over that young girl, Hannah. Someone so like her that Joseph Ricker had chosen her to take Hannah's place. To be the instrument he used to play the strings of her fears.

To torment both of them and make sure that Hannah suffered because for some reason they were connected, and he had never let that go.

The way Hannah never let go of the fact she hadn't seen what was inside Joseph Ricker from the beginning.

She'd gone about her business, walked her beat, and done her job to the best of her ability.

And in the meantime, he was conspiring this whole time. Now he'd followed through.

Both the guilty and the innocent had been punished the day Ricker murdered his family. And unlike the dead who had been laid to rest, Hannah was still paying the price.

Now there was another Hannah out there suffering.

Because of her.

Zander said something to Badger. He shook his head, and she saw tears roll down his face. He swiped back his hair, but it fell forward again. The several days of beard growth on his face needed to be shaved. It added to his gruff demeanor, making him look like a serious threat instead of a man lost in his memories. Overcome by guilt.

Badger shoved away from them and walked around the SUV.

For a second she thought he was going to walk away. Head across the street, and keep going. Disappear from sight so that none of them knew where he was.

But he got in the passenger seat.

Zander called out, "Judah, all in."

Lucia opened the back door of the SUV and ushered Hannah and Nora into the back. She got in the front while Judah got in the driver's side.

None of them spoke. Nora reached over and held Hannah's hand, but she didn't need comfort. She needed to work this case and find that girl.

An innocent person was suffering, and she could do something about it.

And yet, the last time she had gone with what she thought she should be doing, the worst had happened. If she met up with the feds and tried to help instead of sitting down with Badger, apologizing, and trying to help him through it, she might lose what she'd built with him so far.

Maybe it was already gone.

Maybe all she had was a case and not any kind of relationship.

Maybe she would lose it all.

## 17

The car ride was completely silent. Although, the glances between Zander and Andre in the front seats probably meant the two of them had neck ache by now.

As soon as they pulled up in front of the rental house, Badger pushed the door open and climbed out. He watched the other SUV pull in beside theirs on the driveway.

Zander got out of the passenger side, which put him right in front of Badger as soon as he shut the door.

"They came here?" Badger said.

"You think I want my wife somewhere unprotected?" Zander shot back.

Badger shook his head. "I just figured they would take Hannah to the FBI office in Baltimore so she can help out with the case."

That was what she wanted to do, whether he agreed with it or not. They'd been entirely at odds until she had pushed him to the point he yelled in her face. Bringing up things that were better off buried.

What happened with Alexis had defined his years growing

up in Hawaii before leaving the islands for the army.

He'd only been back to go to Zander's wedding, and every second of that, he'd been on edge waiting for someone he knew to spot him. Even though they'd been miles from where he'd lived as a kid, Badger had expected it every single second of his time there. Just waiting for it all to come crashing back on him.

But it hadn't. Instead, he realized it had rested there, inside him. Dormant until Hannah pushed him on why he didn't want to face the fact a girl had been kidnapped.

Seeing her on that video, strapped to the chair and completely overwhelmed by the fear. All he had been able to think about was Alexis.

It was in his mind now, still. The memory of her in that coffin. Lying so still, her body gray.

Then, in his mind, he'd seen Alexis on the chair in the place of that girl. Instead of the teen, Hannah, on the video, it had been Alexis. And there was nothing he could do about it. He'd been faced with his failure all over again—along with his inability to change the horrible things that happened to people around him. Badger couldn't bear if anything like that happened to Hannah. He wouldn't be able to face himself or anyone else.

She was like a wild thing he couldn't pin down. Not that he wanted to subdue her, but having her in his life still felt like trying to catch a wave singlehandedly. He'd tried to be part of her life before, and she had dismissed him. Gone back to her police job and got involved in a task force investigation. He'd gone home with his tail between his legs.

Who was to say that wouldn't happen again? It was probably for the best that she disagreed with him. After all, he would only inevitably fail. Badger had to do the things he knew he could do. Nothing else. He would fall back on his skill set and just do his job. This didn't need to get messy with his past coming up and Hannah's inability to see what was plain.

Her life was in danger, courtesy of whoever had Lana hiring them to keep her safe.

She needed to get with the program if she wanted to live through this.

And that didn't mean going up against Joseph Ricker. Not when he was probably only there to torment her and make her life a nightmare.

The others got out of their car. Hannah didn't look at him.

Badger turned and walked into the house. There was no point making this awkward. He just needed to…

He had no idea what he was going to do, so he found the kitchen.

Zander and Andre cornered him again. The way they had before he got in the car. Determined to get him to tell them what was going on with him.

While the others filed past, headed for other rooms, Andre and Zander blocked his exit from the kitchen.

Badger pulled a soda from the fridge and didn't ask if they wanted one. He popped the top and took a drink. The sweet taste and bubbles ran down his throat, the sensation enough he could concentrate on that instead of everything else.

"Since you came in here before we could finish our conversation outside," Zander said. "The fact is that you wanted Hannah here, so she's here and not at the Baltimore field office."

"Just like that? Because I said so."

Zander folded his arms across his chest. "It's your job, so it's your call."

"You were tasked with protecting her." Andre shrugged.

"I see what this is."

Zander said, "Then tell us. Because we want to know what this is."

"You found Nora." Badger looked at Andre. "You got Lucia back." Even Eas had Karina back in his life now, along with their teenage daughter. "She's family. That's why you want this fixed."

Hannah was part of the group now, whether either of them figured things out or not. It wasn't about Badger making the call. It was only about her being in the fold now, and so they needed Badger to get with the program like he'd decided she needed to.

They thought *he* was the one with the problem that needed to be solved.

"Are you going to tell us what that outburst was about?"

Zander shot Andre a look.

"It's not like you don't want to know," Andre said. "He needs to tell us."

"I figured if he trusted us, then he would." Zander had a guarded look on his face.

Badger had never seen that look before.

"You know the worst of us," Zander said. "But you don't share? We've been friends, squad mates, and teammates for a long time. Longer than a lot of people manage to stay married. It's like you don't even trust us, still after all this time."

Never mind that comment about marriages. Badger didn't have anything to say about that. His own parents got divorced when he was three.

But the rest of it?

Badger shook his head. "Of course I trust you. I put my life in your hands every day, and you do the same with me. How can you even say that?"

Andre said, "Maybe because something is going on with you, and we have no clue what it is."

"You never had Ted look it up?" They knew he didn't share about his past. It was just a fact of their relationship. One he thought they'd accepted.

Now he knew they wanted Hannah in the fold. That meant if Badger had a problem with it, then he was the one who was going to have to leave. Even with the years of their friendship and the respect they had for each other—or, at least what he thought they'd had—family meant so much more than that bond.

Hannah was going to be the one who stayed.

And he would leave knowing he had disappointed Zander more than he ever wished to.

Andre said, "The tortured past thing fits the whole *Winter Soldier* thing you've got going on. But eventually, you're going to have to tell us what it is you had to tell us wasn't your fault."

Badger swallowed down the taste in his mouth.

Andre continued, "Whatever it is, it's the reason why you run from your name. Why you didn't want to go back to Hawaii for Zander's wedding. We thought that might trigger something, but it didn't happen."

"We've been trying to get you to talk to us for a long time," Zander said. "But maybe you never will."

Badger felt the burn of tears in his eyes. The last thing he wanted to do was break down. Getting angry was one thing, but crying was a whole other story. If he told them the truth, they would know he should never have been part of their team in the first place. Badger was nothing. Worse than a disaster, he only destroyed the things around him. And the people. Otherwise, he would have a good history and not the destruction his life had been before he joined the army.

Badger pushed past both of them and headed for the room where they had set his stuff. The side of the house where the sun rose so that he could see the morning.

The kind of friends who had always had his back. Who considered small things to be critical and never backed down when things got bad.

Now they wanted to take that all away from him because Hannah shared Nora's blood. Things had changed. The team was evolving into something new with all the additions and relationships.

Badger didn't want to stick around, knowing he couldn't have it for himself. Which meant he needed to leave them all behind.

Whether he wanted to or not.

---

HANNAH HUNG UP THE PHONE. Lucia had given her a quiet place to make the call to the team of federal agents who were working the abducted girl's case.

When she turned to exit the sitting room, Lucia stood in the doorway. "Feel better?"

Hannah shrugged. "I hope I gave them something helpful. It's hard to tell without seeing their faces. Maybe they just think I'm trying to interfere, but it's not like I barged into their office."

"We can do that later if they don't come up with

anything." Lucia grinned. "Trust me, I know plenty about dealing with federal agents."

Hannah handed back Lucia's phone. "I thought I remembered you being DEA or something like that."

"Office of Professional Responsibility." She said it with a reserve, probably not knowing how Hannah would react to that and bracing herself.

"I have no problem with Internal Affairs." Hannah had never been investigated for anything and didn't plan to be. Although after everything that had happened with Alanson, maybe there would be some follow-up interviews. Depending on what he told Rochester Police Department and Hannah's Captain, she could get written up.

Nora came into view behind Lucia's shoulder. "Ted is about to get on."

They were all amped up to hear what he had to say. The team's technical guru was the best, as far as Hannah could tell. It was like the guy could pull any piece of information from anywhere. She wanted to ask how they'd managed to stumble on him as a resource, but that would have to wait until later.

Right now, there was a teenage girl out there, and despite what Badger seemed to think, Hannah had no intention of ignoring it. She wouldn't be the cop she was if she gave up on someone innocent in danger.

It was the right thing to do. And she knew that because every instinct she had screamed that she should get as far away from Joseph Ricker as she possibly could. Which meant that sooner or later, she would be coming face-to-face with him—and Ricker wasn't going to like the outcome.

Hannah followed them down the hallway into the living

room. She heard the rustle of a foot on the carpet and glanced back to see Badger behind her.

Neither of them said anything, and he didn't meet her gaze.

Hannah followed the women into the living room. Badger obviously didn't want to talk about whatever it was, and part of her wondered why he was still here when he had no intention of engaging with any of them. He only wanted to shut them out and order everyone around so that he could be in control.

But they couldn't even deal with that right now, either.

Nora settled beside Hannah on the couch, Zander on the other side of her. Judah perched on the arm beside Hannah's shoulder. A move of solidarity because Badger stayed over by the kitchen. Andre chose the armchair, and when he tugged on her hand, Lucia tumbled onto his lap. Which only made Hannah wonder how long it would be before the two were having a baby. Not that closeness and comfort, and pregnancy, were mutually exclusive. It just seemed like they were trying to make up for lost time.

Hannah felt the burn of tears behind her eyes as the laptop on the coffee table loaded Ted's image. It didn't matter that she'd never even come close to a relationship like that in her life. She could grieve not having it anyway. Though, it didn't feel like something she would ever have. Just a distant, impossible dream.

Ted smiled. "Hey, guys—"

Hannah cut him off. "Do you know where she is? Did you get anything from the video?"

"You want me to go through every piece of the video and tell you why he's giving nothing away?"

"Not really."

Ted nodded. "Then, no. There's nothing in the video that can tell us where she is. Unless you know something."

She shook her head. "Even the feds don't have anything from the video. They're talking to everyone in Hannah's immediate family and interviewing the guys who were in lockup with Joseph Ricker. Plus the guards. If someone knows something, they'll find out."

But it made her feel powerless, not knowing what was happening to the girl, where she was, or how to find her. She could only imagine how scared the teen was.

"Any other updates?" Zander asked.

"I dug into background on the guy who killed Pearson. The one Badger definitely didn't throw out that window." There was a slight tone in his voice. Hannah didn't know what to make of it. Ted continued as though he hadn't made some insinuation, "And the stuff he said about his brother. As far as I can tell, the guy works for Travers Industries as a contractor."

Nora said, "Where have I heard that before?"

Andre said, "The company in New York. With Karina and the chip."

"Oh, right." Nora nodded.

"And didn't former president Raleigh start working there recently?"

Everyone turned and looked at Judah.

He shrugged. "I get BBC News notifications on my iPad."

Ted spoke then. "He's right. After his wife was killed, Raleigh took a job working for Jerry Travers in a department that is heading up the rollout of that new federal phone system."

Andre made a low *mmm* noise in his throat. Judah shifted in his chair.

Ted continued, "It's the same technology developed that enabled the missile to hit the plane with such accuracy, the technology that killed his wife. I guess Raleigh wants to make sure it's used for a noble reason now. All the phones will be unhackable, so it'll be impossible for anyone to get into confidential federal information."

Andre snorted. "You're working on it, right?"

Ted shrugged. "I have no idea what you're talking about. I'm a very busy person, with little time to try and beat my personal best hacking record. And I'm not at all irritated by the strength of the firewalls at Travers Industries."

Hannah needed to know more about Joseph, not get dragged into banter. "What about Joseph's phone number?" she asked. "The one he called me at the hospital from?"

"Okay, so that's the thing," Ted said. "The number doesn't make any sense. But since Travers popped up in his once already, I'm going to make the leap and say that I think his cell was provided to him by Travers."

Hannah frowned. "Ricker?"

Ted nodded. "I could get into all the technospeak, but suffice it to say there's a solid possibility the two are connected."

Zander said, "So the guy who shot Pearson works for Travers. And Joseph might have a phone supplied by them. That gives us the possible connection between the initial threat on Hannah's life and the release of Joseph Ricker."

"You don't know it relates to his release." Hannah shook her head. "There's no evidence of that unless I'm missing something. All it means is that after he got out, Joseph was maybe given a phone he has no business having."

"There's a pattern here." Zander seemed sure of that. "A connection."

"I deal in evidence. Not theories."

Judah and Lucia both shifted. Sure, she was going toe to toe with the boss. But she'd dealt in ideas before, and it meant people died. Given Joseph was back, Hannah wasn't about to jump in without the facts.

"But I know we all want the same thing," Hannah conceded. "To get that teen home."

Zander nodded.

She couldn't get the image out of her head. That girl, so scared.

The reality of it, like evidence, proved substantial. But in a way that forensics didn't operate. Clinical results were one thing, but the video had overwhelmed her with fear for the girl. It made her want to burst from the couch and run out the front door. Chasing down…nothing, right now.

Hannah focused on Ted. "We have no idea where she is?"

Badger pushed off the counter and strode off down the hall.

Zander pinned her with a stare. "You're the only one he's talked to in all of this."

Hannah shook her head. "Not because he wanted to."

"But you broke through," Zander said. "And sometimes you have to rip off the bandage and expose the wound before it can heal."

If Hannah were honest with herself, that was the last thing she wanted to do right now. But she had always stood by her partners and done the right thing. If there was something she could hand over that they needed, Hannah would give it. Even if she never allowed it to be reciprocated.

She stood and headed after Badger. Before she hit the hallway, she glanced over her shoulder. "Find that girl."

If anyone could save a life, it was their team.

## 18

B adger had just grabbed the strap of his duffel bag when he heard someone in the doorway.

"You're leaving?"

He was surprised it was Hannah. It seemed more like Zander to send Nora in, knowing there was a shot she might be able to change his mind. All of them had protected her since the day they met her when it became so clear she needed their help.

Hannah might be her sister, but the two were very different. Except in some subtle ways. He now realized they had some similarities to their features. He just wasn't going to dwell on that.

"And you're here to convince me not to go?"

"Could I?" She almost sounded like she wanted to.

Badger turned and sat on the edge of the bed. Mostly he'd been ignoring how much his physical body had been through. Hannah looked like she needed a couple of days of rest and a good home-cooked meal made by Zander.

Exhaustion weighed on his shoulders. He ran his hands

down his face and let out a long breath. When he opened his eyes, she had stepped into the room and now leaned back against the wall beside the door, her arms folded as though she could get him to stay purely because of how stubborn she was.

"Are you really going to leave?" Before he could answer, she spoke again. "Do you even know what you have here? What I wouldn't give to be part of this team? This family?"

"You don't mess around, do you?"

As if he wasn't aware that Chevalier was his family. That had been the case for all of them, considering what they had found with each other. Judah was the only one of them who had extended family he had a relationship with. The rest of them had basically no one—except that while most of his family was still alive, they wanted nothing to do with him.

She had parents in the couple who had adopted her. Now she had a half sister and a brother she'd just found out about —all of whom wanted a relationship with her. Now the team was taking her under their wing as well. Whether he wanted it or not, and he would have said he did, Hannah was here to stay as a part of their team's extended family.

Weeks ago, he would've jumped at that, but she'd been the one to walk away from him.

Even though she had leaned on him. Saved his life. Stood by him. Still, Badger wasn't even sure where her feelings were at. Or if he wanted to go there, considering if this got awkward or something happened between them, and it went badly, the whole team would have to deal. He would leave, just so it wasn't uncomfortable for everyone.

He was already failing, so making this thing with Hannah personal would only lead to even more disaster.

"I just wanted to see if you're okay." She frowned. "I'll leave you to it."

Hannah started for the door when he said, "I didn't take you for a coward."

She turned back. "Excuse me?"

There it was. That backbone she had in her, the one that had only increased with her police training and all the things she'd been through. "I know I'm a lot to contend with. I never said this was going to be easy, but when I say I'm going to do something, I finish it."

"And that's the only reason why you haven't ditched the team?"

Badger winced. "I didn't think coming here to protect you was going to bring up so much stuff I never had any intention of telling anyone about."

"Maybe if you just tell me, it'll be easier to deal with." She shrugged. "Or tell Doctor Windermere. Is psychology part of the service he provides for you guys?"

Badger winced. "I think he wants it to be. But it was easier not to say anything."

"Why pretend everything is fine when it's not?"

He blew out a breath. Was she really going to make him do this?

Hannah just waited.

"Timo was my friend. Alexis was his little sister. We were twelve, and she was eight. Her mom made us promise we would look after her, but we wanted to surf, so we parked her on the beach and did our thing. Until we spotted the van pull up, and the guy that got out." His throat clogged.

A knowing expression crossed Hannah's face.

"Yeah." He could barely say the words. "We got back to

212 | LISA PHILLIPS

shore as fast as we could and ran after her. But the van was down the street already. They found her body two days later."

She started to speak, but whatever it was, she held the words back.

"Timo killed himself. On the anniversary of her death." He let his gaze drift across the carpet. "Everyone told me I should do the same."

She gasped. "Because it was your fault that man chose to do what he did? You were a kid. You didn't hurt her or kill her."

"So I shouldn't take responsibility for something I didn't know would happen?"

Hannah winced. "You think that's what I did?"

"You didn't know Joseph Recker was going to burn down his house. How could you have?"

"I should have seen something in him."

"And I should have known my selfishness would cost Alexis her life?"

He realized again that there was a lot they had in common. It made him feel more than ever that he was separate from the rest of the team. They were all good men and women who consistently did the right thing. They had no terrible skeletons in their closet the way he did.

Meanwhile, Badger had always felt somewhat like an imposter. Even in the army—sacrificing for his country. It hadn't made him feel like a good person, even doing the right things. Now he'd been part of this team for years because he'd hoped that who Zander was might rub off on him.

Now he was set to lose all of it. They would realize he should never have been part of their group, and Hannah would become part of the team in the exchange.

"You found your family now," Badger said. "They can help you find the girl."

Hannah's brow flickered. "But you're not going to?"

It was the same as asking if he thought he didn't bring anything to the group. He knew he had skills. In a lot of ways, aside from the physical issues he'd had recently, Badger had been at the top of his career for a while now. He was an integral part of the group. But that didn't mean that with the addition of Lucia and then Hannah, they couldn't learn to get the job done without him.

"You said that when you start something, you finish it." Hannah's brows rose. "That means you can't leave until the threat against me is over."

"Lana hired Chevalier, not just me specifically."

"So you'll walk away, knowing someone out there wants to take me out?" she asked.

"I think they want you distracted. That's why Pearson died, and you didn't."

She frowned. "So it wasn't a hit?"

"Pretty bad assassin if he can't nail the right target. Plus, there's the connection between the brother working for Travers and the phone Joseph has."

"You think there's a connection between the guy who shot Pearson, or at least his brother, and Joseph Ricker being released and seeking me out?"

Badger said, "He only showed up after Pearson was killed and the cops arrested the guy."

Hannah nodded. "Then you can help me find the brother, and we can grill him until he tells us everything. That's the only way to get to the bottom of this."

He was quiet for a minute.

"What is it?"

"I don't have to be the one that goes with you." He met her gaze. "You don't need me to figure this out."

"Maybe I *want* you to help me find whoever's got it in for me. Not because you have some special skill or access no one else has. Or because Lana told you I was in danger."

"Then why?" Everyone already knew how he felt about her. What he didn't know was how she felt about him.

Her cheeks reddened, and she lowered her chin. "I'm not exactly good at this. Even if it was the right time, I might be really, really *bad* at this."

"You already know the worst thing about me. How terrible could it be?"

"I don't know what happened after Alexis died. Or how you were treated." Her gaze softened. "But I do know that when tragedy happens, people look for someone to blame. All the fear and grief? It needs an outlet."

"So now you feel sorry for me?"

"It makes me want to go to Hawaii, look them all up, and ask them why they put all that responsibility on a twelve-year-old."

---

"You're right." Badger still had that guarded expression on his face, as though at any moment she could tear him to pieces. "They were looking for someone to blame. And considering Timo and I were just being selfish, maybe they weren't entirely wrong."

Hannah had a different idea about that. But she wasn't going to get into it with him. Not when he'd only told her the short version.

But the bottom line was that he hadn't done anything to

hurt the girl. The sad truth was Alexis had been a victim, just like he had been a victim of the people around him. Pressuring him and his friend until the other boy killed himself.

She couldn't even imagine.

Hannah had lived a largely solitary life and didn't have a whole lot of close friends. The Chevalier team was the first group of people she actually wanted to be part of. Not just because she wanted to prove to them how capable she was as a police officer. But more than that, they were the kind of people she wanted to have around. Not because she was related by blood to any of them. Just because they liked her.

Admitting that to Badger would be a terrible idea. She didn't want to ever be that vulnerable. And yet, he was edging her toward that place where she opened up to him.

Hannah decided to be plain about it. Because time was running out for that captured girl, and they needed to aid the hunt for her in any way they could.

She said, "I like you. I've been attracted to you since we met, and I respect everything about what you do and how you live."

"So why did you push me away?"

She blew out a breath. "That whole Gladstone thing, and finding out I had a sister? Plus, on top of that, you wanted to tell me what to do." She managed to exhale a laugh about that. "Let's just say being ordered around is a trigger, and we'll leave it at that."

"Now you know why I feel the need to not leave anything to chance. If there's something I can do, and it might save someone's life, then that's exactly what I'm doing."

She nodded. "I do understand that now." But then, there was a whole lot of stuff on her side. "Other people can be just as capable as you."

"I know that. My team—"

She cut him off. "I'm not talking about them."

She had a feeling they needed to figure this out between them, and it couldn't have anything to do with the rest of the team. Or her family members. And yet, even with everything going on, underneath it all was the fact her entire life had been thrown upside down.

She continued, "In the space of just a few months, I've gone from a single police detective with adoptive parents to someone caught up in national politics, whatever kind of crime lord Stephen Gladstone was. Two siblings I had no idea I had, and one I've never met. A mother who doesn't seem to want anything to do with me, but still apparently cares that my life is in danger. And there's someone out there who wants to kill me, or distract me, or make me go crazy wondering which it is."

Her breath came fast.

Badger got up off the bed. "I don't like being the one everyone is tiptoeing around."

"I don't like people knowing more about me than I do."

He gave her a soft smile. "I'm not going to keep anything from you. If I know something, then I'll tell you."

"I'm not going to pull punches," she said. "You can handle a lot more than people think. I just don't want to cause you to hurt if I can avoid it."

He lifted his hand and touched the side of her jaw.

Hannah wanted to lean into the warm touch, but there was so much still unresolved between them even though they'd gotten past this.

"I like you too," he said. "And I've been attracted to you since the first time we met."

"I won't waste my time asking you not to order me around."

"That's probably a good idea," he said with a smile in his eyes. "But my wanting to take charge comes hand in hand with me sticking around through all of this. And I figure we'll find a balance somewhere."

Hannah nodded.

Badger dipped his head. He paused, his lips inches from hers. As though asking permission.

Hannah gave a slight nod.

He started to lower his head the rest of the way.

The door swung open. "Hey, Badge—" Nora let out a soft laugh. "When you guys have a minute, Ted has something."

The door closed again. Badger groaned. He took a step back and let his hand drop, a slight smile on his face.

"It's probably for the best." Hannah winced. "I don't think I'm good at that, either."

Before he could placate her with some nicety, Hannah fled the room like a coward. Back to the living room, where the whole team now stood around the kitchen. Standing next to a laptop that was open on the counter, Zander held a whisk over a bowl of what looked like pancake batter, and the smell of bacon wafted from the oven.

Hannah's stomach rumbled.

Badger came up behind her. She didn't turn much, just enough to know it was him. He squeezed her shoulder, then let his hand linger on her elbow. It wasn't the kind of touch she was used to. But it was nice, feeling like she was connected instead of the way she had always been.

"What is it?" she said.

218 | LISA PHILLIPS

Lucia hopped up to sit on the counter at the far end. "Since there is already law enforcement trying to track down where Joseph took that girl and working the case as an abduction, we figured we'd come at it from an entirely different direction."

Hannah said, "Like tracking down the shooter's brother, the one who works for Travers Industries, and sweating him until he talks?"

"If the guy really is an assassin rather than his brother being the one who is, I doubt we'll be able to break him." Lucia shrugged. "But he might give us something on whoever is targeting you. If we hand over an incentive in exchange."

Badger shifted behind her. "You're going to bargain with the guy?"

Hannah said, "If we find something he wants badly enough, he'll give up what he knows."

He didn't seem so sure. Considering they didn't know what would induce the guy to talk, it was a moot point. Hannah had leveraged a suspect with far less and gained far more in the process. They just hadn't seen her do her job on a good day.

The whole team had her at a disadvantage. Her life was in danger, the worst of her past back in the present. It was the last situation she'd want to be in, especially with people who she wanted to respect her. But now that Badger had told her his story about Alexis and what he perceived as his failure, she knew there was more connecting them than she'd even been aware. He knew how she felt. They understood each other far better than they had.

"You think he can lead us to Ricker?" Hannah said. "I know there's a connection between them, but can it save that girl's life?"

"We can pray," Nora said.

Badger shifted, and she felt his fingers wrap around hers. The strength of his grip, balanced with the warmth of comfort. Solidarity, standing side by side. As far as she was concerned, holding hands was seriously underrated.

A gleam in Nora's eye caught her attention.

Hannah felt the pull of a smile on her lips. "So when do we leave?"

"As soon as Ted—" Zander pulled out his phone. "Here he is. O'Connell?"

She was about to turn away to find her shoes when the expression on Zander's face changed.

Everyone braced.

"Okay." He tapped the screen of his phone and looked at Hannah. "There's a call coming into your phone." It rang before he'd finished speaking. Two rings, and he said, "Ready?"

She nodded, even though she wasn't.

Zander swiped the screen, then tapped.

Badger's grasp on her hand tightened. "This is Detective Yassick."

"Tell me he drowned." Ricker's voice rolled through the phone speaker.

"Sorry to disappoint you." She leaned against Badger's side. "It didn't work."

He barked a laugh. "As if I have time to try and kill you. I've been busy having fun."

Her stomach roiled, but Hannah said nothing.

Lucia motioned to the phone and mouthed something.

Hannah shook her head. She was going to do this her way, and that meant letting Ricker believe she was barely paying attention to him.

"Hannah!" he yelled.

"Sorry, I'm busy doing something right now," she said. "Are you talking to the girl you kidnapped or me?"

Everyone shifted.

Didn't they like her methods? She needed Joseph reacting, not thinking he was in control.

"You need to listen to me!"

"Why? You're only going to lie." She wanted—needed—to know where the girl was, but begging would give him the upper hand.

"Well, you can believe *this*," he said. "I left you a present." His voice rumbled. Was he laughing? "I'll text you the address."

## 19

B adger held her hand in the car all the way to the address Joseph Ricker had given them. Whatever Ricker left for Hannah, they were all going to see it.

As Judah parked the car beside the one Andre drove, Hannah hung up her phone call. "The feds on the case are going to meet us here."

Badger caught her tone. She wasn't asking permission, but she did seem nervous about his reaction. Because the last time she had called in her colleagues, he and Judah both hit the roof? Surely they were past that by now. Then again, he'd basically told her he wanted her to walk away from everything law enforcement for the sake of being protected. It was no wonder she didn't know how he was going to respond.

Badger squeezed the hand he held. "That's good." Not just because he had no intention of giving a lengthy statement. If feds showed up, they would see everything with their own eyes and write their own reports.

They got out of the car.

Badger said, "How long has this gas station been shut down?"

Judah rounded the front of the car. "Ted said a year, maybe more. The land was bought by a franchise coffee place. But they didn't start building yet."

"Maybe she's inside." Hannah scanned the building. No other cars were parked around it, and the windows had been boarded up.

Across the street were the fronts of several businesses. This was an older part of Baltimore, and a block down there was a huge concrete apartment complex that had seen better days, although maybe it had always been like that.

Traffic buzzed past in both directions.

They all put on protective vests and armed themselves.

Zander said, "Andre, Lucia, and Judah, take the back entrance."

"Copy that." Andre headed around the side of the building first, followed by the other two.

That left Badger and Hannah with Zander on the front door.

Nora had stayed behind at the house, waiting for Dr. Windermere to arrive. As much as Zander probably disliked leaving her alone—unprotected as far as any of them were concerned—she would be in more danger here.

Given how he felt about Hannah, Badger could understand protecting the person you cared about most. Except that Hannah was a fully trained police officer and a decorated detective. It was clear to anyone that she could take care of herself. He knew he didn't need to get in the way of her trying to do her job, especially if it was only because of his own issues.

He wanted to tell the guys that, just to prove how far he'd

come. So they would know he was doing better. But they would only give him grief about his feelings for Hannah. Now at least Badger knew she liked him as well—though she'd far more successfully managed to fight her feelings. Until things were squared away between them, he didn't want to do anything that might hinder him and Hannah from solidifying what they had.

Their relationship could be the first one in his life that actually meant something. She was the person he wanted to stick around for the long haul if she agreed. After weeks forcing himself not to get too far and fall for her, there was now practically a green light hanging over that.

The promise of what might come was enough to completely distract him from what was going on around him.

Zander stopped at the door. "You good?"

"Yep." In a way, he was better than ever. Even if the fact he might be able to have Hannah and the entire team in his life felt like smoke he couldn't quite grasp.

They would get there.

She gave him a smile, but the edges were trimmed with worry. As though she knew the likelihood they'd find the missing girl alive was slim. This might not be a rescue mission. It might be the crime scene where Joseph Ricker had disposed of the body—if not the place where he'd killed her.

Badger nodded. "Let's find her."

She replied with a nod.

Zander braced, and Badger knew he was about to kick the door in. Their comms channel erupted to life.

Andre's voice came through at high volume. "Get to the rear parking lot. *Now.*"

They raced around the outside of the building, past overflowing trash all the way to the back, which was little more than an alley where the back door of the building hung open. But that wasn't where Judah, Lucia, and Andre were.

The only vehicle in sight was a rusted-out purple Acura from the nineties, with a young woman in the front seat.

"Is that her?" Hannah brushed past him.

Andre stepped in front of her. "Hold up a second."

"We have to get over there!"

Badger squeezed her arm, assessing the scene to figure out what Andre had seen. "Hannah."

The girl's hands had been duct taped to the steering wheel. There was also tape over her mouth, and her eyes darted around. She couldn't move her head. It had been taped to the seat, as had her torso. She was completely immobilized and unable to speak to them, but Badger understood plenty just looking at her.

Badger moved to look through the windshield so she could see him, then mouthed, *It's okay.* He didn't know what else to say, so he looked at the door. "Let's get her out of there."

Both Hannah and Andre were crouched, his flashlight shining on the bottom of the door. "What is that?" he asked.

Neither answered his question. Judah and Zander stood sentry, probably watching for Ricker. Zander had his phone to his ear, and it sounded like he was updating the feds. Or local police.

"Looks like a detonation cord." Andre lowered himself to the ground on his back. "See anything?"

Lucia responded from the other side of the car. "In the middle, it's tucked up there."

Hannah sucked in a breath. "What is it?"

Badger moved close to her, trying to offer her some solidarity. "I'm guessing if we open the door—"

She finished for him. "The car blows sky high."

Badger glanced at the girl inside. Joseph Ricker had left her like this so that she would die when they tried to get her free. Taking the rest of them with her. "You think he learned how to do this in juvenile detention?"

"Unlikely," Hannah said. "But when do things ever make sense?"

"Andre?" The guy knew what he was asking without Badger having to say it.

Judah glanced over. "Two minutes? Because that would be really good right now. That girl there's probably scared out of her mind."

Andre said nothing. Though, Badger could hear him and Lucia talking low under the vehicle.

"We need to get in there and reassure her everything's fine." Hannah crouched. She patted Andre on the shoulder. "Can I open the door on the passenger side if there are no wires?"

"You want me to check rather than just disarming this bomb?"

Hannah frowned. She rounded the car to the far side.

Badger looked under the car, beside where Andre lay. "Is it bad?"

Surely this was some crude bomb Ricker had researched on the internet. Nothing sophisticated, although that usually meant the device was far more dangerous than it would be if it had been constructed by someone who knew what they were doing. Thankfully, Andre was an expert at bomb disposal. There was no need to wait for law enforcement to bring their people and take longer than they had to try and disarm it. Badger doubted anyone in a bomb suit could even get under this car.

"I need some time."

Given Andre's tone, Badger said nothing. It wasn't good.

"Does anyone have a pad and paper?" Hannah asked.

Judah said, "Maybe in the car."

She let out a frustrated sound.

"Hannah—" Badger started.

Before he could tell her not to, she grabbed the passenger side handle and pulled the door open.

From under the car, Andre yelled, "Whoever that was, you just armed the bomb."

Hannah and Badger met each other's gaze over the roof of the car. He knew what she was going to do. Badger grabbed the rear door handle, swung it open, and climbed in while everyone protested. He ignored it all and shifted to look between the seats. With Hannah on the passenger side, they started to work the abducted teen free of the tape.

"Don't worry," Hannah said. "We're going to get you out of here."

Badger agreed with her.

And the alternative? The car would blow up and take both of them with it.

---

HANNAH KNEW what she was doing. And that the guys of Chevalier disagreed with it—except Badger, who had climbed in the car with her. She was overwhelmed with relief, but there was no time to consider that he'd thrown in with her. Something that was both good and bad.

They needed to get the girl out of the tape. Preferably before the bomb exploded and killed them.

Tugging at the tape that secured the girl's hands to the steering wheel did nothing. "We need a knife."

Badger held out his, but she shook her head and pulled the blade from by her ankle. She peeled back the tape over the girl's mouth first and saw her exhale a sharp breath from her nose. "I know." Hannah winced.

Teenage Hannah cried out.

"It's okay." She got the tape the rest of the way off, and the girl started crying aloud. "We're going to get you out of here."

In her earpiece, Andre said, "I need a couple of minutes, maybe more."

Badger asked, "Do we have that long?"

"Let me work," Andre said. "And no one gets out of the car until I say so."

"Copy that." Badger reached for the tape surrounding the teen's torso. Hannah reached out and stayed his hands. She shook her head but pointed to the tape securing her forehead to the chair headrest.

"Hannah, can you listen to me right now?"

She worked on the girl's hands, cutting them free from the steering wheel.

"I need you to focus on me."

Hannah stowed the knife back in her boot when the girl's hands were loose and took both hands in hers.

Badger worked on the tape around the headrest.

She didn't want him taking the tape from around the girl's torso. It would only give her the freedom to shove the door open in a panic and jump out. Doing that would kill them all, given she couldn't get free of the blast fast enough. No matter how quick she moved, opening the door would trigger detonation. This girl would kill herself along with Badger and

Hannah and Andre, and Lucia. That was the last thing Chevalier needed.

The girl whimpered. "Get me out of here."

Badger pulled the tape from the back of the seat, where her head had been taped to the back of the headrest, and Hannah helped the girl remove it from her forehead.

"There we go. That's much better, isn't it?" Hannah practically crooned the words. "We're going to get out of here as soon as we can."

The girl struggled around the tape, trying to pry it free with her fingers. "Get this off me. Now. Let me go."

"Hannah, I need you to listen to me." She used her cop voice. "The man that took you did something to this car. None of us can get out. Not yet. But there's someone under the car, and he knows what he's doing."

The girl started to cry anew. "I know what he did. We're all going to die."

"Did he tell you?" Hannah wasn't going to mention a bomb until the girl did it first.

"He said you had to die too." She gasped. "That you would come here, and we would die together."

"Did he say anything else?"

Badger sat quietly in the back seat. Hannah glanced over and saw respect on his face. Even given the situation, she was still working. Trying to gather as much intel as possible. In the event they were all killed, Zander could take the information and go after Ricker.

It didn't matter who was left. Joseph Ricker wasn't going to get away with this.

Ideally, they would survive. But Hannah had never counted on that. It was impossible to tell, even on a good day.

Let alone when everything seemed so crazy and nothing made sense to her.

Like waking up one day a police detective with perfectly nice parents who had retired in Texas and going to sleep that night with a half sister. Now she had a mother who evidently wanted nothing to do with her and frequently broke the law to serve her own interests. And a brother she'd never met.

The teen gasped, shook her head, and whimpered instead of speaking. In a way, something similar had happened to this girl. Her life was utterly unrelated to all of this, and yet she'd been dragged in. Picked out because she was adopted, and her name was Hannah.

How Joseph had managed to figure all that out, she had no idea. Plus, he'd found her here in Baltimore when he was from New York—as was she.

The whole thing was just crazy when Hannah took the time to think it through. Too bad there had been no time to do that so far.

"Hannah, look at me."

The girl turned her head and met Hannah's gaze.

"My name is Hannah, too. I'm sorry." She winced. "But that's why he chose you because you were adopted, and your name is the same as mine."

"Do you know who my real parents are?"

Hannah shook her head. "I never knew who mine were. Not until recently."

Behind the team, Badger pulled out his phone and typed on the screen with his thumbs. She figured he was texting Ted, asking what the guy had found out about the abducted girl. She might have a sealed adoption the way Hannah had. But given Hannah's siblings and mom had recently come into her life, the teen might have had family who wanted to meet her.

Or people Chevalier needed to protect her from.

Tears rolled down the teen's face. "I thought this might be…about them. Because he asked me if I knew anything."

Probably just curiosity. But Hannah didn't know. "Do you have siblings in your adopted family?"

The girl nodded. "I"—her voice broke—"have a brother."

"I never had any siblings. I always thought it would be cool to have a brother. Or a sister. Unless they borrow your clothes. That's just annoying." She tried to keep things light.

The teen said, "My mom and I are the same sizes now. These are her jeans."

Hannah nodded. "Cool. I have a pair that looks like that brand. What about shoes?"

The girl shook her head. "She's a size six. I'm an eight."

"Are we really going to sit here and talk about shoes?" Badger's voice sounded far lighter than his expression indicated he felt.

The girl glanced at Hannah, her eyes alight. She tried to laugh, finally settling on a smile. The girl managed to respond in kind, a little. She was pretty cool—the kind of kid Hannah could imagine handing her business card to. Just in case she ever needed a friend who happened to be a cop.

"Maybe we will just talk about shoes." Hannah smiled. "I have five pairs of Vans."

The teen said, "I have seven."

"All different colors and styles?"

She nodded.

"Me, too." Yeah, Hannah was sure she could offer this

girl a friendship. Maybe mentor her. Stick close, even if just via text. Check in often and see if she was doing okay.

Badger's eyes flashed. She figured he'd have made a joke about someone killing him now to put him out of his misery if it wasn't in extremely poor taste. But she'd have laughed anyway.

The girl's humor was short lived.

Hannah squeezed her shoulder. "It won't be——"

"Done!" Andre called through the comms channel. "Get her out."

Badger immediately cut the tape on the back of the chair. Hannah got out and rounded the hood as quickly as possible to the driver seat, which she hauled open. The girl was already free and shifting her legs to get out.

Hannah caught her elbows. "I've got you."

She tugged the girl into her arms, and the teenager allowed herself to be held for a second. Hannah walked her toward Zander, and Judah ran over with a jacket from the car wrapped around her.

"Two minutes. Cops, feds, and an ambulance," Zander said.

Hannah nodded. She glanced at Badger, back talking with Andre and Lucia.

He looked at her as if he'd known her attention was on him. The smile was for her alone.

She returned it, feeling her cheeks heat.

Zander squeezed her shoulder. "You did well with her."

"Thanks."

Cops inundated the area. Teenage Hannah was loaded into an ambulance, and they called her parents. Hannah fought the tide of getting swept up into the fed's conversation. Grilling her about everything and finding out what she knew.

As if she could reach into Joseph Ricker's mind and extract the information.

The entire team was separated. A crowd gathered beyond police tape strung up around the scene. Even the bomb squad showed up, so they could dispose of the ordinance safely. It was a scene so familiar to her. It may as well have been her favorite restaurant. But none of it was right. Not the cops. Not saving the victim or giving a statement.

Not until she scanned the gathered crowd and saw him there. Staring at her.

Everything in Hannah coalesced to a single word.

*Justice.*

## 20

On the periphery of what he could see, Badger spotted the moment Hannah broke away from Zander and sprinted toward the tape.

Zander lifted a hand to the button on his vest. "Badger."

His team leader didn't even need to give that much of a command through their comms channel. He was already running after her. Two feds tried to do the same, and Zander stepped in front of them. He engaged them in conversation so they couldn't follow.

Zander was leaving this to their team to solve.

Badger threaded through cops and other first responders. He ducked under the tape and nearly got snarled up in a couple holding hands. Badger apologized and darted around them, trying to keep Hannah in sight.

Andre's voice came through comms. "Judah, have from your side. You see her?"

It sounded like Andre was running. Which meant Lucia was probably coming with them. The feds had a million questions about Andre and how he'd been able to disarm the bomb.

Now everyone's laser focus was on Hannah.

Badger crossed the street and pounded down the sidewalk on the far side. He keyed the button for his radio. "Hannah, hold up." She needed to wait until they caught up with her. "Talk to me."

He didn't want the rest of the team hearing his unsuccessful attempts to get her to respond to him so he didn't try again. Instead he picked up his pace even more than the breakneck speed he already had.

If Joseph Ricker was up there and did something to Hannah before Badger could catch up to her, he wasn't sure he would ever be able to forgive himself.

It was enough to induce him to pray, even if doing that had never worked for him before. Andre and Zander had faith. They were working on strengthening it, meeting together to read their Bibles and pray with Eas.

They'd invited him, but since Badger didn't know what he was doing, he figured he would only wind up making a fool of himself.

*Keep her safe*, he prayed.

If there really was Someone up there, surely they were powerful enough to do that. But since Alexis had been murdered, he wasn't sure he could reconcile there being a supreme good in the world.

Badger turned the same corner Hannah had. He didn't see Joseph, nor did he see Hannah. He raced to the end of the street and glanced in both directions.

Just more traffic. A couple of homeless people and a guy jogging in a T-shirt and shorts.

He keyed the button for his radio. "Hannah, where did you go?"

Badger heard nothing back, not even a whisper. Her radio had no button. He preferred to activate his own comms. With her being unused to their system, Zander had given her one with an open channel in both directions. That meant the rest of the team had heard everything they'd said in the inside of the car, just without the echo of his radio being on as well.

*Focus. Think.*

He spun around. Where had she gone? This wasn't the time to get distracted thinking about the intricacies of how their radios worked, whether or not Ted was monitoring everything. Which he wasn't right now.

"Hannah!" He called out her name again.

A car engine revved.

Badger spun, pulled his gun, and raised it to aim at the driver. The past washed over his mind so that he saw Alexis being dragged to that van by the huge man who had taken her from the beach that day.

Sand in his mouth. Water in his lungs.

Badger choked on the memories, the powerlessness, and fear.

Joseph Ricker held the steering wheel. He angled it toward Badger, headed straight for him. The way he drove? He hadn't been doing it long.

Badger blinked at what was happening, his mind unable to process the scene in front of him.

The car bumped the curb.

Judah grabbed Badger and pulled him away from the front bumper a split second before the car slammed into him. They hit the ground and rolled, the two of them tumbling over as the car engine revved again, and Joseph Ricker sped away.

Badger's head spun.

Judah shoved him off. Badger rolled to his back on the ground and stared up at the cloudy night sky.

"You can thank me later for saving your butt," Judah said. "Where's Hannah?"

"I don't know."

She could be in the trunk of that car. Incapacitated. Captured by Ricker and taken from him. Murdered. Or so many more, worse things could be done to her before she took her last breath.

Tears rolled from the corners of his eyes.

"Get up. We are not done searching." Judah hopped to his feet and pulled out his phone. "Yeah, Ted. I need a location on Hannah's comms."

Badger swallowed back the whimper. *Don't be dead.*

He couldn't handle it if he lost her. Not after he'd seen Alexis taken. This was the resurgence of his nightmare, the last place he had ever wanted to be again in his life. Now Hannah was going to have to pay the ultimate price for him not being fast enough. Or good enough.

"Copy that." Judah hung up the phone and turned to him. "Get up."

He turned away and headed back down the street Badger had run down already. She hadn't been in front of him. If her comms was down there, it was because Ricker had pulled it from her before he kidnapped her. And how was that possible in seconds? She hadn't been that far in front of him. How could he have lost her?

Badger ran his hands down his face. It felt like everything in him was fracturing.

"Hannah!" Judah yelled. A second later, he motioned to Badger. "Get over here!"

Badger scrambled to his feet, gasping for an inhale, and stumbled down the street.

Judah stood beside a huge dumpster he'd run past, both hands spread wide.

Badger frowned. "What is—?"

Judah took a step back. "Hannah, it's okay."

He peered around the dumpster and saw her. Sitting with her knees up. A bloody knife in one hand. Glassy eyes and a distant expression.

Judah thought she was going to hurt someone?

Badger crouched. He laid his hand over hers. Not the knife he'd given her in the car that she'd returned. Given that one leg of her pants was hiked up, revealing the empty sheath in her boot, he figured she'd gone by instinct.

"Hey." He gently tugged the blade from her hand and passed it to Judah. Badger knelt beside her as he ran his hands from her wrists to her shoulders. "Hey, Hannah?"

"I stabbed him."

Badger gritted his teeth. "Good."

After all, the guy had just tried to kill him. He'd tried to kill all of them, along with an innocent teenager who should never have been wrapped up in all of this.

Tears rolled down her cheeks.

Badger groaned. He wound an arm under her knees, the other around her back, and lifted her. Once he had her settled in his arms, he headed back toward the car. "Get us a pickup," he told Judah.

While the British guy did that, Badger held her close to him and walked them both out of there. "It's okay," he crooned in her ear.

Hannah's breath hitched on an inhale. "I stabbed him."

"I know." Just how deeply was she in shock?

"He said they weren't paying him enough to risk his life."

Badger nearly tripped over his feet and dropped them both to the ground. Everyone had heard that through their comms. It was the only reason he didn't stop right then. The others knew already. All of them would be on this.

Zander pulled up. Andre, right behind him.

Badger put Hannah in the front seat of Zander's car. He buckled her seatbelt and gestured with his hands. His team leader would understand. Badger wanted her back at the house as soon as possible, and he wanted Zander to wait one second.

He closed the door and headed for Andre's vehicle, which was idling behind it. Then he opened the passenger door where Lucia sat and bent down.

"Can you guys go with them?" He pointed at Zander and Hannah's car. "There's something Judah and I need to do, but Hannah needs people around her, and she'll want to talk to Nora."

It was the best decision. She would be safe, and they could care for her. Preferably in Last Chance County, where their home base was located. But for now, the safe house would do. As would her sister, the most caring person Badger knew.

Lucia angled out of the car. "You don't want company?"

Badger shook his head. "We need to go talk to someone."

Andre tossed him the keys. "I'll touch base with Ted and keep you posted."

Badger nodded.

Seconds later, once the car in front pulled out, he made a U-turn in the street and removed his earbud. He should have removed his protective vest, too. It was going to be a long drive.

"Find me an address for the shooter's brother," he told Judah. "We need to get to the bottom of this."

---

"WHAT HAPPENED WITH RICKER?" It was the first thing anyone had said as Zander drove away.

Hannah glanced at him. With her hands clenched in her lap, Hannah had been doing nothing but take deep breaths.

Andre and Lucia were in the back.

Zander looked like he'd been chewing on nails.

Hannah said, "Do you know I've never fired my weapon in the line of duty?"

"A lot of cops don't. Or so I've heard." He didn't glance over, just kept driving.

Hannah didn't even think about where Badger and Judah had gone or why he had deposited her in this car and left in the other one.

Whichever way it shook out, none of them were good.

Lucia spoke up from the back seat. "It's true. It's actually pretty rare for a cop to use their weapon, let alone have to use lethal force."

"But you did today." That was Andre.

Hannah looked down at her hands. She nodded.

"You good with going back to the house?" Zander said. "We can check in with Ted, see what this business is about Joseph being paid to come after you."

"It still feels personal."

"It will," Zander told her. "As much as the guy might

deny it, it's not a business transaction. Otherwise, he wouldn't have taken so much pleasure in tormenting you."

Hannah winced.

Andre said, "Was it lethal force?"

"He'll probably live," Hannah said. "I got his shoulder."

Lucia said, "Andre and I should hit the streets. Find out where he went. If he's bleeding, he'll need medical supplies. That means a pharmacy or a vet office."

"You think you can track him down?" Zander asked.

"Worth a try."

Zander pulled the car over to the side of the street.

Andre and Lucia both moved to get out. Andre squeezed her shoulder as he slid toward the door. "You'll be okay. And we'll find him."

The door shut.

Zander said, "He's right, you know. Think about it. That teen was all set to die, but you got her back to her parents."

Hannah knew he was trying to encourage her. Today had been a success. And it might sink in—later. But right now, his comment only made her think of her own parents and how they would react to all of this. She hadn't even told them she knew who Nora was.

"Is Nora still at the house?"

"The doctor is there now." Zander nodded. "I can imagine he'll want to make sure you're all right."

"I'm not the one who got a knife to the shoulder." Hannah managed to sound hard. Even if everything in her was shaking, it still felt good that she had struck back at Joseph. Revenge had never been her thing. But right now, she could see the appeal.

"What are you thinking?"

Hannah said, "It's time Nora and I spoke with Isaac."

Zander was quiet for a few seconds. "That's actually a good idea. If anyone knows what Lana does about you being in danger, I would imagine it's him."

"Will you tell me what he's like?" After all, she'd never met the guy, and the last thing she wanted to do right now was think about either Joseph or Badger. "I know he walked away from your team, but you must have seen something good in the guy at one point."

Zander headed back to the house. Maybe Badger would be there when they got there, or maybe not—and she figured the latter was more likely. All Hannah knew was that she needed to stand on her own two feet and find the answer herself. She'd been right in the middle of it from the outset.

"He's a complicated guy. And not just because he's former CIA." Zander never blurted anything out. It seemed more like he considered his words before he spoke them. "It's clear he's tied up with Lana and her organization. If he's her son, then it stands to reason why. Although, you and Nora haven't been caught in it the same way."

"That could be by design."

"It wouldn't surprise me at all if everything Isaac has done has been to keep the two of you off her radar." Zander shot her a sad expression. "He only told us about you when it became necessary."

"Because you were arrested for murder?" She could recall the day she had walked into that interrogation room to face him. Summoned there by the higher ups for a reason she hadn't even begun to understand, though she'd had an inkling.

He grinned. "You didn't cut me any slack."

Hannah managed to chuckle. "Would you have?"

"No way." He glanced over, still smiling. "I'm glad Nora will have you in her life."

"Me, too," Hannah said. "Do you think Isaac will talk to us?"

"I'll call the prison and see what I can do to get you in there," Zander said. "After all, it's worth it to the agents putting the charges together to get the full scope of who he is. What he might be involved in."

"But there's something else?"

"It's just that every piece of information we've gotten so far has been cryptic. Pieces of things, like you and how you fit into this."

"Like Isaac trades in information."

"It's probably what has kept him alive all this time."

"Not the fact he works for our mother?" Hannah didn't know for sure that was how they were connected biologically, but she could guess.

Her best estimate was that the three of them were Lana's children. All with different fathers, although she wasn't going to hold that against a woman who had lost the man she loved —Isaac's father. Gladstone had been a mission, although Lana had lived with him for years.

It made her wonder who had taken care of Isaac all that time. And why she'd left Gladstone. Had she met Hannah's father by then?

"Isaac will want to see you," Zander said. "I'm hoping that wins out over any tendency ingrained in him to hold back. Hopefully he'll be overwhelmed enough facing you and Nora together for the first time that he'll let something slip."

She nodded. "I just hope it helps us figure out all of this. Because so far, all we have is a mess of random pieces that don't fit together."

Zander pulled down the street where the safe house was located. "If this was a case you were working on, and nothing made sense, what would you do?"

"Go back to the beginning and run through every single piece of information and evidence bit by bit to figure out what I missed."

Nora came out of the house with her coat on, carrying her purse.

Hannah hopped out of the front seat to get in the back. She pulled the rear door open when Nora said, "Hey."

Hannah glanced at her.

"Are you okay?" Nora spread her arms slightly as though questioning if Hannah might want a hug.

She couldn't remember the last time she'd been hugged. Except for Badger, and there was no point thinking about a man who wasn't here.

Hannah moved to her sister, wound her arms around her, and held on tight. "I could tell." It sounded like Nora was chuckling.

"Yeah, yeah. Smarty-pants." Hannah climbed into the car. "This whole having a big sister thing could get annoying, real fast."

"Until Christmas morning. And then all will be forgiven."

Hannah perked up. "Yeah?"

"I guess you'll have to wait and see."

In the front seat, Zander grinned. He lifted Nora's hand in his and kissed it.

Hannah said, "I hate waiting."

Thankfully Nora and Zander kept the conversation light as they made their way to the prison. By the time they got there, it would probably be the early hours of the morning.

Hannah fell asleep, and when she woke up, the sun had risen above the horizon.

She sniffed in a long breath and blew it out, then realized she was the only one in the car. Nora and Zander stood beside it, close together. Both drinking from paper cups.

She shoved open the car door and halfway fell out. "Coffee?"

Zander juggled. "I think she could use another hug."

"Coffee first."

Nora grinned.

Zander said, "Always," and handed her a paper cup of her own.

It didn't matter that it was barely warm because she had managed to sleep without dreams. Without thinking about Badger. But then the thoughts rushed back, and she had to force them away again.

Hannah chugged the entire coffee and wiped her mouth with the back of her hand. "Can we get in?"

"As soon as you're ready." Nora shifted, a nervous expression on her face.

"I can go in by myself if you want?" The last thing Hannah intended was to make her sister upset. With how Nora felt about their mother, she could easily change her mind about seeing Isaac too.

Nora shook her head. "I want to hear what he has to say."

"Then let's go."

## 21

"We could get in serious trouble if this guy reports us as harassing him."

Badger glanced over at Judah in the passenger seat. "Seriously?"

"I'm just saying. He could make trouble for us."

"That could happen every minute of every day in this job." But what counted was the reason why they did what they did and never backed down. The way Zander had never backed down trying to save Nora and clean up the mess her father had made for years.

"So how do we know this"—Judah looked at his phone—"Peter Benton guy, who works for Travers Industries, really is the assassin his brother said he is?"

"I figure we won't know unless we ask him." Badger scanned the street around where they had parked. Peter Benton's residence was across the street, several doors down. His light had come on twenty minutes ago, a frosted window that was probably the bathroom. He would leave for work soon.

"Seems pretty flimsy." Judah's voice had an edge of disbelief. "Like he was actually there to try and stop his brother killing Pearson or Hannah?" A pause. "What happened between you two in the apartment before he jumped out the window?" The disbelief hadn't gone from his tone. It was still there.

"You seriously think I actually threw him out the window?"

Judah shrugged. "No one would blame you if you did. Far as you know, the guy intentionally shot at Hannah and actually missed."

"Because he's a second-rate assassin, and the brother is the real one? Too bad Ted wasn't able to hack the security for Travers Industries yet. Otherwise, we'd know if he had time to drive all the way down here and back up to New York during that timeframe."

"You really think it was a warning to her, and the guy just happened to hit Pearson by mistake?"

Badger shrugged. "His brother fed me the same line about trying to stop Peter. Greg was the one living with that woman above the bar, and they were all set to go on vacation. He claimed his brother killed her because Greg told her too much. That Peter was out of control, and Greg tried his best to stop him."

"But he didn't call the police or report the fact there was a dead woman in his apartment?"

"Who knows what people's thought processes are in a time like that?" Badger said. "It's hard to say how you'd react. Most of the time people make no sense, but blaming someone else is something I'm familiar with."

"So either the brother killed her and Greg going back there was a cry for help, a way for someone else to find out what happened." Judah frowned. "Or Greg's the one who killed her, and maybe he had you chase him back there for the same reason—so that someone would find her and the police would be able to take care of it."

"What all this has to do with Hannah is the question," Badger said. "I don't care if Greg was overcome by guilt about what happened to his girlfriend. There's a dead federal agent, and if the man who did it isn't in custody yet then why not? At least the feds should have talked to Peter."

Badger frowned. He'd have figured they would have arrested the guy.

He didn't want to think the worst—that the feds had been paid off or advised to turn their backs. Maybe even by someone at Travers Industries. Former president Raleigh certainly had the clout to do something like that if he was so inclined.

"There he goes." Judah motioned to the light, which had shut off.

"I wonder if he has coffee."

They had already staked out the house a couple of hours ago. Dressed as power company employees, he and Judah had ascertained there was a hefty security system in place. Ted had told them how to bypass it.

Badger said, "Let's go."

They would be minimally armed. Guns out of sight, and everything else stowed. Bulletproof vests on because Zander insisted. Badger had learned that if he went into a situation with a weapon in plain view, often he was met with a similar response. But if he kept it out of sight? Usually, things didn't escalate.

He'd rather avoid a fight in this instance. Especially if Peter Benton had some kind of hidden panic button.

"You clear the place. I incapacitate him."

Judah said, "Roger that."

They reached the back door fast and picked the lock. Once inside, Badger leaned his phone on top of the alarm panel and continued down the hall, leaving it there. Ted could use his skills to hack anything in the house with Bluetooth capability connected to the internet, including the security system. If there was a panic button on the alarm system, Ted could circumvent any signal that left the house.

The security company would never know that Peter had attempted to call for help.

A Travers Industries thermos sat on an entryway table beside a set of keys. Shoes had been removed on the floor beside the table. Probably yesterday, when Peter got home from work.

They made their way through the house, down the hall to where the light was on in the bedroom. The kitchen was clear. The light came from the master bedroom and closet.

It wasn't long, just a matter of minutes before he emerged, fully dressed and ready for work. Thankfully.

Peter pulled up short. Surprise clear on his face. "What the—"

Before he could reach for any weapon, Badger strode right up to him. He stopped in the guy's space but far enough away he'd be able to deflect any attempt Peter made to grab Badger's weapon.

"One wrong move, and I shoot you," Badger said. "Got it?"

Peter shifted like he wanted to duck back into the bathroom. He was taller than his brother, stronger and warier. If Badger had to put money on it, he'd say this guy was the killer.

Badger motioned with his gun. "Living room. Now."

Peter walked ahead of him. Judah tapped Badger's shoulder twice, which meant he would go clear the rest of the house, making sure no one else was there.

Badger led the guy all the way to the living room and had him sit.

The guy looked up at him. "Gonna throw me out a window like you did to my brother?"

"I definitely drove for hours just to do that." Badger shot him a look that said everything he needed to know. "You're going to talk, and then we're going to leave. That's it."

"And supposedly that? With this cloak and dagger routine and the fact the two of you managed to disarm my security system?"

"We did more than that, Peter."

Judah walked back in. He handed Badger the phone back. "All clear."

Good. Now that he was in, Ted would worm his way through this guy's network while they spoke to him. Anything he had to say was incidental—the real intel would come through what Ted managed to dig out. Everything Peter had been hiding.

"Your brother claims you're the real assassin," Badger said. "That he was only trying to stop you from killing that federal agent." He figured he didn't need to know this was about Hannah.

Peter glanced away, pinning his gaze on the surface of the coffee table. Three remotes and two magazines by the look of it.

Badger kept his attention on the guy they were talking to. "Is that how it works with the two of you?"

"Greg said whatever he had to say."

Badger shrugged. "Stands to reason. He did tell the feds whatever they wanted to hear so he could get out from under suspicion. But if it could be true, that makes me wonder why they didn't arrest you?"

"There's no evidence I was there."

"So you have an alibi or some electronic record you were nowhere near Baltimore that night? That's pretty handy." Badger paused. "Or since you work for a tech company, perhaps you're just extremely skilled at covering your tracks."

"If you know anything about the tech industry, you'll know I'm far too busy to have a second job as some kind of assassin." Peter tried to laugh, but it sounded rusty.

It didn't matter if he did or not. Either way Ted would find out.

Badger said, "How did you get involved with Travers Industries?"

"I was headhunted." Peter shrugged his shoulders. "You want to see a copy of my resume?"

"Is it going to be any more truthful than what's coming out of your mouth?"

The guy's lips curled. "Why are you asking me questions if I'm only going to lie?"

Soon enough, he would figure it out.

"Tell me who put out the hit on Detective Hannah Yassick."

Peter cocked his head and studied Badger.

"You already know I was there. Your brother shot a federal agent, or you did, and he's going to take the fall for it. Either way, someone will be charged with his murder." Badger studied him right back, not backing down even to blink. "And I think you know exactly how this is going to go down."

THE AMOUNT of red tape Hannah and Nora had to jump over to get face-to-face with Isaac was beyond anything she'd ever faced. And that was after years of being a police detective and lately working with feds. Zander had pulled some serious strings. Now they were being escorted down the hallway toward a meeting room where they would see Isaac. All three of them would be together for the first time in the same place.

Hannah couldn't help thinking this was exactly what Lana wanted.

And it wouldn't be a good thing.

"Why don't you let me take the lead on asking him questions?" Hannah figured it was worth a try. She didn't know Nora all that well but planned on learning everything she could if they were going to get to know each other.

"This isn't an interrogation," Nora replied.

Hannah worked her mouth back and forth. "Can you just give me the benefit of the doubt? Like if I say something you aren't sure about."

Nora nodded. "I understand how it works, the delicate balance of trying to get someone to talk and not revealing your own ideas and agenda."

Given her dad had been Stephen Gladstone, Hannah figured that was probably true. "You think there might be something you can get from him that I wouldn't?"

"It's possible."

Hannah nodded. "You're right. It is."

Nora grinned as though Hannah had given her a gift making her feel like a needed part of this. Something Hannah was going to have to remember. Nora had been passed over and manipulated until her entire life was a fabrication, and nothing she did amounted to anything. Hannah couldn't even imagine how that felt. She lived for the effect she had on everyone's lives. Taking down criminals, bringing justice by gathering evidence, and putting cuffs on the person responsible. The justice system took things from there. None of it was perfect, but Hannah did her part to the best of her ability.

"Right here." The guard motioned to the room. "Call out if you have any problems. Or if you're done."

Hannah nodded. "Thanks."

Nora waited, for which she was grateful. Hannah strode in first with her sister behind her. To anyone watching it was a show of strength.

All she did was enter the room, but the way Hannah did it made it clear Nora was under her protection. She needed that show of strength because the man at the table was nothing like she'd imagined.

Nora gasped.

Hannah gritted her teeth. She took a couple of inhales through her nose, pushed off the sensation, and strode to the table. "What happened to you?" She pulled out a chair and set it a couple of inches away, so Nora would sit, then remained standing. No way would she relax when Isaac had clearly been beaten. Possibly by several people. "I thought you were in solitary."

He spread his hands on the table, his wrists shackled. The chain stretched under the table, where it attached to the shackles on his feet. "Accidents happen."

This was more than an accident. His lip was split. Bruises covered his face, and one eye was almost swollen shut.

"What about what I can't see? Did you get checked out by a doctor to make sure you don't have internal bleeding?"

"Nicked my spleen. He just took it out."

"Sorry we got you out of your hospital bed." Hannah didn't like this at all. He'd had surgery recently?

Isaac said, "Don't worry about it. I'm glad you guys came."

"You know we're both wired up. Everything you say will be recorded." This wasn't an investigation, and she wasn't a cop here. Hannah was a close relative of an incarcerated federal fugitive. Someone who might be able to persuade him to give over information where the feds had been unable to.

He said nothing.

She figured whoever was on the other end was currently cursing at her for telling Isaac. But it wasn't as though he was dumb. Her brother had been a CIA agent and a member of Lana's secret organization for years. Which made her wonder why he'd felt it necessary to walk up to the entrance to the Marine base at Quantico and turn himself in.

Sure, he'd handed back a stolen nuke. But now he was paying the price for its theft.

She wondered if there was someone in here he'd needed to speak to. A reason why he needed to be in cuffs and incarcerated. Or was this simply his personal bid for freedom from Lana—or whoever else had been controlling him for years.

"What do they want you to ask me?" he finally said.

"Do any of us care about that?" Hannah motioned to include Nora. "I just found out you're my brother because they tested your DNA when you landed in here, and I came up as a match. Right now, Nora being your sister is an assumption."

Isaac measured his words. "Which would be correct."

Nora spoke in a gentle voice. "Is Lana all of our mothers?"

Isaac glanced at her. "Yes."

There was a softness to Nora that made Hannah want to take care of her. But on the flipside, Nora had spent the first twelve years of her life with her mother as part of her family. Isaac had worked for her for years, and everyone at Chevalier who had seen them said they had a close relationship—even if it wasn't an entirely functional one.

Hannah had never even met the woman. At least not as far as she was able to remember.

So what made her different from them?

Or, as Hannah suspected from what they'd all told her, was Hannah simply not the means to the end Lana was looking for? Her mother only had a relationship with people that got her what she wanted. A mission, or an item she desired. Like keeping the suitcase nuke safe so that no one else could use it.

Lana had been in Nora's life because her mission was to get close to Gladstone. They'd married, and she'd had a child.

Isaac was a loyal foot soldier in her organization.

It might not be that Hannah meant nothing to her. It could simply be that she didn't prove useful.

"Does she need to be taken down?" Hannah was prepared to do that if it brought peace of mind to the people she cared about.

Isaac shook his head. "Don't get caught up in that. You'll lose. And your life is already in enough danger."

"From who?" Maybe he thought Hannah shouldn't have come here, even if he'd said he was glad she had. "So far it seems like more of a distraction than someone actually trying to kill me."

She'd definitely been through the wringer watching her handler die. Driving off the road into the river and saving Badger. Dealing with Joseph Ricker and saving that abducted girl. And that wasn't counting the clinic and that whole mess with Dr. Mathers.

Lives had been lost. But others had been saved, and she would always consider that the best kind of outcome.

"We are all pawns in this." Isaac stared at the table. "Caught up in a war we were never meant to be part of, between two sides determined to destroy each other. And they are going to use us as pieces they move around the table. Pitting us against each other."

Nora reached over and laid her hand on Isaac's. The guards hadn't bothered telling them not to touch him. They just didn't want Isaac standing up until the two of them left. "We're not going to destroy each other. If someone here is fighting a war, it has nothing to do with us."

"Doesn't matter. We're in it whether we like it or not."

Nora pulled her hand back. "You don't have to worry about Hannah and me. All you need to do is take care of yourself." She winced. "Please tell me you know what you're doing."

He smiled, but it seemed more that he wanted to find the humor in himself. In this situation? "I am going to worry about the two of you."

"So tell us what to watch out for." Hannah hoped he did. "Because someone out there wants to do whatever they like with my life, and I don't get a say in it?"

"Welcome to the club."

"I don't buy that, Isaac."

He nodded. "I know. That's what I like about you."

"At least give me something." Whether it was about Lana, whoever she was at war with, or Hannah's own issues, she didn't much care. "Otherwise coming here was a waste of time." She watched that hit home, knowing it wasn't true. Seeing her brother for the first time would never be a waste.

But it got him to speak.

"Fine," Isaac said. "I'll give you a word of advice. Don't go anywhere near Travers Industries. They're bad news."

## 22

"You're right about one thing at least," Peter said. "I do know how it's going to go down with Greg."

Given his expression, Badger figured the guy spared no feelings on his brother. As for his position at Travers Industries, he'd been listed as working in the Research and Development division. But who knew? Only Ted would be able to tell them all the stuff this guy was into.

Badger glanced at Judah. His teammate gave a tiny shake of the head. Despite Judah handing his phone back, Ted had evidently hit a roadblock. Badger's best guess was that he'd been able to break the firewall on the network at Peter's house and get into his computer system. But going from that to piggyback into Travers Industries had proven a whole lot more difficult.

They would have to keep him talking long enough for Ted to get in from this backdoor.

Badger leaned against the wall beside the TV unit underneath the flat screen mounted not too far from him. "Must be pretty annoying to have your kid brother all up in your business. Especially when it's the kind you do."

"Because you still think I'm some kind of assassin?" Peter shook his head. "Even if I had a double life, it'd be something more fun than killing people."

"Like gambling?" There were other vices a man could choose from. Badger didn't want to get into those, though. "So why do you think your brother has the impression that's what you do?"

Peter shrugged. "It didn't occur to you it might be him that's the murder-for-hire person, and he only blamed it on me to deflect the attention from him?"

"I bet you have evidence to prove it, too. Don't you?" Judah asked. The guy had softened his British accent, probably just so Peter didn't get distracted by it and start asking Judah questions instead of being the one to answer them.

"What if I do?" Peter shrugged.

Badger said, "How about you hand that evidence over to us, and we'll pass it on to the feds with our compliments. Or did you already give it to them?" Maybe that was how he'd skirted out from under suspicion in all this.

If the brother turned up dead in prison, Badger wouldn't be entirely surprised.

That had happened recently when someone else involved in all this was killed. An international criminal and the former director of the Department of Clandestine Service, Stephen Gladstone wasn't exactly on the same level as a guy who was paid five grand to end someone's life. But if Greg was killed in prison, Badger would point out to Zander that Isaac should be put on a special watch. To make sure the same thing didn't happen to him.

It almost seemed like every time they went after answers, the truth was just out of reach.

Peter said, "You think I told them something different from what I'm telling you?"

Badger pushed off the wall. "I'll just bet you did."

But it didn't matter because Ted was in Peter's life, and it was only a matter of time until he would finally be able to hack Travers Industries—if he hadn't already done it.

After that they would have more information, if not the whole truth. The world would be a little bit safer. And the people Chevalier Protection Specialists cared about would be as well.

Judah headed for the door but turned back to provide cover while Badger turned his back on Peter Benton.

They trailed out the way they'd come in, and Judah shut the door behind them.

"I'm just glad Hannah is safe at the house." Badger figured the last thing she needed was to be running around, trying to solve this. That was what he was going to do.

Judah shot him a look.

Badger said, "What?"

"You think she's less capable of solving this than you are?" Judah held up a hand. Badger tossed him the keys, and he continued, "Because I'm guessing she would disagree. And some of the rest of us might as well. I'd argue she's in a better physical state than you are."

Badger grasped the handle and paused. "You think I can't do this? I proved I can."

"You also weren't breathing for a couple of minutes the other day." Judah stared at him over the roof of the car. "So you don't have to pretend you're fine. It is actually okay to take a day off and rest."

"In the middle of something like this?" Badger yanked the door open and climbed in.

Judah settled in the driver's seat. "Okay, fine. I'd probably be doing exactly what you're doing. But that doesn't mean Hannah can't be out here too."

She wasn't, though. She was protected, and somewhere he didn't need to worry that she was unsafe. He could let the worry go and focus on the job at hand. Which was what he planned to do instead of getting distracted by what Zander had said.

Judah drove two blocks, pulled into the store parking lot, and called Ted.

Their tech expert answered halfway through the first ring. "It's actually difficult to talk and type at the same time."

Judah pulled on the lever to recline his seat a few inches, a grin on his face. "I thought you'd invented an interface, so you just have to think, and it does what you want, instead of wasting your time typing."

"Sadly, not yet." Before Badger could ask him what he'd learned so far from Peter's home network, Ted said, "Oh, dang it."

"What is it?" Badger sat forward on the seat as if Ted could see him. Which he couldn't.

"Peter just shut off his computer. He made a call to an unlisted number, and now he's leaving his house."

"So you're out? It kicked you off?"

"No." Ted made a *pfft* sound. "First thing I did was plant a worm to give me access whenever I want."

"And with all your skills," Judah said, "you haven't managed to get into Travers Industries system yet?"

Silence was the only answer he got.

Badger winced.

Finally, Ted said, "It's a cutting edge tech company for one. For two, they have more military contracts than anyone. If it was easy to get into, I'd be worried."

"You're not worried already about what the government is up to?" Badger had served in special ops long enough to know that sometimes it wasn't worth asking questions. He didn't want to know the answer because you can't un-know anything. It wasn't like he could steer that great behemoth in a different direction. As far as he was concerned, the government would do what they were going to do.

He accepted the things he couldn't change, focused on what he could, and prayed that he would have the wisdom to know the difference every day. It was the only way he'd survived until the day he left Hawaii.

"Good point." Ted chuckled.

Judah said, "Can you tell so far if Peter gave us the truth?"

Badger hadn't gotten assassin vibes from the guy he chased. But there also wasn't anyone else there as far as he'd seen. Greg's story was entirely too much like someone trying to pass the blame to someone else. Playing the good guy instead of admitting to what he'd done. Or keeping his mouth closed.

"I'll keep you posted. And I just sent you the GPS for his phone."

"Thanks, Ted." Judah hung up.

Badger pulled up the app Ted had installed on all of their phones while Judah pulled out. They caught up to Peter and followed him across the bridge into New Jersey. Away from his office. So he wasn't going to work.

"You think he's just going to the supermarket?" Judah asked.

Badger glanced over. "Like the grocery store?"

"Yeah, that's what I said." Judah changed lanes. "He's probably just out of milk."

Badger gripped the door handle. "Maybe try not to kill us."

"When you're the only one that doesn't complain about my driving?"

"I've been preoccupied," Badger said. "But as long as you don't lose Peter, we're good."

After the conversation they'd just had with Peter, Badger figured there was no way the guy hadn't called for a meetup. He doubted the guy just confirmed his dentist appointment or whatever other mundane thing it might've been.

"He stopped." Badger gave Judah directions to the spot. Finally, they were getting somewhere. Despite everything he'd said, Badger didn't believe Peter had no clue what was happening here. No way did it only involve Greg and not both brothers up to their neck in whatever had been directed at Hannah.

Didn't matter though. Badger would make sure she was safe either way.

A minute later they pulled up, far enough they could sit and watch Peter's car.

Badger pointed. "Over there."

The guy had parked under a bridge. It wasn't easy to stay out of sight, and they might need to exit their car to find out what Peter was doing. But for the time being, they could see him well enough.

And the town car that approached.

"Let's get nearer."

Instead of responding, Judah just climbed out. Which Badger figured meant he agreed.

They worked their way to the end of the building, where he peered around the corner. Badger heard a shuffle behind him. Judah was getting into position.

His friend made a sharp sound. Badger turned back to check what—

Out the corner of his eye he saw something dark rush at his head.

Pain exploded in his skull, and everything went black.

---

Zander was in the hall waiting for them. "Uh-oh, this doesn't look good."

Beside Hannah, Nora picked up her pace and walked into her husband's waiting arms. He gave her a quick squeeze and asked Hannah, "Did he not talk to you?"

"He did." Hannah wasn't sure what to think about the conversation they had just had with their brother.

The first time the three of them were together in the same place, all able to acknowledge the fact they shared blood. Even if it was through a mother, she for one didn't even know. Hannah shook her head and waved off Zander's concern.

She needed to get off this line of thinking before she was sucked down into depression. It had nothing to do with her. So far as she knew, there probably wasn't anything wrong with her. It was just that circumstances dictated she never spent any time with her mom that she could remember.

That was all.

And given she was a cop, and her mom was a wanted fugitive—or she would be if the police knew about her—it wasn't as though they would get along.

So that was all there was to it.

She would actually enjoy getting to know Isaac. If he wasn't in prison.

Hannah led the way outside. She needed the motion of walking to get some distance from her thoughts, so she strode all the way to the car and turned to lean against it. Nora and Zander walked much slower, talking with each other as they did. Nora was probably giving him the whole rundown.

As they approached, their conversation ceased.

Hannah said, "I don't know why I thought he would just tell us straight out who is trying to kill me. Or whatever they're trying to do." Sometimes it did seem like distraction and not death threats. But what did she know? "He never did speak plainly."

"But that was because Lana pulled his strings," Nora said. "Isn't he out from under her thumb now?"

Hannah shrugged. "Maybe he's in prison because she told him to be there. It could be another operation she has him on."

Nora glanced at Zander. "We could ask Karina if Lana has done this before."

Karina was a new addition to their group, now living with her daughter in Last Chance County. Zander's teammate Eas was the father of Aria, Karina's daughter. Judah had told Hannah that the two of them were dating and taking things slow. Karina was also a former operative working for Lana.

"But didn't she work for her fifteen years ago, not recently?" Hannah asked.

Zander nodded. "She could shed some light. But no one knows what Lana is up to now."

"It would only be supposition." Hannah didn't like it any

more than Nora or Zander appeared to from the expressions on their faces. "Unless Ted can find her."

Zander shook his head. "He hasn't been able to so far. I think he was hoping getting into Travers Industries would give him access to information he doesn't have yet."

Hannah said, "I had heard they were developing a new proprietary phone network so that cops and federal employees could have their own system."

Better for tracking, but also worse for privacy or autonomy. It was why she was glad to be a local cop, not a federal agent. That way she could keep the government out of her business. Not that she had anything to hide, but she couldn't see good things from a government owning its own communications network. Controlling everything, keeping all the records, and knowing where every device was located at any given time.

Sure, he could make people safer. But it also amounted to serious overreach.

Zander's phone rang. He pulled it from his pocket. "It's Ted." He slid his thumb across the screen. "O'Connell." He frowned. "How long?" Zander shifted away from Nora and motioned to the car. "Yes, send that to me." He got in the driver's seat, started the car, and the call connected to the vehicle's Bluetooth.

"...how much longer I'll be connected." Ted's voice came through the speakers. "The second I tried to access it, they saw me coming."

"What happened?" Hannah asked the question before she realized she might have overstepped.

"Badger and Judah were doing surveillance," Ted said. "But both their signals just went dark. I got a backdoor into Travers Industries through Peter Benton, and they saw me coming. So now I'm dealing with all kinds of Trojan horses and worms. They're throwing everything in their arsenal at me, trying to keep me out."

"Take care of the system," Zander said. "But send us their last known location."

"Done."

Zander's phone buzzed. The call was already ended. He handed his phone to Nora. "Tell me how long it will take to get to them."

The concern in his voice settled Hannah. But not much. "Does Ted have to fight off a hack often?" she asked.

Zander shook his head and headed for the highway. "He has safeguards against stuff like that. If they get too deep into his system he can fry the whole thing. He'll have to start over, but he has backups. It isn't like they're going to ruin the business."

But it would mean that Travers Industries knew Chevalier Protection Specialists had the company on their radar. And if they were involved at all in what was going on, the company would double down on the protections they employed.

"Head to the airport," Nora said. "We need to get on the plane."

"Where did Badger and Judah go?"

Nora shifted in her seat to turn and look at Hannah. "They went to interview Peter Benton at his house, which is close to where he works in New York."

"And they didn't take the plane?"

Nora shook her head. "They left it for us, just in case. They drove up overnight."

Zander hit the gas, and Nora turned back around. "Call Andre and Lucia," he said. "Have them meet us at the airport."

Ted never called with an update, not until they were on the ground in New Jersey. All of them, Lucia and Andre included. Four of them disembarked the Chevalier plane at the closest airport to where Badger and Judah's phones had last pinged.

Zander turned to look at his wife. "Will you please—"

Nora cut him off. "Go. I'll stay here."

Hannah gave her a hug, and Zander piled them into a new rental SUV. He drove faster than she would've, even with lights and sirens going to get there. It was still the longest twenty minutes of her life.

The four of them walked in formation the couple of hundred feet from their vehicle to where the car was parked. Maryland plates, a rental just like theirs. Zander was at the front. Lucia and Hannah followed, side by side. Andre protected them all from the back.

The doors of the car were open.

"See anything?" Zander directed the question at Lucia.

She moved to the right side of the car while Zander and Hannah went left. With each step Hannah felt a sense of foreboding. But that didn't mean anything. It wasn't like she could trust her instincts and what they were trying to tell her. Until they looked over this whole place, it could be anything that'd happened to Badger and Judah.

Just because they weren't right here didn't mean something was wrong. Maybe they had pursued Peter on foot.

Lucia said, "There's nothing."

The car was unoccupied. Hannah peered in the back seat. "I've got a duffel bag."

Zander continued on, past the car where the street ended at an abandoned parking lot with cracks in the asphalt where weeds grew. No one had used this place in a while.

There were no cars around other than the one they'd driven to get here. Not a single person or vehicle in the vicinity.

The November breeze blew an empty grocery bag across the lot.

"Ted said they were following Peter Benton, possibly to a meet," Hannah said. "Right?"

Zander nodded. But he didn't look out of the parking lot. His attention was on the last building before things opened up.

She didn't want to ask but had to. "Is that blood?"

The dark spot was little more than a smear, but it was wet and about the level of Badger's head—or Judah's.

"Yes." Zander's voice was thick. "Someone took them."

## 23

"It smells a bit odd in here," Judah said in his thick London accent.

Badger was hardly surprised, given it came out more pronounced when he was stressed out. He turned his head toward the sound of Judah's voice. "I thought that was you."

"Kind of like a cross between Marmite and a wet dog. With a weird edge of cherry between the two."

"Maybe they hit your head too hard. Knocked something loose, so your senses aren't working right." Except that Badger's head was the one pounding. On the right side, at the back just below his ear.

Judah was right about the smell, though. Badger just couldn't do anything about it any more than his friend could. Then again, Badger didn't know for sure that Judah was also tied to a chair. It was a guess, given Badger was blindfolded and his hands and feet were both secured to what felt like a metal folding chair.

Harder to get out of than a wooden one. But not impossible.

Until he was dead, Badger wasn't going to rule anything out. Sure, they'd been hoodwinked following Peter Benton. But that was nothing new. In the line of work they'd chosen, anything could happen at any minute. Something that had been hammered home the last few months with everything they'd dealt with.

Judah cleared his throat.

"You good?"

Badger heard an exhale, then Judah said, "I'm gasping for a cup of tea."

He was about to respond to that when a heavy door opened. The hinges creaked. That was good. He would be able to tell any time someone came into the room. There would be no surprising them with the sudden rush of an attack.

Both of them were quiet as footsteps approached. The sound of rubber soles on concrete echoed, giving him a sense of the expanse of the room they were in.

"I'll make this easy for you so you'll be sure to under-stand." The voice belonged to Peter Benton, though it was unsurprising he was still part of this.

Badger resisted the urge to laugh by gritting his teeth. He was definitely at a disadvantage but considering he was tied to a chair, that couldn't really be helped. Unless he managed to get loose from the ties that secured his hands behind him to the legs of the chair.

Judah said, "Interrogation is part of your job description? Or are you doing this for free?"

Since Badger didn't want them to get off topic, he said, "Why don't you just tell us what this is about, Peter."

After a few seconds of silence, the guy said, "You

breached my home network. But whoever you're working with isn't going to get into Travers Industries."

*Ted could hack anything.* But he wasn't going to tell this guy that because it made his friend a target if he wasn't already one.

Peter continued, "So you've got nothing, but you're going to tell me why you're so interested in the company I work for."

Badger had no intention of that. Not just because he had only slightly more than zero clue what Travers Industries was doing as part of this, but also because he didn't want to. Sure, they'd had dealings with the company before—wrapped up in the whole "Lana" business. But whatever this was, Badger didn't betray the people he cared for.

And he wasn't going to aid those who hurt them.

So he said, "Maybe you should tell me why you're wrapped up in an attempt on a police detective's life."

Lana hadn't asked for Hannah to be protected for nothing. Although, he didn't discount the fact it could be simply a way to get someone from Chevalier close to her so that they could discover a piece of whatever puzzle was forming. It was possible her life wasn't in danger at all, and that was just the story Lana used.

Peter said, "I'm the one asking questions."

Judah picked that up right away. "Yeah, but ours are better. What *is* the deal with Hannah? Sending your brother to try and kill her. And he shot a federal agent. You think that's going to go unnoticed?"

"As if Travers Industries can't take care of one police investigation?" Peter scoffed.

"Oh, so you bribe the cops?" Badger said. "Get the charges dropped, and your brother is released. He mysteriously disappears, or he kills himself in a prison cell." Badger turned his head toward Judah. "Where have I heard that before?" He waited for half a second and then said, "Right, Stephen Gladstone. He gave up a ton of information, and suddenly he's dead? Seems a little suspicious to me."

In a sense, they were answering Benton's question by asking questions of their own. Revealing little tidbits of what they knew, like a possible association between Travers Industries and the death of Stephen Gladstone.

Peter said, "No one is going to kill my brother."

"You think?" Judah asked. "I wouldn't be so sure about that. As much as you might want to protect him, he's in the thick of this. From where I'm sitting, he's expendable."

"Just answer my questions."

"Oh, did you ask something?" Badger said. "Like maybe how Joseph Ricker is involved in this? Did you ask about that because I'd like to know as well?"

"Seems like your brother didn't do much to get the job done." Judah expelled a puff of air. "Guess he's not that much of a hitman."

"If I was Travers, I'd get rid of him." Badger shrugged as best he could with his hands secured.

Judah said, "Can't even hit the right target. He wound up causing more trouble than he should've in just fixing the problem. Seems like a bit of a disaster, if you ask me."

Badger nodded. "I think so, too."

The punch came out of nowhere. Blindfolded as he was, Badger wasn't able to flinch away from the fist that slammed into his temple.

His head whipped to the right, and he sucked in a few breaths while pain wracked his skull. "Ouch."

He could vaguely hear what he figured was Judah,

straining against his own ties. Secure and unable to do anything. Probably blindfolded as Badger was.

"Still not as bad as sucking in a single drop of toxic chemical and being laid up for a month." Badger took a few long breaths. It wasn't like every part of this hadn't been done to him already, through his military training or when they'd been captured on missions. In Delta Force they had to be ready for anything, and that included both torture and interrogation. Fear could be both a hindrance and a tool.

Peter spoke close to his ear. "This can get much worse for you. Don't worry about that."

"I won't," Badger said. "Now, I thought you had questions for us."

He waited, trying to imagine the look on Benton's face. Meanwhile, Badger kept his expression neutral.

"Although," Judah said, "I'd probably be more forthcoming if you made me a cup of tea." There was a second's pause. "I'm just saying."

"That sounds like a great idea." Even though Badger didn't actually like tea without four sugars in it, which kind of defeated the point about drinking anything even though people did it every day with lattes. "Tea for two."

A whistle cut through the room. He heard a shuffle—presumably Benton turning—then he heard footsteps moving away.

He wished he could share a glance with Judah and read what he needed to from the guy's face. Not to mention seeing who else had entered the room. So far it had only been Peter Benton—until the summoning whistle. Maybe someone else from Travers was here. But without seeing them or hearing their voice, he had no idea who it was. Though, given the way they'd summoned Peter the second person was clearly superior.

Keeping the questioning to the person Judah and Badger already knew was involved. Meanwhile, the one behind it all pulling the strings remained in the dark.

Peter's footsteps came back over. But instead of standing where he had been, the guy sounded farther away when he said, "Who are you?"

Badger didn't think the question was directed at him. And it was confirmed when Judah said, "You want my whole resume or just the latest updates?"

"You think we aren't going to find out?" Peter asked.

"Maybe you will," Judah said. "I guess it'll just give us more to talk about."

"After you all tell us more about Hannah." Badger wasn't going to let that slide.

"It's funny you're so set on protecting her," Peter said. "Considering you already let one little girl die. Taken by a serial killer and destroyed like she was? Did you know there's a whole website about how you're the one to blame? It's no wonder you ran away from Hawaii and never looked back." Peter paused. "Do your teammates know what you did?"

"Yes, they do." He wanted to say they didn't keep secrets from each other. But the bile in his throat and the snippet of conversation Peter just had with Judah meant he wasn't sure he could. It was entirely possible his teammate had a secret.

The way Isaac had?

Something that could destroy the tight-knit bond between all of them in Chevalier.

Badger swallowed against the taste in his mouth. "But we obviously don't know what Travers Industries is up to, so why don't you just let us go, and we'll call this even."

Peter said, "You really think you can protect her?"

———————

"PULL OVER." Hannah gasped.

When Zander slowed the car and moved to the curb, Hannah already had one hand on the door handle. They were only a few miles from the site where Badger and Judah had been abducted, or so they thought, but she had to get out and move. She had too much on her mind.

Ted had been trying to dig into Travers Industries, but after sending them Badger and Judah's last location, he'd gone dark to focus on the cyber attack. Travers Industries was attempting to gain access to his system. The last Zander had told her and Nora, Ted would have to wipe everything, then restore the entire system from backups.

The entire Chevalier tech support system could be down for hours. Which meant Badger and Judah needed to be found using old-school methods.

Zander hit the brake.

As soon as the car door unlocked, she launched out and strode down the sidewalk. Maybe she should simply find them on foot.

So many questions rolled through her.

Hannah braced against the November wind and tucked her hands in her pockets. Walking as though she were being pursued but didn't want to run and make it obvious she was trying to flee. She wasn't being chased, except by her own failures.

She was a cop. And she hadn't seen that coming?

Badger might have ditched her and gone with Judah to solve her problems on his own. Or at least that was what

Zander had said. Trying to be all diplomatic, like he might have very well instructed Badger to do that. Even though she was sure he hadn't.

Meanwhile, Hannah should've…what? Stayed home like the protectee she was, instead of confronting her own issues head on? It almost made her want to get her mom's number from Zander—if he had it—and demand answers from the woman who had birthed her and then abandoned her.

But that was reactive. Instinctive. Badger and Judah were in danger, and she was thinking with her emotions.

She needed to be logical, not look to her gut reaction—the one that had steered her wrong until she believed there was nothing but innocence in Joseph Ricker. Then he'd murdered his family. Lately he'd kidnapped a girl with her name and forced Hannah to work to try to save her while she dealt with everything in her life.

Part of her wondered if the cartel Dr. Mathers had ripped off might come looking for her sooner or later. As if she needed that on top of everything else.

If it wasn't hours away, she might've even taken a trip to the house Ricker had burned down years ago. It had been rebuilt, and the newer construction included some elements of the same style as the original. She knew because she'd driven past it before.

The people who lived in that neighborhood struggled to make ends meet, or they had better things to do with their money than getting sucked into the trappings of a mortgage that stretched them too thin.

But for the most part, they were good people.

Could she say the same about herself?

Hannah didn't even know what she was doing out here on the street, on some random spot in New Jersey. The local residents had nothing to do with this unless Benton, or Ricker, chose to involve them. They would be innocent victims.

Joseph Ricker was probably still back in Baltimore. She didn't know why she was looking for him hours from there when she'd gotten on a plane to get here.

Hannah stood on the sidewalk and stared at the building beside her like a creeper. She was probably going to get abducted off the street as he'd been.

Badger was with Judah, so they'd keep each other safe. So far Andre and Lucia had been able to piece together that it might've had something to do with Peter Benton and by association Travers Industries. But instead of interviewing his brother Greg, Hannah had opted to stay on the streets.

She turned on the sidewalk. A man stood twenty feet away. Dark clothes. Hood up. Pale faced, like someone she'd stabbed yesterday and who couldn't see a doctor about it. Who had shown up here, miles from where she left him.

Beyond him, Zander pulled over to the curb with Nora in the front seat. She figured he would want to get out and intervene, so Hannah held up a hand to him. She needed to talk to him without anyone else disturbing them.

Hannah shivered. "How did you know I'd be here?"

"Apparently I'm not done."

That didn't sound good. "You don't look well. You might want to see a doctor."

He'd made it here from Baltimore, finding her on the street at the exact moment she had Zander pull over.

Someone was tracking her.

Joseph took a step toward her, then another.

Zander got out of the rear door of the SUV and crept

around but kept his distance. He wasn't going to approach—unless he felt as though he had to.

Joseph might be injured, but she had no intention of underestimating him again.

She held up one hand while the other moved close to her gun. "That's close enough."

"Not like I'm in any state to hurt you."

Was she supposed to apologize? "Why did you take that girl?"

He'd mentioned a payday. She could only hope he'd elaborate. When he only stared at her, she figured he wasn't going to give up much.

"What will you do now?" Unless she managed to arrest him—which was entirely possible with Zander's help—he had to have a plan. Given he'd approached her, maybe incarceration *was* the plan.

Joseph sniffed.

"You were paid to target me?" By people who could track her every move. Travers Industries.

He gave her a tiny nod, barely distinguishable.

"Who are they?"

"They never said. I just got handed an envelope, and inside was a cell phone. They told me what to do and paid me upfront in cash." He made a face. "Apparently, we're not done yet."

"Oh, we're done," Hannah said. Whoever it was knew Hannah would be all but incapacitated because Joseph Ricker was out there with an abducted girl.

He sniffed again.

"What did you take?"

"It's for the pain." He looked away.

"Yeah, sure." She said, "If you submit to being arrested, you'll get adequate medical care."

"And thrown in jail."

"You think that isn't exactly what you deserve?" She didn't waste time waiting for an answer.

It wouldn't get her anything to help find Badger and Judah.

Ricker shouldn't be free. He should be in jail, giving justice to the teen who had been abducted and her family.

For years that had been what drove her as a cop. Why did it feel so empty now when Badger was missing? He infuriated her as much as he intrigued her, and she had no idea how to find him.

Joseph shifted. He slid his hand from inside his jacket, around his waist.

Hannah drew her weapon. Then she realized his hand was covered with blood. "You're going into police custody."

Joseph's eyes rolled back in his head, and he collapsed to the ground. His head bounced off the sidewalk.

Hannah winced. "That could've gone worse."

At least she would be able to tell the parents of the teen he'd abducted that he was in jail.

Zander jogged over. "Cops are on their way. Nora called them."

Hannah glanced at the front window of the SUV. The way the light hit the glass, she couldn't see Nora but nodded anyway. Her sister had been here for her without putting her own life in danger.

Zander had his own cuffs, so he secured Joseph's hands.

"Thanks."

"You think we'd let you go it alone?" Zander said. "You're a part of this family, aren't you?"

She nodded, her throat too thick to speak.

"We're going to find them."

"I hope so." But when they did, what then? It might be getting ahead of things, but when Badger and Judah were back with the others, where did that leave them? She knew Badger would feel as though he were being pushed to the outskirts now that she was "family," as Zander had said.

Zander straightened. "We will find them. Don't give up hope."

"How do you do that?"

"Stick around. You'll pick it up."

Hannah figured that was probably true. But still, that meant everything she was had been fundamentally altered. Was that what happened when you had a family? She didn't even know.

A police car turned down the street.

She sighed. There was so much to do, and all of it was the right thing. But what she wanted was to find Badger.

## 24

*You really think you can protect her?*

Now there was a question Badger needed to ponder.

The answer to which would be that he *was* protecting Hannah. Even being here was, in a way, watching out for her.

He might not be able to do it physically, considering they were nowhere near each other. However, that wouldn't stop his teammates from doing the right thing—and it would have nothing to do with Lana paying them. As if they would accept dirty money from her.

Badger blew out a breath. The sensory deprivation of not being able to see, and being restrained, had started to wear on him. He was getting antsy. And if he let that continue, he could easily make a misstep and hurt their chances here.

He was on razor's edge. What he didn't need was Peter Benton viewing Hannah as a pawn in this.

"You think I'd be here if my job was to protect her?" Badger said.

"So you guys are just the grunts?" Peter asked.

Badger glanced in his friend's direction. "Jude, we the grunts?"

"Guess so, mate," Judah said. "What a revelation that is. I'm gobsmacked."

Badger was glad nothing had changed there. They still had their banter, which would be vital in keeping their resolve in this. The fact it'd been insinuated that Judah was anything other than the person Badger knew? That didn't need to factor. Judah was fully aware of how the team reacted to Isaac's betrayal, so he wouldn't keep anything from them.

Except that was what Badger had done by not telling them about his role in Alexis's death. He'd known for a long time that there was a website. As if he couldn't imagine the worst already without it being confirmed that people continued to speculate on his role—and blame him for a mistake he'd made as a child.

Even one that had turned into a tragedy.

Badger wanted to believe he was the kind of person who wouldn't put himself above his friend's kid sister, but he'd been selfish. The entire community had paid the price. And despite how he'd tried, Alexis had been taken and killed.

Right now he had to keep his focus and not wallow.

"I'm blown away by everything happening here." Badger tried to sound disbelieving and not allow the fatigue to seep into his tone. "You're right, dude. It's a revelation."

Even if all they'd learned was that Travers Industries responded like this to a tiny poke into their operation, it at least gave them intel.

"You're giving me no choice," Peter said.

"To escalate this from kidnapping to kidnapping and assault…or are we going straight to murder?" Badger wanted to know what they were facing.

"You think I want the backlash of making you disappear?" Peter asked. "Not only do I have to make sure you're never found, but I also have to contend with your friends coming around and asking too many questions."

"Sounds terrible," Judah said.

Badger was inclined to believe his tone more than his words. "What's the plan, then? Cause my butt is numb, and I have to pee."

The punch came out of nowhere, betrayed only by the slight shuffle of clothing.

Badger's chair tipped, and his shoulder hit the floor. He cried out. With his arm secured behind him, the whole joint bent backward with the force of the weight of his upper body behind it.

"What are you doing?" Judah's yell cut through his own. "That's enough! Let us go, and we won't destroy you!"

Badger had a flash of an idea that involved rubble, followed by sowing salt in their fields. Total destruction.

Instead he heard a roar. Metal screeched. Then movement, a scuffle, and the flap of clothing. The soft thud of a fist hitting solid flesh.

Badger twisted his head to his good shoulder as a commotion erupted all around him. He ignored it as best he could, along with the wrenching pain in the other shoulder and the fact his forearm was smashed between the leg of the chair and the floor.

He winced. Didn't matter.

Badger rubbed at the edge of the blindfold with his shoulder until it came up. He got it off one eye and managed to focus.

Two men swept into the room. Judah was pulled off Peter

and dragged to the door while Peter sat there with his knees up, breathing hard.

After a minute he came over to Badger, lifted him up by Badger's elbow, and tipped the chair back onto its four legs.

"Ouch." Peter hissed. "You think that's dislocated?" He wasn't talking to Badger.

Badger breathed through the pain, mostly just trying not to be sick.

"Let's put it back." The voice belonged to someone he didn't recognize. Hardly surprising given the white-hot pain in his shoulder.

The ties securing his right hand to the chair were cut. It swung limp by his hip. They replaced the blindfold, so his vision was cut off again.

One guy grasped his arm. The other put a knee across his lap. He was tempted to bite whoever it was but didn't know what he would get a mouthful of. Plus, he was interested in not feeling this pain in his shoulder.

The hands tightened. He felt a deep pull and heard the pop for a second before his roar echoed through the whole room, filling it like a sudden rush of water that drowned a ship. And then he surfaced, bobbing for a second before he could take a full breath.

Footsteps echoed, moving away from him.

"Yeesh." Peter tugged the blindfold the rest of the way off.

The sounds in the room echoed in his ears along with each inhale he took. As he blinked, the room came into focus. Warehouse. High ceilings. Some kind of maintenance room in a basement. Likely multiple floors, which meant it would take time and navigation to get out.

"Now you can answer some questions." Peter set a chair in front of Badger and sat.

Badger gritted his teeth. "About what?" He took a few breaths through pursed lips while he tried to push away the pain in his shoulder. It didn't feel as strange as it had before— but the wrenching pain lingered.

"Your friend Isaac." Peter stared at him, saying nothing more.

In the distance he heard more yelling, the sound of Judah fighting for his life. What were they doing to him?

How his friend got out of the chair, Badger couldn't imagine. But now it seemed as though he might be paying for it.

Peter was likely not saying anything, so Badger would get all nervous and off his game.

"If you hurt him…" Badger didn't need to finish. Peter could plainly see the look on his face—the one he wanted the guy to see. So he might believe Badger had succumbed to the fear.

Peter said, "Why don't you worry about yourself instead of worrying about your friend?"

"Doesn't work that way."

"Because there's such loyalty in your team? I guess that's why your friend Isaac is in prison now. Or why *his* organization leader has disavowed any connection to him."

"So?" As if he was going to believe what Lana spread around was actually the truth. Badger had no idea if Isaac was working on her orders or if he'd gone rogue. But it didn't matter because Isaac had nothing to do with him anymore.

"Tell me what he told the two of them."

Badger said nothing. Mostly because he had *zero idea* what Peter was talking about.

"The police detective and Gladstone's daughter. What did Isaac say to them when they went to see him?"

First, he had no idea they'd done that. But Benton didn't need to know that. "None of your business."

He figured they'd been out of contact when they did visit Isaac, and after that, Badger and Judah were captured. Ted would've filled them in but hadn't been able to.

Another roar down the hall echoed back to him.

Threatening this guy if Judah got hurt was redundant. There wasn't much he could do if he couldn't get out of the tie securing his healthy arm to the chair. If he got his legs free, he could kick Peter, maybe tackle him. Hit him with the chair attached to his left hand…and dislocate that shoulder as well.

Badger needed a good distraction, and thinking about Hannah fit the bill. "Why's she in the center of this?" The alternative was that he barfed all over the floor. Both were under consideration at this point. He swallowed. "What's so special about one police detective?"

"You tell me." Peter shrugged.

Badger gritted his teeth. "You're the one trying to kill her. Though, that hasn't gone your way so far since your brother missed. Or was that the plan all along? After all, she's just a pawn in a war, right?" He was guessing at best. But maybe this wasn't about Hannah at all. It could be about Lana and whoever she fought against—with Hannah caught in the middle.

"You're smarter than I gave you credit for."

"Great." Badger sighed. "Good to know there's something I can tell my boss when I get back. Otherwise, this whole trip will have been a waste."

The door flung open.

"Did he come in here?" A younger guy with a flushed face stood in the doorway.

Peter turned. "Who?"

The guy said, "Who do you *think*?"

Judah had escaped.

That was when Badger saw a second man in the shadows. Standing there listening.

"Find him," Peter ordered. "He can't get away."

———

HANNAH STOOD WATCHING while the EMTs loaded a handcuffed Joseph Ricker onto the ambulance. The cops had asked a hundred questions about how both of them ended up here, to which she had no ideas.

The breeze whipped at her hair in a way she was sure snow would fall later. She hugged her coat closer around her and didn't take her eyes off Ricker as they got him settled. The cop stepped into the ambulance.

The EMT moved to shut the door.

She would have no chance of finding out if there was anything he hadn't told her.

Hannah burst forward. "Hold up." She'd decided to climb in, regardless of whether there was room inside or not, and got all the way in Ricker's face. "Tell me where they are."

"What are you talking about?" He grimaced, lines of pain around his face.

"Badger and Judah. They're missing. And whoever hired you for this, they took my friends. Where are they?"

"You think I know?"

"You can find out. Call and get them to tell you." Hannah glanced down at the wound she'd inflicted on him.

He was clearly still feeling the effects. "You think I won't do worse to you next time? You already know what happens."

The cop took a sharp breath. Whatever he thought of her methods, it wasn't like she'd crossed the line into police brutality. Nor did she plan on doing it now. But Joseph didn't need to know there was a limit to what she was prepared to do. A cop was what she'd always been, and whether she changed jobs at some point, in a sense she always would be.

Joseph shifted. "Phone."

The cop had it.

"Take it. Doesn't matter if you have it, or I do. They'll still find me."

She wanted to tell him this was the bed he'd made for himself.

Now he was going to have to lie in it. He could've ditched this phone and run far away where no one would've found him. Instead, he'd done another job that meant confronting her. Almost as though he wanted to be discovered.

The cop started to argue with Joseph. "Your personal belongings—"

Hannah took the cell. "I'll make sure this gets where it needs to be. And I'll have my task force supervisor call you to confirm," she said to the cop. Alanson was never going to cover for her, but what did that matter? She pocketed the phone. "You have their info?"

"I'm sure you can use it." He glanced away, and she got the message. What did he care about her friends?

"If you help me find them, I'll put in a good word."

He huffed a breath. "As if I'm going to believe that."

"Good. Because that was a lie."

After he'd terrorized that teen? She would get what she could from his phone, but Joseph Ricker wasn't ever going to get any favors from her. He'd murdered. Terrorized. He could have killed half of Chevalier, plus her and her abducted namesake.

"Have a good life." *In jail.*

She left those words unspoken and climbed out of the ambulance so they could provide medical care to a guy who didn't deserve it. Who might not have had any personal vendetta against her, but the fact was, Ricker had taken money to target her from people who had probably been the ones to orchestrate his release.

But only time, and an investigation into that, would provide her answers.

And when he showed up to trial, Hannah was going to walk up to the stand and testify as to everything he'd done.

He wouldn't be walking free any time soon.

Zander met her beside the car.

Before he could say anything, she handed over the phone. "Can Ted get something from this?"

"We'll see." He got out his phone and held them side by side as he tapped the screen. "His system reboot is complete."

They got in the car. Nora twisted in her seat while Zander climbed in the front. "You okay, Han?"

She nodded. "Let's see if we can get anything from Ricker's phone, so we can find Badger and Judah."

It was a cop line. Reassuring the victim's family, even though that included her. She didn't want to think about what was happening to Badger and Judah, but she had plenty of ideas given the look on Nora's face.

Hannah squeezed her shoulder. "We are going to find them."

Nora nodded, her expression grim. "But will it be in time?"

Zander glanced over. "Pray, okay? I know you are."

"I am."

He leaned over and kissed his wife. "I know." When he looked back at the phones in each hand, he tapped his screen with his thumb. "Hey."

"I'm in the phone. There's not much. It's only been used recently." Ted's voice was tinny, and he sounded irritated. "The number that contacted him isn't registered either, and there's no traceable GPS location, so the SIM card must have been removed."

Nora sucked in a shuddering breath.

Hannah squeezed her sister's shoulder again.

"Tell me if you get anything else," Zander said. "We're going to reconvene with Andre and Lucia."

"Copy that." The line went dead.

While he drove, Hannah said, "Do Andre and Lucia have anything?"

Zander tipped his head to the side, then brought it back straight. "Couple of witnesses, make and model of the car. They're running down the lead with local cops. Finding out if they've had reports of similar vehicles related to suspicious activity."

Hannah blew out a breath. Legwork could be frustrating, as often it took a long time to get a result. But when that result came? The satisfaction was a serious burst to professionalism. It was how police work got done.

Every door knocked on. Every witness spoken to. Every lead that was followed up on. It was the way evidence got collected, and cases were made.

This time Zander was the one who asked, "You good, Hannah?"

"I'm good. Thanks, guys."

Despite her words, Hannah's instincts screamed that Badger was hurt and there would be nothing she could do to save him. Everything in her wanted to give up hope, which meant falling into the trap of fear.

As much as she wanted to hope, Hannah's fears roared strongly inside her mind and heart.

*Badger.*

She couldn't help thinking this was all her fault because he'd been drawn into the threat against her, along with Judah. Both were taken by whoever wanted to target her—the person who'd paid Ricker to torment her.

All because Lana was her mother.

It had to be because of her. Hannah hadn't done anything but be a cop, and that didn't merit this kind of backlash. If it did, Ricker would've acted on his own instead of coming after her because he'd been offered an incentive.

It was her fault.

Hannah sighed. "I don't like clichés." Did anyone?

Zander said, "This isn't your fault."

"Of course it is. They're only in this because of me. Because I was the target." Tears blurred Hannah's vision. "If they die, it'll be on me."

Zander's phone rang. Nora answered and held it up in front of him. "O'Connell."

"Z."

"Judah?" Zander said. "Talk to me."

An audible breath crackled across the phone speaker. "Trace the call. Z—" A grunt filled the air.

Nora had her phone. "I'm calling Ted. We're going to come and get you, Jude."

"Okay," he whispered. "Trace the call."

"We are." Zander gripped the steering wheel, a contorted

look of pure fear on his face. Something Hannah had never seen except in the eyes of victims she had rescued—like the teen in that car, so sure she wasn't going to make it.

A tear rolled down her face. *God, help us.*

"Ted got a location." Nora sounded so sure.

Hannah swiped the moisture from her cheeks.

"We're coming, Jude," Zander said. "Just hang on."

"I have to go now."

"Jude—"

He didn't answer Zander's call. The line went dead, and Nora gasped. "I have maps. It says it'll take—"

"Just put it up. I don't care if half the police force is trying to give us a speeding ticket by the time we get there. That just means more help to get them back."

It took far longer than Hannah wanted to wait. Both cars pulled up at an abandoned building. Then they were putting on vests, and both Andre and Lucia entered with them. Nora stayed in the car, out of sight and safe, relaying information with Ted so she could inform them.

Hannah headed for the front door before Zander even finished explaining the ins and outs. She kicked the door in.

Didn't matter what was in here. She was getting both of them back.

No one should die because of her.

The building was an old school, the building condemned according to the sign on the door. Not yet torn down. Didn't matter.

What mattered was any resistance they might encounter on the way in.

She spotted a guy in the hall seconds later. He fired a shot in her direction, then ducked out of sight. She didn't care that it was an ambush. Hannah raced for the guy.

But the hallway was empty.

She kicked in every door. No Judah. No Badger.

Down a level. More kicking. Clearing rooms, pushing aside emotion, and trying to be methodical.

Until she found him.

## 25

Badger had one useless arm. The other was tied to a chair. Peter Benton and the shadow in the corner had retreated to join the search for Judah. He'd been alone—he didn't know how long—when the door flung open, and a figure stood there.

He blinked to clear his vision. "Hannah." The word was barely a croak from his mouth.

Hannah looked back over her shoulder. "He's in here!" She rushed to him, gun out of the way as she crouched. She reached for a knife that wasn't in her boot. "I need something to cut him loose."

Zander came in. "Bro." He blew out a breath the way he did when he was about to lose it.

Badger hadn't seen him do that but a handful of times in all the years they'd known each other.

"You're good." Zander produced a multitool and cut Badger's hand loose. "You're good. We've got you."

Badger didn't want to break down, but he could feel the lump rise in his throat. "Judah?"

"We don't know." Zander keyed his radio. "Andre, you got Jude?" He paused a second. "Good. But we need Windermere."

Badger looked at Hannah. She didn't meet his gaze, but he saw her swipe tears from her face. She lifted the arm that had been tied to the chair and got under it. She started to tug him to his feet. "Come on. Let's get out of here."

"Let me do that." Zander reached for him.

Badger found his feet. When they were sure he wasn't about to fall, Hannah moved out from under his arm, and Zander took her place.

Badger shook his head. "I can do it."

Zander started, carrying Badger for the most part. Whether he wanted that or not.

"I can walk."

Hannah hurried alongside them. Gun poised, ready to defend them with her skills—and her life. She looked like she wanted to be where Zander was, under his injured shoulder, but said nothing.

"Let us take care of you." Zander shook his head. "We want to help you."

Only because he was helpless and couldn't do it himself. Badger had worked so hard to get back on active duty, a full-fledged team member again. Now he would be down until his shoulder recovered. Which meant until he was healed, he would be useless again. Nothing but dead weight to the team. "Where is Judah?"

"Why don't you worry about yourself?" Zander didn't even sound winded hauling Badger's weight across the room. So much larger than life that it was like he could carry anything.

Meanwhile, Badger could do nothing for himself. "I'm sorry. I didn't tell them anything."

He hated that Hannah was here to see this. She knew about Alexis, and now she was seeing him wounded and useless. Maybe it was for the better that she'd never called or texted back after he'd inhaled that chemical in Vegas. After all, she'd never have shown back up in his life if she had. Talk about hopeless.

Badger sniffed and swallowed against the lump in his throat. "I don't know where they took Judah."

He hadn't been able to do anything to stop his friend from being taken. Now Judah could be dead, and there was no way to stop it. Or he'd been hurt. Or he was…who knew where? He hadn't fought his way back to Badger to help him get out as well.

Where was he?

All the awful scenarios rolled through his mind like a mental replay of the worst a human could do to another human. And it might be happening to Judah right now, at a time when he was powerless.

"Give me a gun," Badger said.

Zander stopped in the hall. He leaned Badger against the wall. "You good to stand?"

Badger nodded. "I need a gun."

"We have no spares. And we cleared the building."

"Where's Peter?" If he was still here, someone could get hurt. Hannah could get hurt. Badger was supposed to be the one protecting her. And he was supposed to leave her undefended? "Benton wasn't here. We killed a couple of guys. They seemed low level."

Hannah watched the hall, prepared for whatever came. Guarding her the way he should be guarding her.

*You love her.*

And why wouldn't he? She was everything he wanted in a woman, but she didn't feel the same. Or she wouldn't, after this.

What were they standing around for—

Zander got in his face. "Look at me."

"I am."

"No. I mean, *look at me.*" Zander barely waited a beat before he said, "How long have we been friends?"

Badger swallowed.

"You don't know me?"

"I do." What was this about?

"So you don't know that I don't care if you're on point taking down the worst person we've ever faced or laid up in bed on pain meds texting everyone in the middle of a mission?"

Out of the corner of his eye, he saw Hannah glance over. Neither of them explained that to her. He probably would later.

Zander said, "You think you're only here for the job you do?"

Badger didn't answer.

"So you think we don't care about you or consider you a friend?"

"It's not—"

"Pretty clear to me." Zander folded his arms, almost nose to nose with Badger. "You think if you can't fight, you're worthless?"

Badger pressed his lips together.

"So who you are means nothing to me? Because that's what you're saying here."

"Z—"

"No. You listen to me now." Zander took a breath and continued, "If you're not a soldier, what are you? Because one day you won't be able to fight. Or you'll hit a point in your life it's not worth the risk, and you've got a different focus. Like Eas, spending time with Karina and Aria. He could be here, but he made a choice to be with his family right now. Outside this team, what do you have?"

Badger wanted to tell him that he'd *tried* to have Hannah in his life, but he'd all but been shot down. He glanced over, but she didn't see it. She watched the hall instead.

Zander got his attention again. "I know," he said, a knowing look on his face. "I know what you have. But you think what you have is nothing. So what do we do about that?"

His boss didn't give him time to answer.

"You're off the team until I say otherwise."

Badger sucked in a breath so hard he coughed it out.

Hannah swung around. Before either of them could say anything, Andre and Lucia jogged around the corner.

"Clear," Andre called down the hallway.

Badger didn't take his focus from Zander, but instead of saying more, Zander turned to Andre. Of course. As his number two guy, it made sense for the two of them to figure out what the plan was.

Badger just wanted to get out of there.

He pushed off the wall and passed Hannah. She reached for him, but he sidestepped and kept going. He couldn't face her when he was like this—injured beyond where he could put any kind of filter on his words or his face. And not just that, but he felt like he'd been broken open to the air like a raw wound he couldn't begin to know how to treat.

Badger walked far enough he was out of earshot.

What was the point in hearing them talk about him? They needed to find Judah.

Badger turned. "Where is he?"

They knew who he was talking about. Hannah and Lucia, both with sad expressions, quit their conversation and turned to him. Zander and Andre looked over.

Andre said, "We cleared the whole place. Found the phone Judah used, but no sign of him."

The energy Badger had left drained out of him. He sagged against the wall, his knees bent, and slid to the floor. Head bowed. All he could hear was Peter Benton's voice in his head while the shadowed man crept around the edges of his consciousness.

Zander crouched in front of him. "Let's get you out of here, okay?"

"Where's Judah?"

"We don't know, B." Zander didn't wait for him to agree. He simply hauled Badger to his feet. "Doctor Windermere is waiting for you. We'll get this figured out."

Zander hauled even more of Badger's weight than previously. As they exited the building, he felt as though he was drifting in and out of consciousness.

Nora helped Zander get him to the car. Badger said nothing. He managed to get in the back seat and lay down. Then his head was lifted, and his cheek hit a pair of jeans. Warm fingers brushed the hair from his cheek. Badger turned his head to see Hannah above him. Those tears in her eyes.

She ran her fingers through the tangles in his hair. It still felt nice.

Badger bent his elbow enough to lay his good hand on her upper arm. He couldn't have said why he did it, but some things didn't need to be overthought.

300 | LISA PHILLIPS

---

AFTER MOUTHING those three tiny but monumental words, Badger passed out. He didn't regain consciousness before Zander and Andre hauled him into the house, and Dr. Windermere closed the bedroom door.

"Come on." Nora took Hannah's hand.

Hannah needed an anchor, so she let her sister lead her to another room with an attached little bathroom. She wanted a shower but had no idea where to find a set of clean clothes.

Hannah sank onto the edge of the bed and slumped. Lucia came in and leaned against the wall, looking like she had something on her mind. Maybe it was a cop-to-cop thing, but Hannah could just tell there were questions.

"You look like you're about ready to drop." Nora sat on the bench in front of the mirrored dresser.

She didn't want to talk about that or anything Badger had said in the car. But Nora and Zander had whispered in the front seats on the way here. "Is there any update on Judah?"

Lucia shook her head. "He was there. We know that. Badger told us they took him out, and he was pretty sure Judah managed to escape. But Badger never saw him, and after Peter Benton left, no one came in until you kicked the door down."

"Where could he be?" Nora's eyes filled with tears.

Hannah didn't think she even had the strength to cry. She was so relieved Badger was all right, but knowing Judah was still out there put a damper on all of it. "Did they recapture him after he made that call?"

Lucia shrugged. "There was no security system to look at.

Nothing on the phone we found, or on the two guys we killed. We called local police about them, by the way, and left an anonymous tip."

"What about the ammo we shot them with?" The gun Zander had given her had to be registered to someone.

"It'll trace back to the company, Chevalier Holdings. We'll get a call and have to go sit down. Tell them what happened," Lucia said. "But that doesn't take precedent on looking for Judah."

"How can we find out if they have him?" Nora glanced between them.

"I've been thinking about that," Lucia said. "I think we should be able to find Benton since we did it once already. If he has Judah, we'll know."

Hannah blew out a breath. "Have you called his sister?"

"I'm going to do that next," Nora said. "I just wanted to make sure mine was all right."

Hannah smiled as much as she could.

"Boy, that's the saddest thing I've ever seen." Nora's lips curled up at the edges. "I'm pregnant."

Both of them moved from their spots. Nora got up. They hugged as a trio, a chorus of congratulations until Nora brushed away happy tears. "I haven't told Zander yet. I only figured it out a day or two ago. Isn't it too soon?"

Hannah shrugged. "You've been married a couple of months now, right?"

Nora nodded. "I wanted you to be there. But it was so early, and I didn't know how to ask."

"I would have come, but you're right. We still don't know each other all that well."

"We will, though. Won't we?"

Hannah said, "Of course. And this little one will be my

niece or nephew, right?" When Nora nodded, she said, "So we'll have plenty of time. I'll get vacation days and come see you."

But would that be enough?

As Nora hugged her again, Hannah wondered if work would even feel the same when she returned to her precinct. She felt like a completely different person, and not just because she'd been working undercover in the medical clinic.

She should call Alanson and get an update on that case. See whether they'd rounded up the cartel or not.

Then there was Badger and what he'd said. "He told me he loves me."

Nora blinked.

Lucia turned. "Badger?"

Hannah nodded and felt the heat rise in her cheeks. "In the car, he mouthed it right before he passed out." She retreated a couple of steps back to the edge of the bed, where she waved her hands. "He was out of it, in pain and delirious. Who knows what he's been through? I doubt it meant anything. He was probably just glad he'd been rescued and worried about Judah."

"I'm going to get on that right now," Lucia said. "After you tell me if you're going to tell him you love him as well, like maybe as soon as he wakes up."

Hannah shook her head, mouth open. She closed it. What was she supposed to say? *I love you, too.* She'd never said those words in her life. Not to anyone, not even her parents. They weren't the kind who spoke about emotion like that. She'd never heard them tell each other.

"Because you do, right?"

Hannah glanced between Lucia and Nora.

Lucia glanced at Nora. "She totally does."

Hannah gaped. "I'm not..." She couldn't even say the words to deny it. "I don't..."

"What?" Lucia flipped into interrogation mode. Hannah saw the change come over her.

She was unable to fight it. "I don't know how to do that."

"It's easy. You just say it." Nora gave her a soft smile. "Now look at me? I'm married and pregnant."

"Easy." Hannah didn't even know what to say. "Sure."

Lucia grinned. "It's about communication."

"I don't know how to do that either!" Hannah was about to run out the door. Only the fact Lucia blocked the way kept her in her seat.

Lucia rolled her eyes. "Girl, no one knows how to do that. We figure it out as we go along."

Nora said, "Hannah, have you ever been in a relationship before?"

Hannah worked her mouth back and forth.

Lucia glanced at Nora. "My guess? That'd be a no."

"Sustained," Nora replied.

The two shared a smile.

Hannah said, "Objection." She'd never admitted it aloud. It might be accurate, but was that the point? They didn't know that she was utterly defunct in the romance department. She had no idea what to do with a crush...or attraction. Dates were only awkward disasters.

"Denied." Nora looked at Lucia. "My guess? She likes him more than he likes her, and when he made it plain, she freaked and ran away to an undercover mission."

Hannah started to object.

Lucia cut her off. "Not just that, but all the Lana stuff"—she glanced at Hannah—"I'm sure suddenly finding out you have a mom who is some kind of international…whatever she is? That must freak you out."

"And me." Nora nodded.

Hannah lifted her hands. "Nora, you're like the *least* of my problems right now." She realized what she'd said and tried to walk it back.

Nora just grinned. "That's a relief."

Lucia said, "Just tell him."

Sure. As if she should go into his room and say the words aloud? That was crazy.

"She's right," Nora said. "Look at me? My life was basically a shell. Now I've got a family that loves me, and Zander and I are having a child. We both want this." She set a hand low on her stomach. "There's no point waiting. Life is far too short."

"And it's definitely too short not to tell him how you feel."

Hannah settled for glaring at Lucia. She wasn't her sister, and as a former fed, she could handle it. Which Hannah knew was true when Lucia grinned.

"I speak the truth."

Nora nodded. "She's right."

"Can we find Judah before—"

Both of them said, "No."

Hannah flopped back on the bed and covered her face with her hands. She would much rather be doing police work or helping Chevalier find their teammate than tell Badger how she felt. She would also rather fall into a volcano, but that wasn't the point.

"I'll go round up Andre so we can get out and find Judah."

"Thank you," Nora's voice was soft.

"My pleasure." Lucia shut the door behind her.

Nora came over and sat beside Hannah on the bed. "I understand. Believe me, I understand better than you ever imagine."

Hannah blew out a breath. "I should do it now before I lose my nerve."

"That's the spirit." Nora grinned.

Hannah gave her sister a quick hug and headed for the door. Lucia stood in the hall, facing the open door to Badger's room.

Lucia put her hands on her hips. "Badger did *what?*"

Andre stepped out of the room. "He had Windermere check him over, took the sling for his arm, and they left."

Hannah must have made a noise because both turned to her.

Andre winced. "Hannah—"

"Don't." She lifted a hand, the pain in her chest like the slice of a knife. The same wound she'd given Joseph Ricker. "Did he say where he was going?"

Andre shook his head. "I'm sorry. He's just gone."

## 26

D r. Windermere drove the car all the way to the prison where Isaac was being held. Badger woke up as the car slowed to a stop and the doctor parked.

Windermere turned to him. "Are you sure you want to do this?"

"Given how much red tape there was just trying to get in there, I'm not going to walk away now." Badger's voice was groggy. His arm was in a sling, and thanks to what the doc had given him, his head no longer pounded. "Especially if it means we find Judah."

He stared at the facility, hardly able to imagine what life was like in a place like that. But Isaac had essentially walked into it under his own volition. His trial wasn't likely to go well.

Badger couldn't help wondering if the resulting charges had anything to do with why he'd turned himself in.

"I'll be here," the doc said.

"Thanks."

"How is your vision?"

"Seems fine," Badger said.

"Pay attention, just in case. Let me know if there are any issues."

Badger nodded. He half expected Windermere to offer to go inside with him, but only Badger had been given permission to go in. Windermere had nothing to do with this, and that was how he kept safe even in his association with the team. Zander called it "Operational Security," and Windermere had never complained.

Even sitting outside a federal prison, the idea that Badger might expose the guy to a dangerous situation didn't make him feel any better than his physical state.

"I won't be long."

Windermere pulled out his phone. "No worries. I have a few calls to make."

Probably to his lady friend, but Badger wasn't going to say anything. He headed inside and worked his way through all the doors and security check-ins until he was finally ushered to a room. Long minutes later, Isaac was walked in.

The first thing Badger heard was the jingle of chains.

Isaac didn't move much more than an awkward shuffle, though it was down to his physical state and not necessarily because he was restrained. Badger saw the second Isaac realized it was him and the resulting surprise.

His friend sat on the opposite side of the table. "Come to chew me out because I talked to my sisters?"

"I'm surprised you're finally admitting it out loud."

"Why would I not? They're the only good thing in my life," Isaac said. "Somehow I haven't managed to ruin it yet."

"There's still time."

Isaac's lips curled up.

"Who caught you by surprise?"

Isaac said nothing. He looked like he'd been seriously beaten. Maybe he'd let it happen because he believed he deserved it.

"I didn't think I should be part of the team," Badger said. "I figured now that Nora's sister showed up, I'd get ditched because me being on the team with Hannah around would be too awkward for everyone." And now he'd gone and said he loved her. At least, he was pretty sure he had.

Isaac frowned. "You're an idiot."

Badger's lips curled. "Look who's talking."

Isaac barked a rusty sounding laugh but quickly groaned. "You okay?"

Isaac shrugged one shoulder.

Badger continued, "Why is Hannah a target? Just because she's Lana's daughter?"

That would mean Nora was a target also, but Lana hadn't said anything about Zander's wife being in danger. So either Lana thought she didn't need to because Zander wouldn't let anything happen to her—and the man would take a bullet for her even on their worst day. Or it meant that Hannah had been singled out.

Before Isaac answered, Badger said, "Are you in here to be out of the way?"

"You think I'd leave my sisters exposed like that?"

"I don't know what to think." Badger shrugged. "That's the problem here."

Hurt flashed on Isaac's face.

"You could've told us at any time. You chose to keep us in the dark so that we were completely blindsided."

"I wanted you guys to know the real me. Not all the

baggage that comes with it." Isaac's expression hardened. "Which I'm sure you know nothing about."

"What's that supposed to mean?"

"Hiding the truth so they'd see you for who you really are, and maybe if you can convince them well enough, they'll forgive you for lying."

"That's not what I was doing." It wasn't far removed. But Badger didn't actually believe the man he'd been in the army and with Chevalier was the real him. Maybe the kid who did the selfish thing and cost a little girl her life was the truth. Isaac didn't think so? "Don't get off topic. Answer the question about Hannah."

Isaac let out a long breath. "That's why you came here?"

"You're the only one who is going to give me a straight answer." Badger was pretty sure Isaac had nothing to lose. "And I need to know, or I can't do my job. How do I keep her safe?"

"Is she alive?"

Did he think something had happened? "Yes. She's fine." At least as far as he knew.

Isaac slumped a little and blew out a breath. "Then keep doing exactly what you're doing."

"Judah is gone." Badger motioned to the arm he had against his body. The guards had kept the sling, so he simply hugged it. "Travers Industries took both of us, but when Chevalier came to find us they only found me."

"He'll show up." Isaac nodded, but the look on his face said maybe he was trying to convince himself.

"What don't I know about Judah? And what does it have to do with Hannah and Travers Industries?" As far as Badger knew, she had no connection to that company. "Or is it Lana that links them?" Although, what Judah had to do with Lana was anyone's guess. Badger didn't think there was a connection.

Was the Brit just another innocent caught in this?

If something was going on with Judah that he hadn't told the team, Badger wasn't going to tell Andre or Zander. Not if he could help it. He might need to know—for the sake of the team—but that didn't mean everyone had to learn yet another team member had betrayed them.

"Don't worry about Judah," Isaac said. "He's as solid as they come, and if something happened to him, then he'll take care of himself."

Badger stared. "You think we won't turn over every rock we find trying to look for him? Andre and Lucia are doing that right now."

"But you didn't do that with me," Isaac said. "Because I didn't deserve it."

"You walked of your own volition," Badger said. "You think we wouldn't have fought for you? But you didn't think you deserved that. Who knows what happened to Judah?"

Isaac shook his head and looked away.

"We all know you believed you had no choice."

"But you don't agree?"

"We can forgive, even if we don't understand it." Badger wanted to forgive his friend. "That's how this group works."

He wanted to believe they would offer that to him as well. Zander had seemed furious when they rescued Badger, all because Badger didn't want to appear weak. Like his boss didn't even understand he needed to be capable—for them all to see him as an equal. As if there was no difference whether he was laid up and out of commission or side by side with his weapon.

Badger scrubbed his good hand over his face.

"Yeah." Isaac huffed. "I'm really feeling the love."

He stared at his friend. Maybe he should say "former friend," like everyone else. "Your sisters came to see you, didn't they?"

Isaac conceded the point, pressing his lips together.

"Tell me what's going on."

Isaac sighed. "She's caught in the middle. Does it matter why they're fighting? All you need to do is keep her safe."

"I'm really getting sick of you giving partial answers and being all need-to-know. But I guess that's how it works with the CIA. If you were ever one of them."

"Instead of blindly following orders? I'd rather think for myself."

"Yeah, really seems like you're free to do that." Badger paused so that could sink in. "I'm not interested in a bandage. I want the war stopped. *That's* what we did in the army."

Isaac stared at him. Finally he said, "My mother isn't wrong. He can't be allowed to take over the company."

*Travers Industries.* Badger thought of the man in a shadow in the corner.

"I told them to look into the company," Isaac said.

"All that did is get us more on their radar. Now Judah is gone, and Ted had to do a whole system reboot." Badger figured his friend knew that would happen.

"That's a good thing." Isaac lifted his chin. "They need to know they can't go on unchecked. If everyone goes after them, eventually they'll fall."

"So now we're on Lana's side?" Badger didn't like the sound of that. "Like the enemy of my enemy is my friend? That kind of thing?"

"If you want to finish this, you might have to be."

IT FELT like days before Badger came back, even though it was only hours. Hannah heard the car outside. Instead of being there waiting when he came in, she opted to go and make more tea. Nora's blend she'd brought wasn't bad, though it didn't hold a candle to precinct coffee that was so thick you could stand a spoon up in it.

There was so much to say, but where did she even start?

She and Nora, along with Zander, had attempted to figure all of this out while Andre and Lucia hunted Peter Benton in the hopes of finding Judah.

Surely if the Brit was out there in the world somewhere, he'd find a phone and call in. The fact he hadn't meant he had to be somewhere he wasn't able to call for help. So it was up to the team to find him.

Zander had assured him they would.

She heard the front door close. Hannah stirred far too much sugar into the mug, and then Badger was beside her.

"Hey."

The softness of his voice drew her. She turned and didn't manage to hide the wince.

"Yeah. I look pretty awesome."

She lifted her tea. "Let's sit down. But...do you want something?" She waved her free hand toward the fridge.

He shook his head. "I'm good."

She couldn't help thinking about what he'd said to her. Did he even remember?

"What is it?" he asked.

"Can we...um...chat? Maybe later on?" Zander wanted them to touch base now, given Badger had been with Isaac.

He nodded, reached out with his free hand, and glanced

his fingers across her elbow. "I'd like that." But there was a guarded look on his face. Maybe he thought she was going to let him down easy.

"It's nothing bad. We just need to focus on Judah right now."

"Sounds good."

He headed to the living room first, and she followed.

Nora looked a little green. She'd told Zander breakfast didn't sit well in her stomach, pushing off his concern for the same reason Hannah had with Badger.

Judah.

Hannah sat and held her tea close to her mouth. But she didn't take a sip. "You should tell him."

Nora glared at her, but there was no threat in it. "I'm going to." She spoke through gritted teeth.

"I mean right now."

Zander was sat beside her. He shifted in his seat and turned to his wife. "Is this about you being pregnant?"

Nora gasped so fast she had to cough. "You *know*? It's been two days!" Before he could answer, she said, "I haven't been keeping it from you, I just only found out the other day, and there's so much—"

He tugged her to his side. "Yeah, I know. We're focused. But I want you going back to Last Chance with the doc."

Hannah looked around for the distinguished medical professional they seemed to have an agreement with. All those frequent flyer miles would get old fast, surely. Though she worked the same neighborhoods year in and year out, maybe a life where she traveled more would be interesting.

Like if she became part of Chevalier the way Lucia had. Though, that was because Andre and Lucia were married.

Who knew what would happen with her and Badger?

"I love you." Nora's face softened.

Her husband touched his lips to hers.

Hannah focused on her tea and heard Badger chuckle.

"Careful," the doctor said. "You'll be hurting later if you move around so much."

Badger shook his head. "I feel like I've slept more in the last few months than I have my entire life. I thought it was supposed to be healing?"

"I wouldn't know," Hannah said. "I just ignore it and go back to work."

He grinned, motioning between them with his index finger. "You see. That's why this works." He immediately blushed.

So he didn't think he'd overstepped, she said, "I agree. It does."

The soft look he gave her was one of the nicest she'd ever seen. There wasn't a lot of softness in police work. Generally she met people on the worst day of their lives. She never got to see them after the fact, when they were relaxed and recovering in a safe place.

"Well, now we've got that settled"—Zander slapped both hands on his thighs—"Doc?"

"I'll escort Nora home."

"Andre and Lucia are following Benton. If he's got Judah or knows where he's being held, we'll find it."

Hannah studied the team leader's face to see if he believed what he said. She was convinced enough. "And if they don't have him, but someone else does?"

"No one can be hidden forever." Zander pinned her with his certainty. "We'll find him."

She nodded.

"Badge?"

He lifted his chin. "Isaac mentioned Travers Industries to you and Nora when you saw him?"

Hannah glanced at Badger and nodded.

"Same with me. And he said this was all so 'he didn't take over the company.'"

"Who?" Nora asked.

Badger shrugged his good shoulder. He looked like he needed a full hot breakfast and another few months of the most sleep of his life. But she also knew he was as determined to find his friend as Zander. "That's the question."

"You guys ran into them before, right?" Hannah asked.

Zander nodded.

"I think Travers is responsible for the death of Stuart Edwards." Badger shifted in his chair. "And if they also killed your dad, Nora, I wouldn't be surprised."

Nora nodded. "It would be good to get an answer on that."

"I can take a look at the case files if Ted can get them for me," Hannah said. "But I don't want it to take away from finding Judah."

"Thank you, Hannah." Zander nodded. "We'd appreciate your input on that."

"I was on the periphery of the Edwards investigation, as you know." She could remember seeing Nora in a car at the scene, though at the time she hadn't believed Gladstone's daughter could actually be her sister. And by the time she got back from chasing after an active shooter, Nora was gone. "But I don't think it's been closed yet. I'll see what they have on both."

"What do we do about Travers?" Nora asked.

Zander bit back what he was going to say. Hannah winced. Probably that there was no "we" when she was in the line of fire. Nora was going home, and considering she was protecting a life inside of her, that was a good idea.

Zander said, "I'll check with Ted. See what he has." He looked at Badger. "Who do you think Isaac was talking about, taking over the company?"

"So far it seems like all this has been linked. Like, from the beginning." Badger thought over his words. "Maybe, if that's the case, we should look at former president Raleigh." He shrugged.

"I was thinking the same." Zander tapped his cell phone on his leg. "He was targeted by Patchuli. Gladstone didn't bother trying to save him, which means he wanted the guy dead. Same with Lana. Could be part of this."

"The former president?" Hannah glanced around. Were they actually serious?

Zander said, "He went to work for Travers Industries a few weeks ago."

"Wasn't his wife killed?"

"That might make him more of a suspect," Badger said. "If he's looking for revenge."

She blew out a breath. This might well be out of her league. They were talking about a national investigation with far-reaching consequences. Going up against a multinational tech corporation.

Whatever that had to do with her, Hannah had no idea.

"I'll set a meeting with Jerry Travers," Zander said. They all reacted. He lifted both hands. "I'll wear a suit and approach him about a business venture. See what he says. That's all."

"Someone should go with you."

"Maybe Ted can get more from the inside. If they even let us in." Zander shrugged. "Maybe they won't."

There were other maybes, most of which involved them being buried where no one would find them. Hannah didn't say them out loud, though it was clear Nora had an idea.

Zander hugged his wife to his side again. "I'll be careful. I promise."

"I'm planning on telling Toni we *are* going to find her brother." Nora lifted her chin. "Make sure that's not a lie."

"I'm guessing the second they hear, she and Jeff will be on a plane," Badger said.

"The jet can bring them back." Zander nodded as though it was a done deal.

As if things were so easy. Though, maybe in freelance work it was.

Hannah set her cup down and stood. She had no idea where to go.

Before she could figure it out, the door flung open, and a bunch of guys raced in. Badger shot up, only to get cold-cocked. The room erupted in noise, shouting, and the ratchet of weapons.

Nora and Zander were on their feet, intruder guns pointed at them. Hannah stepped in front in a defensive position and got grabbed. Her arm wrenched back so hard it took the breath out of her.

Windermere lifted both hands.

The guy who had her stared down at Hannah with eyes so dark they looked black. Or that was simply his soul peeking through. No face masks. "*Vamanos.*"

"Hey!" Zander started to object.

"No!" Hannah didn't need him getting hurt. Or Nora, or any of them. They would be shot and killed, no doubt.

The men held their guns up. Four of them, flanking the door.

Hannah was dragged out.

## 27

B adger gasped as he awoke. He realized two things at once. He was in a fast-moving car, and his shoulder hurt like it had when Benton had put it back in place. He moaned aloud.

"Yeah, sorry about that."

Badger turned his head. "Z?" He was strapped in the passenger seat, his boss driving.

Zander changed lanes, moving fast. "I'll give you a second, then I'll explain."

"I'm good," Badger said. "Talk." He shifted on the seat and tried to get his bearings.

Zander looked at his watch. "Eight minutes ago, five guys I'm pretty sure are the cartel Hannah's undercover crew tangled with busted into the house and dragged her out."

"Where are they?" It had to be a vehicle up ahead if Zander was driving this fast. Like he was trying to catch up.

"White van."

Badger tried to pick it out of traffic in front of them, but his head pounded so hard his vision blurred. He couldn't make out anything.

Badger touched his forehead. He didn't even know what happened to her because he'd been out. "Nora?"

"She's good." Zander looked at his phone. "Hopefully soon I'll get a text to say she and Windermere are packed up and headed to the airport."

"She's really pregnant?" There hadn't even been time to congratulate his friend. They needed to have a party and celebrate…when everyone was back together.

Zander nodded.

"Congratulations."

"Thanks." Zander glanced over the edge of a smile on his face.

"So you hauled out my unconscious self and took off after them?"

"Would you have preferred to wake up back at the house with me and the car gone and no way to find her?"

"No."

Zander shrugged one shoulder.

"Thanks, Bro."

"Thank me when we get her back." Zander's gaze flashed with anger. "And Judah."

The knot in Badger's stomach wouldn't leave. But knowing the team was going to pull together and fight to get their friends back meant a lot.

"Plus, if the back of your head hurts, it's probably because I *might* have hit the door frame."

Badger wanted to smile. "What about Andre and Lucia?"

"On the Peter Benton thing. So we'll know if Travers is involved."

"But it was the cartel?"

"Yeah," Zander said through gritted teeth. "So how did they find us?"

Badger blew out a breath. That was a really great question.

Zander said, "Call Ted."

Badger dialed Zander's phone and put it on speaker.

The kid picked up, breathless. "...figure this out."

"What?" Badger asked.

"I'm back up and running. Kind of skeleton crew for a while, but Nora already called me. She gave me enough description that I dug into the task force files on Hannah's laptop that Judah grabbed from the hotel. From there, I back-traced their servers for a real-time update." That was the first night he'd landed on the East Coast. Felt like weeks ago.

"So you broke in?"

Ted made a high-pitched noise. "Mmm, depends on how you think about it."

"One of these days you're going to get arrested for hacking federal databases," Badger said. "You need to be careful."

"Um..."

Zander glanced at Badger. "He's good."

"Just like that?" He stared at his boss.

"Yes," Zander said. "And let's leave it there."

Ted echoed the sentiment. "It's need-to-know."

"You guys are as bad as Isaac with that stuff."

Zander shrugged a shoulder. "I'll give you the gist at our next meeting."

"Our next *meeting* is gonna be a pregnancy celebration party for you and Nora. So we'd better get Hannah and Judah back, or that's not gonna happen."

"Baby shower." Zander nodded. "Later. When we know for sure everything is good."

Badger blew out a breath.

The phone buzzed.

"That's a folder of photos," Ted said. "Tell me if it's the guys who took Hannah."

Badger swiped to open. Zander took the phone at the next light and scrolled through. Badger hadn't seen them for more than the seconds it took to break in and slam him in the head. He should've pulled a gun out. Even if he hadn't had one on him. But who wanted them shooting up the room with a pregnant woman and two-thirds of the people he cared about in the world? Instead, he'd been rendered useless.

But he'd tried.

The fact he was faced with an impossible situation at the moment wasn't lost on him. Nor was the fact that he couldn't control everything. He'd never have been able to prevent Hannah from being taken without a whole lot of bloodshed. And he'd have carried the guilt of that.

Badger was finding a balance between what he could do and the fact in so many ways, he was as powerless as a person with no skills in the same situation. His hands had been tied. But at least he could say he'd tried.

"It's them." Zander handed the phone back.

"I can call Alanson from the task force," Ted suggested. "Let him know where you guys are. Get you some backup."

"I'll call him. Text me the number." Badger shifted and dug out his phone. Thankfully he'd had it in his pocket since the prison, or he'd be without that safeguard. He only wanted to have it on him if Judah called his number before anyone else—which could happen. That and the fact Ted could find them anywhere were the only reasons he even carried a phone.

"Copy that."

"Anything from Andre and Lucia?" Zander asked. "Or on Travers?"

"They've located and are following Peter Benton," Ted replied. "Apparently there's been an uptick in activity, but since I can't try and hack Benton again without more problems they're reduced to sitting on him until he gets where he's going."

"Judah better be there." Badger gritted his teeth.

"Maybe it's better if he isn't," Zander said.

Despite what he'd originally thought, Badger wanted to tell him what had been insinuated about Judah. "Is there something I need to know?"

"He isn't going to betray us."

Zander sounded so sure. Badger didn't know if he was as confident. "We'd have said that about Isaac a few months ago."

A muscle in Zander's jaw flexed.

Ted said, "I'll keep you posted."

Badger hung up the call and used his own phone to get Hannah's task force boss on the line.

"Alanson," came the reply.

"Hannah was taken by the cartel."

"Ryder...something. Hawaiian, wasn't it?"

"Right." Badger didn't waste time saying his given name. It was already on one report this guy had on his desk. "Like I said, the cartel has Hannah. We're following their vehicle, but it's too far for me to give you a license plate."

"You saw them take her?"

"Yes."

It sounded like the guy was walking. Hopefully toward his already fully armed team or a vehicle. Or the local SWAT people. "Why would they do that?"

"Why wouldn't they? I just want to know how they found her at a secure location."

"Maybe it's not as secure as you think." Alanson continued, not giving Badger a chance to respond, "But why would they take her? They gain nothing. The money is in federal hands, and they can't get to the doctor. Everyone else is dead."

"What about the witness? The girl I pulled from the house."

"Changed her mind, I guess. Walked away from protective custody, like we're going to step in again when she's in over her head and needs help."

Badger had the impression he was partly talking about Hannah. "You're sending backup, yeah?"

"Keep eyes on them. My people do the takedown, so you sit on the location and report in. You'll be relieved when we get there."

"And if they're going to kill her, but I can stop it?"

"You don't engage," Alanson said. "I don't need a bunch of mercenary yahoos screwing things up."

Badger said, "I'll text you the location," and hung up on the guy.

Zander shook his head. "Let me guess. He's getting her back himself."

"I'm pretty sure he doesn't care if she lives or dies," Badger said. "He just wants the cartel."

"Probably just wants the promotion he'll get when he has those guys all in cuffs. The rest doesn't factor much." Zander's disapproval was plain in his tone.

"I'm glad we know a fed we actually like, or I'd think they're all this bad."

Zander chuckled as he made the next turn.

The van was farther away now, threading through traffic quicker than them. Trying to escape with the woman Badger loved. One he wasn't sure loved him back.

But he was going to do everything to get her home anyway.

"Catch up."

"I am." Zander yanked hard on the wheel and took a sharp turn that put them almost up on two wheels.

"Don't lose 'em."

HANNAH LAY STILL, trying to take shallow breaths. The knife tip pressed against her throat. She didn't even have room to lift her hands. But she could feel the end of the blade and the hot sting, along with wetness on her skin. She gasped an inhale as a tear rolled from the edge of her eye.

Her captor planted his free hand beside her head and leaned close. "Payment will be made. In your blood."

"I don't have any of the stolen money."

She couldn't think. Couldn't even breathe.

Hannah needed to get it together, or she would either do or say something she shouldn't. Though, there was likely nothing to be done right now. She had a sliver of hope. Enough to get it together and not completely dissolve.

He looked away, calling out to his friends—or underlings. "Did you lose them?"

The reply came in Spanish, but she understood enough to know it was negative. Who was behind them? It couldn't be cops. Given how fast they'd dragged her out of the house, how could any of Chevalier come after her?

Badger had been unconscious.

Zander would stay with his pregnant wife.

The doctor.

Hannah couldn't think. And right now, she needed to act like Sarah, the medical center front desk girl. Not someone with extensive police training. Even if none of it would come in handy right now. Any fight she got up to would be a losing proposition. She just needed to wait.

For rescue?

More like for a chance to get herself out of this.

She might want Badger to come and get her more than anything. He'd been knocked unconscious, so how could he be behind them now? It was impossible. She'd never been one to wait around for rescue.

These guys were going to take her somewhere and murder her.

Weston's dead body swam in her mind. No hands, no tongue.

*God, help me.*

They were going to do the same thing to her because she'd been in their house when they were robbed.

Her mind wouldn't quit spinning.

How had they found her at what should've been a safe house? Someone had to have told them where she was—a breach of Chevalier's security. It was the only explanation. Otherwise, they'd never have had a chance to snatch her.

And at a time when she should be out helping Chevalier find Judah? That only made her cry more—for a man she barely knew. But she could tell he was a good man, unlike these guys.

The guy looked back at her. She knew who he was, the head of the cartel Dr. Mathers had robbed. José Suarez.

But Sarah wouldn't know that.

Right now Hannah was a scared, idiotic woman who'd gotten in over her head. "I'm sorry."

She didn't bother sniffing because the nose dripping would help. Plus, it was honest. Generally she favored procedure, regardless of her feelings—ignoring her instincts and getting on with her job. But right now, giving in to a little of the fear was realistic. These guys would expect her to dissolve into hysterics.

Hannah repeated what she'd already said. "I don't have your money."

"I have all my money." His dark gaze bored into her. There was no escape. "You think I don't know how to keep track of what's mine? But you tried to take it."

"I didn't have anything to do with—" The knife sank deeper. Hannah cried out.

"So I make a statement. No one tries to steal from me, or they pay the price."

"I didn't take anything." Hannah gasped. "I wasn't with them. They dragged me into it."

"Does that matter? You are nothing, but your death will have meaning, at least." He studied her like she was an insect he needed to step on and be done with. Hannah didn't represent a threat to him at all—which meant he didn't know she was a cop.

That core of police in her expanded, as though trying to escape through the shell of Sarah—her undercover persona.

Like she needed that to happen right now?

Her instinct wanted to fall back on that training, even in an impossible situation. That was how she knew it wasn't right. But as that old way of thinking reared its head, Hannah wondered if it wasn't the right thing.

Her mind warred back and forth between what intuition told her to do and the right thing. The truth of who Suarez thought she was—and those human fears. Or the cop she was, who kept her femininity behind a police shield. It felt in that moment as though she fractured into two people.

Hannah wanted desperately to be both, even if one seemed stronger and more capable than the other.

One could be trusted.

One sought truth and justice.

But the idea she might listen to all the screams in her head—everything in her that wanted to fall back on being a cop—made the scared girl she was even more fearful. She'd trusted Joseph Ricker and an innocent child had died.

Could she trust herself now?

*I'm not nothing.*

And she was the one who fully understood her. Sometimes it seemed like Badger was the only one who even cared to try. Even God, who was supposed to have created her and knew everything about her didn't seem to. Though, that might have been her fault more than His. If she lived through this, she could try and figure it out.

"I'm not nothing."

He started to speak.

Hannah wasn't interested in what he thought she was trying to say. "I'm a cop. A detective, with Rochester PD." She took enough of a breath to say, "I'm on a federal task force, trying to stop that crew from ripping off guys like you."

His teeth flashed. "So you're a friend to the cartel?"

"You're the end game." The knife shifted. She winced as pain burned on the side of her throat. "Taking you down."

"And this should induce me not to kill you?"

"I can *help* you." Hannah couldn't believe she was even suggesting it, but maybe Alanson would agree she had no choice. She could be a double agent of sorts, pretending to be dirty so she could give intel on the cartel back to the feds. Then it would be that much easier for the task force to take them down.

She was willing to try, at least. Even if distracting him gave whoever was tailing them time to stop the van. Plus if he was listening then he wasn't killing her.

"I can feed you intel," Hannah said. "Let you know when the feds are going to hit. Or help throw them off your scent. I can be an asset."

He shifted, the knife still against her throat. His free hand traced a finger along her collar bone. "Is that right?"

She nodded.

"And what else will you be willing to do for me?"

As if Hannah were going to take that bait. But she needed to keep him distracted. She tried to lift her chin as best she could. Maybe he'd think strength was attractive. "Whatever you want."

His lips curled up. He might be persuaded he could get what he wanted.

"I can be useful to you."

The van jerked. Someone up front yelled, "We lost them!"

Suarez called out, "Get us to the truck."

*We lost them.*

More tears rolled from the corners of her eyes. She didn't want to dissolve into despair at the hopelessness. She needed to rally and fight this, not lie here doing nothing.

His gaze returned to her. "When we reach our destination, we will continue this conversation."

Hannah said nothing. Being complicit was one thing until she shed that skin and who she really was reared its head.

The van rolled to a stop, and one of the guys slid the door open. The collar of Hannah's shirt on one side was damp. With blood? She didn't want to think about what her neck looked like, with all the jerking.

Two of them hauled her up by the elbows while Suarez watched—until he felt the need to sample the merchandise for himself.

She squeezed her eyes shut.

Her feet slammed the ground. Hannah got her balance. A split second later as she felt their grips adjust, she shoved both men away and ran for the rear of the van.

Someone tackled her from behind. Hannah tripped, and two hundred pounds landed on her. Black exploded along with pain in her skull. Her jaw. Everywhere. Her senses blanked, and the world flipped over a couple of times.

She heard a low laugh. "This one is feisty."

## 28

"Where is it?" Badger drummed his fingers on the window ledge, watching out the car window as they rolled slowly along the street.

Even though his shoulder hurt like crazy, he wasn't stopping. No matter if Zander gave up, which he wouldn't. Badger's shoulder was going to heal like everything else. He was still here, and that meant he'd do whatever he could. Whatever it took.

Like the hunt for Judah, the only difference was that they had a lead on Hannah's location because Zander reacted fast.

They got honked at for going slow, but neither cared. This wasn't a busy part of town. Probably why the cartel decided this was where they would go. Out of the way, so there were few witnesses when they—

Badger pushed out those thoughts. And the ones about how Zander had reacted with Hannah faster and more effectively than Badger with Judah. Even though he'd been tied to a chair in one instance and out cold the other. Zander was the team leader for a reason, and Badger was proud to call him a friend.

This wasn't Badger's fault, and he shouldn't take it on board as if it was. He'd been unconscious when Hannah was taken. Yet when he closed his eyes, it was Alexis he saw. The whole thing was messed up. The way his head had been for years.

Tragic things happened every day, often with no rhyme or reason.

It would likely take him years to unpack the guilt and shame he'd absorbed, handed to him by other people so they could feel better because they'd laid their own feelings on him. There was a healthy amount of remorse in there, but he needed to figure out what that looked like. A way to accept responsibility for what he should've done differently—even if it might not have changed the outcome at all.

Right now he needed to focus. Find Hannah. Get her back for Nora and for him. Even if she didn't feel the same way, it didn't matter. He would rescue her anyway.

Zander eased past another street, scanning left while Badger scanned right.

Were they going to find the van again? He'd barely been able to breathe when they realized they'd lost it.

The cartel couldn't have gotten far.

Badger saw the van parked at the end. Doors open. "There!"

His friend hit the gas and pulled up behind it with a screech of brakes. No movement.

Badger shoved the door open, no vest. At least he had a gun now.

He held the weapon in front of him and raced over. The back door revealed an empty inside. "Clear."

Zander went to the driver's door. "Clear. Don't touch anything. The feds will probably want to pull forensics."

Badger tried to care about that. In a general sense, he did, but his obligation was to Hannah's life and not any investigation. He climbed inside, looking closer. "Zander!"

His team leader spoke from behind him then. "What is" —he stopped—"that blood?"

"Yes." Badger swallowed.

"Not much. She isn't hurt badly." Badger winced. He didn't like the idea she was hurt at all. "I don't need reassurance. I just need to find her." He climbed out the back.

Zander frowned. "You think I don't know how you're feeling?"

"Nora was taken by her father's head of security. Hannah is in the hands of a group of cartel guys known for cutting off hands and cutting out tongues." As if there was any comparison.

"So that makes my fear less than yours is? Or her trauma?"

Badger blew out a breath. "You know it doesn't, but we don't have time for a life lesson right now."

"There's always time to learn."

"So go be a teacher."

Zander squeezed the back of Badger's neck. "What do you think I do every day?"

Badger sniffed and blinked against the burn of tears he didn't plan to shed. Getting emotional wasn't going to solve this. All it would do was cloud his better judgment at the precise moment he needed a cool head.

Zander said, "We're going to find her."

Badger nodded.

Zander checked his phone. "There's a message. Andre

says Peter Benton is on the move, and he's headed toward us. They're following him."

"He's coming here?"

Zander nodded.

"But it's probably not related to Hannah, right? I mean, it's a cartel who took her."

"And yet, when they should've had no idea how to find her, they knew exactly where she was. How could that be?"

Badger lifted his hands, then let them fall back to his sides. "Am I supposed to know? Isn't that a Ted question?"

"Think it through." As though this was just another one of Zander's tests. Instead of angering Badger, that helped him focus.

"The cartel is a separate thing from Travers," Badger said. He'd rather punch a brick wall than talk about this. Or run an ultramarathon…as long as Hannah was at the end of it.

"Are we sure of that? Travers would be an easy way for the cartel to get that intel."

"So they called Travers and made a deal?" Badger didn't see any way that would happen.

"Or the company gave the cartel the info." Zander shrugged. "The cartel does the dirty work, and Travers gets what they want. Hannah out of commission."

"You really think they're behind the threat on Hannah's life?"

It made sense, at least as far as Badger could figure. So far everything seemed to have involved Travers. The hit on her that resulted in Agent Pearson's death, then Joseph Ricker had been paid to come after Hannah and what he'd done seemed like an attempt to destroy her peace of mind—maybe even distract her.

Zander said, "They seem to have had their hand in everything that's happened so far. Why wouldn't they take advantage and get the cartel to do their dirty work?"

"It didn't work with the shooter or Ricker."

"Pulling out the big guns."

Badger winced, not wanting to think about what was happening to Hannah. "So how do we find her?" He looked around. Wherever they'd gone, it was probably in whatever vehicle peeled out fast enough to make the tire marks on the asphalt. Continuing his scan, Badger spotted a bank across the street, on the far side where it T-boned this one. "Cameras?" He pointed.

Zander put his phone to his ear. "Hey, Ted. Yeah, we need you to hack into the security at this credit union across the street from my location."

Badger took some deep breaths while Zander was turned away. Then he wondered why he was doing that. His boss didn't seem to mind the fact he wasn't a hundred percent. Zander had hauled Badger out unconscious and put him in the car instead of taking care of things himself.

Badger didn't know what to think about it.

He walked back to the van door and looked at the blood again. As though it could somehow lead him to Hannah. He simply wanted to refocus on the search. She was hurt. She was missing.

*I love you.*

Did she feel the same?

This couldn't be about whether or not she reciprocated his feelings, but the fact was she'd given him nothing to go on so far. He'd made it obvious, and she'd...

Badger turned and walked in the other direction.

At the last second he forced himself to turn again, using

the rhythm of a march to center him. The last thing he needed was to bust his gun hand by punching a brick wall.

He didn't want to believe that all of this was about Travers wanting Hannah out of the way. The company, or someone who worked there, had enough pull to use company resources for their personal agenda. The former president fit the bill, but what was the connection? If this was a conflict between Lana and her people with Raleigh and the company, and Hannah was stuck in the middle? That didn't bode well. But all this was speculation. Badger had no way to prove what the connection might be.

"He's working on it." Zander came back over, stowing his phone out of sight. "You think the cartel might've made a deal, and they're handing Hannah over to Benton?"

"I don't know what for," Badger said. "She has nothing they want, or they'd have been trying to snatch her before now. Instead it's been near misses and things that seemed specially designed to distress her. If they've escalated to murder, why do it personally when an experienced cartel can take care of your mess?"

Zander's expression darkened.

Badger read what he didn't say there on his face and nodded. They needed to find Hannah. Like, *now*.

———

THE TRUCK SLOWED. Hannah's stomach lurched. There was nowhere for her to go, sandwiched between two of Suarez's guys in the back bench seat. It was a normal neighborhood as far as she could see. Whose house this was, Hannah had no idea. She might've recognized the address from the task force files, but she hadn't seen the street name, and there was no number on the house or mailbox.

They turned onto a driveway and eased down beside the house, through an open gate to a detached garage with the door down.

The guy beside her shoved the door open and dragged her out by the elbow. Hannah winced. Her legs felt like wet noodles, but she got them straight and with her free hand touched the skin of her neck.

She hissed. It stung now that she was thinking about it and not ignoring the pain.

The other half of the back seat sandwich poked her from behind.

Hannah stumbled between them into the house, where they shoved her into a wooden chair at the kitchen table. The three of them stood guard, guns visible. There wasn't any point tying her up, and she was glad they realized that.

None of them had said anything the whole ride in the truck. They'd lost the van. No one knew where Hannah was.

She had to get out of this on her own. "So we can make an agreement, right?"

Suarez poured himself a drink. He stared at her as he sipped, that dark gaze probably contemplating what he planned to do to her before she went back to the feds as a dirty agent. A pawn. He would try and break her, and if she were honest, it would likely work.

Hannah wanted to set realistic expectations.

Her body flushed hot, then chilled. Sweat gathered at her hairline and dampened her shirt. But she said nothing else. What happened next was entirely up to Suarez. Whatever occurred, she wasn't going to like it. There was no good in this situation. Hannah just had to be able to live with it.

He drank the entire lowball glass, then set it aside as if he had all the time in the world. Maybe he did.

Hannah hoped that wasn't true. But she couldn't allow her thoughts back to Badger, or she would be swept away wanting to see him again. Knowing it wouldn't happen and that it would be something she'd also have to live with as she went back to her life, all so the task force could take down the cartel. However long that would take.

She didn't want to think about whether or not he would wait for her. That wasn't fair to him. Badger couldn't factor into this, or she would make the wrong decision.

"What happens next isn't up to you," Suarez said. "That is the first thing you must learn."

Hannah waited quietly, mostly trying not to freak out.

"Everything that happens is because I ordered it. Your life now belongs to me."

She resisted the urge to squirm in her chair. At least he—probably, hopefully—wasn't going to cut her hands off.

Hannah caught a flash of color outside the window.

She didn't look over or acknowledge that she'd seen anything. It was one of the hardest things she'd ever done. Before he could speak again, the door busted open. It flew back and hit the wall as the cavalry barreled their way in. At almost the same time, the door from the hall opened the same way.

The cartel guys swung around.

Gunfire cracked and popped like fireworks in the cramped kitchen. Light flashed with the blast from every muzzle.

Hannah clapped her hands over her ears, shoved back in the seat, and moved but also slightly fell off the chair onto the floor. She crouched and scrambled to the wall, moving away too fast. Her shoulder slammed the wall, and she heard herself cry out, the sound only in her mind.

A body dropped to the floor on the far side of the table. A hole in the center of his forehead.

The others dropped as well, including Suarez.

Hannah stayed where she was until a hand touched her shoulder. She flinched away from it and fell from her crouch to her behind on the floor.

"Hey."

Hannah lifted her head and realized she was breathing hard.

The woman in front of her was blonde, with her hair tied back. Maybe in her fifties, but it was hard to tell. She looked like an aging Hollywood actress, except she wore black fatigues and had a rifle across her back.

"Hannah, can you hear me?"

She also bore a striking resemblance to Nora, in a way. An older version of her but with some features Hannah also had. And Isaac.

*Lana.*

"Come on." Lana grabbed Hannah's elbows and hauled her to her feet. There was no resisting it even if she wanted to. "Let's get out of here, get some air."

Yes, air was good. Hannah gasped.

Lana led her over dead bodies to the door. Then they were outside, and she could lean against the truck.

*You saved my life.*

"You know who I am?"

Hannah stared at her birth mother. Despite the cacophony of thoughts in her head, she had no words on her tongue. Her chance to say everything she'd ever wanted to tell her mother, and she couldn't force but one word from her mouth. "Why?"

"You think I was going to let Suarez kill you? Or turn you?" Lana shook her head. Her people exited the house, and she glanced over her shoulder. "A minute."

One guy lifted his chin, and they headed to the front of the house carrying stuff—laptops, and phones. Taken from the cartel? So Lana hadn't just come here for Hannah. Or she'd seized an opportunity for intel on Suarez and his family dealings.

Lana turned back to her.

"I know who you are."

Her mother nodded slowly. "Nora probably told you, right?"

"I know Isaac is our brother." It was still partially a guess, but when Lana nodded again, she knew she was right. "One big happy family, right? Except for the fact you had to hire Chevalier to keep me safe, instead of having the guts to call and tell me yourself."

Now that her tongue seemed to have unstuck, the words were flowing.

Hannah continued, "So thanks for the heads-up, I guess. You probably think I owe you my life now." She waved at the house. "And since favors are currency to you, I guess I'll be seeing you—or one of your people—sometime. When you decide you want something from me."

"You think that's what this is?"

"It's who you are." The former Soviet double agent had informed her home country to the American government in exchange for a life here, no doubt. It seemed like the woman had never stopped operating. Now she was just doing it privately while the government had no idea. "And I doubt you even want that to change, do you?"

The corner of Lana's lips curled up. "I've always liked you, Hannah."

"Funny. I didn't even know you existed until a few weeks ago."

"I've followed your whole life. School performances, grade reports. Who you dated. Your first job in that ice cream shop. Your boss was a real tool." Lana shook her head. "College. The police academy. Every case you ever worked, right up to this one."

Hannah already knew this woman was formidable. After all, she'd followed Karina's whole life in a sort of private witness protection, which should've been secure. But somehow, Lana had breached that. She'd known where Karina was the entire time—something the accountant's office was still trying to figure out.

Hannah should've been scared, but Lana did everything to benefit the people she protected in her own way. No matter the consequences.

Lana pulled a gun from the back of her waistband, still in its holster. "Unregistered." With her other hand, she pulled a roll of cash from her pocket. "To get you where you need to go."

Hannah didn't accept. She only stood there unmoving. "You think that makes us even?"

"Not even close." As if Lana planned to make things up to her. Likely not, but it was a scary proposition if she did intend to do that.

Hannah said, "I don't need anything from you."

Lana's radio crackled, and a high tone split the air. Like a whistle. "I guess you don't." She strode away, leaving Hannah standing there wondering what had just happened.

The second after Lana's vehicle pulled away from the curb, a convoy of SUVs and cars stopped in front of the house. Some pulled onto the driveway.

Badger scrambled out of the passenger seat of a car and landed on hands and knees in the grass. He pushed off and ran to her.

Hannah met him halfway, and they slammed into each other.

Then she let go of everything she'd been holding back for hours. Because she was finally safe.

## 29

B adger didn't care about his shoulder, but Hannah still seemed to remember he was hurt. Probably down to the sling. She burrowed one arm under his good one, which was wrapped around her back. The other she snaked up and around the back of his neck. Holding onto him as tightly as she could while she cried.

Badger hung on, feeling the burn of tears in his eyes. He shut them and buried his face in her hair, even though he probably shouldn't. But taking a moment for himself seemed like the right thing to do just now. After all, he might not get another chance. She could remember any second that he was seriously attracted to her and feel like she needed to back off, to save his feelings. But she didn't.

Hannah shifted a fraction until they were practically nose to nose. "Are you okay?"

He couldn't believe she was asking him that. "If you're okay, then I am as well."

She nodded. "I'm okay."

But he saw the cut on her neck. "You need medical attention."

He wanted to hear the whole story. But he also just wanted to keep hugging her, saying everything that needed to be said without words. Hannah had been outside when they rolled up. What happened, and how did she get out? He knew she could've saved herself, but he wanted all the details. No matter that it would make him want to kill José Suarez all over again.

"Not yet," she said softly. "Later."

Over by the house, he spotted Zander emerge from inside with Alanson. Both of them headed toward Badger and Hannah. Zander shook his head. So everyone inside was dead.

"What happened?" Badger asked. He needed her to give him the story first, so he could help her do damage control with the feds if necessary.

Her task force supervising agent was headed this way.

While she looked past his shoulder and formulated her thoughts, he saw Zander tug on Alanson's arm and say something. The fed stopped his forward progress. Good, Zander was buying him some time with Hannah first.

And that meant his boss was also respecting Badger's need to take care of Hannah himself. Without interference from the feds. Even though he was injured, he was still able to do what felt like an imperative.

And Zander, his longtime friend and team leader, was giving him the space to do it.

She lowered her arm but left her hand on the side of his neck, though she didn't put any pressure on his injured shoulder. She stared at him with those blue eyes.

"What is it?"

She gave him a small smile. "I love you, Ryder Samuel Huaka'i."

Badger frowned. Had it come over her this fast? That didn't mean anything good. It wasn't like a person didn't feel something for somebody, and then after one dangerous situation, they suddenly were in love. More likely she knew now how capable he was of protecting her and she wanted to feel safe.

Hannah stiffened in his arms. "I don't have to use your real name if you don't want me to."

"What happened?" He shifted to get a closer look at her neck. "What else did Suarez do?"

"This isn't about him," she said. "I'm sorry, I won't use your real name if you—"

"A few days ago I wouldn't have liked it, but right now I can honestly say I don't mind."

"Really? I didn't want to overstep."

He knew what she'd been trying to do. Accepting the person he was all the way to his core. "You love me?"

"I didn't know if you remembered telling me."

"How could I have forgotten?"

She smiled. "I just wanted to tell you because I couldn't let myself even think about it when I didn't know if I was going to survive. But I've never been sure of anything in my life."

She increased the pressure on the back of his neck a tiny amount. Badger lowered his forehead to touch hers, unsure what she was asking from him. He didn't want to be too presumptuous when she had just broken free of an intense situation.

She knew how he felt, and now he knew that she reciprocated those feelings. But it was hard to say what the future was going to hold. Just because they loved each other didn't mean there was a happy ending in store for them the way it had happened for Zander and Nora. Andre and Lucia. Eas and Karina, with Aria completing their family.

Their situation was different, with Hannah living on the East Coast and working as a cop. If they were going to make a relationship happen, one of them would have to give up their job and move across the country.

And right now he couldn't ask her what she was going to do.

It was too soon to talk about that—before she'd even received medical treatment.

Hannah lifted her face and touched her lips to his. Badger's whole body tightened, and he held her closer to him. They could venture into dangerous territory pretty quickly, judging by the lightning that seemed to whip through him. Thankfully Hannah was more aware than him because he felt her smile against his, and she pulled back a fraction. "Well."

Badger grinned. "I don't think it's ever felt quite like that. But this might not be the time or place for it."

Her cheeks flushed pink. It was better than the pale tone when she'd first run to him. "Part of me can't even believe it's done. First I thought he would kill me in a horrible way, and then I managed to convince him that he could use me as a dirty cop. That I would feed him back information." Something crossed her face. "And other favors."

Badger didn't like the sound of that.

"Then she came in with her people. And now they're all dead, but I guess that's how they operate."

"Hannah…" She wasn't saying what he thought she was. Please.

"She was here."

"Lana?"

Hannah nodded. "My mother. I guess she saved my life. Maybe it wasn't for the first time."

"She got you out?"

"Killed them all, and walked me outside. We talked a little bit."

Badger waited for her to tell him.

"Maybe she wanted to do it out of the kindness of her heart. But that's not really how she operates, is it?" She pushed out a slow breath. "I didn't really know what to say to her after all that with Suarez. Then she tried to hand me cash and a gun, like I can just take off and disappear."

"Well," Badger said, "you always need cash and a gun. But it could be she thinks you're still in danger."

"Great." Hannah sighed. "I'm not sure."

"Maybe you want to get as far from Travers Industries as you can."

"What does that company even have to do with me?" She started to pull back. "I've never had any interaction with them or anyone that works there. But you guys all have. So was I targeted because of my connection to Chevalier?"

"It's possible. But I'm not sure." He didn't want her to think it was bad to get to know him or the team. Or her sister. Isaac, considering he was currently in federal prison, might be an entirely different thing. "I do have an idea about what it *might* be about. I just don't want to throw around speculations when we have no evidence."

She nodded. "Thank you for that." She blew out a breath. "I have enough to deal with in front of me."

He was in front of her, but she motioned over her shoulder to all the feds milling around.

348 | LISA PHILLIPS

"I don't need to wonder about unknowns," Hannah said.

"If I find out for sure, I'll tell you."

She touched her lips to his. "Thank you."

Badger hoped she would do that more as she grew more comfortable in her feelings for him, and their relationship found steady footing.

"I like that look on your face."

"It's not going anywhere, anytime soon," he said. But right now there was a lot of paperwork and procedure to deal with. Alanson was getting antsy even with Zander trying to keep him in a conversation. "Do you want to sit in the car, and Alanson can come to talk to you? I'll go see if an ambulance is on its way."

"Is Windemere still here?"

She would rather be treated by their team doctor? It was great to hear, because it meant she was embracing their team along with him and her sister. But she would have to wait on that one. "He took Nora back to Last Chance County."

A wistful look came over her face. "I'm going to have to visit that place one of these days."

Badger couldn't help smiling. "I was hoping you would."

HANNAH WANTED to stand there and gaze into his eyes, as though her life had turned into some kind of sweet Hallmark movie that would normally make her want to barf. Now she'd become everything she disliked. But maybe that was what happened when a person fell in love for the first time.

Later, when she got a chance, she was going to phone Nora and ask her. Maybe when her sister met Zander, the same thing had happened.

But then Alanson cleared his throat, and she started to pull away from Badger. He turned so that she was under his good arm. That kept them connected, at least in a sense, even if it seemed like Alanson disapproved. Not that either of them cared what he thought.

Before he could launch in on whatever he was going to say, Hannah started. "All of Suarez's people are dead?"

"Did you kill them?"

"Did you find a gun somewhere, or am I holding one?" If she had killed them, there would be a weapon somewhere.

"Maybe you tossed it in a drain before we got here."

Hannah had no idea whether she was going to throw Lana and her people under the bus. Part of her wanted to protect her mother from possible charges, but that was only a sense of nostalgia that she shouldn't hold onto. Not when that woman hadn't ever been a part of her life.

Sure, Lana had saved her life today. If Suarez had even been about to kill her, which was debatable. Still, she hadn't been looking forward to what would've happened in the process of her becoming an agent on Suarez's payroll. Who knew what the currency might've been?

Hannah settled on the truth. Somewhat. "A group of people all dressed in black fatigues busted in. The doorframe is probably splintered. They took out all of the cartel's guys, including Suarez. I'd never seen any of them before."

That was true.

"I'm supposed to believe strangers rescued you?" Alanson said.

"It doesn't matter what you believe or not. Evidence will point to the truth. And I doubt anyone will cry over the Suarez cartel dissolving in the power struggle over who is going to take José's place in charge." He had no siblings, and most of his family was dead. She couldn't see a clear contender for his replacement among any of his surviving men.

Who knew what would happen to the cartel?

Likely Lana would sweep up all their assets, though for better or worse she had no idea. The kind of person her mother was remained a mystery.

Alanson frowned. "I expect you in the office first thing tomorrow morning to look at pictures and identify all of them."

She nodded. "Yes, sir."

"Get yourself some medical attention." He strode away.

"Well, I guess that's that." Hannah felt her cheeks heat.

Zander wandered up to them, and she didn't quite know what to say.

"Nora is okay?" she finally asked.

"Until I tell her she isn't going on any more missions."

Hannah winced. "She's going to understand that you don't want her in danger."

Zander said, "I have a feeling it isn't going to end anytime soon. You?"

Normally Hannah wouldn't have put much stock in her feelings. But now that she was so sure of how she felt about Badger, she had to learn to trust that part of herself.

"I'm hoping I won't be a target anymore. Maybe Lana will do me a favor and take care of that." Hannah shrugged one shoulder and felt Badger squeeze the outside of her arm in an attempt to comfort her. "But I'm not going to go looking for trouble. I'd rather get to know my siblings." There was more, but she didn't know if it was the right time to say it.

Zander studied her with an unsettling gaze. "How about helping Chevalier figure this out?"

"You should." Badger tugged her fraction closer. "Judah is out there, and we need all the help we can get to locate him."

"He's still missing?" she asked.

Both of them nodded.

"Of course I'll help you look for him." Given everything that had happened, it would seem strange to go back to her job in homicide. Plus, she would wind up thousands of miles from Badger.

Was she really thinking about putting in for retirement from the police department?

She didn't dare speak that nascent thought out loud. Not when there was still so much to sort out.

Zander's phone buzzed. He looked at the screen. "I should take this." Then he wandered off into the sea of federal agents and first responders.

Badger turned her in his arms. "Doing okay?"

She nodded. "I could use a pot of coffee, but I'm good."

"I need a cheeseburger. We should find somewhere that serves both."

His boyish expression made her grin, and he kissed her again. But briefly, the way it had been before. Just the warmup, the prelude to a show that was going to leave her breathless—and just might last the rest of her life. That was the magnitude of the promise in that simple touch.

Zander called out, "Badger—"

They turned to him together. But Zander wasn't what caught her attention.

A man approached, striding toward them with his hood up. His face in shadow.

He brought a gun up. "You ruined everything."

His eyes blazed with fire, and it was directed at Hannah.

The whole front yard erupted into noise and motion as the feds realized this had shifted to an active-shooter situation. "Put it down! Hands above your head!"

Before anyone could reach him, the guy pulled the trigger. The muzzle flashed, and the gun cracked.

Badger shifted in front of her at the last second. His body jerked, and he fell.

The flashbang of multiple weapons followed for a second —like a war zone in the heat of battle.

Hannah caught Badger before he hit the ground, slumping onto her lap.

Shot.

She screamed.

---

## 30

One week later

W hether he was awake or sleeping, Badger didn't know. His body somehow disconnected from his consciousness. In a way he didn't like.

He fought for the surface, kicking and thrashing until he broke through.

Then he felt it.

The touch of her fingers on his and her lips against his cheek. "I'll be back soon."

HE AWOKE WITH A START—AND a groan.

"We just landed." Across the aisle, Dr. Windermere unbuckled his seatbelt. "How are you feeling?"

Badger made a face.

"You're allowed to tell the truth." Windermere sat on a

seat facing him. "You were shot in the chest. That's a traumatic event, and no one expects you to bounce back like nothing happened. Even Karina stayed in bed for a week when she got here."

Except Karina had been stabbed eight times. He'd taken one bullet, but Badger knew what the doc was saying. Windermere apparently didn't know this had nothing to do with the tight ache in his chest—if you could call it that when it was like calling a collection of pebbles a quarry.

"At least the Xbox is still in my room." If Badger was going to pretend it didn't bother him that Hannah hadn't shown up in the hospital, or since, he'd need plenty of distractions.

All he had was that elusive dream, the one he didn't know was real or not. He needed to quit thinking about it.

Badger got himself out of the chair. Kind of. Stars blinked at the edges of his vision.

"Once you get back to the house, we can give you more pain medication."

"Thanks, Doc."

Windermere walked him to the door.

The whole team waited at the bottom of the stairs, but it wasn't who he wanted to see. Andre and Lucia, who'd shown up seconds after he was shot because they'd been following Peter Benton—his shooter, who had been killed seconds after he pulled the trigger on Badger.

The story they'd told was that after he and Judah were tied to those chairs and grilled, and Judah escaped, Benton was essentially kicked out of Travers Industries. His brother was dead, a statistic of prison suicides.

Badger wasn't convinced Benton had done the deed of his own volition. Peter blamed Hannah as the cause for him being ostracized and had come after her—which meant he hit Badger because he'd been doing his job protecting her.

The woman he loved.

Who'd left as soon as he was stable and hadn't called or texted since.

Badger gritted his teeth and descended the stairs. Zander was there, along with Karina and Eas. Aria and her dog. Even Ted and his brother Dean, who were both looking worried. Nora stood off to the side, talking on her phone.

Windermere said, "I'll bring the car over."

Zander shook the doc's hand, then moved closer, put his hand on the back of Badger's neck, and leaned down to look in his face. "Good?"

Badger nodded. He couldn't form the words even if he'd wanted to tell Zander that he'd be back to full operation as soon as he could make it happen. Mostly, he was just glad to be alive. Even if Hannah wasn't here.

*I love you.*

So where was she?

The rest of them either shook his hand or squeezed his shoulder. Karina kissed his cheek. Aria swiped away a tear, so he gave her as much of a hug as he could.

"Nothing on Judah?"

Zander jerked back around from looking at Nora, who'd hung up. "That's what you want to talk about?"

"Yes." They didn't think he was going to air the conversation about Hannah to everyone, did they? Badger didn't even want to talk about her. The last time she'd ghosted him, he'd moped around for weeks. As if he'd do that again? No way. If she was gone again, it could be for good for all he cared. Even if she was Nora's sister. It didn't have to have anything to do with him.

Nora hung up her call. "Badger, how are you?" She kissed his cheek.

"Good." He glanced at Zander. "And ready for you to answer my question."

"No, there's been nothing on Judah. He wasn't taken, and he hasn't called in. There's literally no chatter anywhere about him—or even what *could* be him. It's like he's disappeared off the face of the earth."

That wasn't an option, but Badger didn't know what alternative it could've possibly been. "We need to find him."

Zander's eyebrows rose.

"Fine, you guys find him. When I'm good, I'll help." In the meantime, Ted could get him a laptop. He had people he could reach out to. See if they'd do the legwork.

Zander blew out a breath and nodded. "That would be good." He looked worried.

Nora ducked under his arm and hugged his middle. He kissed the top of her head.

"Come on," Andre said. "Let's get back to the house."

Badger nodded. He and Lucia tried to get him to sit up front in their car, but he just got in the back with Windemere. Badger closed his eyes because he didn't want to talk to anyone. Nor had he looked at his phone. Not since he woke up and she was gone.

What was the point when he would only see that she hadn't called or texted?

When they got back to the big house they all shared, Badger just stared at it out the vehicle window. It wasn't like he had anywhere else to go, but it still felt weird being here. Everyone would know how spectacularly he'd failed again with Hannah. That old pull toward trying to convince everyone he was doing fine when he wasn't reared its head again.

Badger pushed off the sensation and let them help him walk inside, all the way to his bed. Just to prove a point to himself that he didn't need to fall back on those old tactics.

*Where is Judah?*

They all needed to know where he was. If he was okay.

Badger didn't like not knowing any more than the rest of them did.

He eased back onto his bed, feeling like a different person than the last time he'd been here. In a lot of ways, it was true. But maybe he should simply accept this was where he was meant to be.

It seemed like everyone came by to ask if he needed anything.

Eventually it slacked off, and then a fist rapped on the door.

"Yeah?"

The door eased open, and Ted stuck his head in. "You awake?"

Badger nodded. "Did you do it?"

The young man blew out a breath and ran his hand through his hair. "You realize how illegal that was, right? I mean, I've got some push with what access I have to a lot of things, but that might've been crossing too many lines."

"We needed to know."

Ted leaned his hips against the dresser. "You're right about that."

"Because it was a match?"

"We need to have a meeting," Ted said. "The whole team. Get everyone together so we can discuss what this means and what we're going to do about it."

"We're not doing anything about it." Badger shot him a look. "Tell me what the results are, and then don't tell anyone else unless they ask."

Ted said nothing.

"I was right." When he still said nothing, Badger continued, "Lana's so protective of Hannah, and Travers is on the other side. He works for the company."

"Just took over a major division of research and development."

"Someone capable of pulling all those strings. Benton's brother, then Joseph Ricker, then the cartel."

Ted nodded.

"Former president Raleigh is Hannah's father."

Ted looked at the floor.

"You tested her DNA against his?"

Ted lifted his head. "Yes. And no one is ever going to know how I got it."

Badger nodded. "At least now we know why."

"I should call her. Tell her, so she can take precautions. This isn't going to go away."

Badger looked at the blanket Nora had laid on him, giving him a weird look as she did. But she hadn't said anything. "Do what you feel like you need to."

"Good, because I already called her."

"Great."

"Where's your phone?"

"Backpack." Badger waved across the room, where Andre had put it.

"I'll get it for you."

"Don't bother," Badger said. "I don't want to be disturbed."

"What if she—"

"Love you, Bro. But don't."

Badger closed his eyes. Ted got the message and left his room.

Too bad sleep never came. Not even when the door opened again, and whoever it was moved the laundry off his armchair and sat. Badger didn't want company. They would leave, too. Eventually.

Just like Hannah.

And he would get over it again like he had before.

―――――

HANNAH FELL ASLEEP WITHIN MINUTES. Made sense, considering she'd driven a total of twenty-nine hours to get here, spread over two days. She was exhausted. Ted's call had shocked her, at a time she hadn't believed she'd been capable of being any more shocked about who she was—and the people she'd come from.

Her father.

Hannah had no words.

While she slept, her mind flitted from dream to dream. The gunshot, and Badger falling in her arms. A hospital scene where he coded and they called time of death like they did on TV. Only that hadn't happened.

Him lying in his bed, pale with that dark hair falling over his forehead.

She'd had so much coffee and bad restaurant food her stomach never settled. She shifted one way on the chair and then what seemed like moments later had to turn the other way. She couldn't get comfortable on an armchair, no matter how hard she tried.

Badger needed to rest. She should probably find somewhere else—

"Would you—" His growl cut off.

Had he hurt himself? She sat up, blinking. "Badger?"

"Hannah?" He blinked at her.

Tears filled her eyes, and she nodded.

"I'm asleep."

She got up and moved to his bedside, sat on the edge, and laid her hand over his—the way she had at the hospital. "You're not asleep. Neither am I, even though I drove for two days straight. Slept in my car. Ate way too many chips and drank too much diet soda." *Brooded about my existence.* "I'm kinda wired."

His brow crinkled.

"I took a photo every time I stopped. So you'd be able to track my progress all the way here." And yet, it looked like he had no idea what she was talking about. "Didn't you get my messages?"

He hadn't replied to any of them. But Nora's updates said he was doing okay at each stage of his coming home, so she'd figured she would talk to him in person.

Badger said, "Get me my backpack."

She brought it over. He seemed kind of mad. Did he not want her here? Given they'd told each other how they felt, and then he'd been shot saving her, plus everything since then…she'd figured he might at least be happy to see her.

Badger rummaged for a phone, then shoved the backpack off the bed so it flipped and hit the floor. Half the contents spilled out. She was going to put that stuff in the laundry when he fell asleep. It'd been in the bag too long.

He stared at his phone. "You did." His thumb swiped the screen. "All the way here."

"Of course." She sat beside his knee. "I wanted you to know I was headed to you."

With romantic notions that he'd be waiting. Or that knowing she was coming would somehow help him heal.

Apparently, it didn't work like that.

"There's a moving truck that should arrive tomorrow. I guess I'll need a storage unit to put all my stuff in. I just brought the basics with me."

His eyes widened.

"Until I figure out what I'm going to do next."

"What do you mean?"

She winced. He wasn't making this easy for her at all. "I quit my job. I was already done with the task force, although I spent two days writing reports and attending meetings, and we aren't done yet. There is more to wrap up in a week or so. But then I figured I had enough vacation days, so there was no reason to go work a few more cases as a cop just to ride out my time."

She took a long breath. "I'm done. I packed up my house and came here because I know you love being part of Chevalier, and I would never ask you to give that up. Last Chance is where my sister is, and soon my niece or nephew. Why would I be anywhere else?"

"You gave up your whole life?"

Hannah looked down at their fingers, intertwined now. Despite the fact he was recovering from being shot, there was still so much strength in him. "I love you." She looked up. "My life didn't seem all that great. It was actually kind of lonely."

He tugged on her hand.

Hannah braced herself with a hand on the bed, so she didn't land on his chest.

He smiled. "You'll have so much family you won't know what to do with them all. They're going to drive you crazy."

"Good."

"I love you, too."

"Good." She returned his smile. "Because they might be the reason I'm in Last Chance, but the reason I'm here"—she motioned between them with their joined hands—"is you."

"Sweetest thing I ever heard."

"Badger…" She didn't want to push him if he was hurt. He probably needed rest.

"My mom called me Sam." He shook his head. "It's too wrapped up in everything that happened there, and I'd rather not be reminded of it." He lifted their hands to his mouth and kissed the back of hers. "You should call me Ryder. Only you. No one else."

She smiled.

"I love you."

"I love you, too…Ryder. Everyone is going to get sick of us saying that to each other."

He grinned. "I don't care."

Hannah touched her lips to his.

"You want me to ask Zander if he's hiring?"

She'd thought about that, but she also had another idea. "I'm thinking something slightly different."

"Yeah?"

"Nora will be here, right? She won't be traveling so much with the team, so I thought maybe I'd work in town. See if the Last Chance County Police Department is hiring. Maybe they need a detective."

"There are already two girl detectives. And both are blonde like you."

Hannah laughed. "Or I'll get a private investigator license. I heard there's one of those in town as well."

"I'm sure you'll find something."

She nodded. "I think I already did. The rest of it?" She shrugged. "I'm not worried."

"Maybe I'll hire you to find Judah since we can't."

Zander hadn't given up, and neither had anyone else. "Of course I'll help." She kissed him again. "He'll show up. I just know it."

## 31

Abuja, Nigeria
Three days later

Judah held one hand on his side, just under his ribs. Despite the blood and the stabbing pain every time he breathed, he ran anyway. If he didn't, he was dead.

He just needed a cup of tea. That was all. Then he'd be fine.

His bare feet slipped on the concrete. Judah slammed into a wall and pain sliced through his middle. Maybe he needed more than tea.

He squeezed his eyes shut and slid down the wall to curl into a ball between the dumpster and brick, out of sight. Hidden in the darkness.

"Where is he?"

"That way!"

"Go. You find him!"

They pounded past his hiding place while Judah held his

breath. He had no phone, no weapon. No shoes. Just a T-shirt soaked with blood on one side and a pair of shorts.

The noise receded.

*Get to the safe house.*

It took minutes to talk his legs into straightening. He was out of strength. Out of options. Out of time.

If he waited here too long, those men would double back and figure out where they'd lost him. He'd be staring at the barrel of a gun for a split second before he met his Maker. His only regret? He hadn't called his friends and told them he was alive.

Soon enough, he might not be. But until then, he wasn't going to drag them into this. Things were too far gone.

Judah pushed off the wall and ran for the safe house.

He could never go back.

———

I hope you enjoyed *Last One Still Standing*, please take a moment to leave a review, it really does help!

The Story finishes in book 5: Last Line of Defense, turn the page to find out more!

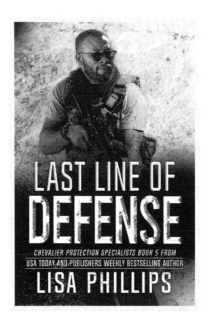

THE FIGHT IS ALMOST OVER.

Reporter Soraya Adams tried to tell the world about Travers Industries and wound up losing everything. Disgraced by a tech company reshaping law enforcement communications, she is forced to flee or be killed.

Judah Havig found a family in Chevalier Protection Specialists, but like everything else in his life it will eventually go bad. When British Intelligence calls in a long overdue favor Judah has to choose between loyalty and a future.

Enemies become friends. Tragedy strikes when it's least expected. And the entire team is put to the test as Chevalier takes on Travers Industries.

Everything is on the line in the final installment of this high-stakes series.

.  .  .

*LAST LINE of Defense* releases Dec 2021, Find it On Amazon

## ALSO BY LISA PHILLIPS

Chevalier Protection Specialists series continues!

Book 4: Last Man To Survive – Nov 2021

Book 5: Last Line of Defense – Dec 2021

Find the whole series here:

www.lastchancecounty.com/chevalier-series

Find out about Lisa's other books at her website:

authorlisaphillips.com

Other series:

Last Chance County

Northwest Counter-Terrorism Taskforce

Double Down

WITSEC Town (Sanctuary)

Love Inspired Suspense titles

# ABOUT THE AUTHOR

Find out more about Lisa Phillips, and other books she has written, by visiting her website: https://authorlisaphillips.com

Would you also share about the book on Social Media, leave a review on Lisa's page and share about your experience? Your review will help others find great clean fiction and decide what to read next!

Visit https://authorlisaphillips.com/subscribe where you can sign up for my NEWSLETTER and get free books!

Made in the USA
Middletown, DE
28 December 2021

57178300R00222